CRIMSON

VALE

A Modern Gothic Love Story

JENNIFER HARLOW

DEVIL ON THE LEFT BOOKS

COPYRIGHT

ALSO BY JENNIFER HARLOW

THE GALILEE FALLS TRILOGY
Justice
Galilee Rising
Fall of Heroes

THE F.R.E.A.K.S. SQUAD SERIES
Mind Over Monsters
To Catch a Vampire
Death Takes A Holiday
High Moon
The Sin Eater

THE MIDNIGHT MAGIC MYSTERY SERIES
What's A Witch To Do?
Werewolf Sings The Blues
Witch Upon A Star

AN IRIS BALLARD THRILLER
Beautiful Maids All in a Row
Darkness At the Edge of Town

Verity Hart Vs. The Vampyres: A Steampunk Adventure

For all of us who fought your demons and won

CHAPTER ONE

It's happened. It has truly happened. I have finally gone mad.

God help me.

I knew it would happen eventually. I knew the madness was in there, biding its time. *Tick, tock, tick, tock.* All my life I've heard that sound, the sound of the clock winding down towards zero when the invisible bomb would blow apart the walls of my mind. *Tick tock, tick tock.* You attempt to put the doomsday chime out of your mind, distract yourself to have some semblance of a life. You keep yourself busy with work, friends, love, with the day-to-day monotony of living. You volunteer, you take up ridiculous hobbies like glass blowing, or keep the television on at all times to drown out that sickening, soul-crushing noise. The inevitability of your destruction. But that knowledge leaks through in dreams, when your guard's down, when there are no more distractions. When you have nothing and no one. That bomb finally detonated, leaving nothing inside me but insanity. In truth I didn't even put up much of a fight. I was too weak. Worse, there was no need. At least my madness won't destroy innocent lives. That's the only good thing about being barren.

Perhaps that's why God cursed me. He knew *this* was on the horizon just as, deep down, I did as well. Perhaps I forced the seven miscarriages. My subconscious at work because I knew any child sprung from my flesh would have to endure the cycle I did. Is that why it always happened while I slept? Owen and I endured every test imaginable. My eggs, my uterus, his sperm, even our chromosomes. Some abnormalities but nothing to explain why it kept happening. But I knew. I just couldn't face it until now. It was me killing our babies. But I wanted them *so much.* I did. I still do. It was all I wanted in this world, to be a mother. Ever since I was a child, I would have the same dream. Me in a billowing white sundress standing on that blue painted porch holding my son. That blessing staring up at me with the brightest, bluest eyes I've ever seen as I kissed his soft blonde hair. I live for that dream now. Thank God most nights I have it. Actually every night for the past three weeks. As long as…*no*. The dream is not bad. It *can't* be. The whispers, yes. Feeling as if someone is beside me, even breathing on me? Absolutely. But not the dream. My only solace won't be taken away from me too.

Three weeks? Has it only been three weeks? Is it possible to wake up insane one night? Is that what happened to Mama? I was too young to remember much, and Aunt Helen and Uncle Robbie would barely speak of her "for fear of bringing the devil back." Oh, I wish they were alive for so many reasons. Though in this situation they'd just tell me to pray. Which I have. I have been down on my hands and knees rolling those rosary beads between my fingertips for so many hours I've lost count, and like the Xanax and Zoloft, it barely helps. I was already taking those drugs when the whispers began and have been too afraid to inform Dr. Bramble about this new level of insanity in case she phones Owen, and he has me committed. According to my divorce attorney, he still can. I mean, the whispers are not terrible. They don't tell me to harm anyone or myself, at least I think not. I can rarely make out the words. And they're not happening all the time either. But I decided if either of those events occur, Owen won't need to commit me, I'll do it myself.

The telephone rings in the kitchen. I let the machine get it. Only four people call me now: my best friend Melissa, my attorney, my agent, and Owen. If it's Melissa she's phoning to give me an hour long pep talk in-between flights. My lawyer will just want more documents or to inform me of the continued progress in the divorce I truly don't want. My agent will read me the riot act as to why I haven't finished the illustrations for *Sherlock the Mouse*. And Owen, well…we'll either get into a fight or worse, he'll know there's something amiss and rush over. Any one of those four options will end with me in tears.

And the winner is..."Jane, it's Owen. Are you there?"

Even his voice brings the tears. My soon-to-be-ex-husband is a man of few words, but when he talks, you listen. He doesn't waste a word. I love that about him. Almost as much as I love how we never really needed words, how his mere presence put me at ease. My rock for the past twelve years. Gone now. That's what I don't understand. Why now? Why didn't my mind slip away four months ago when he did the same? Why not when he told me about the affair? It makes no sense, but I suppose that's the definition of madness.

"Jane? If you're there, please pick up. *Please*," he pleads. "I'm getting worried here." He sighs. "We have to talk about the house. My lawyer's pressing me for an answer. Will you please just call me back? If I don't hear from you by tonight, I'm coming over." He pauses. "Please just call me, Janie. Please. Call me."

One more thing to worry about. This house. This ugly, pre-fab, overpriced piece of junk. I hate this house. I hate Los Angeles. I hate the smog, the traffic, the plastic people who look down on you for not being the same. At least *she* wasn't one of them. The harlot. I met Violet a few times. She looks a lot like me. Same long blonde hair, though mine is natural, Caribbean blue eyes, and hearty Midwestern frame. I'm taller than her at five-eleven but not by much. He claimed that's why it happened that once, because she reminded him of me. Not sure if that makes it better or worse. Of course I'm not sure of anything at present.

The house, the house, this freaking house. When we first bought this four bedroom with fenced yard, we were still so full of hope. I'd only had two miscarriages then. Five more to come. Three empty rooms never filled. A mausoleum that now seems like a prison as well. We should just sell it. Should have years ago. But where would I go? I barely go anywhere now. Just to the grocery store, Dr. Bramble's office, drug store, and occasionally my lawyer's. And that was *before* the whispers. Before seeing the grocery checker sprout boils that popped pus all over my celery before, in the blink of an eye, returning to her normal self. Dr. Bramble too. I haven't been to a much needed session in two weeks since I looked down to get a tissue then up at the doctor, instead greeted by a creature with shark teeth, red eyes, and blood dripping from every orifice. I ended the session then, feigning a headache, and drove home as if the devil were chasing me. I haven't made it past the mailbox since. I just lie here on the paisley couch Owen and I bought in Santa Barbara in my yellow sweats watching television and willing and praying myself sane.

The knock on the front door makes me leap a foot off the couch. I'm not expecting a food delivery. Oh God, what if it's Owen? I haven't showered or brushed my hair in four days. There are yogurt cups, empty chip bags, and Chinese cartons all over the beige carpet. He hasn't set foot in our house in over a month. He can't see the house or me like this. I won't let him in, I just won't. He'll go away. He will. I'm not opening that door.

Open the door...

I gasp and my body locks up. That's the first time I've understood it. Him. That was him, not her. And he's here. Behind me. I would spin around, but the past hundred times I have, there's been no one there. This time though…it was as if he were right by my ear. I could all but feel his breath on my earlobe. I glance back and sure enough nothing but emptiness. Another knock.

Open the door, beloved.

"Mrs. Harrow? Mrs. Jane Harrow?" the man on the other side of the door asks.

If it will shut the voice up, I'll do anything. I pull the quilt off the back of the couch, wrapping it around myself before moving down the hall to the front door. Photos of happier times lie face down beside two weeks of unopened mail. I check through the peephole and see a mailman on my porch. I crack open the door, letting in the light. The drapes haven't been opened since Owen's last visit, so I'm momentarily blinded. What this stranger must think of me, pale and all but hissing at the light like a vampire. "Yes?" I whisper.

"Are you Jane Hines Harrow?" the man asks.

"I am."

"I have a registered letter for you, ma'am. I need to see some ID."

Which means more legal documents. After I locate my purse and sign, I retreat back into my gloom. Davenport & Davenport, Attorneys at Law. Not our divorce lawyers but still vaguely familiar. The return address gives me pause. Crimson Vale, Louisiana. Aunt Helen's hometown. And Mama's. What on earth?

I return to my couch and rip open the envelope, finding a single sheet of paper and a photo of a house inside. When I view the snapshot, my breath catches.

Home...

It's a grand two-story boxy Antebellum Greek revival plantation house made of white painted wood with covered wraparound blue painted porches supported by columns and iron railings. The windows, almost a dozen on one side alone, are either bay or have pointed arches. The lawn appears dead or on life support with the grass brown as dirt and bare in patches, yet the tall oaks with Spanish moss dripping from them, and weeping willows scattered around detracts notice from the ground, as do the bursting white magnolias. It's so beautiful, but that's not what stops my breath. It's the fact I've seen this house before. In my dreams.

Home...

The letter quakes in my hand as I read it.

"*Dear Mrs. Harrow,*

It is with deep regret that I must inform you that your grandmother Felicia Fontaine Cowan and your uncle Jerome Fontaine Cowan passed away September 9, 2018. Everyone at Davenport & Davenport offers you our deepest condolences for your loss. As executors of your grandmother's Last Will and Testament, we have written this letter to further inform you that *per her final instructions you, her only known living relative, have inherited the bulk of her estate including her savings of $26,783, stock portfolio with as of September 22, 2018 totaling $987,234, and the house at 187 Fontaine Lane and all its contents last valued at $2,369,147. The $200,000 to St. Theresa's Bayou Hospital and $200,000 to St. Jude's Catholic Church have already been distributed and your loved ones have been cremated per their requests.*

I apologize for the late notice of their deaths. We were not able to locate you until one week ago, and have made multiple attempts via telephone to reach you since. To claim your inheritance you or your attorney will need to contact our law office at the number and address listed above. Once again, we are sorry for your loss. Your grandmother was a respected woman in the parish. She will be missed. We look forward to hearing from you.

Regards,

Bramwell T. Davenport Jr, Esq.

P.S.-Enclosed please find a recent photo of Fontaine House. We will continue to pay for utilities from the savings account until you inform us otherwise."

It's waiting for you...

"Shut up!" I snap.

I re-read the letter three more times then pinch myself to make sure I'm not hallucinating. This is a mistake. They have the wrong Jane Harrow. Aunt Helen told me her sister Felicia was killed the same night as their father. And they never mentioned a Jerome, who was apparently mama's brother. Not that she or Uncle Robbie really ever liked talking about the past. Whenever I'd ask about other relatives or her upbringing Aunt Helen would reply, "We're the last, that's all you need to know. Leave the past in the rearview as God intended."

Once or twice she'd wax nostalgic, talking about her cotillion or my grandmother following her around like a tiny shadow. My grandmother. I've had a grandmother and uncle up until three weeks ago—

Three weeks ago.

I can pinpoint the exact moment I truly went mad. I sat in my studio fixing Sherlock the Mouse's deerstalker when I heard the first whisper, the woman's faint pleads for lack of a better word. I couldn't understand her words, but even now when I hear her, a fear and sadness envelops me from inside out. I walked around the house to make sure no one was inside or that I'd left the TV on. Nothing. Though still unnerved, though those pleas continued, I began back upstairs to the studio. That was when the man's voice overshadowed the woman's. "Finally."

Then I felt it. Behind me. Close. I spun around and though it was 6:30 in the evening, there was darkness at the bottom. Inside my house. Mere feet away. A black…thing staring up at me about as tall as a man with no features, no clothes, no face, only an inky void. A primal, soul crushing terror gripped me, but underneath was a familiarity. I'd seen it, felt its unnaturalness before. That was still there but overshadowed by its excitement, its pure happiness like a child on Christmas morning holding a puppy for the first time. Then it was gone. Vanished right before my eyes. I must have fainted because the world flashed as black as the shape, and when I came to, the sun had set. That was September 9th. The shape hasn't returned, but I sense it all the time. Watching me. All but breathing on my neck, goosebumps plumping from its fervor.

Like now.

I now take those same steps two at a time to my studio where easels with my paintings, station with my paints and pencils, drafting table with computer fill the small room. I shrouded my latest paintings because they scare even me. The black shape, the grocery clerk, even Dr. Bramble stared back at me. Monsters all. I thought art therapy would help, but I was wrong.

Sherlock the Mouse gets minimized on the computer before I pull up the internet. I type in "Felicia Fontaine Cowan" and "Jerome Cowan." First entry is an obituary dated September 14th in the *Lafayette Advisor*.

"CRIMSON VALE, LA-Services for Felicia Fontaine, 73, and Jerome Fontaine Cowan, 56, will be held on Sept. 16 at St. Jude's Catholic Church with Father Raymond King officiating and cremation to follow. Both entered into rest Sept. 9 and resided in Crimson Vale all their lives. Felicia was the daughter of Cotton and Cecile Fontaine, sister of Helen Hines, wife of Daniel, mother to Jerome and Juliette. In lieu of flowers, please send donations to St. Teresa's Bayou Hospital."

That's it? It doesn't say how they died or anything about me or Jerome's family, wife, kids, and whatnot. I click on another few articles and glean nothing new. I back up to the obituary to study the photos of my long, now forever, lost relatives. My grandmother must be about seventy with her hair pulled into a bun, my straight nose, pointed chin, full lips, weary blue eyes, hard wrinkles covering every surface, and sour glower for the camera. Heck, she looks as if she's never smiled in her life. Aunt Helen looked much the same, though she had hazel eyes and larger nose.

In contrast my uncle appears born to smile. He sits on the steps of the porch, grinning from ear to ear. There's even a halo around him, though it's made of blonde, curly hair. Grow his hair out, add a few pounds, and he could be me. The same big eyes, pointed chin, nose, high cheekbones though he does have thinner lips and longer jaw than me. The newspaper chose a photo of him as a teenager. I only have a few pictures of Mama but once again the resemblance between them, between us all, is uncanny. How old would she be now? I do the math. Fifty-six. Same as him. They were twins.

A trillion questions crisscross my mind. How did they die? Why didn't my grandmother or uncle ever contact me? They knew about me if they put me in the will. What…? Oh God. Everything I ever knew about my family is false. A lie. I thought my great-grandfather and grandmother died in a car crash and that's why Mama went to live with Aunt Helen in Missouri. Aunt Helen never mentioned a Jerome. Why did they use a photo from so long ago?

Home…

"Will you please be quiet?"

Great, now I'm chastising my delusions. Soon we'll be having full conversations. I stare at the photos on the screen of my kin for a minute just feeling…numb. Maybe they were all terrible people. Great-Grandfather Cotton was a tyrant, I know that much. I could tell by the way Aunt Helen spoke about him on those rare occasions. That had to have been it. She was protecting me from them. That's why she made me swear on the Bible never to visit Crimson Vale. I thought her vehemence odd, but with all the drugs they had her on at the end, she was barely lucid. She didn't want me to find them because they were wretched people. I can understand and condone that. Yet…a deep anger fills me from my clenched stomach out. How dare she? I had a right to know them, to meet them, horrible or not. Now I can't. I was cheated. First Owen, now Aunt Helen and Uncle Robbie. Everyone betrays me.

I can't look at those people a moment longer. I shut the browser and take a deep breath. Then another. A migraine's driving up the path. It's creeping up behind my eyes. I grab the letter and portable phone from the desk before walking next door into my bedroom. Like the rest of the house, it's a mess with an unmade bed, clothes piled up on the hamper, and remnants of food packaging littering the rug. Some of my better paintings and drawings line the walls, mostly landscapes. There are a lot of bare spots with nails hanging out because I took down the portraits of Owen. I pause as I pass a drawing of Aunt Helen shelling peas in our old kitchen. Her salt and pepper hair is pulled into its usual tight bun and mouth set straight as she concentrates on the task. She was always so serious, so tightly wound as if she let her guard down for a moment, the world would crumble. She loved me though, I don't doubt that. Of course so did Owen, and he betrayed me too. I take the frame down to add to the gallery of liars in the hall closet.

After I pop a pill to stave off the migraine, I climb into bed. The meds will knock me out. Thank God for small favors. I do love my pills now. Perhaps too much. I'm unconscious about sixteen hours a day now. Before I drift off today, I need to make a phone call.

"The law offices of Davenport & Davenport. This is Betsy, how may I assist you?" the woman says with a Cajun accent. It's as if she's talking with honey in her mouth.

"Um, my name is Jane Harrow. I received—"

"Oh, Miz Harrow! We finally tracked you down! Mr. Davenport is just about to step out, let me see if I can catch him. Please hold."

A few seconds later a Southern man says, "Miz Harrow?"

"Yes."

"Jane Harrow, formerly Jane Cowan?"

"Uh, Hines. My maiden name is Hines."

"But you were born Jane Hallie Cowan, birth mother Juliette Cowan then adopted by Helen Fontaine Hines?"

"Yes."

The man sighs. "Missy, you are a hard woman to find, I tell you what. We had two P.I.s scowering the country for you, girl. You're in Los Angeles, right?"

"Um, yes."

"Thought so. We've been calling and calling the numbers listed for you, leaving messages for three days. You didn't receive them?"

That's where I've heard of Davenport & Davenport. Their messages on my machine. I heard the word attorney and assumed it had to do with the divorce.

"Never mind," the man, I assume Mr. Davenport, says. "Got you now. I assume you received the letter and photo?"

"Yes, but I'm just confused. I—"

"Listen, I'm sorry. I'm already late for a meeting, and my son is at a deposition, so I can't get into specifics now. Brass tax is your grandmother left you everything. I know it's a shock. Was for us too. No one in town knew you existed until my son presented her new will. Just give it time to sink in, think about what you want to do with the house, talk it over with your husband, whatever you need to do. When you're ready, you can either come down here or go through your lawyer. I will tell you the Historical Society has shown great interest in Fontaine House. With them you won't get full value, of course, but the undervalue is tax deductible. But take your time. The house and money aren't going anywhere. Okay? I need to go, I'm sorry. Bye."

"Wait," I say. "Mr. Davenport, I-I-I don't…" I can't find the right words. "How-how did they die?"

There's silence on the other end for a few seconds. "Your uncle went peacefully."

"What about my grand—"

"Miz Harrow, I really have to run. I'm sorry. Good-bye."

He hangs up on me. And I thought Southerners were polite.

I shut off the phone and set it on Owen's side of the bed with the letter. Well, it's no mistake. I am a millionaire. Most people dream of something like this, inheriting a vast fortune from a long lost relative. Instead I feel like bursting into tears. Everything I ever believed, everyone I ever believed in, has lied and cheated me.

I won't…

"Shut up, shut up, shut up," I shriek, covering my ears with my fists. I flop my head on the pillow and grab another to press over my other ear. "Please leave me alone. Please, please, please. Just go away. Go away. Go away."

Come home, beloved. Come home…

I shut my eyes tight but the tears still escape. Weeping turns to sobbing as I curl into a ball under the covers until the drugs sweep me away into oblivion, as his voice caresses me like lapping waves. *Come home. Come home. Come home…*

To me.

*

The gray of the sky stretches on forever, infecting even the air with its oppressive gloom. It's hard to breathe, hard to even move without the gravel on the drive cutting into my bare feet as I stroll up the drive toward my home. The still air stirs as if my body slices through it like a knife. It doesn't want me here, the house, the property. Its fear, its melancholia attempts to repel me like a magnet of the same charge. I continue against it, the house decaying with each step, paint chipping then falling like snow all around me. Vines and kudzu snake around the once white columns now yellowing, like tentacles of a Kraken strangling the thick, sturdy structure until they groan and crack. Until windows shatter and rafters crumble. I continue on, past the hanging oak branch with ravens sitting wing to wing, their beady eyes and heads revolving with me as I persist. The alligator sitting on the dead grass opens its long snout to bare its teeth. I ignore it, I ignore all, even the crimson trail my bleeding feet leave in my wake. Nothing matters. Nothing else matters…

But him.

He waits at the top of the stairs of the porch, the decaying debris narrowly missing him as if he's sheltered by an unseen force. He doesn't notice. As the house disintegrates around him, his eyes never leave me, not for a moment. Oh, he's as beautiful as he was in the photo, golden hair haloed not by the sun but by his own ethereal, vital glow. That brilliant smile never dimming. I pad up the cracked steps to the porch, to him, leaving bloody footprints on the blue paint. As I take the final step up, our eyes meet. The intense longing and love that passes between us makes me weak in the knees, but if I fall I know he'll catch me. He'll always catch me. Tears spring from his eyes as he hesitantly lifts up his thin hand to my face. His icy hand caresses my cheek, giving me goosebumps over every inch of my flesh.

"Finally," he chokes out.

He envelops me in his arms, hugging me so tight no space remains between us. He kisses my hair, my forehead, down my cheek until his hungry lips find mine in a deep, probing kiss. Perfect. His taste, his fit, the hard press followed by the tender caress of those lips. *Perfect.* My body responds, lust escaping my every pore. He clings to me, fingers digging into the flesh of my buttocks hard enough to leave bruises. I don't care. He could flay me alive right now as long as he doesn't stop kissing me. Because I was made for this. For him. Even when I taste the blood, even when his fingernails slice through my skin, even as the porch crumbles underneath my stinging feet, I cannot pull away. I wouldn't dare. If I do, all is lost. He breaks our kiss first, all but tearing my soul from my body. When I open my eyes, he's gazing down at me as streams of blood pour from his red eyes to the gray cracked veiny skin of his cheeks and out his mouth. "Finally. You're home."

I awake with a gasp. Jesus wept. I sit up in my bed and take several deep breaths to calm my racing heart. I can still taste him in my mouth, sense the press of his lips against mine, savor the warm sensation he brought between my legs. My eighteen-year-old uncle. Who I just made out with. Even for *my* dreams that's disturbing.

It takes a few seconds to return to reality, but when I do, I realize the dishwasher downstairs has just started up. My delusions have never done dishes before. There's someone in my house. As burglars are as likely to do chores as much as imaginary figures are, I don't feel the need to grab the baseball bat or .38 Owen made a point of leaving for me. Still. Cautiously, I tip-toe down the stairs until I spot a trash bag by the side of the couch, and the quilt folded on top in its proper place. A cabinet shuts in the next room, and a second later, my husband steps out of the kitchen carrying another trash bag. Our eyes meet and my stomach clenches.

I was hoping to avoid this very moment since the day he moved out. The moment he realizes I'm falling apart without him. My husband appears as he always has, calm and in control. He must have just come from work as he's dressed in chinos and green golf shirt with his gun and shield clipped to his belt, the DEA uniform of choice. Agents always look ready to jump from meth lab to golf course, which Owen has done multiple times. At least he has the decency to look tired with dark circles under his light brown eyes. Even the best of circumstances, he's not handsome in the classical sense with a bulldog face, hooded eyes, uneven nose from all the times it's been broken, and graying brown hair shorn in a military cut. Once a Marine always a Marine. Even without the gun and underlying killer training he'd be imposing at six-two and over two hundred pounds of bulk. Most people's first instinct is to shrink away from him. Mine included. At least now.

He fills the doorway, face the usual granite. Even after twelve years together, eleven of those married, I still have a hard time knowing what's cycling through his head. He has only two facial features: the glare and the blank. The few times I've ever viewed a glimmer of emotion were during our highest highs and lowest lows, and once I noticed them, they vanished. I'm receiving the blank now, so I must not look as bad as I think I do.

"What are you doing here?" I ask, smoothing my frizzy hair.

"You didn't get my messages? I've called you three times this week."

I glimpse down at my feet to escape his gaze. "I've been busy."

"And I've been worried."

He's been worried about me since the moment we met at a college friend's wedding. With one glance of me sitting alone at my table, watching everyone dance, something inside him screamed that it was his job to take care of me. To protect me. What I needed protecting from at a wedding, I don't know. I suppose it's his version of love at first sight, but with fewer hearts and flowers.

"It's not your job to worry about me anymore, Owen. I'm fine. Thank you. You can go now, please." I snatch the garbage bag from his hand and walk into the living room, setting it next to the other.

"You don't look fine, Janie," he says, following me.

"I had a migraine earlier and got some bad news. I'll be fine. I'm better already."

He surveys me as he must do his perps, trying to decide the correct angle to go in for the kill. "Like hell you're fine, and don't blame it on the damn migraine. There's trash everywhere, you haven't showered in days, there's unopened mail from two weeks ago, and your eyes are bloodshot."

"I've been…sick is all. The flu."

He scoffs and shakes his head. "Then where are the tissues? The empty medicine bottles? The only empty bottle was for Xanax." This is the problem with marrying a member of law enforcement: you can't get away with anything. "Stop bullshitting me, Jane. How many Xanax do you take a day? From the empty wine bottles I assume you've been mixing booze and pills. Are you out of your fucking mind? Are you suicidal, is that it?"

"Of course not. I would never…it's a mortal sin, you know that."

"So you're playing with fire and hoping for a happy accident? Jesus Christ, Janie."

"Do not take the Lord's name in vain," I say quietly.

My husband stares at me, but underneath the apathy I can see the sadness creeping through his eyes. I look away. "I'm fine, Owen. Please. Just. Go. *Please*," I almost pray.

Come home to me.

My head jerks toward the voice to my right, but there's no one there.

"Jane?" I glance back to Owen. There it is. That glimmer of fear radiating through his defenses. He can't even hide or push it back this time. The last time I saw him this frightened was during my last miscarriage. I was losing so much blood we had to call an ambulance. I was a hairs breadth from undergoing a hysterectomy. My big brave husband looked so helpless as our baby geysered out onto our sheets. I think that's his only fear, helplessness, and I've made him face it time and again. My poor darling. This time the fear vanishes in an instant. "Sweetheart, what the hell is going on? You are scaring me. *Really* scaring me."

"I…I…"

"Sweetheart," he says with a step toward me. He's going to embrace me. God help me, I want him to. I want to collapse into his arms as he hugs and kisses the pain away like he always has.

No. Remember Violet.

I leap back at the mention of her name. "Owen, leave," I say with untapped strength. "I want you to leave right now or I will call the police. I swear I will."

Fear is replaced with determination as the scowl of death crosses his face. It works on drug dealers and artists alike. "I am not going anywhere, Jane."

"Fine." I walk past him into the kitchen where the other phone is. "I warned you." I pick up the receiver.

"It's a waste of time," he calls from the kitchen doorway. "This is still as much my house as it is yours, remember? I'm not trespassing. They can't remove me."

He's right. I remember my lawyer telling me that too. "Just go, Owen. Okay? Go."

"I am not leaving you like this. I am not leaving this house until you tell me what is going on with you."

"Well, if you're not leaving, I am," I blurt out. "I will. I'll go. You can have the house, I don't care."

"And where exactly will you go?"

"I-I-I'll go..." *Come home, beloved.* "Home. I'll go home." When those words leave my mouth, it is as if the gloom that descended on this house like smog lifts. I can breathe fresh air again. A flash of a smile crosses my face for the first time in a month.

Owen's eyes narrow. "Home? This is your home. Right here."

"No, this is our *house*. It's not home anymore. It hasn't been one for a long time. I'll move out. You can stay here, you can sell it, I don't care. I'm leaving as soon as I'm packed."

My husband remains impassive. "You're just going to pick up and leave? Just like that? That's crazy."

"Don't call me crazy," I snap through gritted teeth. "I am not crazy."

"Sweetheart, I didn't say…" He sighs to buy time. "Where will you go?"

"My grandmother and uncle died."

Now his eyes narrow to pinpoints. "Sweetheart, your grandmother died a long time ago, and you don't have an uncle."

"I do. Well, I did. I got a letter from a lawyer in Louisiana. They left me a house, stock portfolio, a savings account. I'm going there. Tomorrow. I just have to pack."

"That is insa—" He bites his tongue, "that is ridiculous. Some long-lost relative dies and leaves you a fortune? It's a scam, Jane."

"Give me some credit. I saw the obituary, I spoke to the lawyer, it's real. I'm driving down there to sign some papers tomorrow."

"Down where?"

"Crimson Vale. It's near Lafayette."

"So you're giving me our house, leaving behind everything and everyone, to drive across country to stay in a house you've never seen based on a letter, and a phone call from a total stranger claiming to be a lawyer?"

Trust…

"I guess I am." I put the phone back and walk toward him. "There's nothing keeping me here now," I say as I brush past him.

He follows me into the living room toward the front door. "This is…you can't do this, sweetheart."

"I don't need your permission, Owen. I'm doing it."

"Then I'm going with you," Owen says.

No.

"No, you're not. I don't need you to baby-sit me. I don't need you to protect me anymore. So just stop trying, okay? I am perfectly capable of doing this on my own, and even if I wasn't, I wouldn't want *you* there to have my back," I lie. I open the front door. "I promise to call you when I get there. Now go." He doesn't move, so I shove his arm. "Go!"

"At least give me the name of the lawyer. I'll check him out before you leave."

"There's no need. Goodbye."

My husband stares at my stony face, much like his and quietly sighs. He steps out into the warm night. "If you need anything…" His square jaw sets. "It's not a chore, worrying about you. And it's not something I can control. Here, there, married, divorced, it won't matter. I love you. Always have, always will. So if you need me, I'll come running. I don't care what it is, or when it is, I will be there. Even if it's to save you from yourself." He pauses, the sides of his mouth twitching. "I love you. Have a safe trip."

Owen turns his back on me and walks to his SUV. I can tell by the slight slump in his shoulders and hands in his pockets it's taking his all to leave me. It goes against his every instinct. And I still love him. I do. But I just can't stand to be around him anymore, and not only because of the one night stand. We've just been through too much, most of it soul scaring. Worse, most of it is my fault.

Distance. That's what we both need. To get away from my life, from all the bad memories. This trip might be the perfect solution. Things happen for a reason. It's God's plan.

As I watch my husband drive away, for the first time in years I feel…right. Hopeful.

Like I'm finally going home.

CHAPTER TWO

When Owen and I moved from St. Louis to Los Angeles, we drove. Bruce Springsteen, Bob Dylan, Tim McGraw all blasting on the radio as we coasted down the interstate, eating beef jerky, Twizzlers, and playing license plate Bingo. It was the middle of summer so I was in a tank top and shorts. I caught him checking out my legs and cleavage more than once. My legs have always been my best feature. Long, toned yet curvy even though I don't work out. Right over the California border, I convinced him to pull off the highway. We parked on a dirt road, yanked down our pants, I climbed onto his lap, and we made love like we never would again. I guess we never did again, not with that level of passion anyway. Soon it became more mechanical, choreographed for maximum reproductive optimization as our fertility doctor called it. But that day it was just about us. Our love, our pleasure in each other's bodies, our bright future in sunny California. When I pass the state line this time, I take a moment to mourn that Jane. The shell of her drives on. Who knows, maybe she'll rise from the ashes in Louisiana.

After Owen left that night, a new vitality filled me. I swept around the house like a twister grabbing everything I thought I'd need. I used all three of our suitcases and loaded four additional boxes in my Kia since I didn't know how long I intend to stay in Louisiana. Still don't. At five the next morning, I left that house without looking back. I've never been an impulsive person—I plan a grocery visit days in advance—so just packing up my car and driving into the unknown has been thrilling. The excitement overshadows any fear or doubts that creep into my thoughts. More important the whispers have almost completely stopped. Only once or twice I've heard the woman and her fearful mutterings, but I just turn up the radio.

After two and a half days on the road, stopping only for gas or sleep, I drive through Lafayette and forty-five minutes later that find the first sign to Crimson Vale, the green marker shot up by buckshot. They sure do enjoy doing that in this state. There have been more vandalized signs than not. The only time I've ever been to Louisiana was when Owen and I visited New Orleans on vacation once, and we never ventured out of the city. I am definitely not in Southern California anymore. This whole state's very flat with grassy fields filled with sparse trees, cotton fields and decaying buildings. Former homes and barns with half roofs collapsed and the only pristine wood covering the shattered windows. The poverty America finds itself in is as evident as it was in Missouri. Such a shame. The two-lane, pothole filled road to Crimson Vale is prettier than most of the state with dense forests, a field with white tufts growing out of the perfectly straight rows, yet more abandoned, even rusting small homes and even farmhouses like the one I grew up in. I sold it to a corn consortium after Uncle Robbie died. The moment I signed the papers they bulldozed the house and barn. I'm sure my foster parents rolled over in their graves. At least now I can release the guilt I've had about that for years. There are worse crimes.

I've been trying hard not to think about Aunt Helen and Uncle Robbie with little result on this lonesome. I still haven't come up with a reason for why they lied. They abhorred lies. I once had to say five Hail Mary's and five Our Fathers for fibbing about eating cookies when I was eight. "Lies make Baby Jesus cry," she told me a million times. Yet lying about my heritage was perfectly acceptable. From that one lie come a million questions. Why did Mama leave if she wasn't an orphan? The most obvious reason paralyzes me. *Me.* I only have the words of a liar that my father was some solider named Doug Mama met on the way to Missouri. I had no reason to doubt them then, but I sure as heck do now. I could have a father in Crimson Vale, one who doesn't know I exist. I could have brothers and sisters, nieces and nephews, even other grandparents. Reason enough to make the journey. As I drive over the Morningstar Parrish line with a carved wooden sign welcoming me, I say a prayer for God to forgive me for breaking the promise I made on the Bible. I know He will. After all He is the one who guided me here.

I pass across an iron bridge with fishing boats floating on the brown water below with hollowed out cypress trees on the bank and in the middle of the river. A bayou. An honest to goodness bayou.

When I cross that bridge, the modern world seems to vanish. Houses at least a century plus old, most the same architectural style as my new home with some Victorians and Georgians thrown in for variety. The grander houses grow more frequent as I reach the town proper with a large white water tower keeping sentinel over it. This oasis of small town commerce is prettier than some of the others I've driven through, especially when I turn down Sugarcane Lane with a tidy downtown area resembling the French Quarter with two-story brick buildings, the top level lined with iron porches. I pass a sign that informs me this is the Crimson Vale Historic District. In the center of the square of buildings is a park with hanging oaks and a large wooden pavilion with benches spread around for people to enjoy the grandeur. I was imagining some rundown place with boarded up shops like Cornwell, where I grew up, not a Southern Beverly Hills.

The GPS on my phone tells me I've reached my destination on the west side of the square. The law offices of Davenport & Davenport sit at the end of the line of wooden doors. Like most of the other shops there is a hanging sign with the name carved then painted on, though theirs looks freshly painted white and blue lettering. I park right in front, shut off the car, and sigh. I don't know how such an innocuous building can conjure such fear inside my body. My hands tremble as I remove my seatbelt. I'm here. I'm actually here. I did it. Now I just need to get out of the car. Two thousand miles and it's the last twenty feet I can't manage.

I stare through their window. The lights are on inside with a pretty forty-something woman with pageant big, blonde hair sitting behind a desk talking on the phone. I should have called. The lawyer's probably not even there. And I've been driving since seven am almost non-stop, so I must look a mess. I check myself in the mirror and cringe. I forgot how bad humidity makes my hair frizz. The bane of curly hair. I need lipstick too. I retrieve my purse from the floor and pull out my brush and make-up. As I apply lipstick, the woman from inside walks out toward me, mouth set straight. She's dressed in a tight blue cardigan stretched over obviously fake breasts and gray short skirt. I drop my lipstick when she knocks on the window.

"You can't park here," she says. I recognize her voice from the phone.

"Oh, I'm sorry," I say. "I-I didn't know."

"These spaces are for clients. The metered spots are down the street."

"Oh, um, I'm a client."

"No, you're not," she says, eyes narrowing.

I get out of the car. "I'm, uh, Jane Harrow. I think we spoke on the phone?"

The woman studies me, face falling. "Oh, my dear Lord. I-I'm so sorry, Miz Harrow. We didn't know you were coming! Did you drive all the way from California?"

"Yeah. Sorry I didn't call. It was just sort of an impulse, and…I'm sure Mr. Davenport isn't in. I don't—"

"Are you kidding? He's been chomping at the bit to hear from you. You're the most exciting thing to happen to this office in years. Come on in, he ain't busy."

No choice now. "Thank you."

I follow her into the office with its high-end white walls lined with photos of the town, suede arm chairs, chestnut desk with Mac computer, and gleaming hardwood floors including the stairs. "I'll just call up to him, let him know you're here," the secretary says, picking up the phone on her desk. "He's gonna be so surprised!" I sit in the comfy suede armchair as she dials. "Mr. Davenport, you have a walk-in." She listens. "No, sir you're gonna wanna see her. It's Jane Harrow." She's quiet. "Really. Okay, sir." She hangs up. "He'll be down in a minute. I'm Betsy, by the way. Betsy Champlain-Thibodaux. You look like her."

"Who?"

"Juliette. And Jerome, though I only remember him from when I was a child. My older sister Liza had a huge crush on him, but so did all the girls at Immaculate Heart."

"Immaculate Heart?"

"The school. We all went there. Your Mama too." She pauses. "I'm sorry."

"For what?"

"You know, her death. We didn't know she'd died until we were searching for you."

"It was a long time ago," I say with an uncomfortable smile.

"Still," she says. "What a way to go. Such a shame. So young. And suicide? I'm so, *so* sorry."

"Um, thank you." I need to change the subject. Fast. "And thank you for getting Mr. Davenport to see me on such short notice."

"Nothing to do with me, hon. He's real excited you're here. Bram will be too. He was real close to your granny toward the end there. Even put up some of his own money to find you. Took two private investigators."

"Oh."

The creaking of the stairs draws my attention away from this uncomfortable conversation. A dapper elder gentleman in his seventies dressed in an expensive double breasted pinstripe suit descends the stairs. I wouldn't call him attractive, closer to imposing, with gray hair, small brown eyes trained like guns on me, stocky build and thick jaw. Betsy lights up when she lays eyes on him. He barely notices her, not with me in the room.

"Miz Harrow?" the man asks. I rise as he walks over. "I am Bramwell Davenport, Jr." We shake hands. "This is a pleasant surprise." He releases my hand. "Mrs. Thibodaux, you may make the last of those calls then go home. Please include my wife, telling her I may be delayed. Oh, and also call Bram. He should know about our newest client." He looks at me. "Miz Harrow, please come upstairs."

He ushers me up the stairs to another narrow hardwood hallway and into the first door on the right. His office is as nice as the rest with large antique mahogany desk, and old maps on the walls amid his diplomas and awards. I sit in the brown leather armchair across from him.

"I apologize for just showing up like this," I say.

"Think nothing of it," he says, flipping through the files on his desk. "If I'd just inherited a fortune, I'd want to get my hot little hands on it as fast as possible too." He opens a file. "There's a lot of paperwork you have to fill out. Taxes need to be dealt with before you can receive the stocks, and deeds of transfer, but I've started the ball rolling. It will still take one or two months in probate. I don't see any problems on the horizon though. You should have a lawyer look over all of these."

"I've been through the process when my uncle died."

"Good. Makes things even smoother." He stares me down, eyes narrowing. "You look like them. The Fontaines. You're the spitting image of Felicia at your age. She was a damn fine looking woman in her day. Juliette too."

"Thank you," I say with a weak smile. I'm getting the feeling this man flirts with anything in a dress. I demurely look away. "I, uh, have some questions."

"I'm sure you have more than *some* questions, Miz Harrow. Just know you may not like the answers."

I nod. Okay. Here goes. "How did my grandmother and uncle die?"

He folds his arms across his broad chest. "Miz Harrow, I don't know how much of your family history you're privy to."

"None. Until your letter I was under the impression my grandmother died thirty-seven years ago in a car accident. I didn't even know I'd ever had an uncle."

"I'm sure there are reasons for that, Miz Harrow."

"Do you know those reasons, Mr. Davenport?"

His thin lips purse as he decides the best way to impart what I fear is terrible information. "The Davenport family has been in this town almost as long as the Fontaines, over two hundred years, and for about a hundred of those, we've always been your lawyers. Why your great-great Aunt Lavinia was betrothed to my grandfather, but she died before the wedding. Cotton was my godfather. There was even talk about me marrying Felicia, but your granddaddy Daniel got to her before I grew up enough."

"Sorry."

"Alls well. My point is I know your family well, which is why it was such a shock to find out about you. It was a well-guarded secret, even from me. Seems Felicia only ever told my son, and that was only when he drafted her will a few days before she died. I gotta ask myself why that is."

"Me too, sir."

He nods again. "Before I tell you what happened, there are some things you need to understand about your grandmother. Despite being beautiful, sweet, and coming from the richest family in the parish, she did not have the easiest life, Miz Harrow. Her mama Cecile died when she was a little girl, and Cotton was...a hard man."

"I know. Aunt Helen told me a little about him. How he was never around, and when he was, he used to abuse them."

"It wouldn't surprise me. There've been all sorts of rumors about Cotton, depending who you ask. That he got a fifteen-year-old servant pregnant, that he killed his wife, his son-in-law, that he trafficked with the devil, was into hoodoo, you name it. Everyone was scared to death of him, but his money kept this town going during the Depression and after the war. At some point before Felicia started selling it all off, the Fontaine's owned almost every building downtown. Cotton was a shrewd businessman, no question of that. What else did Helen tell you about him?"

"Just that he died in a car accident."

Davenport chuckles and shakes his head. "You know it was Helen who told me I'd go to hell for telling lies? She used to watch us kids when our parents got together. So damn serious and pious all the time. She stay that way?"

"I guess."

"You poor thing."

His pity rankles me. My mouth sets straight. "She was good to me," I state defensively. "They both were."

"I'm sorry," he says all the mirth draining from his face. "I spoke out of turn. Forgive me."

I nod. "So how did my great-grandfather really die?"

"No one knows for sure. He disappeared. There were only your grandmother and Hallie's accounts. But the official story is Cotton attacked Felicia for whatever reason. She might have just breathed wrong. Who knows? Hallie tried to stop it, but got beat for her trouble. I saw them after, it was real bad. Concussions, Felicia has a broken nose and ribs, it was bad. But what he did to them was a paper cut compared to what that bastard did to your uncle. Jerome walked in on the assault. He came home from celebrating his eighteenth damn birthday, and found them and confronted Cotton. He…they fought and your uncle was hit several times in the head with a fireplace poker. No one knows what happened after that. Cotton, all the money in his safe, and his car all vanished. He was never heard from again."

"Where was my mother during all this?"

"In the house. She was supposed to go out that night with Jerome but had a migraine. Took some pills and slept through the whole thing. She woke up when the ambulance came. She was still pretty out of it when they questioned her. I know, I was there. Hallie called me and the doctor before *I* called the police."

"Why?"

"It wasn't like it is now. The most Cotton would have got, especially with all the endowments to the Sheriff's office, was a slap on the wrist. And the beatings had been happening for so long. That was just the night your uncle decided to try and stop it. And look what happened."

"What did happen?"

Davenport's back straightens again, and I prepare for more bad news. "Irreparable brain damage. He was in a permanent vegetative state for the past thirty-seven years, close to the world record. There were rumors he woke once five years in but quickly fell back into the coma. Such a shame. That boy was going places. Captain of the soccer and debate teams. Good student. Hell of an artist too. One of his paintings won some state contest. He even got into some art program in New York City. I thought Cotton would have a problem with his only grandson becoming an artist instead of taking over the business—I had to read my own son the riot act when he had similar notions—but Cotton just laughed. 'I'm not worried. He'll have a change of heart when he becomes a man, you mark my words.' Jerome didn't even know he got into the program. The letter came after."

"That's terrible."

"Oh, it gets worse," Davenport warns. "Felicia never gave up hope on that boy. Hallie either. They moved him and those machines into the house, and besides a part-time nurse here and there, they took care of him all these years. Became recluses. Got worse ten years ago when Hallie died. I don't think Felicia left that house once in three years. Besides Father King, my son Bram was one of the few who ever visited toward the end. When Lulu, the new nurse, found them dead, no one was terribly surprised. It was bound to happen sometime."

I take a moment to ready myself for what is sure to be a horrific answer to my next question. "What was bound to happen?"

Davenport frowns. "As best as we can piece together, Felicia gave her son a lethal dose of sedatives then shot herself in the head. Lulu found them the next morning."

"Oh my God," I say.

"There's no concrete proof his death was pre-meditated. In fact, she'd been fixing up the house. Bram said she was even cheerful at times. She was even livelier than she'd been in decades."

"Then why?"

"They found a very high dose of barbiturates and alcohol in her system at the time of her death. The official story is, due to her altered state, she accidently overdosed Jerome. When she realized what she'd done, when it hit her he was really dead, she shot herself. We managed to keep the details quiet, at least from the major papers."

"Thank you," I say in a small voice.

"I know this must be a lot to process. Do you have any further questions or I don't know, clarifications?"

I wrack my overwhelmed brain. "Um, do you know why my mother was sent away?"

"Your mother wanted to leave. Hell, she wanted to leave *before* that night. You have to understand, Felicia was a mess, always had been since your grandfather Daniel died when the twins were two. Hallie raised those kids pretty much on her own, and when he got old enough Jerome took over the rest of the heavy lifting with Juliette. They were so devoted to one another, close to inseparable even in the damn womb. With Hallie overwhelmed, Felicia focusing on Jerome, it was the best thing all around for Jules to go."

"Who is Hallie? You keep mentioning her."

"Hallie Platt," he says with an amusing grin. "Her family worked for the Fontaine's longer than mine, since before the war between the states. Slaves who stuck around afterwards. Hallie's mama Ada was the cook for the Fontaine's until she died. And if rumors can be believed, Cotton was her daddy. When Cecile, your great-grandma died, Ada first then Hallie took up the child rearing and ran the house. Neither stopped until they dropped dead."

"What about…" the words choke in my throat. This is the question I'm scared of the most. "Madness? Is there any insanity in the family?"

Davenport just stares at me for a moment, incomprehension slowly filling his wrinkled face. "Girl, have you been listening to a word I've said? They were *all* insane. Every damn one of them right on down the line. Ending right with you, Jane Harrow." He raises an eyebrow. "Ending right with you."

CHAPTER THREE

After signing a few papers and taking the rest with me to look over later, Davenport Junior, or D.J. as he asks me to call him, agrees to take me to Fontaine house, though I insist on driving myself. I didn't like the way he kept grinning at me, staring at my chest, practically licking his chops like I was a veal cutlet. I'm young enough to be his granddaughter.

Compared to the other towns in this state, Crimson Vale seems to have gotten through these harsh economic times and various natural disasters relatively unscathed. As we venture farther into the woods, the Georgians and Victorians with pristine lawns and landscaping are once again replaced with ancient oak trees, magnolias, even weeping willows. I've never seen one in real life. They're beyond beautiful with the gray hanging moss amid the mix of orange, yellow, even red leaves as far as the eye can see. California is a brown wasteland in comparison. I have missed the seasons.

Not even the majesty of the surroundings can keep my mind from wandering to my family history. At least my anger toward Aunt Helen has waned. My great-grandfather was a murderer, abuser, and possible molester. My grandmother possibly murdered her comatose son then blew her own brains out. My uncle was kept in a coma for almost four decades. No wonder my mother ran as fast as she could away from them. I would have too. I do still wish I could have met my grandmother. I would have helped. Somehow. At least visited so she wasn't all alone.

No...

I hear the woman's faint whisper and turn up the radio. That's the first time I've understood her. What if she starts being as loud as the man? I don't need two people yelling in my head, though he's been silent since I left California. Maybe my delusions decided to take turns tormenting me.

D.J. maneuvers his Mercedes down a gravel road. The trees grow denser here with a few hollowed out cypresses visible in the distance. We must be near the river. The road continues for about a quarter mile before we reach the clearing and house. Fontaine House. *My* house. It's even grander than the picture let on. A warm glow spreads through me like nothing I've ever felt, like a part I never knew I had was now filled. I beam as bright as the sun. My smile doesn't fade even as when I climb out of the car, I notice a large black snake slithering on the dead grass. I'm just glad there are no alligators.

"Exquisite, isn't it?" D.J. asks as he strolls over to me. "It's over a hundred fifty years old. Built right after the Civil War when the old plantation house was destroyed by the Yankees."

"It has electricity?"

"Oh, yes. Internet, cable, even indoor plumbing, ma'am. In the last few months, before her passing, Felicia began a massive restoration. Painting, repairs, refurbishing. It was almost as if she knew you were coming, Miz Harrow," he says with a gleam in his eye.

I half smile before walking to the house. The moment I step onto the cornflower blue porch a sense of déjà vu stops me in my tracks. It takes me a moment to place it, but when I turn back around toward the driveway, my breath is knocked out of me. My dream. The one I've had since I was a child of me holding my baby in my arms. The trees, the iron railing, the white wooden chairs, the cornflower-blue painted hardwood floor, the door with the stained glass "F" in it, it's all the same. Unease pushes away the sunny excitement from before. There is no way I could know this place. All the details, from the spears on the black railings and placement of the magnolia tree just below a second story window to my right, are so exact.

"Miz Harrow, are you alright?" D.J. asks as he steps onto the porch. "You look like you've seen a ghost."

"I, uh, I'm fine," I lie. "May we go in, please?"

When he opens the doors, the faint smell of paint and musk like that in a museum wafts out. You can literally smell the history. We step into the foyer, the hardwood floor with a red and gold Persian rug creaking as we do. There's a sweeping staircase with the same patterned rug up the middle to the second floor.

"There are eight bedrooms with two downstairs for servants off the kitchen and six upstairs. Five bathrooms, two living rooms, dining room, and study."

"How big is the property?"

"A hundred acres. Twenty-five on land, and the rest in the bayou and little islands behind the house. Let me give you the fifty-cent tour."

I follow him to the right into the first living room complete with a red brick fireplace and huge bay windows framed by thick red curtains pulled aside with a white sash. The furniture is a mix of wicker and antiques, all the wood faded but still beautiful with ornate carvings including a six-foot red French velvet Louis XV sofa. There's even a grand piano in the corner.

"Who played?"

"Your grandmother. Your mother too. She could bring tears to your eyes, your mama. Auditioned at Julliard. Do you play?"

"No."

Staring at that piano, I can imagine Mama sitting at that bench for hours on end as a teenager, blonde hair swept up in a ponytail swishing from side-to-side as she got into the spirit of the music. A memory comes to me. Mama, with her greasy, unbrushed hair I never saw another way, sitting at the piano in the farmhouse with her eyes closed playing Beethoven's mournful dirge "Moonlight Sonata" over and over again as little four-year-old me watches her from under our coffee table. Not that she would have noticed me had I been right in her lap. For hours she never moved from that piano, hadn't stopped playing for even a second. Aunt

Helen finally came home with a bag of groceries, aghast at the sight of my mother.

"Are you still playing that same song? Have you been playing it all this time?"

Mama ignored her, thumping on the keys hard enough to break her fingers until the song ended. Just as she had three dozen times before, she began the song anew. Aunt Helen called Mama's name four times but was met only by Beethoven. Concern filled my aunt's face, but she walked past my mother to me, set the bag down, extended her hand to me, and lead me away from my possessed mother. Mama played until I fell asleep.

"Lost you again," D.J. says, bringing me out of the memory.

I shake my head to clear it. "Sorry. Let's keep going."

Next is the dining room with a table that seats a dozen with a small crystal chandelier hanging above. Too bad I don't know anyone in town. I throw a mean dinner party. The kitchen is through the swinging door. Large but almost bare with only a few appliances such as an ancient fridge, gas oven, coffee maker, and microwave on the dark gray linoleum counters. By a window overlooking the porch and bayou sits a small, circular table with four chairs with pressed herbs in glass frames scattered along the walls. So far this is the homiest room in the place. The heart of the house. Through another door near the fridge are rooms as big as jail cells with twin beds, small dressers, an ancient TV with rabbit ears, and bathroom between them. There's dust over everything, and when I begin to sneeze, it's time to retreat.

Our next stop is another smaller living where, along the far wall, are glass enclosed bookcases with leather-bound books inside. Through the next door is a study with more bookcases, a huge globe, and paintings along the wall of battles and maps. The mahogany desk with a chair similar to the ones in the other room behind it is another antique with curling carvings in it. The desk is bare with no picture frames or papers on it. A man cave. Cotton's domain. Surprised the walls aren't dripping blood. When D.J. pulls open the double doors, we're back in the foyer.

Halfway done. So far so wonderful.

Upstairs the long hallway is divided with two doors on the right and five on the left. We move left first as D.J. points out the various portraits of my ancestors. Great-Aunt Lavinia, Great-Great-Grandmother Josephine, Great Uncle Tucker, Great-Great-Great Grandfather Francois all with the family's curly hair and pointed chin. The first two bedrooms are as personal as a hotel rooms with the same four-poster double beds, chifarobe, dresser, and rocking or lounge chair by the window with gauzy white curtains. Guest bedrooms. Not surprisingly they appear pristine, as if no one ever used them. Probably never did.

As I examine the second one, D.J.'s cell phone rings. He unclips it. "Have to take this."

"Okay."

He nods before walking toward the staircase. Thank goodness. I could sense him staring at my bum more than once when he wasn't touching my arm as if I were blind and needed a guide. Oh, I wish Owen were here. If a man even glanced my way, my husband shot the offender the glare of death. It worked every time.

When I hear the front door shut downstairs, I move onto the next room, a bathroom with a tub/shower combo, but the next bedroom is more interesting. Downright odd. Faded blue and white striped wallpaper lines the walls with the matching blue curtains drawn, but even in the dim light I can still make out the details of pendants from Immaculate Heart Prepatory and paintings on the walls. After checking out the tiny ensuite bathroom, I move back into the bedroom. The paintings are interesting, ranging from one of the house as the sun sets over the magnolia trees to those of a familiar teenage girl sitting in a rocking chair outside, her long legs stretched onto the railing. My mother. No matter the painting "J.C." is scrawled in the corner of each. This was my uncle's room, left untouched. The bed's even made. Is this where they died? I don't see any blood or bullet holes. Regardless, I want out of this shrine.

The room right across is as unnerving as the previous one. The walls are wallpapered pink with tiny white bows that match the bedspread. There's a white vanity desk with big mirror next to a huge armoire also painted white. Along the walls shelves hold trophies with my mother's name on them amid many, many China dolls. First and second place for musical achievements. The paintings on the walls bear the same initials as the others, but these are all of my mother. Her dressed as a gypsy. In a boat with a white parasol. On the stairs with brown-haired girl, arms over each other's shoulders. Mama at the piano with a stream of light hitting her hands. Uncle Jerome certainly had a muse. The only one not of Mama is of a light skinned African American woman kneading bread in the kitchen downstairs. I'd place her in her forties with an afro barely contained in a floral handkerchief that matches her red apron. He even captured her pointed chin. Hallie.

Just standing in this room sets my nerves on edge. This is where Mama grew up. Played with dolls. Fantasized about boys. Did her homework. This was her oasis away from her mother and grandfather. She probably lay on that bed talking to her best friend or brother about school, about her dreams for the future. I doubt those dreams included a comatose brother, Cornwell Missouri, getting pregnant at eighteen, insane by nineteen, and dead at twenty-one. I can practically sense those shattered dreams clinging to the walls like black mold, hidden but slowly eating away at the structure and causing untold harm to those who linger. I think I'll avoid this room as much as possible.

Two more rooms to go. Let's get this over with.

There are more portraits on the walls on the right half—Arabella, Emily, Richard all with the Fontaine chin and curls. There is also an antique carved armoire filled with towels, sheets, even a few quilts. I recognize one or two from when Aunt Helen crafted them in our living room. I guess not all contact was cut off. Not sure how I should feel about that. Nothing. Those two shrines broke a fuse inside me. Thank God. I shut the door and move onto the next bedroom.

This one is a bit bigger than the others, about the size of our old master, and more lived in with a King-sized, four-poster bed with another familiar quilt, this one yellow and purple in the shape of a daisy that offsets the light blue walls and white curtains. The paintings in here are watercolors of the grounds, house, or vases of flowers with "J.C." in the corner of each. He was prolific. There's even a flat-screen TV with DVD player, a hairbrush, comb, and Vera Bradley bag filled with makeup on the dresser. In the corner, near the bay window overlooking the second-story porch, is a roll-top desk. I find ledgers, a laptop, a checkbook, some bills and other loose papers I'll have to review later. Next to the bed on the nightstand is a pair of glasses, P.G. Wodehouse novel, and remote controls with a Vera Bradley purse on the floor. I have to strongest urge to poke around inside it and all the dressers and end table too, but this seems wrong. This is the only room with a tinge of life left in it, as if my grandmother just stepped out. Even the bathroom with the divinely deep claw-footed tub still has her toothbrush and shampoo. I leave everything as is.

As I walk across the hall, I hear the crackling of gravel outside. Oh, thank God. That awful man must have gotten called away. Thank goodness for small mercies. I walk through the double doors of what I find is the master bedroom. It's large, easily the size of my entire first apartment, yet almost empty. There is next to no furniture, just a folded up cot in the corner, a worn green lounging chair with another Vera Bradley bag full of knitting needles and yarn, a bare armoire and dresser, and nothing more. Even the windows are bare. The walls as well, nary a painting or decoration on the beige walls. Even the high ceiling appears freshly painted. As I move around, I notice the industrial plugs in the walls for the medical equipment. This room has been sanitized.

This must be where it happened. My uncle lay in this room for close to forty years with my grandmother by his side, apparently knitting as the tubes and respirator kept him…I wouldn't call that alive. Undead. What on earth was she thinking? Waiting one year sure, but thirty-plus? Giving up her own life to watch over a comatose man? Insanity. It really must run in the blood. I only hope—

Creaking in the hallway startles me out of my dark thoughts. Darn it, I guess he didn't leave. I'm not sure how much longer I can handle social niceties. I'm exhausted from the drive, not to mention out of practice with people, and would derive great satisfaction from smacking that letch with my purse should he glimpse down my shirt again. I just want to take a shower, get into my pajamas, and sleep for a week. Have to get him out of here first. I walk into the hallway.

Everything stops.

My lungs, my heart, even my ability to blink stops the moment I set eyes on *him*. If it were storming outside I would swear I'd just been hit by a bolt of lightning. Time stands as still as we do, just staring at one another with the same awestruck expression. The stranger my age is a few inches over six foot with a lean body encased in an expensive gray suit with matching tie and vest. He could grace the pages of a magazine with that suit, wavy dirty blonde hair with a lock brushing his forehead and coiffed to appear slightly disheveled, big blue eyes, feminine lips, straight nose, and strong jaw ending at a pointed chin. He's around my age, but as our eyes meet and another wave of whatever this is jolts through me, he seems a century older and I've known him every moment, every millisecond of that time. I'm scared, exhilarated, unnerved all at once. But deep down there's a …recognition peeking through the strum and drang.

I never believed in love at first sight, and I don't know if that's what this is, but every atom of mine senses, every atom of his calling to me, screaming for me to sprint over to this stranger, tear off our clothes, and have him rut me like a beast right on the hardwood floor. To feel him stretching me, thrusting inside me. My most sacred place pulsates and grows wet just from the mere thought. *What the heck is happening to me?* This stranger must be suffering the same torment because those blue eyes grow ravenous like an anorexic faced with prime rib. No one's ever gazed at me like this, with pure unadulterated, hot, wild, salivating lust. The same way I'm gazing at him. My resolve to remain on my side of the hall cracks with each passing moment. His fails. He lets out a soft grunt and takes a stride toward me. *Thank God.*

"Mrs. Harrow?"

Those two words break whatever enchantment engulfed me. I somehow pry my eyes away from the stranger toward the creaky stairs. Suddenly I'm freezing and trembling as if in shock. At least I can breathe again, though only in short bursts. D.J. takes the final step up into the hallway. "Oh, good, you found her," he says to the stranger.

"Yes," the man says, quiet voice cracking a tad, "I did."

"Mrs. Harrow, may I present my son, Bram. He's the one who tracked you down." D.J. glances from his son to me, eyes narrowing in confusion. "What the hell is the matter with you two? Y'all look like you've seen a ghost."

"We're fine, sir," Bram says with only a faint trace of a Southern accent. "Just got a chill. Old house and all."

"Oh. Well, you can get someone to fix that, I guess. Bram can give you the handyman's name and number. He's been the one taking care of things. Hey," he says to his son, "I've been meaning to ask. What happened to all those weird looking creatures and symbols that used to be on all the walls and tables? The gargoyles and such? There were still a ton of them even after the renovation."

"I, uh, had them removed." Bram turns to me. "I hope you don't think I overstepped my bounds. I had them remove the medical equipment too and clean up. I just…wanted to cheer the place up for your arrival."

"Um, thank you. For thinking of me."

"Your grandmother would have wanted me to, um, make things as comfortable for you as possible."

"You're very kind," I say, blushing. I'm sure as red as a fire engine. I look over at D.J. "Both of you."

"So, have you decided what you're going to do with the place?" D.J. asks me.

"I haven't really thought that far ahead."

"But you're planning on staying, right?" Bram asks with urgency. "At least for a while?"

I meet his eyes again, instantly overpowered by the intense fear in them. I can stand it for only a millisecond. "Um, I-I guess."

"Well, you are welcome to stay here while the will's in probate. Or the Cypress Hotel is lovely. There's also the Crimson Vale Motel, but it's a tad low rent."

"Um…" Do I really want to spend the night alone in this house? Two people died here, and those are just the ones I know of. I don't believe in ghosts—your soul either enters heaven or hell—but this house feels as if it's under an enchantment. Frozen in time by an evil witch. But it's mine. I came all this way, and if I don't stay in this house tonight, I never will. "No, I'll be staying here. The letter said everything was still turned on?"

"It is," Bram says. "I-*we* kept the utilities up to date for when you finally arrived."

"Thank you. Both."

We stand in silence for a few awkward moments. I sense Bram staring at me, waiting for something, but I can't return his gaze. My eyes remain glued to the floor. "Well," D.J. says, "we'll get out of your hair. You're probably tired from your trip. Bram?" The son follows the father down the hall and stairs with me three steps behind to show them out. Bram glances back, each time his mouth opens to say something, but he thinks better of it each time. "You have my card if you have any questions," D.J. continues. "Don't hesitate to call, even if it's just for the name of a good restaurant."

"Thank you."

The men step out onto the porch, but I wait at the threshold. "Remember. *Anything*," D.J. adds as he ambles to his BMW.

All I want is for you to leave now. "I will. Thank you."

His son moves toward his own BMW SUV, but halfway there Bram suddenly stops, doesn't move for a moment, then spins around to face me. For some reason my stomach clenches from nerves as he does. I grip the door handle in case he's about to finish what he started in the hall, whatever that was. "I, um, I…" he says. His mouth clamps shut again to find the right words. If possible, he's as unnerved as I am. He shakes his head to clear it and smiles. "Welcome home, Jane."

Those words send a cascade of warmth through my body like warn rain just washed over me. I haven't a clue what to say back. All I can manage is a weak smile before retreating inside like a mouse into a hole. The moment the door shuts, I turn my back to it and rest against the wood with a sigh. What is the matter with me? Have I replaced voices and seeing invisible people with nymphomania? I remain pressed against the door until I hear both men drive away, the tension waning as the sounds fade, leaving nothing but glorious silence. The house is still. *My* house. Mine.

Home.

CHAPTER FOUR

Hurrah, there is food in the pantry. Ramen, canned peaches, Vienna sausages, spaghetti, plus an apple and beef jerky I have left over from the trip to fill me up. I sit at the small wooden table in the corner of the kitchen with four matching chairs that has probably hosted more meals than the lavish dining room. The silence lost its appeal after ten minutes, so I eat with the radio playing. Classical music that the radio was set to. I can almost see my grandmother sitting at this very table listening to this same song before having to return up to her comatose son. God, how lonely she must have been. I've only been here an hour and I feel its oppression pressing on me. The walls are coated with isolation and misery. I'm going to do my utmost to purge those if it's the last thing I do. I just left a house like that, I refuse to live in another.

After cleaning up my feast, I start unloading my car. I can't believe how much I brought. All three of our suitcases, four tote bags, and three boxes, not to mention the cooler and overnight bag. By the time I deposit everything in the larger guestroom I'm covered in sweat and my arms and legs ache. Maybe first thing I should do here is join a gym. Didn't realize I'd gotten so out of shape. I can't imagine what Bram was so responsive to. I have no muscles, heck I'm little more than a scarecrow. Even my breast went down a cup. The fact I actually care shocks me.

Shower and pajamas are next on the agenda. I find myself locking the bathroom door. Okay, guess I'm not as comfortable here as I thought I was. I use my last bit of energy washing the road and sweat off. Good thing I went around the house checking it was secure before the shower. Those stairs are too much for me now. I slip into bed and grab my cell on the nightstand for my final task of the night. I promised I'd phone him when I arrived.

"Jane?" Owen asks over the phone. "Is that you?"

"Yeah, hi, it's me. I'm here. I made it."

"You're at the house?"

"Yeah. It's…beautiful. Even better than the picture. And so quiet. You'd love it."

"So there were no problems?"

"It wasn't a scam if that's what you mean," I say with an undercurrent of anger.

"That wasn't…I just meant the drive, dealing with the lawyers, that's all."

"Oh. No, it was all actually a lot easier than I thought it would be. The Davenport's were very," –gorgeous, spellbinding, frightening—"accommodating."

"Did they tell you what happened to your grandmother and uncle?"

I sigh. "Yeah. My family makes yours look like the Walton's." I tell him the whole sordid history.

"Do you think it's all true?" my always skeptical husband asks at the end.

"He has no reason to lie."

"Still. I'll look into it. See if I can access the incident reports, autopsies—"

"Owen, no. Please don't."

"There's got to be more to the story than what he told you. You don't want to know what he left out? What—"

"*No*, I don't. What good could it possibly do now? They're all dead. It doesn't matter. I don't want to know any more horrible things. I've discovered enough for a lifetime. I just want…peace, okay?"

There's no sound on the other end of the phone as he mulls this over. We've been married long enough for me to know he's already made up his mind to do it anyway, if he hasn't already. Still, he says, "Whatever you want, sweetheart."

"Thank you. And I'm sorry about the other night. I was rude."

"You're forgiven."

He's already forgiven me for far worse crimes, why not that? "How are things with you?"

"Same old, same old. Still building a case on that motorcycle club in San Fernando."

"They don't want to send you undercover again, do they?" I ask anxiously.

He went undercover for six months with another club when we lived in Missouri. With his massive physique, hard-edge attitude, and air of violence everyone but I seems to notice, he fits right in with that crowd. I barely saw him, once a week at most, and almost lost my mind with worry. It got him a promotion though, and enough money that we could finally afford to try for a family. I simply failed on my end of the bargain.

"Would you care if I did?"

"Owen, of course I would care! It's so dangerous. Last time you were almost shot."

"I haven't said yes. Yet. They just brought it up today. I wanted to…talk it over with you before I gave them an answer."

Meaning do I still want to continue with this divorce nonsense, and I'm going to risk my life if you are. One would think a man who used to make sport of starting bar fights in his youth wouldn't be so passive aggressive. Only with me. With everyone else he's just aggressive-aggressive. Don't know which is worse.

What else can I say but the truth? "Well, I'll probably be here for awhile, so do what you want. I can't stop you." There's more silence on his end. It's oppressive. "So, did you move back into the house yet?"

"No, not yet. Maybe this weekend," he adds. "I guess you're planning to stay there then?"

"At least for a few weeks. Get the paperwork in order. Fix up the house."

"To sell?"

"Probably. I don't know," I say quickly. "I just got here. I'm exhausted. I haven't made any decisions yet."

A pause, then, "You're actually considering staying there permanently, aren't you?"

"No, not seriously. I don't know, Owen. I'm not capable of making life changing decisions tonight. When I know so will you. I promise."

"Okay," he says with reluctance. There's more silence on his end. I never used to mind these. In fact one of the reasons I agreed to marry him was he was one of the few people I felt comfortable with just being alone in a room in complete silence. We could sit in a car or restaurant not saying a word for minutes without a moment of awkwardness. Of course the last year that silence became torturous. I'd either chatter about the weather or other nonsense to fill the maddening void. He'd never contribute.

"I'm gonna go, okay? I'll talk to you later."

"Okay." He pauses. "I love you."

"I lov—" I catch myself. A reflex, nothing more. "Bye, Owen."

I end the call. Now I'm *beyond* exhausted. That man takes it out of me. I shut off the Tiffany stained-glass lamp on the nightstand and close my eyes. The only noise emanates from my breath and the spinning fan above. Not ideal conditions when attempting to keep thoughts at bay.

I can't believe he's considering going undercover again. The one and only time he did, a meth head took a shot at him during a drug deal. I swore I'd divorce him if he ever took another assignment like that again. I know his job's dangerous. The first year of our marriage my heart leapt into my throat as he stepped out the door. I've attended two funerals for agents lost in the line of duty, but working undercover is like running toward a bullet. How dare he attempt to blackmail me like that? Stop the divorce or I'll put myself in grave danger? I never thought he'd play dirty.

He must be getting desperate. Probably didn't think I'd take it this far. Of course neither did I. Most days I can't answer why I don't fire my lawyer and ask Owen to come home. Because I love him. We're all each other has. But we've just hurt each other *so* much. We've wiped away all trust. And it's as much my fault as his, if not more so. After all, I betrayed him first.

I can pinpoint the exact moment our marriage truly began to crumble. It was right after the sixth miscarriage, a little over a year ago. We were in with the fertility specialist who, like the previous two others, had no real answers for us. We'd both tested negative for all major chromosomal abnormalities, and when they tested the fetal tissue, it was healthy as well. I was fertile. Getting pregnant wasn't the issue, staying that way was, especially since my uterus now has scar tissue. The specialist was adamant that for the sake of my health I should either use a surrogate or stop trying full stop and look into adoption. That the next miscarriage could result in a hysterectomy or worse. That it was over.

That was it. The moment. I had failed us both.

But I wouldn't give up. I couldn't. As Owen filled out the adoption applications I refused to even touch, I pretended to go back on the Pill. Four months later, I was pregnant again. Owen was livid. That was the only time I was ever afraid of him as he screamed and railed against my subterfuge. My idiocy. My lies. He slept in the spare room for a week. And it was all for nothing. Number seven lasted nine weeks before my poor womb revolted. Tried to kill me with a massive hemorrhage. I lost a third of my blood volume and was a hairsbreadth from losing my uterus. In the hospital Owen could barely look at me. When I was strong enough, physically at least, he went away on "business" for a few days. A week after he returned I found a pamphlet in his truck about vasectomy aftercare.

When I confronted my husband, he didn't deny it. He said he knew me too well, that I wouldn't give up until I was dead, and he wouldn't stand by and let that happen. That was when we started to live as roommates. We slept in the same bed, I kept the house and made him dinner the few nights he wasn't at the office, but that was it. Even pecks on the cheeks seemed too intimate. We attempted marital counseling, then individual counseling, but my heart wasn't in it. I was too depressed, too hurt, too exhausted to care. To fight. We continued in limbo for five months until his one night stand. He drove right home from her apartment, shook me awake, and told me what he'd done with tears in his eyes. The final nail in our coffin. I may have been the one who filed for divorce, but I miss him every minute of every day. Earning that rare smile. Holding onto him as we ride his motorcycle. Tracing his scars, his tattoo of my name over his heart, the Celtic cross on his left shoulder, "Semper Fi" on his bicep, and my favorite: the Claddagh with its heart and hands forever pointed down on his ring finger. Heck, I even miss his snoring. When I don't down pills, it takes me forever to fall asleep without it. Don't think that'll be a problem tonight though.

I drift off to sleep in my new home with the image of my husband alone in his car, staring up at the freeway signs wondering how far he could drive tonight before stopping to come rescue me from myself once more. Old habits die hard. I hope he's burying this particular habit once and for all. For *his* sake.

*

It's him. He's here. I've found him.

Finally.

Despite the snap of the alligator's jaws as I step onto the cracking porch. Despite the corrosion raining down around me from the collapsing house, the moment our eyes lock, that hunger and longing radiating from both his and mine blows away the rest of the world. There is only me and him. As it always should be. "Finally," Bram whispers as his warm hand caresses my cheek. *"Finally."*

That one touch is the only tenderness he can afford. His mouth collides against mine, tongue invading my mouth, almost pinning it in a dominance match already won. At the same time, one arm wraps around my waist, fingers digging into my back as his other snakes under my skirt, fingernails clawing up my thigh to my bare buttocks. I fear he draws blood. I don't care. Let him skin me alive as long as he never releases me. I close my eyes and kiss him back with equal intensity, clinging onto him like a woman dangling off the edge of a cliff. That familiar throbbing between my legs begins, increasing in intensity with each passing instant. I'm dripping already. His arousal grows against mine until I'm sure we're both going to explode.

Not yet. Our lips still sealed, he backs me against the column before. His hands leave my body to work on his pants button and zipper. I refuse to let those lips escape mine as he pulls his pants down. I couldn't stand not having him touch me now. This is what I was made for. Him.

He braces me against the column, hoisting me up so I can wrap my legs around his bare waist. The tip of him presses against my thigh already as wet as I am inside. The throbbing is unbearable now. Maddening. But he doesn't move. Even his kisses cease. "Jane," he whispers.

With that one word, I realize everything has chilled. The air, the wall behind me, but especially Bram. The arms holding me steady, his thighs next to mine, even his manhood are all as cold as the grave. What…? My eyes fly open. Dear God. Instead of my beautiful Bram, it's my uncle gripping me. My uncle with blood running from his every orifice down his gray, cracked skin. "Welcome home."

Before I can scream, the corpse impales himself inside me, tearing me in half.

I jerk awake with a yelp, heart racing but far more disconcerting the sensation of him, the agony of the violation still throbbing between my legs. I glance wildly around the unfamiliar room for my assailant. It takes a moment to establish where I am, that it was just a dream. It *was* just a dream. Somehow I manage to steady my breathing, climb out of bed, and splash cold water on my face. It was just a dream.

Be it the dream, the cold water, or my own crazy brain, when I crawl back into bed, I realize I am wide awake now. Normally I'd watch television but my room doesn't have one, only the living room and my grandmother's room do. Do I want to watch that badly? I lie in bed staring at the ceiling for a few minutes, willing sleep to return. Almost impossible when whenever I close my eyes I see my uncle's bloody face. Yeah, I want to watch that badly, and I have to go in there sometime. It's my house now. I need to begin feeling comfortable in it. I yank the quilt off the bed, wrapping it around myself, before I venture into the dark hall. The silence is deafening so when I hit a creaky floorboard it echoes throughout the house. At least no one will be able to sneak up here without my knowledge.

Felicia's bedroom is as stuffy as the rest of this place, so after I turn on the TV I open the window, breathing in the crisp, humid air. Much better already. Her bed is far more comfortable than the one in the guest room, one of those Temperpedic type that's like sleeping on a cloud that molds to your body. We had to throw our Tempurpedic away after the last miscarriage. Looked like a pig had its throat slit on it. We went through so many mattresses through the years.

The last thing my grandmother watched was *Fox News.* Seems I come from a long line of Republicans. The hits keep coming. I change it to the always mind numbing *Real Housewives* and settle into the pillows. They still smell of Chanel #5. Aunt Helen wore it on special occasions like dates with Uncle Robbie or Christmas parties at church. I wonder what else the sisters had in common. Did they enjoy the same foods? Fold towels the same way? What did my grandmother used to think about when she laid? There are a million, billion unanswered questions that will forever remain that way. It hurts my head just thinking about a few of them.

The Housewives bicker over who is the fairest of them all, and for once I can't seem to pay attention. The perfume is overwhelming. I change pillows but the smell doesn't waver. She must have spilled some. I get up to open the other window, but even from here with a fresh breeze the odor is overpowering. Maybe I should strip the bed. Make sure—

The air changes.

Subtle but the ripples make the hairs on my arms tingle. I think someone's…I near about jump out of my skin when I hear creaking in the hallway. It only happens once but is loud enough not to be the house settling. I stand stone still, staring at the open bedroom door. I should climb out the window onto the porch. I should find a weapon, right? When no one appears after a few seconds, I know I have to go looking. God, I wish Owen—

There's another creak, farther away but still loud enough to get my adrenaline spiking. I glance around for a weapon, finding only a knitting needle. Better than nothing. I yank it from the yarn, get my cell phone, steel my spine, and charge out into the hall.

Oh, I really wish I'd paid attention to the location of light switches. The glow from the TV provides enough illumination for me to peer down the hall to the staircase. Empty. I really have no desire to go room to room with nothing but a knitting needle. I quickly move to the light on an end table underneath Aunt Arabella, and when I switch it on, my tension level lowers. Until I hear a creak downstairs. Fudge. I should call someone. The police. Yeah, I'll become very popular here if I phone them every time I hear a noise. It's nothing. I know it's nothing.

"If there's anyone down there, you should know I have a gun," I call out. "You have five seconds to leave before I come after you. I've already contacted the police."

Nothing. Crud. Tomorrow I'm turning this house upside down for a gun. This is the South, my grandmother was Republican, there's bound to be one around somewhere. It's dark downstairs, but I manage to find the light switch by the front door. Nothing. I move through the study, small living room and kitchen, even the servants room without locating so much as a mouse. Just in case, I exchange the needle for a butcher knife. Really I shouldn't have either. Owen told me when fighting an opponent with superior physical strength the weapon is often used on the victim. Clutching this large blade makes me feel better though.

Of course both the dining room and larger living room are vacant because I am just a paranoid freak. There are no open windows or unlocked doors. No bogeymen lurking in closets or dark corners. I plop myself down on the piano bench with a sigh, setting the knife on the keys. Aren't I lucky? A new symptom of insanity manifesting itself: paranoia. I'm literally jumping at shadows. I sigh again and stare at the piano. The keys are dusty. I hit a few. Out of tune. Guess Grandmother didn't play. She—

What was that?

The now familiar experience of being watched returns, but this time is accompanied by the unmistakable odor of cigar smoke. I…movement. Out of the corner of my eye. My throat shuts off my air supply. Holy God there really is someone here. The intruder doesn't move again. Maybe he doesn't know I know he's here. Okay, just do it. Three…two…one! With one quick movement, I grab the knife and spin around, brandishing it at…nothing. There is nothing there. An empty doorway. The smell's dissipated as well. Crud. *Crud.* I can't stop panting as I lower the knife. Great, now I'm smelling imaginary scents. Maybe I have a brain tumor. I think that's one of the symptoms. Not sure which is worse, tumor or insanity. Six of one, half a dozen of another.

I complete another sweep of the house, including the bedrooms before I return to the Housewives, feeling like an idiot. I've lived alone before, heck I've been doing it for months now, but one night here and I'm ready to call in the National Guard. I fall back into my grandmother's bed, pulling the quilt tight around myself. The knife is placed on the pillow beside me. Just in case. Like the locked bedroom door.

My first night in my new home. Fight with Owen, horrific dreams, paranoid delusions coming in full force, and horrible television. No matter how far you get from where you began, there you are all over again.

CHAPTER FIVE

Lord, it's cold. Why is it so cold? A chilled breeze stirs me from slumber. I open my eyes, and see it's a little past eleven. The TV's still on, that horrible real estate show playing. If the cold didn't entice me out of bed, the TV does. I shut it off and close the windows. Darn it. It's gray outside. The only thing I enjoyed about LA was the weather. Sunny and warm over seventy-five percent of the year. It's days like today I want to stay in bed with the covers over my head. That impulse is intensified by the fact I have to venture out into my new town today. Grocery shopping to do. Blah.

After the usual morning rituals, I change into blue jeans and long sleeve pink shirt, pull my hair into a ponytail, and shut off all the lights I flipped on last night. A few more nights with them on, and I'll blow through my inheritance before I officially have it. I find a plethora of cleaning supplies under the sink but sadly no food has materialized in the night. My list ends up being as long as my arm. Best get this over with.

Per my GPS, the nearest grocery store is ten miles away in an actual shopping center with a Walmart, Books-A-Million, Starbucks, and clothing boutiques. Finding civilization sooths me to no end. Just like home. It being a weekday the majority of the shoppers are women with tiny children and overflowing shopping carts. Most pay me no never mind, but a few, the older ones, I catch glancing at me with questioning eyes. I lower my head and continue shopping as if I don't notice. I lived in a small town, even smaller than this one growing up, so this could be a normal reaction to my being a garden variety stranger. I hope it is.

Normally I loathe grocery shopping, but in spite of the glances, it feels good to be here. It's so…normal. The few people who I actually look at don't morph into bleeding corpses and there are no whispers. I'm starting to feel a little like myself again. Maybe instead of cleaning I'll get some work done on the book. The illustrations are due in a week, and I'm not even half done. I've never missed a deadline, I don't want to start now. Yes, that's what I'll do. The quicker I fall into my old routine the better off I'll be. Normalcy, that's all I want. Boring, humdrum, monotony. It's not—

The smashing of glass down the aisle pulls me out of my thoughts. Not four feet away a woman in her fifties stares, slack-jawed, at me with red pesto all around her feet like a pool of blood. "Oh, dear Lord," she gasps almost horrified at the sight of me. She's overweight with reddish hair shorn short, pug nose, and clothes two sizes too small. Before I can turn around to flee, the wide-eyed woman pushes her cart toward me. "I-I-I'm so sorry but, you-you look so much like someone I used to know. I thought you were a ghost for a second. You are Juliette's daughter, right? I-I didn't even know she had a daughter until Mrs. Cowan died. You-you, God you look just like them. Maybe him even more than her even. My God."

I have no idea how to respond. "And-and you are?"

"Oh Lord," the woman says, smoothing her hair, "I'm sorry, what you must think of me. Crazy woman at the Winn-Dixie, right? No, I'm Tammy Charbaux, well now. I was Tammy Strickland when I knew your mama. My sister Janet was her best friend since kindergarten. She and Jerome practically lived at my house when we were growing up. She was so sweet. They both were. It was terrible what happened to him, to both of them. Hell, all of them," she says with a scoff.

"Yes," I say with a half-smile. "Wait, your sister's name is Janet?"

"Yeah, Janet Strickland, now Janet LeClerz. She lives in Baton Rouge. She's a doctor. Well, a psychologist. When I told her about you, she was so shocked. Juliette never answered any of our letters after she moved away. We didn't hear she died until a year after. Damn near broke Janie's heart."

"I'm sorry."

"I know she'd love to meet you," Tammy says. "It's rude of me to ask, I know, but could I get your telephone number to give to Janie?"

"Of course," I say, pulling out a pen and paper from my purse. I write down my cell number since I don't know the house number yet.

"So, how long are you in town for? I'd love to have you over. I make a fine meatloaf. Just in case you get lonesome in that creepy old house."

I hand her the paper. "I'd love that. Thank you."

"Anything for Juliette's little girl. She taught me the piano, you know. Can't remember a note now, but she was so nice. So beautiful. So talented. They both were. We all thought for sure Jerome would come to his senses and realize he was in love with Janie, but it didn't happen. Guess a lot didn't," she says with a sad smile. "All such a waste." Tammy shakes her head. "Anyway, I'll make sure to give this to Janie and call you about dinner."

"Thank you so much."

"Of course." We stand looking at each other for an awkward second before she half smiles again. "Well, best tell them about the spill. I'll see you around." She pushes her cart away after another smile, and I move the opposite direction.

Well, that was a pleasant surprise. I locate my mother's best friend and am offered a free dinner all in one stroke. This is a sign, it has to be. There are no coincidences, they are only signposts on God's path. Maybe my biological father *is* here. If anyone would know, it'd be Janet. Janie. I must be named after her. This revelation brings a smile to my face. Mama named me after her best friend, and the woman who raised her, Hallie. For some reason, I swell with pride. I have roots. "Thank you, God," I whisper.

The rest of my shopping trip is uneventful with only a few more glances, but I finally loosen up when I return the safety of my car. There isn't a doubt in my mind people will gossip about my excursion to their friends. They probably feel the same as Tammy, like the ghost of Juliette Cowan has risen from the grave to purchase lettuce. *I'd* be unnerved if I were them.

About halfway home, as Bonnie Raitt gives people something to talk about, my cell phone rings in my purse. The theme from the movie *Halloween*. Melissa. She programmed it the last time she visited. Guess I've put off talking to my best friend long enough. If I'm sane enough to shop I'm sane enough to get through a conversation. At least I hope so. "Hello? How goes the book tour?"

"Forget the damn tour. You've moved to Lousia-fucking-ana and didn't tell me?" my always colorful friend asks. "What the hell, Jane?"

"I guess Owen called you."

"You bet your ass he did. I would have called sooner but I lost my damn phone in Seattle and just got a replacement. He left me three messages begging me to talk some sense into you."

"Owen doesn't beg."

"Well, it was his version of begging. The fact he called *me* should show how worried he is about you."

"There is absolutely no reason for either of you to be nervous," I chuckle. "I'm fine. I'm great."

"The hell you are. You're in the middle of a divorce with a man you're still in love with, you just found out you have long lost relatives who murder-suicided, and you dropped your whole life to move halfway across the country on a whim. Plus I've been calling and calling this past month, and you haven't called me back once. That's not like you. None of that is like you."

"Okay, first, I've been getting divorced for months, I have more or less come to terms with it. Second, yes it was a shock to discover I've been lied to for years, but I didn't know my uncle or grandmother, so I'm not exactly mourning them. Third, I haven't made a decision if I'm staying here or not, so I haven't moved. And the reason I didn't phone you back was I knew you were on tour and didn't want you to be distracted by my silly little problems. I did e-mail you, remember? I am fine. I feel better than I have in years. Really."

Her end is quiet for a moment as she mulls my lies over. "Tell me exactly what happened with this Louisiana mess."

I tell her about the phone calls and letter, the arguments with Owen, the drive, the family history, leaving out only my descent into insanity and almost throwing myself at a perfect stranger. I love Melissa to death, have since we became roommates in college, but she makes everything a drama. It's a wonderful trait for a writer but can be annoying in a friend. When I'm done with the saga, I've reached home.

"Holy crapballs, J. And you're staying in that house alone?"

Juggling the phone and grocery bags, I manage to unlock the door and step into my stuffy house. "Yep. You should see it, Mel. It's gorgeous like *Gone With The Wind*. Over two hundred years old. I'll send you pictures."

"I don't care how gorgeous it is. At least two people you know of died there. Recently. Have you saged the house?"

"What?"

"To cleanse the negative energy. It don't get more negative than a murder/suicide, babe. You just buy a sage stick and walk around every room saying a blessing. I'll mail you one."

I set the bags on the counter. "You know I don't believe in that stuff."

"Then get a priest out there. I'm serious. Remember my cousin Wendy? She bought a house where a guy was murdered, right? There were all these nasty smells, doors closing on their own, whispers, even hands holding her down on the bed. She burned sage, even called a priest, but finally she just had to move. That was a serious haunting, maybe even a demon. Just nip that negative energy in the bud right away before it spreads and festers. Trust me on this."

"Mel, this isn't one of your novels. There are no vampires in the attic or ghosts haunting the halls. They even cleaned the blood off the walls. It's a perfectly wonderful house. You'd love it. There's hardwood falls, a study—"

"It's not the floors or architecture I'm worried about, babe. It's the fact that everyone who lived there went batshit crazy. That can't be a coincidence."

I stroll back outside to retrieve more groceries. "What? You're saying the house killed them? My grandmother was stuck in here alone with her comatose son for almost forty years. *She* decided to do that. *She* was the one who shot herself, not the house."

"Okay, did you just hear yourself? There was nothing about what you said that could be considered good. If you had half a brain you'd get in your car, hightail it back to LA, rip up those stupid divorce papers, and throw your arms around your big lug of a husband like you know you should."

"Excuse me," I say as I walk back inside, "didn't you say a few months ago I should castrate him for stepping out on me?"

"Yeah, that was before he told me his side of things. Tricking him into getting you pregnant again? Withholding sex for months to punish him?"

I stop dead in my tracks in the foyer. "He told you all that? What, are you two talking about me behind my back now? How long has this been going on?"

"We're both really worried about you, especially now. You can't keep running and hiding from your problems, J. They're still there when you decide to return. But Owen may not be. In spite of all the bullshit you two have gone through, he has stuck by you. Even now. You are the best thing that happened to each other. You *need* each other. Don't throw that away because of fear or pride."

"I'm not-I-I'm not taking marital advice from a two-time divorcee, okay? I gotta go." I pull the phone from my ear and hang up. The nerve! She—

THWACK!

A screech escapes me as I leap inches off the floor and drop the bags and phone in fright. Oh Jesus Christ! I pivot around and see the door has slammed shut on its own so hard the glass panes on either side of the thick wood still rattle. What the…? Clutching my hand to my pounding chest, I walk over to the door. I throw it open again, expecting to find someone on the porch, but nothing. No one. Impossible. You have to be standing inside to close it that way. There are no windows open in the house either. How…?

A chill runs down my spine. There is no way…*no.* Stop. No. There *must* be a window open somewhere inside, end of story. Flipping Melissa and her crackpot theories are getting me all worked up. I shut the door.

Oh, darn it. When I return to the parlor I find my phone broken and bread flattened. Perfect. Now I have to get a new cell phone. At least I have a legitimate reason not to speak to Owen or Mel and defend myself. Maybe I'll get some peace and quiet. That's all I really want. Is that—

I hear the same creaking from last night right in front of me as the door to the dining room moves open a little, the smell of flowers and sugar wafting in. I stare at the empty space, not moving a muscle. I can't even blink.

Get out of this house, the woman whispers.
THWACK!

The kitchen door slams shut right before my eyes. That wasn't the wind. Jesus help me.

Get out.

So much for peace and quiet.

CHAPTER SIX

I wish I believed in ghosts. It would make my life so much easier. I know little about them but I do know they don't usually leave the location they're haunting. They stick to where they died, they *don't* travel thousands of miles to bother someone they never met. The timing is odd I'll admit but logic wins out. And that logic scares me more than any ghost ever could. Logic dictates that I'm hallucinating either due to a psychological break or brain tumor.

After quickly putting away what absolutely had to be, I fled that kitchen and didn't look back. The only location with internet connection is my grandmother's room. She didn't believe in Wi-Fi. It doesn't feel right using her computer so I unplugged it and attached my laptop to the LAN line. I add wireless router to my list of essentials to purchase. I'm happy to discover I don't have any other symptoms of a brain tumor. No headaches, no numbness, weakness, or seizures. Good because I was just getting used to the idea of being insane. Hate to think I was wasting my time on the wrong cataclysmic disease. Guess black humanoid voids have been replaced with pretending to see doors move on their own. Can't decide which is worse.

I lock the bedroom door and crawl into bed with *Top Chef*. Nothing numbs the brain better than reality TV. Padma, Kim, Heidi, Gordon have become my best friends in the past few months. My only companions. If I could, I'd never leave bed. But today even Padma's failing to keep my mind from racing. I thought, I was *positive*, things would be different if I came here. It was a stupid hope, so stupid. I'm such a moron. I'll just keep with my current plan: ignoring it all. The voices, the hallucinations, it began out of the blue and it could end that way too. No need for powerful drugs or a padded cell. Yet.

At least if I'm here I can keep up the family tradition of going nuts inside the walls of this house alive. Until I murder someone or blow my brains out. Or do both. Murder/suicide seems to run in the blood as well. Felicia and Jerome. Mama tried but only got it half right. Maybe that's another reason God cursed my womb. My bloodline includes liars, molesters, murderers, suicides, and downright crazies. I knew about the crazy. My earliest memories are of my mother's descent into it right before it swallowed her whole, almost taking me along with her. Aunt Helen seems to be the only member to have escaped the family curse, but even she was obsessive at times. Hours spent praying the rosary and making me do the same, especially around my birthday. We'd be hours at St. Michael's praying for Mama, for our immortal souls, for strength when facing evil, for sins of the past. I'd have bruises on my knees for a week after, and my hands ached for days. I still prefer Helen's brand of crazy to mine though.

I've skipped church the past month for obvious reasons, but I have prayed. A lot. Perhaps I should start going back. I spied a large Catholic Church in the center of town. I should go Sunday. It always makes me feel better. Cleansed. Exercise too. When Owen and I lived in St. Charles, a suburb outside of St. Louis, I had a walking partner. Carmel and I would go walking around the neighborhood every morning, gossiping and venting about our husbands. I've missed those walks a lot in the past five years. The gym isn't the same and nobody walks in LA. I could go for a stroll now. Check out the property. Get some fresh air to clear my head. Yes, that is exactly what the doctor ordered.

I pick myself up and brave the hallway to my bedroom, grabbing my maroon hoodie and sneakers. Just as I tie the second lace, there's a knock downstairs. I immediately sit straight up. "Oh, come on," I whisper to myself. It isn't real. Just ignore it. But as I rise from the bed, there's another round of knocks. *Ignore, ignore, ignore.* I step into the hall as three more poundings echo through the house.

"Mrs. Harrow?"

Okay, either my hallucinations have decided to adopt a thick Southern accent or there is a real live person at my front door. When I walk downstairs, I spot two figures through the window panes by the front door. My tension wanes as I breathe a literal sigh of relief. The welcome wagon has arrived. I'm back in a small town. I'll probably get a lot of pop-ins. Maybe they'll even bring food. It is the South. I smooth my hair and plaster on a smile before opening the door.

Two women, one in her seventies and the other surgically altered to appear in her early forties, wait on my porch. The younger woman's large hazel eyes grow in time to her collagen filled lips forming a perfect "O". The stranger is vaguely familiar with dirty blonde hair with highlights, straight nose, and thin to the point of emaciation yet still attractive in khaki slacks and white cashmere sweater complete with pearls. The older lady appears much friendlier then the gawker with a genuine smile on her wrinkled face. Like Mrs. Frosty behind her, the woman is dressed conservatively with a blue cardigan and pleated black skirt.

"May I help you?" I ask the nicer of the two.

"You must be Jane Harrow," the woman says with a Southern accent. "I'm Edwina Taylor, and this is Daphne Davenport." Edwina extends her hand. "It is such a pleasure to make your acquaintance."

I shake the hand. Mrs. Davenport begrudgingly extends her perfectly manicured paw, giving me a limp wristed shake with a look of disdain added for good measure. She yanks her hand away as if I had poop on mine. What a lovely woman.

"You both as well," I say.

"I knew your grandmother. We attended Immaculate Heart together a lifetime ago. I'm so sorry for your loss. She was…most unique. Very beautiful. You look quite a bit like her. Like your mother too."

"Thank you." Both women stare expectantly at me. I don't…oh. "Would you like to come in?"

"Yes, thank you," Edwina says, stepping inside. When Daphne passes, she scans me up and down, not pleased with the sight judging from her pursed lips. I know I'm a hot mess, but that's just rude. I smooth my hair again as I shut the door. "I hope you'll forgive us for popping in without an invitation. We tried calling earlier, but there was no answer. We left a message. We're from the Crimson Vale Historical Society."

"Oh! Yes, um…sorry. I forgot I even had a working phone let alone an answering machine," I chuckle nervously.

But they aren't paying attention to me. Both glance around the foyer as if taking mental pictures of the room. Edwina even taps her toe against the hardwood floor, making it creak. "Huh."

O-kay. "Um, may I offer you both something to drink? Coffee maybe?"

"That would be lovely, thank you," from Edwina.

"We both take fat free cream and Splenda," Daphne adds. "If you don't have those, bring me a mineral water."

Yes, your majesty. "Be right back."

Shaking my head, I fire up the coffee pot. Lord knows what those women are doing in there alone. Mentally selling the antiques? Examining the moldings for cracks to bring the value of the house down? Judging my grandmother? I fill the coffee machine and rush back to find my guests. They're in the larger living room continuing their investigation. Edwina knocks on a wall as Daphne stares at a painting, another watercolor of the house, though this one is much darker in color and tone than the others. In fact it makes the house resemble something out of a Poe story with foreboding shadows emanating from every tree like phantoms about to envelop the structure. Daphne scowls at it while playing with her pearls.

"The coffee will be ready in a few minutes," I say.

Both women cease their activities to glance at me. "Thank you dear," Edwina says.

"Would you care to sit down?" I ask, gesturing to the sofa. As they sit, I lower myself into the matching arm chair.

"You're probably wondering the cause of our extremely rude behavior," Edwina begins. "We don't usually barge into people's homes like this. I do apologize again."

"Accepted," I say with a smile. Some of the color drains from Daphne's face as I do. "Are you okay?"

Edwina turns to her friend. "You are wan, dear."

"I-I'm fine. Really. I'm just tired."

"The coffee will be ready soon," I say.

"I'm fine," she snaps.

Edwina clears her throat. "As I was saying, the Historical Society is one of the oldest institutions in the Vale. Your great-great-great-grandmother was a founding member. Your great-grandmother Cecile was also a member. She was instrumental in restoring St. Jude's after the hurricane of '26. We extended an invitation to your grandmother, but…you know. She had other concerns. We understood." Both women frown. "It was an absolute tragedy what happened to them. We are so sorry for your loss."

I am getting sick of people saying that. Not only is it insincere on their parts but also mine. I didn't know them. I've lost nothing. But I still say, "Thank you."

"So you *were* in contact with Felicia," Daphne declares. "We were under the impression you had no idea you had family here."

"I didn't."

"You had no idea? Really? I find that hard to believe," Daphne says.

"It's true. Why would I lie?"

I don't think I've ever encountered someone who hated me so fast.

Daphne opens her mouth, I'm sure with another insult, but Edwina cuts her off at the pass. "You wouldn't. No one is accusing you of that," she says, glaring at her friend. "It was all just surprising. The deaths, your reemergence, you moving into the house so quickly. We just…are not quite sure what to make of it."

"Why do you need to make anything of it?"

Edwina clears her throat. "Excuse me. My heartburn's acting up. May I use your bathroom?"

"Um, upstairs, turn left, second door on the right."

With a smile, Edwina stands and walks out, leaving me with Cruella de Vil. The room grows uncomfortable the moment Edwina vanishes, for us both judging from the way Daphne begins picking lint from her trousers. My recessive Southern genes boot up after about ten seconds.

"So, um, are you married to Mr. Davenport, the lawyer?"

"Yes."

"He seems…competent at his job. How long have you been married?" I ask for lack of something better.

"Thirty-nine years."

"Wow. Impressive. What's your secret?"

"Mutual understanding," she says with a scowl.

Okay, guessing this is a sore subject. Moving on. "And Bram must be your son. How nice it must be having two lawyers in the family."

"If you say so."

And we fall back into the quagmire of horrid silence again. "Well, um" I say, rising, "I'll go check on the coffee. Excuse me." I don't care if she steals all the antiques, it'd be a small price to pay for getting away from her.

The coffee's done enough. Since I have regular milk, sugar, and no bottled water she'll just have to take it black. Dreadful woman. Suppose if my husband cheated and flirted with everything in a skirt I'd be unpleasant too. Or it could be her natural state. Wouldn't surprise me. As I prepare Edwina's drink, I realize I never did get a straight answer as to the reason for their visit. Not that I care anymore. At this point I just want them gone. I pick up the mugs and return to the interlopers. Daphne turns her fake nose up at my offering, but Edwina says, "Thank you, dear."

"You're welcome," I say, sitting again. "Hope it makes you feel better."

"It shouldn't, but I'm still drinking it," Edwina chuckles. "The house really is remarkable for its age. I'm surprised to see Felicia kept it in such good shape."

"I told you Bram convinced her to renovate a few months ago," Daphne says.

"I know, but I didn't realize to what extent."

"It was bad before?" I ask.

"Oh, yes," Edwina answers. "The paint was chipping so badly if a breeze blew you'd swear it was snowing. The weeds in the yard reached your knees. Half the wallpaper was missing—"

"Don't forget those gargoyles and crucifixes and whatever those strange symbols were all over this place," Daphne adds with another sneer. "Disgusting. Thank God Bram knocked some sense into that old bat's head or the entire house would have been condemned. He did everything, you know. Hired the contractors, oversaw the whole project."

Just the thought of him made my stomach flutter. "The next time I see him, I'll have to thank him."

For a fleeting second I notice something akin to fear pass over Daphne's face. "So you intend to remain in town? Live in the house?"

"I intend to stay in the house as long as I'm here, yes."

"And how long will that be?" Daphne asks with enough frost in her tone to bring about another ice age.

"I don't know."

"Indefinitely?" Daphne asks.

"I-I don't know. I haven't decided yet."

"Have you received any offers on the house yet?" Edwina asks.

"Have I…no. I've only been here a day."

"Good," Edwina says with a sigh. "We'd like to put in a bid. We know how much it was appraised for, but we can't offer that much, I'm afraid. I—"

"Wait, wait," I say, holding up my hands, "I think this conversation is a tad premature. I have no clue what I'm doing with the house yet. I've barely thought about it."

"I find that hard to believe," Daphne says.

"And why is that?" I ask with a hard edge.

"Daphne," Edwina warns quietly.

"Look, Mrs. Davenport, I feel as if I've done something to anger you, and—"

"You haven't, dear," Edwina cuts in.

"Of course you didn't," Daphne says snidely. "You just stole the house from us."

"*Excuse me?*"

"Felicia promised us this house," Daphne spews out.

"What?"

"This house. It should belong to the Historical Society. Those were her wishes. It was in her will for decades. Then all of a sudden, a few days before she dies, there's a new will with you— who no one knew existed—inheriting the lot? I find that *highly* suspicious, Ms. Harrow."

I'm too shocked to find the appropriate words, but I'm sure even if I could I wouldn't say them out loud without needing to run to confession. From her smug smile, this was precisely her intention. I stare her down, both sets of eyes narrowing.

"Ma'am," I say, "pardon my language, but I could give a fiddler's fart what you think or believe about me. But for the record, I did not steal this house from you. I did not go behind anyone's back to convince a woman I never met to give me this house. And if you had proof I did, I'm sure you would have contested the will by now. However, if memory serves, it was your son who drafted it. Do you intend to call him a liar as well? Accuse him of fraud and collusion like you are me?" Her eyes narrow with contempt. "Didn't think so." I stand up, my back ramrod straight. "When I decide what to do with *my* house, I promise to take your offer under consideration. Now, please leave. I'm very busy today."

Glaring as if it could turn me to stone, Daphne rises, smoothing her designer trousers to regain some dignity. Edwina at least has the grace to appear mortified by the turn of events. "We're so sorry for bothering you," she mutters before moving toward the door. Daphne's sub-zero expression remains on me for a second more before she follows her friend out with me a few paces behind. I wait at the door to watch them climb into Daphne's black Porsche. Edwina shoots me a sympathetic smile before climbing in. I suspect this meeting did not go as she'd anticipated. We are judged by the company we keep.

After the Porsche pulls out of my driveway, I shut the door and rest my head against it. I've never kicked anyone out of my house before. Heck, I've only ever raised my voice a handful of times. But the nerve of that woman…just because you're miserable doesn't mean you should make everyone join the party. Now I *really* need to take a walk.

After locking the front door in case they sneak back, I take off at a quick clip trough the dying clearing toward the back of the property. Even with the rain showers the grass is one shade away from brown. Shorn but neglected none the less. It might need reseeding if I sell. I should start making a list.

The clearing is half the length of a football field, ending right at the edge of the black swamp. Wow, I own an honest to goodness bayou. Murky water with specks of green on the surface, hollow at the knees cypress trees spread around with branches hanging heavy with gray Spanish Moss. Various bugs skim the still water, and if I'm not mistaken at least one set of eyes peeking out of the dark water. Those eyes stop me from getting any closer. There are probably snakes too, which scare me more than the alligators. Squirmy, hidden until they pounce, then injecting you with their venom after a painful prick. I shudder simply thinking about them.

I continue my walk about five yards from the shore toward the tree line. Right at the edge where flat clearing meets tall oak and maple trees, I notice what was once a dock and boat both half submerged under the water, now nothing more than rotting wood poking out of the black water. The painting of my mother sitting in a boat surrounded by cypress trees comes to mind. I can just imagine Mama and her brother running through that clearing, green grass as far as the eye can see, before hopping into that boat. Jerome rowed them away from that house from their abusive grandfather and drug addict mother. Just the two of them alone on the tranquil bayou. I should replace the dock. Buy a boat. If I chose to sell, it could only help with the price. *If* I put the house on the market.

The woods, *my* woods are dense, despite the fact the leaves have just begun to shed for winter. Branches crackle and shake all around as squirrels scurry about, preparing for winter. I stroll along at a quick enough speed to get my heart rate up to help pump away the negativity.

Darn you, Daphne Davenport. I've never encountered such a horrid woman before in my life. Five minutes of conversation and she accused me of being a thief, a con artist, and if I'm not mistaken, there was even a thinly veiled accusation I had something to do with their deaths. It was as if my mere existence was an affront to her. How is it my fault the house came to me? Felicia was *my* family, my blood. The house is rightfully mine will or no. End of story. And I don't condone cheating, especially after being on the other end of the situation, but I'd probably step out too if I were married to her. Nothing is ever good enough, nothing is ever *enough* for women like her.

Though it's October, the humidity sticks to my skin. I'm sweating after a few minutes, but I don't mind one lick. This is exactly what I needed: solitude, quiet, an activity, and no voices or hallucinations. Perhaps keeping busy is the key. Maybe that's been the problem, lazing about. With nothing to occupy my mind, the delusions had free reign. I'll find a project. Wait, I have a whole house full of projects. Cleaning, repairing, the lawn. I'll be busy for weeks. I—

Who is that?

About eighty feet away, a tall, thin man with a mess of curly brown hair, sharp cheekbones and thick horn-rimmed glasses, stands beside an oak tree staring at me. He's young, early twenties, dressed in camouflage pants and jacket with an orange vest. A hunter. I didn't realize there was anything to hunt here besides alligators. But he doesn't have a gun, his hands are empty save for a wedding band.

"Hello," I call.

While no words pass his lips, his expression speaks volumes. Though he's in plain sight the boy seems shocked I've acknowledged him. His face falls, especially the corners of his thin mouth. His head moves side-to-side to check for another person.

"It's okay," I say. "I don't mind you're here."

The boy opens his mouth to speak, but then it snaps shut as he gazes over my shoulder. Shock morphs to horror, his mouth gaping open and eyes bulging enough I notice it even behind the glasses. I spin around to see what's got him so spooked. Nothing. When I turn back *that's* when I receive a fright. The boy's gone. Vanished. I literally looked away for a second. Unless he's The Flash he couldn't have gotten far enough away to be out of sight. No sounds of cracking branches or footsteps. I even glance up in case he climbed a tree. Okay…now I'm hallucinating nerdy hunters. Wonderful.

My walk now ruined, I decide to head home. A moment's peace, just a frigging moment's peace, and I can't even give myself that. I start back toward the house, checking over my shoulder in case he decides to reappear. I've never hallucinated an entire human being in such detail before. I mean, his clothes crinkled when he moved. He had sweat on his brow. *Just stick with the plan, Jane. Ignore them. Ignore them, ignore them, ignore them.*

I make it to the house without incident, either real or imagined, only to find fresh heck waiting on my porch. I stop dead at the tree line, smoothing my, I'm sure, frizzy hair on instinct. I'm a fright, all sweaty and red faced, though now for an entirely new reason. Bram, on the other hand, resembles a movie star sitting in one of the white rocking chairs with his cell phone pressed to his ear. Even if I didn't get a flash of last night's dream, the feel of his lips on mine, even the taste of him on my tongue, he'd take my breath away in that dark blue suit and perfectly coiffed blonde hair. I no doubt resemble a wild-eyed, sweaty, swamp monster. I could just turn and slink back into the woods. He'll leave eventually. Lord knows how long he's been waiting. For me.

Too late. I must catch his eye as he turns my way with a large smile affixed. I half smile back. Darn it. As I slowly stroll toward the house, he finishes his call and slips the phone into his pocket, that sunny grin never wavering. "Hi," Bram says as he rises. "Did you have a nice walk?"

I stop at the steps to keep my distance. "Yes, thank you."

"Beautiful, isn't it? The bayou? The perfect blend of untamed nature and serenity."

"I suppose," I say quietly.

He takes a step toward me before leaning against the pillar, just like… I avert my eyes to keep that particular memory at bay. "You grandmother told me she used to love going out on the water when she was a girl. She said she never felt more at peace than on that tranquil water with nothing but the birds and gators keeping her company."

"Maybe I'll get a boat then."

"Does that mean you're staying?" he asks, if possible his grin growing.

Okay, I am officially sick of that question. "You know what? None of your business, okay? What I do is none of yours or anyone else's concern. I will stay here as long as I want. This is my house now. I may choose to bulldoze it or live in it forever, I don't know yet." I take one step up. "But I do know that if you're here on behalf of your mother, whatever you say to me will fall on deaf ears. I do not appreciate either of you arriving uninvited, making cruel insinuations, and—"

"Wait, wait," he says holding up his hands as he bridges the gap between us. Despite my anger the smell of his cologne and his personal scent all but intoxicate me. I'm suddenly hungry, turned on, and weak in the knees. How I maintain my glare is beyond me. "I'm not here to plead my mother's case. Far from it. I had no idea she was coming here. None. She called me right after she left and told me what happened. I am…*mortified* by her behavior. I am so sorry she treated you like that. There is no excuse, *none*, for her actions. I came over after I hung up on her."

"Why?"

"To apologize. To make sure you're okay. To…see you, I don't know," he says with a nervous chuckle. "Seemed like the right thing to do at the time. Rethinking that now, though. Anyway, I'm, uh, sorry I've disturbed you. I'll go." He can't look at me as he walks past down the porch steps.

Great, now I've insulted him. He's attempting to be kind, and I insulted him. "Mr. Davenport, wait."

"Bram," he says, spinning around. "Please. Call me Bram."

"Bram. Look, I'm so sorry I yelled at you. It's been a rough…while. Would you like to come inside? The coffee's probably still hot."

"I'd love a cup. Thank you," he says coming toward me with that bright smile of his. It could light up the Vegas strip if not the whole of Nevada.

As I unlock the door, with him so close, goosebumps rise in an attempt to get even closer. Oh God, I realize I just invited a man in for coffee. It's been over a decade since I've been on a date but I do remember what coffee is code for. Oh, I hope he doesn't think I invited him in for that. Perhaps he does because when we step into the house his hand presses lightly on the small of my back. I don't utter a word but make sure to keep my distance to the kitchen.

"How do you take it?" I ask.

"Lots of cream and sugar," he says with another smirk. "I've had a huge sweet tooth lately. Been eating and drinking like a pig as well. I'm sure my cholesterol and insulin levels have skyrocketed."

I pull out the last two mugs from the cupboard. There are precious few cups and plates in this house. Suppose Felicia only required one set. No throwing dinner parties in my near future. I rather wish I had no company now. I was on edge before, now I have to concentrate on keeping my hands from shaking. I sense him watching my every movement. He smiles like a cat who killed a canary when I turn back around. I smile shyly back before moving to the fridge. "Would you care for something to eat? I can make you a sandwich."

"I can make it," he says. As I pour the coffee, he strides toward the fridge. "Would you like one too?"

"Um, okay." He opens the still empty fridge. "Um, I think the cold cuts are still in the bags along with…everything else. I was interrupted before I got to put much away."

He moves toward me before handing me the milk. "The first things first," Bram says with another lovely smile. His hand lingers on the carton, waiting for me to snatch it from him. When I do, his hand moves up enough to brush my fingers with his. The moment flesh touches flesh, my cheeks fire up, sending the inferno to every nerve-ending. I'm blushing, I know it, and his smile grows. At least I don't whimper.

Bram steps away toward the bags on the counter as, with my shaking hand, I pour the milk. Maybe it's because I haven't been touched in months—not even a simple brush against the skin like that—but I have goosebumps up and down my arm, not to mention a tingling. I'll just have to make sure I don't do that again, no matter how wonderful it felt. As I add the sugar, Bram removes the food from the bags. I watch as he puts the cereal with my grandmother's leftovers, the fruit in the basket I didn't notice before, and the soup with the other cans. He knows this kitchen. I forgot he used to come here. He probably even made my grandmother sandwiches too.

Bram closes the cupboard as I put his mug beside his hand. "Here."

"Thank you," he says after a sip. "Perfect." I half smile before walking to the farthest part of the kitchen to finish the groceries. "So, how was your first night?"

"Fine. A bit spooky at first."

"I'll bet. Every kid in town is scared of this place. I should probably warn you Felicia told me that sometimes teenagers will sneak around or into the house. Just keep the doors and windows locked. Or if you get really concerned call the Sheriff. Or me. I'll protect you," he says with a wink.

"Thank you."

"Least I can do after what my mother did. What she insinuated."

"It's not your fault."

"No, I should have seen it coming. She said the same things to me when she found out about the new will. She wanted me to investigate you, declare Felicia incompetent, even burn the document. Today was the first time I'd spoken to her in a month. She wants this house. Always has. She used to bring me out here when I was a kid just to look at it. The grandest house in Crimson. The jewel in the crown. I think she plans on putting up most of the money for the Historical Society and living here in the guise of taking care of the place."

"Will she contest the will?" I ask.

"She's discussed it with Dad, but she doesn't have a legal leg to stand on. That won't stop her though. She's not one to give up. Ever. I get that from her," he says with another wink. I'm beginning to get the feeling I'm in the presence of the town flirt. Like father like son. My ardor for him wanes a tad after this realization. But only enough for me to be able to look at him without blushing. "But she is the woman who gave me life. What

can you do? Can't choose your family." I'm about to reply when
his face falls. "Oh, shit. Sorry. That was insensitive."

"It's okay. I wasn't offended."

"Still. I know D.J. told you about…everything. I feel I
should prepare you for some of the opinions that might be shared
about your grandmother especially. I got to know her well toward
the end. She was shy, almost painfully so. I thought it was just
because she'd been out here alone for so long, save for a long line
of nurses, but apparently she was always like that. Even before
Jerome's accident she barely left the house. Too drugged up.
That's what I heard, at least."

"Why?"

"We never really spoke about it, but I got the sense there
were problems with her father. I think she got worse after Daniel
died."

"Daniel?"

"Your grandfather Daniel Cowan. She talked about him a
time or two. His death devastated her."

"How'd they meet?" I ask.

"He was a waiter at the country club during her debutante
ball. She said it was love at first sight. For him too. They had to
keep it a secret, of course. Cotton Fontaine's daughter being
courted by a shrimp boat captain's son? The old man never would
have stood for it. Of course when she got pregnant a few months
later, Cotton had no choice but to allow the marriage." Bram
scoffs. "Of course he only allowed it for all of two years."

"What do you mean?"

"Daniel was shot dead. Hunting accident, and I use that
last word loosely. Stray bullet when he was hunting in these very
woods with friends. No one admitted to being the shooter, and no
one was charged either."

"Let me guess, the scuttlebutt was Cotton had a hand in
it."

"Of course. Felicia never said it, fairly sure she refused to
talk about Cotton outright, but I could tell she believed it too."

"Why didn't she leave then?"

"She had no place to go. She had two babies, she wasn't even twenty, and she had no skills. She had no choice but to live with that man until the night he beat the shit out of her and effectively killed her son. And she never got justice, not for any of it. Maybe that's why she refused to give up on Jerome. To punish herself for not stopping him."

He sips his coffee and starts on the sandwiches, moving around the room as if he owns the place. It should bother me, how at home he is when I'm not, but the novelty of someone making me something to eat is too great to ruin.

I move around to the other side of the island to watch as this gorgeous man makes me a sandwich. "Do you think she meant to kill him?" I ask, sipping my coffee.

"Jerome? I saw her the day before, and I didn't get that sense. She was completely normal. For Felicia. No, it was an accident. Jerome was her whole world. I can't see her hurting him, not after all that time. I know she drank, but I didn't know about the pills. Not that I can say I'm surprised. I just…the whole thing, it breaks my heart. In spite of everything, all the hell that was her life, she still cracked jokes. She still sat down and talked with me. She'd listen for hours as I droned on about my shit, and she always knew the exact right thing to say. Not to mention she was a hell of a cook. She could win prizes for her chicken fried steak and blackberry pie. I really liked her," he says with a hint of regret. "She was a real lady. Very giving. No matter what others say, you keep that in mind. They didn't know her. They never gave her a second thought."

"Why did you?"

"Because I'm a hell of a nice guy," he says with a mischievous grin.

Bram passes me the sandwich, our eyes catching for a moment. Once again a shiver of lust snakes down my spine strong enough to stop my breath. If I didn't know better, I'd think he senses this because the grin grows. I avert my gaze to the plate.

"You felt sorry for her," I say.

"Well, it was hard not to. But I did like her. And I *am* a hell of a nice guy. You'll see. How's your sandwich?"

I take a bite. "Delicious. Thank you."

"Just one of my many specialties. I hope to show you more in the future," he says, chomping on his sandwich.

My face heats up again. Safer topic, please. "What else can you tell me about her?"

"You have her smile. It only came out on special occasions but when it did, the room lit up. Just like yours." Though I keep my eyes down, I sense him studying me. "Actually, I think you have a lot of her in you. You're both so damn beautiful but…sad. So sad. And someone as beautiful as you shouldn't feel a moment of sadness. Not a one."

I have no idea what to say. He sounds so earnest, as if he wants to vacuum the melancholy out of me himself. First my grandmother, now me. He must have a savior complex. He's like St. Jude, the patron saint of lost causes. "Everyone gets sad sometimes," I offer.

"Not that level of sadness. It's in every gesture. Every look. Hell, you can *feel* it around you. It's almost oppressive. I think it's stuck to the walls here. The few people who come in can sense it in this house."

"I don't."

"That's because you're used to it." He pauses to sip his coffee. "If it makes you feel better, so am I. Felt it the first time I ever set foot in this house. But not just that sadness. It was as if…it knew me. That I belonged here. The energy connected with me. Weird, right?"

"Not to me. I know exactly what you mean." I sip my coffee. "But you don't seem sad. There's certainly nothing oppressive coming from you." Quite the opposite in fact.

"I've gotten good at hiding it. Learned to from a very early age. Hell, I'm so good I even fool myself sometimes. You know how it is, having to keep a smile on your face while inside you're raging and crying to the heavens for salvation. How you're worried you won't be able to keep the storm bottled up a moment longer. How you're worried the agony, the desperation, the fury has festered into your brain, slowly making you insane." I'm staring at him, mouth agape. It's as if he's reading my mind. Or soul. "Like your grandmother."

"Was she? Insane?"

Bram considers this for a moment. "According to my mother and the rest of the Vale, she was a fruitcake. But no. As far as I saw, she never had hallucinations or violent tendencies. But she sure as hell wasn't healthy. She barely left the house except to take Jerome to the hospital once a year for tests. I offered to take her out to dinner a few times, but she seemed almost afraid at the prospect. Like I said, after that housekeeper died, her only visitors were the nurses, Father King, and Doc Gage every couple of months. This house was her whole world."

"Maybe she just liked it that way," I offer.

"Nobody likes misery, not really. It's a pit. Sometime's it's hard to climb out alone, that I'd understand, but when you're thrown a lifeline? Only the completely bereft of hope refuse to take it. I speak from experience. I tried to be that for Felicia, but…she just wouldn't save herself."

"You seem to know a lot about unhappiness," I say not as nonchalantly as I would like. I study his face to see if I've offended him, but he remains impassive.

"This surprises you? You met my parents. Imagine being raised—and I use the term loosely—by them. The occasions they deigned to acknowledge my presence, it was only to tell me how wrong I did everything. Nothing was ever good enough. If I got an A- I should have studied harder. I was running back not the quarterback. I dared to apply to Pratt Art School. I even got in, but no, I'd be cut off if I didn't attend his Alma Mater and become a lawyer. D.J. went through three wives and only got one son, had to make me count, right? Someone had to carry on the illustrious family name and tradition," he says with a scoff. "And Mother, well, I think she would have sacrificed me to the gods if it meant she could remain Mrs. Davenport. Anything so she never had to return to the swamp from whence she came. I mean that literally. She grew up one of seven kids in a three-room shack on the bayou. My grandfather was an alligator hunter and craw fisherman, not to mention a mean drunk. The only times I ever saw Daphne afraid was when D.J. threatened to send her back to Jupiter Gulch when she made waves about his extra-curricular activities.

"And somehow, I made it all my fault. Their problems, my problems, it was all on me. If I was better, *more*, all they wanted me to be, then maybe they'd actually love me. It fucked me up, pardon my language. But it did. I was trapped in this darkness with no way out. I'd bash against it, and bash against it, but I couldn't escape. It was so frustrating. Beyond frustrating. Hell. It was pure hell. Drugs, women, gambling, I did whatever I could to fill that whatever-shaped hole inside. If I'm honest, it's only been a year or two, after my DWI and car accident, that I've gotten even a little better. I found some help, or really help found me. I got tossed that lifeline, and I grabbed it with both hands. Now, especially now," he says with a bright yet still seductive smile, "the future looks so very beautiful and bright."

He tells this wretched tale so calmly and with such ease those emotions are infectious. This man, this stranger is baring his soul, all his ugly scars, as if it were the most natural thing in the world. He's as comfortable as if he'd known me all his life. No one's ever been so honest and open with me before. It's unnerving but…

"My mother went crazy and tried to drown me in the bathtub when I was four," I blurt out before I can stop myself. "She'd been depressed to the point of psychosis since my birth. Maybe even before. Maybe *I* did it to her. I don't remember much, thank God, but I do remember the water filling my lungs. Fighting. Scratching. Flailing. But I couldn't sit up. I couldn't…it hurt. My lungs, my hands, legs, my head as she held it underwater, it all hurt. Then she screamed. It was loud even under the water. And she let me go. She let me go and ran shrieking into the next room, broke a mirror, and slit her throat from ear-to-ear. It was the best thing she ever did as a mother. It's horrible to admit but that doesn't make it any less true.

"I was raised by my Great Aunt and Uncle. They were good people. Strong, stable, and they did love me, but they were strict. *So* strict. Everything was a sin. I couldn't go to the movies, I couldn't sleep at friends' houses, I couldn't talk to a boy without a lecture. We'd go to church three times a week without fail. But they were good to me. I loved them. Just like I loved my husband. Our life was wonderful for a while, close to perfect,…until the first miscarriage. Then the next, and the next…until the seventh. He never said it, but how can he not blame me? It was *my* body that expelled them. My *lie* that finally pushed him away. I was so immersed in my failure as a woman, so lost in that dark pit you were talking about, I couldn't bear to look at him, let alone have him touch me. So we're in the middle of a divorce neither of us truly wants but probably needs. I've lost the only man I ever loved.

"And to top it all off, I just found out I was lied to all my life. I have to question everything the people I trusted the most in this world ever told me. I have to consign myself to the fact I have not only crazy people along my bloodline but possibly molesters and murderers. And it's not that surprising because…I'm going crazy too. Truly crazy. For over a month, I've seen people's faces melting off. I've heard voices. Which means I either have a brain tumor or I'll end up drugged out of my mind, not knowing who I am, and no one will care. No one. Owen will move on as he should, my best friend has her own life, so I will continue to be as I am now. Completely, utterly alone, with my madness. Family tradition, I guess," I say with a mirthless chuckle as I wipe a stray tear from my cheek. "I don't think there's a lifeline for the hole I'm in, Mr. Davenport. And…you're the first person I've told this to, and I have no idea why." He stares at me, almost as miserable as I am. "Please. Say something."

Bram doesn't move, doesn't say a word, he just stares at me with tears in his eyes. As if I've broken his heart. He sets down the mug and slowly moves toward me, never losing that agony my story inflicted upon him. I shrink away little by little as he comes closer. He stops about two feet in front of me, just staring. Part of me wants to sprint away, but I can't even move my eyelids to blink. I can't pull my hand away as he hesitantly places his on top. This simple touch sends countless bolts of lightning through my whole body. There isn't an inch of me not covered with goosebumps each pulsing in time to my racing heart. I haven't recovered from my body's hurricane when he wraps his arms around my stiff body, swaddling me with his warmth. His compassion. All of *him.* I can't recall the last time I was held. Just held. Months? Maybe a year? He's so strong and solid, not to mention he smells astonishing. Better than chocolate, better than roses, better than a newborn baby. I have the strongest desire to lick him. This total stranger. I should push him away before I forget myself. Before I lose the strength to leave this majestic place. But I haven't an ounce of fight left in me, especially a battle I'm loathe to lose. I rest my head against his pounding heart and hug him back. He squeezes tighter. We just stand here for a few seconds like the world has melted into nothing, and we're all that's left. There are no problems, no worries, only us.

More tears stream from my eyes onto his shirt. "I'm here," he whispers. "Believe me. Please believe me. Everything will be alright now that I'm here. I promise. You aren't alone anymore. I'm here."

I believe him. I felt it yesterday when I laid eyes on him, but now I'm sure. This is too good to be true, so it must be. This man has been sent to tempt me like the snake in the Garden of Eden. His words, his eyes, all of him wants me to believe that love at first sight has us in its grips, but I'm too rational to trust it. To trust him. He's probably done this before with emotionally vulnerable women all over town. This, me, is nothing special. He just wants to sleep with me.

Don't trust him…

I pull away and wipe my eyes, refusing to look at him. "I, um, don't want to ruin your suit."

"It's okay, I don't mind."

"I do. Um, I'm grimy after my walk. I need a shower." I move around the island to the drawers, opening them one by one in search of saran wrap. "I can, uh, wrap up your sandwich to go. I—"

Bram walks over to the last drawer and removes the wrap. "It's here." We stare at one another for a moment before I look away, though his eyes remain on me. "Did I do something to—?"

I gaze up again. "I'm married," I blurt out.

"I thought you're getting divorced."

"It's not finalized yet."

"And you're still in love with him."

"I don't…" I avert my eyes again. "I don't want to talk about this."

"Okay," he says. "I don't wish to pressure you to do anything you don't want to. That's the last thing I desire. Truly."

"Thank you," I say quietly.

"I simply…you…" He shakes his head. "I'm selfish. Anyone in this town will tell you that. I am one of the most selfish bastards ever to walk this earth. I admit it myself. But the second I saw you, I just had this, I don't know, *need* to watch out for you. To take care of you. I haven't been able to stop thinking about you, not even for a minute. I was so distracted today I almost forgot to file an injunction today. And…as I'm hearing myself talk, I realize how nuts this sounds. You're probably gonna want to get a restraining order after this." He laughs nervously. "I'm only telling you this because I don't want you to get the wrong idea about me. About what you, this, means to me. You'll hear things about me, most of them true I'm sad to say, but please don't judge me too harshly until you get to know me. And I hope you will, in whatever capacity you're comfortable with. If friends is all you want, all you can handle, I can live with that. I think we both could use one. So if you need anything, from a cup of sugar to a rescue from my mother, don't hesitate for a millisecond to call me. Day or night. I don't sleep much, so I'd probably be up anyway." He steps toward me. "Really. Whenever. You call me, and I'm here."

"Thank you."

He nods. "I'll just wrap this up and get out of your hair." He wraps the sandwich as he glances at me. When he's done, he gives me a smile that lights up the room. "Thank you for the sandwich and…for listening to my babbling and not judging me."

"Ditto."

Bram steps toward me again, and if I hadn't already backed into the counter, I would now. "And remember what I said. No matter what, no matter when, I'll come running."

"Thank you."

For a moment he just stares down at me with tenderness, and I think he's going to kiss me. My lips plump in anticipation. I've never wanted anyone to kiss me more than this man in this moment. But he doesn't. He steps away, and I can breathe again. "Thanks for the sandwich and talk. Hope to do it again soon. *Very* soon."

With another sly grin, he strolls out. I don't relax, I barely breathe, until I hear the front door shut. So this is the famous Southern hospitality. I'm sick of it already. I really don't think I can handle any more guests. Either real or imaginary.

God, please let me be left alone. Please. *Please.*

CHAPTER SEVEN

As always the pills help keep the demons at bay, at least for the night. I doubled my Lunesta dose so nary a bad dream, sexy or otherwise, disturbed my slumber. No visitors either. I wake late the next morning groggy from the pills. The weather does nothing to improve my mood. Hard rain. Cleaning the house is about the only activity I'm capable of doing today, even after two cups of coffee and a cold shower. I pull on my yoga pants and Owen's ancient USMC shirt I purposely hid when he packed up. I lived in it the first week of our separation.

The kitchen, definitely the most labor intensive room, is first on the agenda. All the counters, the cabinets, the fridge, along with mopping the floor, it takes over an hour to complete. I waste another two hours just dusting and polishing the entire downstairs. There are so many antique figurines and paintings that appear centuries old and therefore expensive. In fact this whole house could double as a museum. During the vacuuming, a large crack of thunder makes the lights flicker. Crud. If that little boom was enough to cause a disruption, the larger storm on the horizon arriving tonight will surely cause problems. Fudge, I need to locate the electric company's number, not to mention flashlights and candles. In all my rummaging, I haven't found either. What I have found are guns. A Glock, a Beretta, two revolvers, a gun in each room and all loaded. I don't dare touch them.

After a salad and Lean Cuisine, I move to the second level with all my supplies. I start with the guest bedrooms, changing the sheets, dusting, and vacuuming, but once again leaving the guns in the nightstand. When I reach Jerome's room I hesitate. Who am I to disrupt the shrine? But if I decide to sell it all has to go anyway. I should just box up the whole lot, selling or not. It's morbid. Both rooms are. The twins have been gone decades yet it's as if they popped out for the afternoon. I'll just give them both a little dusting for now. The thought of dismantling whole rooms is a bit daunting today.

The air in Jerome's bedroom is thick as only someplace that hasn't been aired out in years can be. I open the window and the breeze from the storm stirs the dust like a whirlwind. For the millionth time today I sneeze myself snotty. Ugh. After my fit I flip on the lights and get back to work. Uncle Jerome wasn't a clutterbug so my job is relatively easy. His bookcase takes the most time. He loved art books along with the Hardy Boys, H.P. Lovecraft, and Edgar Allen Poe. Someone had a dark side.

His nightstand proves more interesting. Inside I find a thick sketchbook with a few stray baseball cards, and a Bible. The drawings, mostly done in charcoal and pencil, are very detailed and lifelike. They feature my mother a great deal. Her studying. Playing the piano. Reading on her bed in her pajamas. His muse. The others are of Hallie sitting in a rocking chair on the front porch. My grandmother asleep in her bed with a bottle of pills on the nightstand featured prominently. What looks like a graveyard with cracking headstones and crypts amid tall grass. The last is a self-portrait in this very room as he stood in front of the mirror above the dresser. This is the only one with any imagination or artistic license as behind him a dark figure looms in the shape of a tall man right behind him. Probably represents depression or his dark side. I wonder how long before the attack he drew this. I place the pad on the bed.

Mama's room is more time consuming. And unnerving. Mostly because she has almost two dozen China dolls, all with those large dead staring eyes, all in dire need of cleaning. Aunt Helen hated these things too. Uncle Robbie brought one home from a church bazaar and before he even handed it to me, my aunt, ripped it from his hands and smashed its head into a million pieces as if it were emitting poison gas before storming out of the farmhouse. Uncle Robbie rushed outside after her. Through the window I watched as Aunt Helen berated him, screamed at him, then burst into tears. He hugged her for over five minutes as I swept up the doll's shattered head. Yeah, these are the first thing to go.

I'm almost afraid to open her drawers and closet. I hesitate but do eventually dive in. All those nerves for nothing. No diary, no photos, no, "Jane, this man is your real father," letters to me. Just polyester clothes, white socks, and a banjo in the closet. I do find more drawings on index cards from Uncle Jerome. He shows his sense of humor in these. A sketch of a bloated man about to burst with "Grandfather" on top. A woman lying on a bed snoring while there's a fire around her with "Mom" written above. Mama at the piano with a smile on her face. A black woman with a graying Afro throwing a peace sign with one hand and holding a pie in the other. Each makes my smile grow. I hope they made Mama smile too.

With Mama's room as done, I come to the fork in the road: Felicia's bedroom or the master. I know the crime scene clean-up crew took care of the worst of the mess, even painted the walls white, but still. Two people recently died in there, one violently. Not to mention the other night's…hallucination. Which is why I force myself to do the room first before I lose my nerve. I switch on the overhead light. No visible blood or even any indication an invalid was ever housed here for almost forty years, save for the industrial wall plugs. I vacuum, dust what little there is, examine where the blood splatter might be for places the professionals missed. None. As if it never happened.

All that remains now is the room I occupy. Felicia's. It feels like more of a violation going through her drawers and closet than my mother's. As if the old woman's looking over my shoulder with disapproval as I violate her privacy. I proceed regardless, vacuuming and dusting, before tackling the bathroom. Oh, I'm exhausted. Bone weary. Shower, quick dinner, and then straight to bed. As I scrub the tub, a giant boom of thunder jolts me and the lights flicker again. I finish the bathroom with a sigh. One more task to complete. Find a flashlight and candles.

Closet first. Hurrah, an electric Coleman lantern among the clothes. Felicia's clothes are all dull. Beige and primary colored shirts all worn, most with large holes or stains all over them like an Avant-garde painting. I don't think she bought any new clothes this decade. Goodwill won't take most of these. That's so sad. That she let herself go so much. That she had no reason to try anymore. I know how that is. I'm on the slippery slope right now. Well, no more. Time to get off the slide. Tomorrow I should go out and buy a new outfit. Get my hair done. Heck, maybe I'll just have them cut it all off. Simplify my life. I could use some simplicity. Right now I'll settle for candles and another flashlight.

I open the nightstand drawer. Right on top I find a Bible as worn as her wardrobe, along with tissues, an Agatha Christie novel, and photos wrapped in a blue ribbon. Mama and Jerome as children sitting at the piano. An older black and white one yellowing at the edges of two little girls in saddle shoes and floral dresses standing on the stairs. I recognize that scowl on the older of the girls. Aunt Helen. So serious, even as a child. The next is of Mama and Jerome on those same stairs, him dressed in a tux and her in a sleeveless white chiffon dress with white gloves. Her coming out into society. A few months later she was shipped off. Went from debutante to pregnant farm girl in a few scant months. That couldn't have been an easy transition.

The next photo gives me pause. Mama sits on our old couch beside Aunt Helen, who actually smiles as she holds an infant in her arms. Me. There's another where I'm a year old and Uncle Robbie cradles me on the tractor all bundled up in a pink sweater. There are more of me: school photos, my First Holy Communion, my Confirmation. Even one of my wedding. Owen's arm is around my waist with Aunt Helen and Uncle Robbie on either side of us. I stare at this one for awhile.

I barely remember my wedding, only fragments. Melissa and I at the beauty parlor. My first ride in a limo to the church with my family. Walking toward a teary-eyed Owen on Uncle Robbie's arm. Sitting at the dais wondering why we paid so much for food that tasted of nothing. The spike of apprehension every time my new husband touched me. Drinking way, way too much and puking the moment we entered our honeymoon suite.

I was petrified, absolutely petrified for months every time I thought about the wedding night. I knew about sex but knowing and putting said knowledge into practice are two very different things. Owen and I had fooled around but only made it to third base. At twenty-three I was still *virgo intacta*. I pledged my virginity to my husband as a child, the man I pledged to love forever before God. That man was Owen Harrow. On the elevator ride up I'd never been more scared in my life. I was shaking, still nauseous, heck, I could barely breathe. The booze didn't help. After my upchuck, Owen didn't say a word. He simply held my hair and wiped a cool washcloth on my forehead until I passed out in his lap in that bathroom. I woke the next morning still in my white dress with my husband snoring in bed beside me. I was so relieved, yet guilty. *So* guilty. I'd ruined our wedding night. I'd failed in my first wifely duty. My husband didn't utter a word of recrimination.

We flew to Hawaii on our honeymoon. For two days in paradise we slept in the same bed, held hands, kissed, but nothing more. On our third day we decided to take a hike to a secluded waterfall a friend of Owen's told him about. It was worth the trek. Rocky crags, thick tropical foliage, a cliff where water fell into a clear blue lagoon like something only seen in movies. Of course being the accident magnet I am, I cut my foot on a jagged rock on the bottom. Blood pouring out, Owen collected me into his arms and carried me to shore. As he wiped my blood and tied his bandana around my foot, I stared at him. My huge, frightening, rugged husband. His hair was wet and tangled, his chest bronzed from all our sunbathing, but it was really how concerned he was for me over a silly cut. It moved me. The care he put into not just that act but everything to do with me. He was so patient with my fears, so loving not just then but since the moment he'd entered my life. It was the moment I realized he would never, ever hurt me.

That I had nothing to fear from him. That I truly loved him. That I *wanted* him.

My husband secured the bandana on my foot and looked up at me to see if I was all right. What he saw in my eyes, he didn't seem to believe. Owen didn't blink until I reached across to caress his cheek. He didn't move. I untied my bikini top, and he stopped breathing. Nothing until I placed his large, rough hand on my breast and kissed him long. Deep. With passion I didn't think myself possible of. It was me who lowered us onto the sand, me who slid off our trunks. It hurt, no question, but the pain didn't last as long as I thought. He was slow, gentle, lovely. He kept asking if I was alright, if he should continue. I kissed his doubts away. Even after that first time he'd wait until I gave him a look or smile, before he'd touch me. It took him about a month to realize I wasn't going to break apart or run away in terror.

I flip the picture over. I can't look at it anymore. I miss him. I miss him so much right now that pain brings tears to my eyes. This is supposed to get better with time. When will I stop feeling this deep, soul-crushing sadness whenever I think about him? The man betrayed me. He lied to me. He got a secret vasectomy. He cheated on me. Maybe if I just replay those facts on a loop, it'll help. It hasn't yet.

I'm about to put the photos back in the drawer when I notice a few loose ones at the bottom of the drawer. My grandmother as a teenager sitting on a horse with a tall man, a cigar dangling from his mouth, holding the reigns. With the pointed chin and big eyes, I'd guess this is my great-grandfather Cotton. Even in middle age he was a handsome man. Imposing even sporting a smile. Monster. The next photo features Felicia, only a few years older maybe, holding two babies with Hallie and a familiar young man by her bedside. Must be my grandfather Daniel. I wouldn't call him handsome, he's too lanky for that, and with those prominent cheekbones and glasses…

"Oh, sweet Jesus."

The photo drops from my hand as I all but leap away from it. No way. Not possible. I-I-I my mind is playing tricks with me again. I must have seen a photo of him before, even if I don't remember doing so. When I was in the woods yesterday, I just imagined him. My stupid, crazy brain conjured him from that forgotten memory. There was no man in the woods. Or he was a cousin. Likeness skips generations. It wasn't Daniel. I'm nuts for even considering the possibility. Guess I'm just nuts period.

There's another boom and the lights flicker again, for longer this time. I'm done. I'm done cleaning, I'm done finding things that I don't want to find, thinking things I don't want to think. I pick up the photos and toss them back in the drawer, slamming it shut. *Enough.* I quickly turn on the bath, peel off my clothes, and finally slide into the tub. Oh, those strawberry bath salts smell amazing. Calming. I found a huge supply under the sink in half a dozen flavors. My grandmother's one luxury after a long day alone with her comatose son. One takes life's joys where we can find them.

When I'm as limp as a noodle, I climb out of the bath and return to the kitchen to throw a frozen pizza in the oven and watch the news as it cooks. Massive thunderstorms, floods, murders, God is not happy with Louisiana today. Even with the TV on, the pitter pat of the rain on the windows is audible. Should I be worried about flooding? The bayou is close and it has been pouring all day. Even with the house on the elevated brick foundation, it is possible. I step out onto the back porch. Even partially shielded by the awning I'm sprayed by cold water. Crud. The backyard has a good inch of water and rising. One or two more and it'll begin to seep inside, ruining the floors and today's hard work. I don't know what to do. Is there anything I *can* do? No. Nothing. Nothing I can do. Such is the story of my life. With a sigh, I return inside.

After dinner, I return to my bedroom. Just as I step through the threshold, the house is plunged into darkness. Brilliant. I have to call this in. I saw an electric bill in the desk. I retrieve the lantern and rummage until I find the bill. Shoot, my phone's downstairs. Bill tucked into my waist, I grab the lantern, my iPod, the quilt, and Felicia's copy of *Pride and Prejudice.* Mr. Darcy can keep me company on this dark and stormy night. I move downstairs to the living room with the only comfortable looking piece of furniture in this place: the thick, velvety couch. I drop off my stuff before retrieving my new cell from the kitchen. And I forgot to charge it. It doesn't even try to turn on. The rotary works fine though. Small mercies.

As I'm listening to the automated message from the electric company, I stare at Bram's card on the fridge. I've done an excellent job of keeping him from my thoughts this past day. I slipped once or twice while I scrubbed, replaying the strange conversation we had in this very room. He was so sincere. So open. If the tables were turned, and he told me all the crazy things I told him, I would have slowly backed away from the lunatic, praying never to see them again. I don't know, I got the sense…he almost reveled in the fact I was so damaged. Probably because it makes me such easy pickings for a self-proclaimed womanizer. Or because he's as damaged as I am and saw a kindred spirit in me. Perhaps both. Either way I believed him when he said he'd come running if I needed him. Hope I never do. In truth, deep deep down, I don't want to ever see him again. I don't like how I am when I'm around him. On edge. Irrational. Wanton. Wet, as Melissa calls it, between my legs at the mere sight of him. God, even now, even simply thinking about him, I sense the titillation prickling that forbidden area. I look away from the card.

After finally reporting my outage, I flop on the couch with my book and iPod. With Chris Isaak crooning, the lightning flickering outside, and star-crossed lovers coming together, my ever present tension begins to wane. So much so, by the time Elizabeth visits Pemberly, my eyes grow heavy. The last thing I remember before falling asleep is Elizabeth flirting with Wickham and thinking she should know better.

What…?

The overpowering reek of cigar smoke draws me out of slumber. It's as if someone blows it right in my face, but there's no breeze. My eyes open. I wish I hadn't. Oh my God. In the doorway to the dining room, a man in a three-piece suit stares at me, one hand rubbing the exposed penis poking from his fly while the other hand holds the cigar. His grunts and heavy breathing ring out louder than the howling wind outside. Jesus God help me. My stomach, my throat, my lungs all clench in abject terror. On instinct, I throw the book at the pervert. My fear heightens as the book passes right through him, but the figure remains as solid as the doorframe around him. That's when his laughter begins echoing inside my mind. Hearty, mocking laughter as the pervert hand pistons faster on his manhood.

As a whimper escapes me, I leap up, grab the lantern, and back away from the cackling, masturbating monster. He—

I get into the foyer and yelp. A dainty woman—more of a girl really—with curly hair and thin, long, white nightgown stands on the staircase sobbing into her tiny hands though no sound comes. The woman removes her hands to look at me, but I can't return the gesture. The sight of the blood still running down her cheeks from her black eyes proves too much for me. I swallow the rising bile just in time.

Get out, dear...Save yourself... a sweet, Southern girl whispers into my mind.

I'm asleep. This is a dream. This has to be a dream. I pinch myself but don't wake. I want to wake. Please wake up.

Want to suck it, pretty girl?

I twirl around and can't hold back my scream this time. The man is close enough I should sense his breath on me, his body heat mingling with mine, but I don't. The stench of cigar remains so overwhelming I don't want to breathe anymore. *Run, dear. Save yourself...*

Yes. I dash toward the kitchen for the phone as a burst of thunder rattles the house down to the foundation. Police. *Runrunrunrunrun...* Police. Car keys. *Runrunrunrun.*

I reach the kitchen, pick up the phone, and am about to press "9" before I stop myself. What am I going to tell the police? Whatever intelligence the fear hasn't overshadowed knows these intruders are just illusions my psychotic brain has cooked up. The book flew *through* him.

Runrunrunrunrunrun.

But I don't want to be alone. I don't want to be alone. I want Owen. I want him to hold me until they go away. I want Owen. I want Owen.

Gohomerungohomerungohome.

I cover my ears but her warnings don't cease.

Gohomerungohomerun.

"Shut up!" I shriek.

Gohomerunrunhomehome.

Another thunderclap booms around the house, but her words continue as loud as ever. The house shudders again, dishes and glass rattling right along with it. Jesus—

Something hits my bare foot, and I yelp again. When I reach down I find a magnet and card. Bram's card.

Call him, the man whispers.

Nonononogohomenorunnogohome.

Both voices start blending together, *noyoucannotnocallhimnocallhimgohomerun.*

"Shut up!" I cry but they only grow louder, trying to compete with one another.

Callhimnononocallnogocallhome.

"Stop it, please stop it," I sob. "Stop—"

Like it was shot out of a rocket, the toaster flies off the counter onto the floor. Oh, God. Oh God. Before I can stop myself, I dial the number on the card. *Nononononononononononono.*

"Hello?" Bram asks on the other end.

"Bram?" I whimper.

"Jane? What's the matter? Are you okay?"

"No. No," I answer, voice trembling as violently as my body. "There may be people in this house or I've gone crazy.

They-they-I-I-I'm so scared. The toaster…the toaster just moved on its own. And I can't see them. I don't want to but I know…I-I feel them watching me…" I glance around the room, seeing no one but sensing their eyes glued to me. "They're here."

"Jane, listen to me. I am on my way, okay? I am coming to you right now. Just get out of the house. Wait for me in your car and—"

The phone jerks from my hand by the unseen force, skidding and clattering on the floor. I scream, pick up the lantern, and dash the opposite way. Car. Car.

Gohomedeargohome.

The moment I open the front door, the howling wind whips the cold rain against my body. That doesn't stop me. Nor does the lighting, the thunder, or the ankle deep water like quicksand, I trudge through. I don't care. I am driving the heck…oh, no. *No.* When I reach for the spare key under the wheel well, I notice both tires on the driver's side are flat. How…? No. No, come on. Oh God. A snake glides a few feet away in my direction. Oh God. Having no other course of action, I just climb into the dry car.

Gohomedeargohomerunleavedontleavethisisyourhomehel ovesyougohome.

Three voices, no four now, they won't stop their torture. Through my sobs I groan in frustration and cover my ears to no avail. "Leave me alone. Just leave me alone. Why won't you leave me alone?"

Owenlovesyougohomerunhomeyoubelonghereleavegohom ethisisyourhomethisisabadplaceyoubelonghere.

They won't stop. Why won't they stop? Please…stop. I rest my head on the steering wheel and sob until my throat and eyes ache. Shut up, shut up, shut up, shut up. Why can't I make them stop? Just stop. I hate this. I want to be normal again. Why is this happening to me? What have I done to deserve this? Why is God punishing me? Why? These questions cycle through my head as fast and loud as the voices. So loud. So loud. I cry and cry and cry as the concert continues in my head.

A crack of thunder like a leather belt snapping booms even louder than the voices and jolts my gaze up in time to watch as a jagged bolt of pure light makes contact with a tree twenty feet away, splitting it straight down the center like an ax. But my mouth remains open in a silent scream, not from this show of raw, savage nature but because of the man standing not three feet away staring at me as intently as I am him. There's only an instant of light before the bolt dissipates, but I recognize him instantly from the glasses and dry hunting attire. Even when the light fades I can make out his outline. Still there. Still watching me. It's him. Not a cousin, it's *him*. The man from the photo. My grandfather. Daniel.

ItsnotsafesugargohomegotoOwennonothisisyourhomegoh omedear.

There's another flash of light, and this time I see the bullet hole in his forehead. "Oh God." No more. I shut my eyes and curl up like the frightened madwoman I've become. I can't continue this way. I can't. I'd rather die. God is supposed to be merciful. Why doesn't He take me now? I've earned His mercy. I've been good. Pious. I've obeyed all his commandments. *I've been good.* But he's forsaken me. He has. Why? What have I done to deserve this? What? They won't stop talking. They won't leave me alone. Leave me alone. Just let it end. Let it all end. Anything is better than this.

I don't know how much time passes as I pray for death. As those voices vie for supremacy until they're all I hear. As I hold my ears and rock back and forth. God, take me now. Take me now. I don't—

Aagh!

My eyes fly open when there's a knock on my window. At the same time, there's silence. Blissful silence. The voices. They've stopped. *They've stopped.* Why...? I look to my left and see a man in a yellow raincoat with his face pressed against the glass peering in with a flashlight in hand. "Jane?"

Those blue eyes, that melodic voice. My angelic savior. "Bram."

I open the car door and launch myself into his awaiting arms for something solid, something real to anchor me. My hero doesn't hesitate. Those strong, warm arms envelope me as I sob into his shoulder. "It's alright, beloved. I'm here now. I've got you. I have you now." He kisses my wet hair a few times to reassure me further. "Everything will be fine now. I'm here."

"There-there-there are pe-people inside and they won't be quiet and my tires are flat and I want to leave," I vomit out before the sobs begin again. "Take me away from here. I want to leave. Please."

"Jane, I barely made it here. The road's too dangerous. It's flooded, and there are trees and power lines down everywhere. We can't chance it."

"No, no," I beg. "I want to go. I need to go. I *need* to go."

He cups my cheeks in his cold hands, bringing my head toward his lips before he kisses my temple. "I won't let them harm you, beloved. I'll protect you. I'll keep you safe. I swear on my life, Jane. I swear it." He gives me a quick peck on the lips that reenergizes my nerve endings. "We have to go back in the house now."

"No!"

Those blue eyes find mine, all determination and comfort. "They won't hurt you. I won't let them. I *won't.*" I almost believe him. Maybe I do believe him because I put up no resistance as he wraps his arm around my waist and leads me through the water toward the house. I glance where Daniel stood, but he's vanished. "It's alright. Nothing's going to harm you. *I* have you now."

My breath catches as he opens the front door. Nothing. No people. No voices. No scents. It's as quiet as a crypt. "Hello?" Bram shouts. Only his own voice echoes back. "Come on," he whispers as he pulls me inside.

Be it the cold water permeating through my skin to my bones, the adrenaline crash, or the fear, I'm trembling so violently if Bram weren't holding me I might collapse.

We venture into the foyer, past the staircase, but the woman's gone. Oh, God. I really am crazy. There's no trace, nothing, that proves she was ever there. Humiliation overshadows the terror within me. I made this wonderful man risk his life to save me from my imagination. If something happened to him on the way here…I push the thought away. Bram leads me into the living room. All that's amiss is my book on the floor. "Oh God," I whimper.

"What?"

"I just…I…I'm so sorry. I shouldn't have called you. I—"

The stench of cigar assaults my nose again. "What's that?" Bram asks. He spins us around, both our mouths dropping in unison. The man in the suit stands in the foyer doorway grinning like the Devil ushering Jesus toward the gates of hell. Bram's grip around my waist tightens, fingers even digging into my flesh.

"You…see him too?" I ask, voice barely audible.

"Yes."

One word. One syllable and a weight lifts from my very soul. Bram sees him. The man's really there. I'm not crazy. *I'm not crazy*. I'm not crazy…

Not releasing me, Bram takes a step toward the man, jaw set as hard as his glare. "Get out." The intruder's grin grows before he begins silently chuckling. We take another step. "You will leave this house," Bram orders, voice like titanium. "I banish you from this house! You will leave this house at once! You are not welcome within these walls! *You will leave*! Leave! *Now*!" he roars.

It's as if I blink and the man fades. Dissipates into nothingness. Gone. I let out another sob as my legs finally give out. Bram catches me in his strong, capable arms. "It's okay," he whispers, petting my hair. "Don't be scared. He's gone." I just keep sobbing. "Don't be frightened."

He doesn't understand. I sob not in fear, not in anger, but sweet, sweet relief. In happiness. I've never been this happy before. Where laughter isn't enough, though I do laugh through the tears. "You saw him," I laugh. "He was real. They were all real. You saw him. I'm not crazy. *I'm not crazy!*"

Bram holds me tighter, chuckling right along with me. "No, my beloved. You're not crazy. You're not crazy at all." He lifts my head up to kiss my lips before smiling. "You're haunted."

CHAPTER EIGHT

Is Owen making bacon? That's so nice of him, especially since it's my turn to make him breakfast in bed. It's the least I can do. He works so hard. I open my sore, raw eyes and realize my mistake. I keep forgetting where I am. Owen's thousands of miles away, so who…oh, Lord, I let a man I barely know spend the night in my home. He slept in a guest room, but I don't recall locking my door. I glance over. Heck, I didn't even close it. For all I know Bram could be a rapist or multiple murderer. I check myself. Pajamas, panties, both present and accounted for. Still. Not wise.

I throw off the covers and climb out of bed. I do have a guest after all. The clock is blank which means the power is still off. Great. I quickly brush my teeth and stare at my reflection. Even with dim lighting, I look wretched. Red, puffy eyes. Blotchy skin. Lank hair. Part of me, the intelligent part, tells me I should go downstairs as is. That I shouldn't care how I appear to a man who isn't my husband. But I find myself smearing on concealer and lipstick before brushing my hair into a high ponytail and slipping on my robe.

The house is so quiet save for the crackling of fat and clattering of pans that grows louder the closer I move to the kitchen. Bram's hard at work at my stove swishing around the bacon and eggs in wrought iron pans I didn't even know I owned. The tea kettle whistles just as I step in. The sunlight streams in, hitting his golden hair, giving it an angelic tint. How can a man be so handsome and pretty all at the same time? There's no other word for him besides beautiful. Simply beautiful. Especially when he's acting domestic. I sense my stomach tighten, among other regions, as he cooks. I got pregnant the first time on our kitchen table after watching Owen doing this very task. I restrain myself now.

"Good morning," Bram says as he spins around. "Tea'll be ready in a minute. No coffee. Sorry."

"Tea's great," I say, stepping in. "I think I saw some—"

He holds up a tray filled with various tea boxes. "Got it already. Felicia was a tea connoisseur. Pick your poison."

"Um, Earl Grey. Cream and sugar," I say as I sit at the table in the corner. "I keep forgetting you know this place better than I do."

"You'll learn," he says, prepping the tea. "The power's still out, I'm afraid, so no toast either. I already spoke to a friend at the power company. This region's been moved to the top of the list." He walks over with my tea. "Should be fixed in a few hours. I also phoned about your car. Jesse'll come by with his tow truck when he can."

"Thank you. For everything. You've been…words cannot express how…" I shake my head.

"It's okay," he says, saving me once again. "I like being your knight in shining armor. Never been one before. It's kind of thrilling. Braving the elements, fighting off ghosts all for the love of a beautiful damsel in distress. I could get used to it. Need any dragons slain?" he asks with a smile.

I half smile back. "Probably." I sip my tea. Perfect. "You really think I have ghosts?"

"That or last night was a mass hallucination." He shuts off the gas burners and begins dishing. "But really—and I can't believe I'm uttering this sentence—ghosts make more sense. This house…everyone in the Vale knows to stay away. Cold spots, invisible eyes following you, thumps. Hell, the stories go back generations. Confederate soldiers, slaves, even French trappers have been seen. There's something about this land, I guess, that draws and keeps them here. I'm sure the Hoodoo practices didn't help."

"Hoodoo? Is that voodoo?"

Bram brings over the plates and forks before sitting across from me. "Voodoo's a religion, hoodoo are magical practices. The town gossip is Hallie's grandmamma, her mama Ada, even Hallie herself were practitioners. That curses, human sacrifice, even raising demons all happened at Cotton's request right here on this land. Not a lick of proof was ever uncovered, mind you, but it is possible. I do know before we cleaned up this house for your arrival, there were all sorts of symbols and sigils painted on the walls along with charm bags and trinkets in every corner. The master bedroom was the worst. Four dozen icons covering every inch, even the ceiling. It was intense going in there. Even without the decorations. That poor man. Your poor grandmamma too. I really liked her, I did, but…" He shakes his head. "I don't want to speak ill of the dead, especially in light of recent occurrences."

"Did she wear Chanel #5?" I ask.

"Yeah. She doused herself in it. She said it was her one attempt at luxury and civility. Why?"

"I started…hearing and seeing things the day she died. A woman's voice, then a man's, and once a black figure. Then the smells: cigars, Chanel. Those didn't begin until I arrived at this house though. Neither did *seeing* them save for the black figure that appeared once in California."

"The man I saw last night was Cotton Fontaine. No question."

"And he's been here all this time. Watching me and…" The image of playing himself sends a shiver down my spine. "They shouldn't be here. They're abominations. How do I get rid of them? How do I usher them into God's paradise? Should I call a priest or—"

"Felicia had Father King in here every month to bless this house. Since they're still here, I don't think it did much good. I already put a call into my mother. She has a woman who cleanses houses of negative and unnatural energy."

"I don't know," I say. "I'm not really comfortable using witchcraft and—"

"It's not witchcraft. It has nothing to do with good and evil, it's about energy. Physics. Why do you think he disappeared when I told him to? My concentrated energy forced him away like your fear made him stronger. The energist does what I did but also changes the general energy of the house, making it less hospitable for them."

"I'd really be more comfortable with a priest. I'm sorry."

"No, I completely understand. His number's around here somewhere, I'm sure. Until then, if you see or hear something, just ignore it or do what I did: order it away."

"Okay." I eat my eggs. They're divine. "How do you know so much about this stuff?"

"You're not the only one whose encountered things you can't explain." He shovels in his eggs. "Take last night. Right before you called, this…intense fear gripped me from out of nowhere. It woke me up even." He gazes across at me with a mix of sadness and longing. "Don't know how or why but, I just *knew* you were in danger. I was putting on my shoes when you called. I can't explain it. I…feel this tie to you. There hasn't been a minute since we met you haven't overwhelmed my thoughts. My dreams. Hell, even before then." Bram stares down, face turning red. "I can't believe I'm telling you this, but I dreamed about you. Before we met. The same dream for over a decade. It was at this house. I was waiting on the porch, leaning against the pillar as it cracked, as the house fell apart all around me, but I didn't move. I couldn't. Then I saw you, and I knew why. Because when I saw you walking towards me, your white dress billowing as you stared at me, you stopped my breath and yours. You didn't even notice the—"

"Alligator?" I ask, voice quaking. "R-ravens everywhere?"

He looks up, eyes growing wide as his mouth slowly opens. "How-how did you know that?"

"Did-did you ever have one…with a baby? On the porch—"

"A blonde woman has her back to me, holding something in her arms. And all around me, coursing through me, is pure, unadulterated love at the mere sight of her. I approach her and somehow that love doubles when I see the baby with huge, aquamarine eyes staring up at me. Our son. I wrap my arms around her, the love of my life who gave me that most precious gift she cradles. No being ever has or ever will be as happy as I am in that moment."

It's my turn to glance away from his heated gaze. My mouth opens, but I don't know what to say. That's impossible. Two people can't have the same dreams, especially when they've never met. I gasp, attempting to draw breath, but it's almost as impossible as every horror that's come before. Ghosts, psychic links, family curses, hoodoo, it's all too much. This is too much. I almost wish I were crazy. *I can't...I can't...*

Bram leaps up and rounds the table as I continue gasping. He drops to his knees and takes my hands in his. Just his touch calms me more than an entire bottle of pills. He draws my fingers to his dry lips, kissing them one by one, bringing my fear level down further with each caress. "It's okay. It'll all be okay. There's no reason for fear, Jane. Can't you see? This is...phenomenal."

"Phenomenal?"

With a breathtaking smile affixed to his beautiful face and eyes rimmed with tears, he presses my hand to his cheek. "We're linked. Your God or the universe or whatever has brought us together. Don't you see? We...are meant for one another. I-I-I've never been more sure of anything in all my days. I was even before. When I first saw you in that hallway. This just proves it. And you sense it too. I know you do. It's written all over your face. Every time you look at me. Every time you touch me, you recognize this one universal truth. You do. Jane...please. Am I wrong? Tell me I am, and I'll go. I'll leave you alone until the end of time itself." My mouth opens to say the words, but I can't lie. He presses my hand in harder, clutching it so hard I hear tendons snap yet perceive no pain. Agony, horror, fear don't exist in this new realm of ours. "Do you know how miraculous you are to me? How miraculous this is? Us?" He leans forward so our mouths are a mere inch apart. Still too far away. "Tell me I'm wrong," he whispers. "Tell me you don't feel it too. Tell me…" A centimeter. My lips plump even without him touching them, "…you don't want me."

Bram barely utters that last word before what little resolve I have left shatters. My lips assault his. In a day full of shocks, the biggest one by far is how the moment our lips join, every cell recognizes how much I crave this man. None more so than my most sacred place. Like my lips it becomes engorged, pulsating, as this man, this veritable stranger, kisses me back as if I were providing air to a drowning man. Greedy. Hungry. He grabs the back of my neck, pulling me closer into him. His tongue finds mine, teasing me. I'm overwhelmed by him. His taste. His touch, hard to the point of pain, including his savage lips. His smell, clean but with a smoky undercurrent like he's been kissed by fire. I'm so intoxicated by him I almost fail to notice his arm wrapping around my waist. He draws me from the chair so I'm kneeling in front of him until he lowers me onto the floor. His knee parts my legs without a shred of resistance. In fact I wrap them around his waist. He's as enflamed as I am, that engorged bulge instantly grinding against my own sex with only the thin fabric of my pajama pants separating us. One thrust wretches up my madness further to the point it actually burns deep inside. With one hand still grasping my hair, he uses the other to untie my robe. That same hand moves under my tank top to my breasts, tracing the outline of my nipple, sending waves of pleasure rippling though with each rotation. It's—

I cry out as he pinches the nipple. Hard. The burning reaches atomic proportions at that moment. I writhe against his erection as he meets me stroke for stroke. Circle, circle, squeeze, moan. With each round the countdown to detonation grows closer, and we're still dressed.

He moves to remedy that. He releases my neck, deciding his hand is better used down south. With so many pleasurable sensations I barely notice as he lightly traces the sensitive skin, tickling it right above the rim of my pajama pants. But as he continues his march south, and barely brushes my clitoris, I really do come close to losing my mind. I break our kiss to throw my head back and cry out. Both hands work in tandem. Circle, circle, squeeze. Pleasure, pleasure, glorious pain. As above so below. Close. Close. So close—

Glass shatters beside us.

We both stop our exploration and jerk our gazes that way. What…? A coffee mug. It fell from the table. Thank God. Thank God because the accident returns me to my senses. What the heck am I doing? "Get off me. Get off me!" I pant as I push him away. Though shocked, he removes his hands from my body, and I scoot away. "I'm sorry. I'm sorry. I can't do this. It's wrong. This is wrong. I'm married. I can't do this. I'm sorry."

We just sit on the floor, panting the frustration and lust out as best we can. Bram stares at me with those agonized eyes but I keep my gaze down on the shards of the mug. "I'm sorry," I say again.

"There's nothing to be sorry about," he says after a pause. "I understand."

"You do?"

"We barely know each other, and I don't want this to be another…I want this to matter. Because to me you're the only thing that does. We'll take this as slow as you need."

"Okay," I say for lack of something better. "Thank you."

"I'm going to…" he moves to rise but only makes it to his knees. "I…I don't want to leave you in this house alone. They're still here. You're not safe."

Oh God, he's right. The question is what am I more afraid of? The ghosts or being around the man who makes me forget my morals and lose all control? Without hesitation, I say, "I know what to do now. I'll be fine. I'll get the priest here as soon as I can."

"Okay," Bram says, not hiding his disappointment. He finds his feet. "I'll go then. I should go."

I pull my legs to my chest. "Yes."

"I'll, uh, call to check on you later. If anything happens…"

"I'll phone. I promise."

Bram nods before starting toward the door. When he reaches the threshold, he spins back around. "I'm not wrong, am I? At least…give me that."

"No. You're not wrong."

His smile lights up the room like a second sun. "Then for you, beloved, I can wait until the sky turns green and the moon no longer rises. But please, I've already waited so long. Please don't fight this. Please don't fight us. I'll take care of you, Jane. I'll be good to you. I'll never cheat on you. I will never abandon you. I will do everything in my power to make you happy. To give you everything you desire and more. All you have to do…is let go. Give in. Say yes." That angelic smile of his grows. "Say yes, Jane. Say yes."

And he walks out, leaving me alone with my guilt, my shame, my longing so deep it reaches the center of my soul. I can still feel him on my lips, taste him, smell him. I close my eyes to savor it, and the moment I hear the front door shut, I whisper, "Yes."

*

I've always found such comfort in church. Aunt Helen insisted we attend at least three times a week. The scent of incense, the hymns, the stillness and quiet when you're alone in the house of God as I am now, it all sooths not only my mind but my soul. Even now. Especially now. I've been sitting in this pew for over half an hour at St. Jude's praying the rosary, asking God for the strength to resist temptation, for forgiveness of my sins, for mercy for the trapped souls in my home. I pray that He's listening as well.

Not ten minutes after Bram left, I grabbed my Bible and walked around the house citing Bible verses aloud for an hour straight until the tow truck arrived. I could see the church from the garage so while they attached my new tires, I decided to meander over. Find some peace. Just a shame Father King wasn't in. Again.

But still. It's worked. I am no longer a raw nerve. I've even managed thirty whole seconds without replaying that smut scene in my kitchen. His tongue teasing mine. His fingers playing—

I pray harder to banish the impure thoughts once more. *Not in God's house, Jane.*

A shutting door and footsteps draw my attention away from my self-flagellation. I glance up just as an ancient priest, easily in his late eighties, with a gray beard, short hair, and hunched shoulders walks down the aisle. He takes one look at me and his mouth drops open. I am growing quite annoyed with everyone reacting as if I were a circus freak. At least after last night's revelation *I* don't consider myself one anymore. "Hello," I say to the awestruck man of God.

My speaking seems to knock him from his daze. "Oh, sorry. I just—"

"Are you Father King?" I ask, rising from the pew.

"I am. And you must be Jane. I was going to come visit next week. Introduce myself. You…look so much like your mother, it's uncanny."

"You knew my mother?"

"Of course. I christened her and your uncle both. I'm so sorry about his passing. Your grandmother's as well. She was a wonderful woman. Such a huge heart."

"Yes, I heard you visited her quite often."

He begins up the aisle toward me. "Yes. She…didn't like to leave the house, especially after Hallie passed."

"I'm sure you gave her great comfort."

He steps into the pew in front of me. "I hope so. She was a special woman. I miss her."

"Well, you met with her once a month for decades. That's understandable. You were probably the person closest to her in the whole wide world."

"Yes, I suppose I was," he says with an uncomfortable smile. "As I suppose you have certain questions for me. I'll do my best to answer them."

This isn't what I came for, but I best not look a gift horse in the mouth. "Was she insane?"

He's visibly taken aback by my directness. As am I. Definitely not myself today. "I don't know how to answer that. She had certain eccentricities, I suppose."

"She shut herself away for almost forty years with her comatose son, covered the house with religious relics, then she kills her son and herself. I also heard she believed the house was haunted. I really think those go beyond mere eccentricities."

"Felicia had a hard life. Any joy that found its way to her was snatched away. Mother, husband, children, all gone too soon. Grief and loneliness do strange things to people, especially to those with delicate souls."

I nod. "She never got over my grandfather?"

"No. I officiated their wedding, you know. You could see the love passing between them as they said their vows. Before that even."

"How did he die? Was it really a hunting accident?" I ask.

"That was what the police said," Father King replies.

"But Cotton really murdered him, didn't he?"

"I can't say without breaking the sacred pact of confession." Which means yes. "However, if ever a soul was bound for hell, it was Cotton Fontaine's. All that really mattered was that your grandmother did. Cotton loathed Daniel. If he did have him killed, I'm surprised he waited three years to do so. Then he all but murdered her son and scared away her daughter and granddaughter. If she was crazy that man drove her to it. May God have mercy on all their souls," he says, crossing himself.

"On the topic of souls. Is it possible from them to be trapped on earth?"

"You're speaking of ghosts."

"Yes. I understand you blessed the house once a month. Why else would you do that if not to keep them away?"

Father King once again simply stares instead of answering, attempting to find the right words. "Yes, Felicia believed certain souls were trapped in and around the house. I don't know if you believe in such entities but—"

"I didn't until both Bram Davenport and I saw one last night. Cotton Fontaine to be precise. My grandfather Daniel too. Felicia may be trapped as well. I want them gone. I want them to cross over. Is that possible?"

"I would like to believe so. But I've performed all the rites multiple times, and per Felicia, the spirits returned. There isn't much more I can do. I'm sorry." Not the answer I was hoping for. I sigh. Maybe I should go Bram's route. An energist. Which means I'll have to contact him.

But perhaps the Father can aid me in another matter. "Did my grandmother ever talk about me? About my mother? Why she never made contact? Why she sent her away?"

"You know I cannot break the sacrament of confession," Father King says again. "What I can tell you is that she loved your mother more than words can say. When Juliette died, Felicia refused to leave her bed for weeks. Hallie called me to try to comfort her but to no avail. She never truly got over it. I never heard her utter your mother's name again."

"So why did she send my mother away?" I ask.

"To protect her. To get her away from that house, from what became of her brother. They were so close. Twins, best friends in every sense. I saw Juliette the day after the accident. She was catatonic. A living ghost. Everywhere she looked must have reminded her of her brother."

"So it wasn't because she was pregnant?"

"I…" he says, stunned again. "I do not believe so, no."

Darn it, another dead end. Useless. This man couldn't help my grandmother why did I think he could help me? Wishful thinking. Owen did chide me about managing my expectations more than once. Every time I got pregnant I immediately wanted to paint the spare room and buy a crib. After the third time, when he gave into my whim we had to live with a blue room and our son's baby items for months until Owen couldn't stand the sight of it and dismantled all my hard work. He never let me do it again. He was right, of course. Guess this world has no use for an optimist. In my experience we're always, *always* let down. I should have learned this lesson by now.

I rise from the pew. "Thank you for your time. And your honesty." With a half-smile, I move out of the pew.

"Jane?" Father King calls. I spin around. "If you ever need to talk—"

"Thank you," I cut in.

The storms may have passed but the wind and overcast gray sky remain in their wake. This kind of day seeps into your soul, dimming its light. The church is literally the centerpiece of the town with all the stores surrounding it in a square, including the Davenport office to the south. His car's there. It was when I entered and remains now. I hurry the opposite direction back to the garage.

If he was watching me, I'm soon lost in the sea of townsfolk crowding the streets. Now safe from the storm, not a citizen of the Vale isn't out in search of supplies or camaraderie. Groups chat about their lack of power or property damage that is until I pass by. Even with my head hung I can sense their eyes on me as their conversations grind to a halt then become whispers after I've passed. Small wonder Felicia became a hermit.

I cross Sherman Way, but just as I reach the other side, a horn honks. When I turn around, a Mercedes pulls up beside me. Another honk stops me dead. The window rolls down, revealing my least favorite person in town. "Get in."

"I beg your pardon?"

"I need to speak to you," Daphne Davenport says. "I'll take you wherever you're going. Get in. Please." The truck behind her honks. "I'm not moving until you do."

The man honks again and leans out the window to glare, but Daphne ignores him. She stares at me, determination and ire pulling me in. Crud. I climb inside before we cause a major traffic jam. "I'm going to Jesse's Garage. My car—"

"Let's take a little drive first."

Oh wonderful, I've been kidnapped. "I—"

"How are you liking the Vale so far?" she asks, ignoring me.

"It's fine. I haven't really—"

"And the house? Enjoying the house? The storm didn't cause much damage, I hope."

So that's what this is about. The house. I'd admire her tenacity if it weren't so tinged with hostility. "No. It might have lost some shingles but nothing too severe."

"Good. Excellent. I'm not surprised, though. Good bones, that house. It'd probably survive an atomic bomb." She turns the car onto Blake Street, the exact opposite way from the garage. "My mother worked there as a maid for a spell. I baby-sat the twins once or twice too. I loved wandering the halls. Taking in all the grandeur, the history pretending it was all mine. Even now it's the finest house in the parish. Two point five million."

"I'm sorry?"

"I will give you two and a half million dollars for the house and all its contents. I'm aware of its estimated value, but the furniture is mostly antique, so I added a generous sum. I'll take it as is, no inspection required. Believe me when I say there is not a single person within this state who will offer you more. It has a…reputation almost as tarnished as your family's. Judging from the call I received from my son this morning, this reputation is not unwarranted. I myself often encountered cold spots and spied dark figures out of the corner of my eye. Clara can clear them out though. She's the best energist in the state. The governor used her. What I've offered is more than a fair price. The only caveat is you pack up in the next two days, and that you have no further contact with my son. Return to your husband, to Los Angeles, or *not*, I truly don't care. But you leave my son alone. There's nothing for you here anyway. Nothing but ghosts. Literally."

I stare at this woman, mouth agape not only at her audacity but at her lack of emotion during this proposal. "Why do you want the house so badly?"

"Because it's the best. The grandest. The brass ring if you will. I've wanted to live there ever since my mother scrubbed its toilets when Cotton Fontaine wasn't fucking her in the master bedroom. Where the same thing happened to me ten years later. One good thing I'll say about that son-of-a-bitch, even at his advanced age, that man could fuck like a stallion. Runs in the family, I guess," she says with a smirk. What does that... "So, what do you say? Is two days enough? I can have D.J. whip up a contract and send it to your lawyer in LA today. Please do know this is a one-time offer which expires at the end of the day, or sooner if you inform my son of our bargain. That last condition goes from now until the contract is signed and finances transferred. If I hear you have made so much as a phone call to Bram in the interim, I pull the offer. With probate, escrow, it should take months. If I know my son, and if his past is any indication, he'll find someone else pretty to obsess over, and you will be nothing but an afterthought. So much like D.J. He chases anything in a skirt as well.

"You are not special, Mrs. Harrow. I tell you this not to be cruel. Quite the opposite. You strike me as a sincere if not innocent woman. I love my son, I do, but more often than I care to admit, I do not like my son. My fault and D.J.'s. He was our only child. We indulged his every whim. Now he does it himself. Drugs, drink, women. He can't commit to a houseplant. He's not for you Mrs. Harrow," she insists. "Nor is this town. Too much history. No one here will think of you as anything but the daughter of madness. Your mother was sent away, you were *kept* away, for a reason. Take the money. Go home, Mrs. Harrow. Here we are."

I've been so immersed in this strange proposition by this strange woman I failed to notice we've gone in a circle and have arrived at the garage. She timed this perfectly. "Um, I'll think about it."

"There's really nothing to think about. I'm offering you the deal of a lifetime. Don't allow emotion to cloud logic. That path always leads to nothing but misery. I look forward to hearing from you."

Guess that's that. With an awkward smile, I climb out of the car. The door barely closes before Daphne drives off. Okay…that was very uncomfortable and odd. She really wants the house. And me away from her son. I cannot say I'm not incredibly tempted, especially after this morning. Thousands of miles from Bram might not be a terrible thing. Neither is becoming a millionaire. Almost seems too good to be true, yet I believe her. At least I believe in her desire for the house. Two and a half million. I could start over, *really* start over, anywhere in the world with that kind of money. Paris, Cairo, heck I could travel the world until I find the right place. Plant roots wherever feels most like home. I—

Oh, who am I kidding? *Here.* Here feels like home. This town. That house. I sense it in my bones. My soul. I'm connected to this land. It's my birthright, ghosts and all. Can I just sell that to the highest bidder? The weight of this decision makes me sigh. Storms, ghosts, infidelity, now this. It's enough to drive a woman mad.

CHAPTER NINE

New tires, new cell phone, new quandaries, I'm exhausted by the time I return to the house. The power's back on at least. No strange smells or whispers either. Maybe my Bible reading did the job. Or they're drained from last night's theatrics and needed to recharge before unleashing further horrors. That's at least what one of the books I skimmed at the store mentioned could happen. I bought two on the subject. Something to distract me tonight.

After quickly grabbing a snack—I can't bear being in the kitchen after this morning—I rush upstairs to the relative safety of my bed and check my voice mail. Three messages.

"*Hey sweetie, it's Mel,*" says my friend. "*Just calling to see what's up. Love you. Bye.*"

"*Jane, it's Corrine,*" my agent says. "*Still waiting on those illustrations. I need an ETA. The publisher and author are getting nervous. Call me.*"

Crimeny, I completely forgot about the illustrations. I have to get those done ASAP.

"*Hi Jane, it's Marty,*" says my divorce attorney. "*I understand there have been new developments in your living and financial situations. Please call me so we can discuss your options. Thank you.*"

A fifty dollar phone call that.

Finally, "*Um, hi. This is Janet LeCherz. My, um, sister Tammy told me she ran into you and gave me this number. I don't...I don't know what to say,*" she chuckles nervously. "*I-I want to meet you. And I'll bet you have a million questions for me. Um, my number is 555-7852. Please call me. If-if you want.*"

I can't. Not right now. There are pressing matters in the present far more important than rehashing the past. There's only one person I can talk to who'll give me an unbiased recommendation of how I should proceed. I need to talk to my best friend.

"Oh, thank the gods," Melissa says over the phone. "I was actually getting worried. It's so bad for the skin, you know."

"I broke my phone. Sorry I worried you."

"Not just me. You need to call Owen too. He's freaking. You run off to God knows where at least have the courtesy to return our calls and texts so we know you're alive," she chides. "Him especially. You know how protective he is of you. You used to think it was adorable, remember?"

"I'll call him. I promise."

"Good. So, what's going on? What's up?"

"I need your advice." Where to start? "Um, what do you know about cleansing houses of ghosts?"

"This again? Jane, what the fuck? What is going on? Are you...I think maybe you should go see a shrink. Babes, if you're seeing and hearing things—"

"But I'm not! I-I-I thought I was going crazy, I really did, until Bram saw the same ghost I did last night. My great-grandfather. There might be three more, including my grandparents. I know you believe in them. Ghosts."

"I mean, I sort of do. In theory. I've never seen one myself but...wait. Did-Did you say you had a man over last night?"

"Can we please stay on topic?" I ask. "Ghosts?"

"Um, burn sage and call in a paranormal investigator, at least that's what I saw on the *Discovery Channel*. You know what? Read a damn book about it," she snits. "Now, who is this Bram and why was he at your house late last night?"

"I was scared. He's...my lawyer."

"And you needed him to what? Sue the ghosts?"

"No. He's just, he's been nice to me."

"How nice?" Melissa demands. I don't answer. "Janie, you are very, *very* vulnerable right now. You're seeing things—"

"He saw them too! He described the man I was seeing down to the suit color. It was real. It was a ghost. I'm not crazy."

"Janie, I'm not saying you are," Melissa says desperately. "I'm saying don't do anything with a man just because he shows you a little attention. I know you. You'll regret it."

"I'm not…it-it's complicated."

"Oh, don't give me complicated. You're scared, you're damaged, you're exhausted, you haven't gotten laid in almost a year, and this man can probably smell that on you. I'm all for strings-free sex, but not in your case. Especially not now. You love Owen, and despite his boneheaded move with that whore, he loves you too. Stop punishing the both of you. It is not your fault you cannot have children. *Owen* doesn't blame you, so for Christ's sake stop blaming yourself. You know I love you, and I'm always on your side, but you pushed that man away with both hands. He reacted. Badly. But he is only human. Forgive him. Forgive yourself. Put that damn house on the market and go back to your husband. Start over."

"Mel, that's exactly what I'm trying to do. I-I just can't leave yet. There's still so much I have to learn. About my family, about my parents. My-my father could be here."

"Jane so far all you've found out is they're murderous, molesters, or just plain nuts. You've opened enough cans of worms, one more and you could drown in the fuckers. When it comes down to it, your family's dead. You're alive. You're alive with a husband who would die a million deaths for you and a successful career thousands would sell their mother for. Go home, kiss your husband, adopt a damn baby, and live happily fucking ever after. I really, *seriously* can't fathom why you aren't packing your things as I yell at you." Mel pauses. "Do you love Owen? The truth now."

Without hesitation, I say, "I'll always love him."

"Then go the fuck home. *Now*."

This is why I called her. She may be rough, she may be blunt, but she is rarely wrong. I think I needed it said aloud for it to penetrate. I mean, two and a half million dollars. I really would be crazy to turn down an offer like that. And I do physically ache for Owen. That's probably why I reacted so violently to Bram. I'm dying for physical companionship. To be touched. Heck, I'd probably hop into bed with a blender if it crooked its finger. Home is where the people I love are. I'll be a rich woman. I can have someone else dig into my family trash.

"I'm sorry if I'm being harsh," Melissa offers. "I love you. You're my essential person. Have been since college. I just, I see you running toward an inferno when there's a Ferrari waiting to take you to Ice Cream Mountain. Just don't let lust or fear cloud common sense. That's all. Promise?"

"I promise," I say, biting my lower lip. "And I promise I'll call Owen."

"He's never been my favorite person, you know, but he is yours. Next to yours truly. Too bad we're not lesbians. So many problems solved, right?"

"Right."

"You call me day or night, okay? Hopefully from the road on your way back to Cali. I love you."

"Love you too. Thank you." I hang up.

Okay. It's decided. I'm selling the house to Daphne. I'm never seeing Bram again. Life can return back to normal. Maybe the ghosts will leave me alone now. They wanted me to come, I did. I acknowledged them, and when the house isn't mine anymore, they'll leave me in peace. Daphne will get them to pass over come heck or high water. If anyone can scare the dead away, it's Daphne Davenport.

I should sleep on this, a decision this huge, but I know myself. I'll think up a million reasons to stay just because it's the easier move. The safer route. Hiding. Running. I've done enough of that. Phone still in hand, I go in search of Daphne's phone number but realize she never gave it to me. Crud. Instead I return to bed and call the law office. "Davenport Senior, please. This is Jane Harrow." Betsy puts me through.

"Well, hello, Mrs. Harrow. What can I do you for?" D.J. asks.

"I was actually looking to get in touch with your wife. I don't have her number."

"Daphne? What on earth for? She's not trying to rope you in on one of her projects, is she?"

"No, it's about the offer she made on the house."

"The what she what? Daphne put an offer on Fontaine House? When? For how much?"

I'm stunned silent for a moment. She didn't discuss it with her husband? "Um, today. For two and a half million dollars."

"Jesus wept," D.J. mutters before he's silent as well. He clears his throat five seconds later. "Well, Miz Harrow, I think I need to speak with my dear wife before you do, if you don't mind. We will have to get back to you. But I assume you do wish to sell?"

"I...yes. I do."

"Alrighty then. We'll be in touch. You have a nice rest of your day." He hangs up.

Wonderful. My millions vanish as quickly as they came. I should have known it was too good to be true. Yet he didn't seem too adverse to the idea. Even still, if they do withdraw the offer, I'm still selling. I'll leave in the next day or so. Everything can be handled from California as it always should have been. I let out a long sigh. The hard part's over. The decision is made regardless of who I sell this tomb to. All else are minor details and annoyances I will handle as they come.

No, the man whispers. *Sta—*

"Oh, shut up."

*

Oh, I have missed being productive. Accomplishing something and having the physical proof right in front of me. I may actually finish *Sherlock the Mouse* on time. I've finished three illustrations in an hour. Three more left. God, I love creating. Drawing an image, a thought from my imagination, and making it a part of the world. Concrete. It's magic in a way. A gift from God.

Sherlock may not be the Mona Lisa, but I still put my all into his adventures fighting Molearty. I wonder if Uncle Jerome got the same thrill when he sketched that I do. I'm definitely going to take all his paintings and sketches with me. The photos and a few trinkets as well. That will be tomorrow's project, boxing up what I think Daphne would just throw out. At the very least I owe my family that. They—

The doorbell rings. I take off my headphones and save my work before rising from the dining room table. The bell chimes again. Ugh, I thought people in the South had manners. Coming over to a person's home without calling is one of the top ten no-nos, at least per Emily—oh, no.

As I pass the window, I spot a familiar SUV in my driveway. I stop in my tracks. Of course. The last person on this planet I have any desire to see is on my porch and not just because it'll void the offer. I wonder if this will count against my bargain with Daphne, if it still exists. There was no proviso if *he* came looking for *me.* I remain still, even when the bell chimes again, followed by a knock.

"Jane?" Bram shouts. More knocks. "Jane, please answer the door. Please? We need to talk." He waits a few seconds before knocking again. "I know you're here. I know you can hear me. Please talk to me. *Please*," he pleads so desperately my stomach physically wrenches. "I am not leaving until you talk to me. I will camp out on your porch all night if I have to." More silence. "Fine."

I hear his footsteps on the wooden porch moving this way. Crud. I duck back into the dining room as Bram passes by the window, peering in as he passes. Hiding in my own home. Can I be more pathetic? He moves to the next window.

I have to go out there, don't I? Rip the Band-Aid off, Jane. I smooth my hair before stepping from my hidey hole and walking to the front door. After a deep breath, I step outside.

Bram's nowhere in sight. He wouldn't give up that easily. "Bram?" A second later I hear running footsteps around the corner before he steps into view. As always as he moves closer and closer toward me it's as if Tesla coils were sparking through and around me like Frankenstein's monster coming to life. *Just lust. Nothing but lust. Ignore it, Jane.* "Wait," I say, holding up my hand, "don't-don't come any closer."

He stops ten feet away. "What? Why?"

"Just stay there. Please. Just-just say what you came to. From there."

His mouth opens from the confusion he has to be feeling. "Okay. Whatever you want. I just…I don't understand. You're selling the house? This morning you didn't say anything about leaving."

"I didn't have an offer then."

"But-but I thought you planned to stay."

"Things change."

He stares at me, those blue eyes appraising me so intently I have to avert my own gaze to the ground. "Things being us," he finally spits out. "*Me.* You're leaving because of me. Because of what happened this morning. You're scared."

"I'm not—"

"You're scared of loving me," Bram says, taking a step toward me. "Because you do, you know?" Another step. "I see it in your eyes whenever you look at me." Another step. "Look at me, Jane. *Look,*" he demands, all but shouting. Somehow my eyes move up to meet his. An almost cruel grin stretches across his face as he takes another step. "Yes. It's there now. I gaze into those cool pools of yours and see the boiling below. Scorching my soul." Another step. "Awakening something I never knew myself capable of. Intense, all encompassing, pure, true, love. And it's…astounding. Amazing. Bewildering. Frightening. But now I've found it, I never want to lose it. *Never.* And I will. If you turn your back on me, on us, I will be lost. Dead in all but body. And so will you." He's finally reached me. We're so close I smell his aftershave, the coffee on his hot breath. Before I can stop it, my body instinctively arches toward his, centimeters from impact. Thank God for that distance. "Don't do this to me. Don't do this to *us.* I need you. I need you like plants need sun. Like fish need water. Like a needle needs a vein. Like you need me. Please…" He slowly raises his hand to my face, caressing my cheek, sending cascades of liquid heat through my every nerve ending. Damn him. "We are made for each other. We are meant to love one another. It is a universal truth. Just accept it. Give into it. Stop fighting fate, beloved. I beg of you. Don't leave me. I beg you." He leans in, whispering, "*Please.*"

He doesn't kiss me. His lips hover less than a millimeter from mine, so close we share the same breath. He's waiting for me to make the fateful move. I want to. I'm *dying* to, but if I do, all is lost. I'll never leave this man, and I *need* to leave. God grant me the strength.

He does.

I whip my head to the side and take a step backwards. "Go away. If you care, really care like you say you do, you'll go and never come back. You need to leave me alone. You need to forget about me. Never contact me again. Just *go*."

And I rush inside the safety of my home, locking and bolting the door. I rest my head against the wood and close my eyes. I'm still a live wire, vibrating and ready to spark with the potential to ignite any—

"Jane! Jane, please! Jane!"

The sudden pounding on the door makes me shriek and step back. Bram continues to assault my door while shouting my name. With every pound, every onslaught, I take another step away in fear. Not in fear of him but fear of me. His voice, so pained as if he were a drowning man calling to a departing life raft, cracks my resolve. But I can't save him. If I do, I'll drown myself. There is only one thing I *can* do. I turn my back on the wailing man and return to my work, replacing my headphones to let Adele drown out his misery. Not good enough. I close my eyes and the whole wretched world fades to black.

Good girl...

This is the right thing to do. I know it. I do.

I just don't know why it feels so absolutely wrong.

CHAPTER TEN

His endurance proved astounding. Thirty minutes straight he continued his violent onslaught. Bellowing, pleading, banging to be let in. I was surprised there weren't streaks of his blood on the door. Be it the stress, my nerves, or…who am I kidding, the deep well of sadness exploded out of me in another fit of tears around minute ten. How is it I had any left? I rushed upstairs, shut my bedroom door, turned on the TV full blast, and crawled under the covers to hide until the noise finally ceased. Only then do I crawl out of my hole like the coward I am.

I can't work anymore. I can barely think. I'm about to jump out of my skin again. After taking a Xanax, I slip into a tub of vanilla scented bubbles. I need to leave as soon as possible. Tomorrow. Forget the repairs, forget finding my birth father. If Daphne's deal is viable great, if not, I'll hire a real estate agent from California. My stomach lurches again. I ring out the washcloth and place it over my eyes. California. Back to California. Back to my old empty house. Or not. I can go anywhere. Chicago, Santa Fe, even Paris. If I'm smart I'll never have to worry about money again. I can paint full time. Maybe try and find a gallery to show my work. In Paris. Owen and I always spoke about going to Paris. A visit first though. It's the smart thing to do. Just like leaving this house. This town. *Him*. The smart course of action. At least according to my head.

No, my head wins this round. I feel crazier and more confused than when I left California. Ghosts, premonitions, soul wrenching love at first sight, I think I preferred believing I was merely insane. Pills and therapy have a chance of fixing that problem, but what do you take for a spiritual crisis? How do you forget the literal man of your dreams who swears it's his life's mission to please you? Whose kisses make you hear angels sing?

That now familiar fiery lust bubbles up just thinking about him, starting in my sex before infecting the rest of me. I attempt to ignore the inferno by filling my thoughts with the Eifel Tower and baguettes, but as I stroll through the Louvre, I turn to look at the Mona Lisa and Bram's beside me, sliding his hand into mine before leaning in for a long, lingering, sensual kiss as beautiful as all the art in the world combined. The pulsing between my legs becomes overwhelming as our lips caress. Our tongues explore one another. He may as well be in this very room, lips teasing mine. Toying with me. Making me pay for my betrayal.

I move my fingers inside my wet, silky folds as my thumb teasing my clitoris. No, not my fingers. *His*. Like this morning. He's here, right now, fingers caressing and tickling as if I were a violin and he a virtuoso, stroking in perfect time to my body's rhythms. My whimpers and moans add to this symphony of pleasure. Faster. Slower. Press. Pinch. Feather light strokes. He brings me closer and closer to bliss with every stroke he bestows upon both magical spots God gave women. The tension, the heat, the madness intensifies in time to my moans until that sweet release jolts through me. I have to pant to catch my breath, but I'm limp as a noodle. Oh, it may be a sin, but it's just what I needed. At least I'm no longer crying. I say a quick prayer of contrition before draining the water.

After I slip on my pajamas, I meander to the kitchen to prepare dinner before the Xanax begins working its magic. As I'm adding the dressing to my salad, the telephone rings. I pick it up. "Hello?"

"I just got off the phone with my son," Daphne says, none too happy. "Forgetting the abuse he spewed at me, he informed me you two had just met."

"He came over without an invitation, and I sent him away. I told him under no uncertain terms to never contact me again. I am taking your offer and all it entails. Is it still on the table? Your husband seemed to have no idea you'd made it."

"We spoke. He's…amenable to the idea. The price is his only concern. I'd suggest you hire a realtor to act as your emissary here. *After* you leave."

"Precisely what I intend to do."

"But you're definitely selling?"

"Absolutely."

"I'm happy to hear that. And you'll be vacating the property soon?"

"Within a day or two."

"Then congratulations. You are about to become a wealthy woman, Mrs. Harrow. The whole wide world waits at your fingertips. Take advantage, dear. Good-bye" She hangs up. That is one strange woman. I cannot tell if she loathes or likes me. Suppose it doesn't matter as long as her check clears.

I'm about half-way through my salad when the phone rings again. I'm so popular all of a sudden. "Hello?"

"Is this Jane?" a woman asks.

"Yes. May I ask who is calling?"

"This is Janet LeClerz. I-I knew your mother. I called you earlier?"

"Right. Yes. I'm-I'm sorry. I meant to call you back, but my phone broke and the storm…I'm sorry."

"It's fine. I can't…" Janet says breathlessly before taking several seconds to calm herself. "I can't believe it. I can't believe you exist. She never mentioned she had a baby in her letters."

"I don't think she told anyone here. I was a deep, dark secret. Seems the family had a lot of them."

"Yes. You come from a colorful bunch, that's for sure," she chuckles nervously. "They weren't all bad, though. Your mother was an angel. An absolute angel sent straight from heaven. Romy too. I loved them both dearly. I did. And I miss them to this very day." She pauses and chuckles nervously. "I want to meet you. I *need* to meet you. I'm sure you have a million questions for me. I know I have a million for you. I'm, uh, actually coming to the Vale tomorrow. Are you available? It doesn't have to be tomorrow, if-if—"

"No. Tomorrow's perfect. Would you like to come to the house for brunch?"

"I'd love to see the old place. Ten?" she asks.

"Great. I can't wait to see you."

"Me too. 'Til tomorrow. Bye." She hangs up. As do I.

That was lucky. If anyone can fill in the gaps about my mother, it'll be her best friend. I plop back down at the table with a grin. Money, answers, freedom all in one day. All that a woman could want.

And yet...

I realize I'm sitting in the same spot as I was this morning, gazing across at the most beautiful man I have ever met. In my mind's eyes I see him leaning at my feet, waiting for my permission. To kiss me. To love me. Oh, how I wanted him to. I wanted it more than all the money, all the answers, all the freedom God could provide me. And God help me, I think I still do. That I always will. God help me stay strong.

God help me.

CHAPTER ELEVEN

The baby dream. Why did it have to be the baby dream? He was in my arms. Staring up at me with his huge blue eyes, gurgling and reaching up for me with his tiny fingers. Even as I wake I still feel him in my arms, still smell his newness. Best scent in the whole universe. It covered my whole body. Not even a shower washed it away.

At least I got eight hours. Thank you, Xanax. I don't have to greet Mama's best friend resembling a pasty swamp monster. Getting the house and myself ready for my move helps keep my mind off the dream. I consider going into town for flowers and croissants but spend too much time picking an outfit and doing my hair. She'll think I was raised with no manners. I do my best with what I have: glazed donut holes, apple slices, and coffee.

At least I look amazing. Beige wool skirt, black turtleneck, black tights and boots. The house shines too, literally in some places. As I complete my final sweep, pride with a twinge of guilt grows with each room. I know I've only been here a short time, but I do feel as if it's mine. My ancestors, even my mother, chose every piece of furniture with care. Generations of Fontaines helped create this masterpiece, this legacy, and I'm selling it to the highest bidder. Literally. I came here in part to learn my history. *This* is my history. Within these walls. I passed seconds thoughts five minutes after I hung up with Daphne. I think I'm on one thousand twelfth thoughts by now.

I'm working on Sherlock when I hear the sound of wheels on gravel outside. My nervousness level spikes. Here we go. The key to finding my father just pulled up. Owen once told me when he walks into an interview room, when he asks a suspect a question, he keeps his goal in the back of his mind. He *will not* leave that room until said goal is met. I have only one goal: find my father. Let's get on with it, Jane.

The woman on my porch is nothing like I pictured. Guess I imagined she'd resemble Mama, but she's a head shorter and thirty pounds heavier. She is definitely the sister of the woman from the store with auburn hair and pug nose, though she's dressed better in white slacks and purple sweater. I should be used to dropping mouths and bug eyes when people see me, but I doubt I ever will. Another reason to leave town.

"Dear God," Janet whispers.

"I know. I look like her."

"Actually, you look like *him*. Jerome. Of-of course they both resembled one another, but really it's unnerving."

"So I've been told," I say with a crooked smile.

Janet shakes her head. "Sorry. Sorry, that was a rude thing to say."

"I'm used to it," I lie. "Come in."

The moment Janet steps inside, her mouth drops again as she gazes around the foyer. "It hasn't changed," she says as I shut the door. "At all. It even smells the same."

"When was the last time you were here?"

"God…inside? Over thirty years. I used to stop by when I was in town, but your grandmamma and Hallie always entertained me on the porch. This place held up good."

"There was a massive renovation a few months ago."

"Lucky you. It was resembling a slum house last time I popped by," she says, strolling toward the stairs. When she reaches it, she runs her finger down the banister with a grin. "Can't tell you how many times I watched your uncle slide down this thing. Always drove Hallie up a wall. Of course that's why he did it." She lowers her head. "Lord, there are a lot of happy memories within these walls. They outweigh the bad ten to one, you know."

"I hope so." I gesture toward the kitchen. "I've set up coffee and donuts in the kitchen. Is that alright?"

"When have donuts ever been wrong?"

I lead Janet through the dining room to the kitchen. The entire time it's as if my guest were touring the Smithsonian, mouth agape as she strolls down Memory Lane. Chasing each other around the table as children. Doing homework. Stories and laughter at dinner. Things she hadn't thought of in years.

When we enter the kitchen, I ask, "How do you take your coffee?"

"Cream and sugar please," Janet responds. As I prepare her coffee, she sits at the small table. "It's so odd being back here. In this room. I can't tell you how many hours we spent in here helping Hallie with dinner with jazz playing on the radio. Or her going over our math homework. She never finished high school but had a knack for facts and figures. None of us would have passed Geometry without her. Romy still barely did."

I carry our coffee to the table. "Romy?"

"Your uncle. It's what everyone but Mr. Fontaine and Mrs. Cowan called him."

"You were friends with him as well?" I ask, sipping my coffee.

"Met them on the first day of kindergarten. Even then they were a package deal. Might as well have been Siamese twins not fraternal."

"I didn't even know she had a brother," I say.

"That's a shame." She smiles sympathetically. "It's all such a wretched shame. I wrote and wrote her, but your mama never wrote back. I had to *beg* Hallie to give me reports whenever I came home from college. She never told me about you, though."

"I guess if my grandmother hadn't put me in the will, my existence would have died with her."

"Mrs. Cowan never contacted you? Never? Not once?"

"No. I thought they were all dead, or that's what my aunt told me. There was no reason to doubt her."

"How old were you when your mama died?"

"Four."

"Do you remember her at all?" Janet asks.

"Bits and pieces. Her lying on the couch watching soaps. Her in our old Packard, head pressed against the window watching the world go by. Her playing the piano for hours and hours and hours." Her screams waking me in the night. Whispering to herself. Her shrinking away when I tried to hug her. The night she died and tried to…well, Janet doesn't need to know about those. *I* don't even want to know about those.

"I'm glad she kept up with the piano. Jules loved to play. She even applied to Julliard. We had this grand plan," she chuckles. "Julliard for Jules, the conservatory for Romy, Columbia for me. The three of us taking on the Big Apple together. Guess life had other plans, huh? Was she happy? Until the accident?"

"Accident?"

"The car crash? That killed her? That is how she died, right?"

I stare down at my cup. If I want honesty, I have to give it in return. At least the majority of it. "No. She, uh, killed herself. Slit her…" The sides of my mouth twitch. "Anyway. I'm sorry."

A ripple of emotion cascades across Janet's face, lip and nose twitching as the news penetrates. "Dear God," she whispers. "What…no. *No.* I don't want to know."

I do. "Was she ever depressed when you were friends? Did she ever act insane? See things that weren't there?"

"What? No! Not like you mean. Stay too long in this house and everyone starts to see and hear things. Even me. Dark figures, whispers. Just ignore them like we did. And she was never depressed, not clinically anyway. If I had to live with Cotton lurking about or throwing his weight around and Mrs. Cowan drugged all the time, Jules couldn't help but be down about life sometimes. But never in a million years would I have thought she'd take her own life. Never."

"People change," I offer. "She'd apparently been through a lot."

The stranger reaches across the table, squeezing my hand. "I am *so* sorry, dear. I'm so sorry you never really got to know her.

She had this light. When she turned it on, it was like you were standing by the sun. Despite her actions, I am sure she loved you."

That makes one of us. "Thank you," I say pulling my hand away.

Janet sips her drink. "So, tell me about yourself. Start from the beginning. I want to hear everything. What was your father like? Did he resemble Burt Reynolds? Jules always had a crush on him. She had this idea that when we moved to New York when he came to town she'd stalk the poor man until he fell madly in love with her. Hallie was always saying Jules' head was full of stardust. Was he nice, your father?"

"I don't know. I never met him. They told me he was a solider she met on a bus, saw a few times, then he faded away."

Janet's eyes narrow. "That doesn't sound like her. I mean, she was barely allowed to date and even then it was only dances at the country club, which were chaperoned."

"So she didn't have a boyfriend?" I ask.

"Not really. As far as I know she only ever made it to second base with Tommy Brown when we were sixteen. Mr. Fontaine and Hallie kept them on a mighty short leash. They didn't even like me being alone in this house with Romy. I mean," she says, playing with her cup, "we kissed once but...it was like kissing my own brother, you know? I swear I was the only girl in school who wasn't in love with him. All the boys had a thing for Jules too but she never gave them any opportunities to act."

"Could she have had a boyfriend without you being aware?"

"I really doubt it. We told each other everything." I can't help but frown. This isn't going as well as I'd hoped. Janet's expression matches mine. "You thought your daddy was still alive and in town, didn't you?"

"The timing fits, yeah. I thought they'd shipped her off because of the shame, you know, of being an unwed mother."

"No, they sent her away a few days after the attack because she couldn't stand to be in this house. She was a wreck.

They only let me see her once the day after, but she was damn near catatonic, just lying on Romy's bed staring into space. I got her to take a shower and eat something, but she went right back to that bed, clutching onto his sweater like a teddy bear. I left the house and burst into tears on the ride home. That was the last time I ever saw her."

"Still. I could have been a factor, right?"

"When's your birthday, hon?"

"July twenty-fifth. Why?"

"Because the attack happened on September twentieth. Their eighteenth birthday. It is entirely possible she met your daddy on a bus, he was nice to her, and in her fragile state she found comfort where she could. I believe that scenario more than she was carrying on with a local behind all our backs. The girl had no guile. You could read her face like a book."

Darn it. I was really hoping she'd know who he was. If anyone it'd be the woman across from me. Like every only child I desperately wanted siblings. Even one that came later in life would be lovely. Christmases. Nieces and nephews to spoil. Looking at another human being and seeing parts of myself in them. Just not in the cards. Maybe my father was just a deadbeat solider. Maybe one thing they told me about my roots was actually true. There is one other, horrific possibility. "What about Cotton? Could he have…you know? Did he ever come after her?"

"No, and believe me, I heard the rumors too, I did ask. That man was a letch, even hit on me a few times, but Jules swore on her daddy's grave he ever laid a hand on her. Hallie and Romy made sure about that. Mrs. Cowan though…that's why Romy went into the coma. Hallie told me years later. Mr. Fontaine tried to rape her again, she fought back, and he beat her. Poor Romy heard and tried to stop him." Her face suddenly becomes hard as a diamond. "That man was pure evil. You could sense it on him. He literally made my skin crawl. That's why the twins all but lived at my house." She shakes her head. "I don't think he touched her, I really don't, but I can't be a hundred percent sure I guess."

Dear God, what if he did? What if I'm…I don't want to even consider it. Owen and I were screened for genetic abnormalities but only the basics like spina bifida and Down's syndrome. We couldn't afford the comprehensive battery, but we did come back compatible. I could always call the doctor and get tested again. This thought sours my stomach. No. No, I *really* don't want to know. What good would it possibly serve now?

Janet squeezes my hand, bringing me away from the dark thoughts. "Are you okay? I know this is a lot to digest."

"What's the matter with this family?" I ask not just her. "Are we cursed or something?"

"Yeah, but that curse's name as Cotton Fontaine, and unless he made a deal with the devil to stay alive forever, he's dead. He'd be in his hundreds by now."

"He is dead," I say. He's probably watching us right now. Feels as if someone is. Of course it always does in this house.

Janet's eyes narrow again. "Have you seen him? In this house?"

I pull my hand away. "I…"

"If you are seeing things, people and whatnot, don't worry. Everyone does. Mostly out of the corner of our eyes, you know, but once or twice…" She actually shudders. "That shadow one. I still get chills whenever I think about *him*. You'd turn a corner, look up, wake up, and he'd be there. Just this figure of absolute darkness. Watching us. Romy told me just to ignore it or tell it to go away. It usually worked."

"Doesn't really matter now. I had an offer on the house. I'll be leaving within a few days."

Her face falls as much as it can filled with Botox. "So soon?"

"The buyer's motivated. Plus there's nothing for me here. I thought there might be, but…" I shake my head. "A large part of me wishes I'd never come in the first place. Everything I've learned run the gamut from stomach churning to downright horrific. There's nothing here for me but ghosts. Literally. I should have kept my promise to Aunt Helen. I swore on a Bible I'd never set foot in this town. God's been punishing me ever since I broke that promise."

"It wasn't all bad," Janet offers. "There was a lot of joy in this house too. Laughter, music, art, love, this house had it in spades. That's what I remember. One horrible act cannot erase all the good, not if you don't let it. You are not anyone else's past. You do not have to pay for any sins but your own." She takes my hand again. "And despite what she did, I know your mama loved you. How could she not? Look at you. She'd be damn proud to see what a beautiful, kind woman you grew up to be."

"Thank you," I say, genuinely meaning it.

She squeezes my hand again before pulling it away. "Anyway, I've taken up enough of your time. If you're leaving I'm sure you have a million things to do." Janet rises from the table and I follow suit. I usher her from the kitchen. "Now, don't be a stranger. You have my phone number, I expect you to use it. Any questions you have, anything you need, you just pick up the phone."

"Likewise. I don't know how much more I can tell you, though."

"Just that you're happy. Did your husband come down with you?"

"Um, no. He's back in LA."

"Do you have children?" she asks, face lighting up.

I always hate this question. I give her the stock answer. "Not yet."

"Well, God willing and the creek don't rise, huh? Nick and I had trouble too, then we had triplets, God help us. It'll happen." We reach the front door. "And even if it doesn't, you got each other, right?"

"Right," I say as I open the door.

"May I…give you a hug?" I nod yes. Janet wraps her arms around me and gives me a tight squeeze. I quickly return the gesture before stepping back. I want her gone so I can be alone and think. She takes the hint, giving me an awkward smile. "If I don't see you before you leave, have a safe trip back. Remember what I said, okay? Call me anytime."

"I will. Thank you."

With one final grin, my mother's best friend steps outside. I don't shut the door until she's in her car. I rest my back against the wood, close my eyes, and sigh. Well, that's it then. No more hope. Coming here was officially a bust. No siblings, no aunts and uncles, no father. I am well and truly alone in this world. The end of the line. I have no one all over again, and no chance of that ever changing. It isn't until this very moment I realize how much I wanted to find someone, to find that missing link that would unite me with something bigger than myself. People I could count on and who could count on me. Gone. Nothing but an illusion. I haven't even been chasing ghosts, I've been chasing air. Nothing there. Nothing *here*.

I open my eyes and walk straight to my purse for my cell phone. He picks up just as I curl up in the creaky rocking chair on the back porch. "Hello? Jane?"

"Hey."

"Are you okay?" my husband asks.

What a question. "I'm…I don't know. I wanted to hear your voice."

"It's good to hear yours too," he says, voice softening a smidge.

"I just wanted to apologize for not calling until now. My phone broke. I didn't mean to worry you."

"Thank you."

"So, how's work?" I ask for lack of something better.

"It's work. How's wherever the hell you are. Crimson something isn't it?"

"Vale. And it's been…a nightmare. I don't know what the heck I was thinking coming here."

"You wanted to get to know your family."

"And I now know they're rapists, molesters, drug addicts, murderers, and possibly Satanists."

"Well, I have a UFO chaser for a sister and my aunt is a professional dog dancer," he offers.

"Hey, I like your sister. Don't compare her to my rapists and Satanists," I say, mock serious. "I absolutely win the 'my family is fudged up' contest here, Owen Harrow."

"You are right. I concede the trophy on that one," he chuckles.

Oh, just listening to his laugh make me physically miss him. His smell, his taste when we kiss, the way he clings to me in his sleep. I do. Mostly I miss this. I miss being friends. Talking and laughing over nothing. According to everyone, I'm the only one he ever laughs around. At least I can give him that. A joyous heart when I wasn't breaking it.

"Jane, you still there?" he asks, bringing me out of my mind.

"Yeah. Sorry." I shake my head to clear it. "I, uh, I've got an offer on the house already."

"So you're coming home?"

What a loaded question. "I don't know," I answer truthfully. "Maybe. Probably. I haven't really thought past packing up the house."

"Do you want me to fly out and help you?"

Yes. God yes. I want you here so badly I'd give my eye for it. But I'm done being selfish. This man has been taking care of me for over a decade, when we should have been taking care of one another. Giving and giving and getting precious little in return. My head is so messed up right now I don't think I can give him what he wants. Not fully. I certainly don't want to give him false hope. I don't want to hurt him anymore than I already have. Because I do love him, even with all the hell we put one another through, I love him and I always will. Even at our worst, I never doubted that.

"Owen, I…"

"No, it's okay. I shouldn't have—"

"No. No, I just, one step at a time, huh? Let me get through this first."

"I understand. Just know I'm here if you need me."

"I do. Believe me, I do."

"Okay. Love you."

"Love you too," slips out before I can stop it. "I'll call you tomorrow."

"Promise?"

"I promise. Bye."

I hang up before I dig myself into a bigger hole. I pull my legs in tighter to my chest to hug myself. Am I being stupid? Stubborn? I have this amazing man waiting for me. Stable, supportive, kind. He's seen me at my lowest, endured my most despicable, and he still wants me. Still loves me. And our life was great, save for that one gaping hole. I just have to accept it will never be filled. Pushing him away won't close it. If anything the hole just doubled in size. If it grows any bigger there'll be nothing left of me. I'm just terrified it'll swallow him up as well. It almost did before. If I do go back to him, I have to do it whole. He deserves nothing less. He actually deserves a heck of a lot more. I just don't know if I can give it to him. Maybe all that's left of me *is* darkness.

I am a Fontaine after all.

*

 Regardless of where I end up, I have a mission. I research appraisers and hire one to examine the furniture in case there are Tiffany lamps or a Picasso then pop out for boxes and bubble wrap while trying in vain to get in touch with Daphne and D.J. I leave each a message at every number I have for them. After wolfing down a Big Mac and fries, I begin culling the house. Definitely taking the quilts and the majority of Uncle Jerome's paintings, at least those featuring family members. I should probably pack the trophies and pendants as well. I don't want them at the bottom of a landfill. I have to speak to the Davenports before I call an inspector and realtor in case they insist on their own. I leave them each another message. Oh, I hope they're not avoiding me.

Many, many hours and every box filled later, I focus on unfinished business. Poor neglected Sherlock the Mouse finally beats Molearty and I e-mail the files to the publisher. Just under the wire. I'm sure they'll have revisions, but I do indulge in a celebratory glass of wine as usual. Okay, I have four while removing the paintings from the walls. I should take them all but I'm not sure what I'll do with the ones I've already chosen. In truth I have no idea what I'll do with any of these possessions. It seems so wrong to just leave them here at Daphne's mercy. I stare at the painting of Mama in the boat under her parasol in the living room and sigh. These are Uncle Jerome's babies. The only thing he left behind. His legacy. In a hundred years there'll be nothing to prove he ever existed but these. I kind of know what that's like. Crud, I'm going to take them all, aren't I? Yep. He deserves that at the very, very least.

It takes another two hours and three glasses of wine, before his legacy is stacked downstairs in the living room. All thirty. They won't fit in my Kia so I'll have to ship them to Los Angeles along with the already filled boxes. I need to buy more. I need to hire a mover. Okay, I need to figure out where to send them first. Wait, no, first I need to wait for the appraiser before I hire the mover. It's past eight anyway. Ugh, I really need to speak to the Davenports. Stupid Davenports. Selfish, rude, a-holes. How they ever produced such a beautiful, sexy, sweet, sexy son I don't know. Sexy. God, is he sexy. I...am tipsy. Okay, I'm drunk. I am not going to be a happy camper tomorrow. But today is not tomorrow. Today I'm going to finish off the bottle and pester the dastardly Davenports until they motherflipping call me back.

After pouring the rest of the wine into my glass, I pick up the phone and dial. Again. No answer at the law office or D.J.'s cell, so I try their home. The line's busy. Someone's home at least. I hang up, cut up an apple, and down the rest of my wine before trying again. Thank the Lord someone picks up this time.

"Davenport residence," a weary Betsy says.

"Betsy, it's Jane Harrow. I've been trying to reach the Davenports all day."

"Oh, Mrs. Harrow, I am so sorry. I-I got your messages and was going to call you back tomorrow, it's just been crazy today what with the police and funeral arrangements. Everything's up in the air now, even if I did call I wouldn't have an answer for you."

"Wait, what funeral? Who died?"

"You haven't heard? Oh, dear. I'm so sorry. There was a car accident last night."

My knees just about give out as I hear those words. *Bram.* My Bram. Bram could be dead. He could be dead and it would be my fault. He was so upset. Wailing. Pleading. Heartbroken. I may have sent him away to his death. If he got behind the wheel and died because of my rejection, because I wouldn't let him inside, I will never forgive myself. *Ever.* Please, you've taken so much from me already. Not him too. Fearful my legs might give out, I slump to the floor in a preemptive strike, clutching the phone to my ear as I gain the courage to whisper, "Who?"

"Daphne."

I breathe a literal sigh of relief and wipe a stray tear. Thank you, God. Thank you. "Oh," is all I can manage.

"She was driving from Bram's last night and must have swerved to avoid a deer or something. She hit her head and crashed into a swamp. Drowned before anyone found her. It's all so terrible."

"So terrible," I parrot back.

He's still alive. Thank you. *Thank you.*

"D.J.'s been so strong. So focused."

"And…Bram?"

"He's, I don't know. I only saw him once since we got the news. Looked a wreck, like he hadn't slept all night. Poor thing. They didn't have the best of relationships, but she was still his mama."

"Yeah."

There's silence on her end for a few uncomfortable seconds. "Anyway, I know they were talking to you about something, but I'm afraid with the accident…"

"No, I understand. I understand. It'll just, um, tell them I give my condolences."

"We're asking in lieu of sending flowers you make a donation to the Historical Society."

"Okay, I will. Thank you, Betsy. Bye."

It requires effort, but I get to my wobbly feet and hang up the phone in its cradle. Even in the wine haze my mind moves a hundred miles a moment. Does this mean the deal's withdrawn? Will D.J. want to live here alone? With this economy, it'll take ages for this place to sell. Can I still leave?

Ugh, what is the matter with me? D.J. lost his wife. Bram lost his mother. Oh God, my poor Bram. He must be devastated. Judging from the state he left in yesterday, and Daphne's call last night, I can't imagine their last words to one another were kind. The desolation, the guilt he must be experiencing…but he's alive. I'm being selfish again, but I am relieved it was her and not him. Strange considering not twenty-four hours ago I swore I'd never set eyes on him again, and I meant it. With all my soul, I meant it. Yet the mere thought of him not being on this earth…unbearable. It makes my body physically hurt.

He needs you…

Oh, not again. "Shut up," I say to the voice.

This is partly my fault, isn't it? I know I didn't run her off the road, but I did set in motion the events that lead to her death. They wouldn't have quarreled if not for me. Lord, if I'm feeling this guilty, what poor Bram must be putting himself through? I should cal—no. No. An entire bottle of wine and phoning a man you lust after is *not* a good idea. But still…one phone call. Just to let him know I'm thinking of him. That I'm sorry for his loss. That I'm sorry for everything. I'm always so sorry, aren't I?

He needs you…

The memory of him on that porch yesterday, so desperate, in agony, begging to be loved. The *need* exploding out of him. And I turned my back on him. It's just a phone call. He saved me the night of the storm, risked life and limb to reach me, at the very least I owe him a freaking sympathy call after his mother died.

Before I can talk myself out of it, I grab the phone and dial. God smiles upon me once again. Voice mail. "Hello, uh, Bram. This is Jane. Harrow. I just, um, I heard about your mother. I am so, *so* sorry for your loss. From the bottom of my heart, I'm sorry. I know what it's like to lose your mother. I lost both of mine. No matter...the fights or how open ended you left things, she was still your mother. Deep down she loved you, and you loved her. Never doubt that. She loved you." I pause to think of what to say next. Okay, to find the courage to say this next. "And I'm sorry. I'm sorry for any pain I may have caused you. I never...I don't want to hurt you. Ever. That's the last thing on this earth I want. Just know you're always in my thoughts and prayers. And if you ever need me, *really* need me, I am here for you. Even if I'm not *here*, I'm here for you. Tomorrow, a year from now, just...I'm here. I hope you're okay. I'm sorry. Bye." I hang up before I can make a bigger fool of myself.

He probably hates me. I'd hate someone who accepted a payoff never to see me again then literally turned their back on me. Unconscionable. Unthinkable. I stumble over to the fridge to retrieve my other bottle of wine, so I don't have to think about it.

I collect my computer and retire to my bedroom. If the wine doesn't keep my mind off my crimes then staying busy will. Realtors and movers to research. Ugh. I've sold two houses before. This is old hat. Of course now I'll have to wait until the will's out of probate to officially sell. Could have avoided that by selling to my probate lawyer. The realtor can handle those details. Just have to hire one, finish packing, and head to...fudge. I'm going back to California, aren't I? Seems the best course of action. Seems the only course of action. I want out of here. I want to be gone three days from now. I *need* to get out of here.

Maybe I'll meet a realtor at church tomorrow. I hope so because I can't seem to focus on the screen. The words are blurry. Okay, everything's kind of blurry. Never could hold my liquor. Wonder if that's genetic too. Insanity, low alcohol tolerance, depression. I do have a great immune system. Colds and flus always seem to pass me by. Hangovers not so much. Good thing I'm not sticking around town. When I show up to Sunday Mass tomorrow morning looking like a hag and reeking of wine their already wagging tongues will probably dislodge from their mouths. Of course considering my family's reputation as long as I don't shoot someone or run screaming naked through the pews I'll be considered the normal one.

Oh…eff it. I close my laptop, set the alarm clock, and scoot under the covers. Jennifer Aniston's voice is too darn loud, so I shut off the TV too. Ah, the sounds of silence. Well, almost silence. I will miss the crickets and croaking frogs. Their lullaby sure beats ESPN or the infomercials I usually fall asleep to. I shut my eyes, and wait to gain my entrance into the Land of Nod.

Knocking.

Knocking draws me out of slumber I don't know how much time later. Why…? What…? More knocking. It isn't until the second rapping I realize there's someone at my window. By the third, I realize there is *someone at my window.* Fear freezes me in place, all but my eyelids, which I shut to keep the monster at bay. If I fake sleep whoever it is will most likely leave in time. Please let him leave. He'll—

"Jane?"

My eyes fly open at the sound of his voice. Acceptable on the phone, frightening outside my window late at night. He knocks again. And again. Non-stop as he did on my door that horrible afternoon. Even without the lingering alcohol clouding my thoughts, I don't know what to do. Letting him in is stupid, really terribly idiotically stupid. But the pounding's bringing on a headache, and the last time I ignored his pleas, his mother died. I swore…darn it.

I throw aside the covers and totter toward the window, the world rocking back and forth like a pendulum as I do. No more wine orgies ever again. I didn't shut the curtains and though it's dark, in the moonlight I see a disheveled Bram crouching on my upstairs porch. His hand's still raised to knock again when I open the window. Oh, Lord the smell of whisky wafting from his body, no doubt the cause of his untucked shirt and wild hair, would intoxicate me if I weren't already. Two peas in a pickled pod us.

"What are you doing here? How did you get up here?"

"The tree," he says, pointing toward the other end of the house.

"What? Why didn't you just ring the doorbell?"

"This…seemed like a good idea at the time. Dramatic. Romantic."

"Stupid," I add.

"You make me lose all sense," he says with a grin. "I do adore you for it."

"That's not a good thing, Bram. You-you could have broken your neck."

His smile wanes as he stares at my frightened face, morphing into almost a snarl. "Yes, I could have. Would you have mourned me?"

"I'm sorry?"

The snarl intensifies, changing the air around him, charging it with violence. Desperation. Fury. "Would you have thrown yourself into my grave as they lowered my casket into the cold, wet, lonely earth?"

"I don't—"

"Would you have given even the tiniest shit if you could never see me again?" he asks, voice as cruel as the twisted mouth those words came out of.

"Of course!"

"Liar," he hisses. "Yesterday you broke my fucking heart, shattered it to nothing but ash, and today you said if I needed you…"

Out of nowhere he grabs my wrists. I gasp from the shock even before the pain begins. "I need you. Do you hear me? *I need you.* I have always and will always need you. And you need me."

"You're hurting me," I whisper.

His grip tightens as I try to extract myself from this madness. "You need me, Jane. You may not know it, but you do. No one will ever love you, not like I do. I am your willing slave. I would tear this universe apart, destroy and rebuilt it just to be with you. Do you believe me? *Do you believe me*?"

"Yes," I gasp. Pain radiates from the marrow up and down my arms like a guitar string vibrating beneath the skin. He pushes me backwards as he steps through the window into my bedroom. He doesn't stop until the back of my knees hit the edge of the bed.

"We are made for each other. We were placed on this earth to be together. You feel it. I know you feel it. It's in your eyes when you look at me. Your lips when they caress mine. The way your skin prickles, the way your soul, your body enflames when I'm near. I just don't know why you won't trust it. Trust me. Trust yourself. Why you don't give into what you want. What you *know* is right. Give into the madness. Give into the chaos. Give into *me*."

With nary a touch of tenderness, his lips assault mine. I should be repulsed by the pain he's intentionally inflicting, by the taste of whisky on his breath, the violence in all his behavior. Part of me is. All I've been taught, all the morals instilled, want me to thrash against him. Kick him in his already engorged groin and threaten to call the police. But the real me, the primal me at my core, the only one *he's* ever brought out, bludgeons that Jane to death the moment our lips connect. She forces her tongue into that intoxicating, velvety mouth of his. The taste of him, *he* makes me so weak with pleasure as he lowers me onto the bed I couldn't fight him even if I wanted to.

I don't.

Bram releases my wrists, but still not trusting I won't escape, locks me down with his kisses, his caresses as he yanks my pajama pants down. As I fumble with his button and zipper, he bites my neck hard enough I wince, then again as he pulls on the thin skin over my collarbone. Not even this distracts me from removing his pants and boxers. He ceases his meal of me to lift off my top then remove his own. In the glow of the moon we gaze at one another, his face as full of awe as mine. He is the most exquisite thing I have ever viewed in my life. Alabaster skin over taught muscles with nary a blemish. Bruises wouldn't dare mar that skin. His erect penis, a sight that I normally shy away from viewing, now stops my breath. It's as long and thick, as perfectly in proportion as the rest of him. He's Botticelli's paintings combined with Michelangelo's sculptures. A work of art.

I'm only granted a second to appreciate this beautiful creature because a second is all we can stand to remain apart. Those lips, those hands, those teeth are upon my feverish flesh again, toying with me, scratching down my thigh as he lifts my leg around his hip, biting on my sensitive nipple hard enough I momentarily fear he'll rip it off. Shivers of sweet agony cascade through my nerve endings. My punishment. My punishment for making him wait. It's just the beginning. There's no gentility, no preamble as he forces himself into my pulsating, slick folds. One thrust and our bodies collide with the intensity of two cars crashing. My scream, my burrowing nails on his back are ignored. Instead, as if I were a rag doll, he raises my legs, removes that thick, maddening instrument of glorious torture only to thrust deeper into me. To my very end.

Harder.

Again and again, each stroke reverberating in my womb. Pain and pleasure dissolve into one. My sex, my bruising thighs, deep in my belly, I close my eyes to savor every sensation, Every surge like ten tsunamis reaching the coast with equal devastation cascading through my body. Teeth on my neck. Teeth on my breast. Suckling my nipple. Rolling his tongue over it. Biting again. Harder.

Again.

Agony. Sweet agony.

Again.

Again.

My body, my traumatized and brutish body meeting him thrust for cataclysmic thrust. Claw for claw against his skin. Shockwaves all through me. Damaging me. Breaking me. Filling me. Ripping me apart. Making me whole. I'm being forced, being molded, being loved into total surrender. He wants to possess me, and with every hammer, every strike he fuses us, infects me, until there's nothing left but *him*. But I don't care. All that matters is the pleasure. The pain. Heaven and hell. I'm dizzy with the rightness of this, of him inside me. My slick flesh against his. His tongue massaging mine. He was right, we are made for this. For each other.

The heat, the tension that's been tightening between my eyes, in my toes, in my sex, grows until I fear I may shatter. I thrash under him, nails and teeth drawing blood as I try to anchor myself from the swirl of sensations. Too much. Again. Again. Faster. Stringer. His. *His.*

It builds and builds with each strike until…until…he wins. When the orgasm hits, I'm gone. Skinless. Boneless. I cease to exist only as myself. He takes possession of my head, my heart, my soul and I know I will never be able to extract him. That I never want to. I cry out to God and bow my spine to the heavens as I spasm in the most extreme ecstasy anyone ever has or ever will experience in the history of time. I touch the divine. A moment later Bram joins me, spilling himself inside me, matching me spasm for spasm.

Neither of us can move for a few seconds as we return to our own bodies. He comes to his senses first, rolling off me. The sudden absence of him from inside me hurts more than when he was there. My legs, along with the rest of me, crash back to earth.

Be it the cold of the room or aftershocks from the orgasm, I tremble. Goosebumps poke out of my sweaty, still sensitive skin, stinging as if a pin has pricked my every inch. True agony. I'm in agony until Bram wraps his arm under my shoulder and presses his warm, naked body against mine, enveloping me. Saving me once more from the hell of this world. The pain fades and a minute later the world fades as well. I drift into dreamless sleep listening to his steady heart that somehow beats in time to mine.

As one.

CHAPTER TWELVE

What on earth is that horrible beeping? With every squeal, my temples drum as if a hammer hits them. But that I could live with. I can't even stretch out my legs without the area between them sending a wail of anguish up and down my spine. My legs, my neck, my thighs, my breasts all send similar signals as I attempt to shut off the alarm. At least one problem's solved when the room falls into silence. Why did I set that thing? Wine and alarms go together like vinegar and baking soda: a volcanic mess. Why…church.

I pry my eyes open. 9:33. I must have hit snooze without realizing it. I'll be late even if I leave now. I could skip again. My attendance has been spotty in the past month what with the hallucinations. God will understand, right? But this thought makes me cringe. I've sinned. I've sinned *horribly*. I know myself, I'll feel unclean until I confess and get absolved. On the subject of unclean…his sticky seed and my own wetness remain inside and on my thighs. *He's* still there. I've never needed a shower more in my life. First I'll cleanse my body, then my soul.

I've been so distracted by the pain it isn't until I sit up I realize I'm alone. The other side of the bed isn't even warm. The only trace he was ever here, besides my ravaged body are the rumpled sheets streaked with semen and blood. Jesus wept. Staring at the pinpoints of blood from where I tore at him and he at me, I'm mortified and wracked with guilt at the mere thought of what we did. I can't imagine how much the sight of him would amplify those. Get to church. *Now*.

As I hobble to the bathroom it's as if I have splinters in my sex. Ow. Ow. I trudge on and shut the bathroom door. Then I make the mistake of catching my reflection in the mirror. Dear God. Matted hair like a feral dog's, my lips are double their normal size, swollen from his kisses and bites. My neck, my shoulders, my thighs are dotted with deep bruises, two of which, those on my collarbone and breast, are also rimmed with red raw teeth marks. There are even red welts down my thighs where he clawed me. Where we pounded against each other. I look like I've been to war. With a shudder, I turn around and start the shower. Clean. Get clean.

When the scalding water hits them, the bites and scratches sting, but I don't care. I scrub last night away. I scrub *him* away and that woman he made me become. A harlot. An animal. I never knew sex could be so bestial. Consuming. Owen's always been so gentle and courteous. Slow and steady but he always won the race. He never…*fucked* me as Melissa would call it. It was intense but even that word falls short. Fanatical. Extreme. Astonishing.

And it can never happen again.

The shower is short lived. Five minutes later I'm toweling myself off and attempting to find a turtleneck to cover my shame. Twenty minutes after that, I'm scrambling to locate a parking spot within a quarter mile of the church. My stomach clenches when I pass the law office to park three spots away. God driving the spike in deeper. At least his car isn't there. As I hustle to the church as fast as my still aching body can, a horrible thought comes to me. What if he's in there? In church? I'll leave. I'll go Methodist just this once. Then I'll drive home, throw as much into my car as I can, and leave. Pack up. I don't care about the house, I don't care about anything but leaving this vile town. I leave *today*.

The congregation is a verse into "Nearer My God to Thee" when I slink in five minutes late. Of course after a quick survey the only spot available is in the third pew which means half the town's eyes are on me as I move there. Heads actually turn as I walk down the aisle. I know they're gawking because I'm the long lost Fontaine heir, but I still feel as if I'm wearing a scarlet "A" on my white cashmere sweater. At least Bram isn't here. Of course his father sits one pew up with Betsy by his side. I keep my eyes to the floor, then the hymn book as I add my voice to the revelry. Still, I can sense their gazes appraising me and even hear their gossipy whispers. I cannot leave this town fast enough.

The choir concludes the hymn and Father King resumes his post at the pulpit. "May I begin today's service by sending the entire congregation's deepest condolences to those of you who lost loved ones this week, including the family of Emily Billings who succumbed to her battle with Alzheimer's on Wednesday, and the family of Daphne Davenport whose life was cut short Friday evening in a car accident. May we all take comfort in knowing their souls have rejoined our Lord in his divine kingdom. The Billings and Davenports are in all our thoughts and prayers during this difficult time in their lives."

I glance at D.J., who nods as Betsy whispers to him and rubs his arm. The portly man sitting to their right scowls as she does. Must be Mr. Betsy. I'm sure he just adores the fact his wife is now glued to D.J.'s side. Poor Daphne, not even in the ground and the auditions for her replacement have commenced. It wouldn't surprise me if a year from now D.J. was hitched to a twenty-something. She wasn't the nicest of people, but Daphne deserved more than this.

Father King begins his sermon about the healing power of God and after a minute I really miss Father Ruiz, my priest in California. Where Ruiz was animated and dynamic Father King is monotone, as if reading from a script. After ten minutes my brain's as tortured as my body. More divine punishment. I can't sit still for other reasons as well. The Advil helped take the edge off, but I still hurt inside from my opening all the way to my belly. It was the same in the car. No matter how much I squirm I cannot find a position where I don't ache. The woman to my left shoots me annoyed glances each time I wiggle. I don't blame her. The four-year-old beside her isn't as restless as me. This was a bad idea. I'm not fit to be around people today.

I do receive a bit of luck. The sermon only lasts thirty minutes. Hallelujah. I'm the first to rise, eager to catch the priest. Unfortunately, just as I reach the altar, an elderly woman in purple along with her friend in pink step in front of me. "You're Juliette's girl, ain't ya?" purple asks.

"Uh, yes. I'm Jane."

"I taught your mama at Sacred Heart. English her sophomore year. Your uncle too. You are the spitting image of them."

"Thank you."

"They were sweet kids, two of the sweetest I ever taught. Courteous."

"Such a shame. All of it," the pink one adds.

"And you're alone in that big house now?" purple asks. "You're a brave thing."

"Not really. I'm leaving today." I smile. "Excuse me, I need to speak to Father King. It was nice meeting you." I spot three others, all elderly with their eyes trained on me just waiting to pounce as I maneuver through the vacating throng to the priest. He's chatting with an altar boy when I tap him on the shoulder. "Excuse me. Father?"

The old man spins around. "Yes?"

"I-I'm sorry to bother you, but I was hoping you'd hear my confession. I—"

"Confession is on Wednesday and Saturday, three to four."

"Oh, well I was hoping—"

"I'm sorry, I can't today if that's your next question. I have to be in Baton Rouge by one. Call my secretary and set up an appointment, alright? Sorry."

He returns to the altar boy. Guess I'm dismissed. I miss Father Ruiz more and more by the second. I'm also regretting the forty dollars I put in the collection plate. I should have known better. You cannot buy absolution. With my head hung and eyes down, people seem to get the clue I'm not in the mood for socializing. Let them think I'm stuck up and fill in their blanks from there. I don't plan on seeing them again. God willing.

My stroll up the aisle unmolested may be because the busybodies have new prey. Right by the exit, a group of kindly old women have cornered D.J. with Betsy still by his side. Mr. Betsy is nowhere in sight. I'm one foot out the door when I hear, "Mrs. Harrow!" boom from inside.

D.J. extracts himself from the bereavement society when I glance up. He moves my way. Crud. Whatever he wants to say, I am in no frame of mind to hear. I pretend not to hear and keep walking outside. A second later a hand clamps on my shoulder. Didn't even make the outside steps. Double crud. D.J. manages a smile, so I shoot one back. "Hello, Mr. Davenport."

"Mrs. Harrow. I'm glad you're here. I was going to call you later today. I received your message from yesterday. Thank you for your kind words."

"Of course. I am so sorry for your loss. Mrs. Davenport was a…strong woman."

"That she was. Would have to be to put up with me, right? She was a good woman too. A good wife. I'll miss her."

The words are there but the delivery leaves something to be desired. He's so blasé, so emotionless, one would think he were speaking of an acquaintance not his wife and partner of almost forty years. "I'm sure you will," I say with a fake smile.

"Well, the reason I stopped you was I just wanted to get on the same page vis-a-vi the offer on the house. Daphne and I were still discussing it when she passed. And I'm sorry, but two and a half mil is far too much. I don't know what she was thinking. And at the end of the day *she* wanted the house. I don't. I'm gonna have to rescind the offer. Quite frankly I don't know why she was so obsessed with that place. Probably some childhood thing. Anyway, I'm sorry for any trouble this may have caused you."

"It's fine. I was expecting this."

"Good. And if you still want to sell the place, I recommend Rosa Grilaldi. She's handled several of my properties. She has well off clients all over the state, she'll get it off your hands right quick. The house is still in probate, but I'll make sure you get around that. Least I can do."

"Thank you. I'll look her up when I get home."

"You're welcome. We're planning the funeral for Thursday at ten AM here. If you're still in town, please come. I know Daphne would have liked you to be there. Bram too."

"That's nice. But I'm—"

"Speak of the devil," D.J. cuts in.

My eyes trace his line of sight over my right shoulder and down to the sidewalk. Dear Lord. There is not a muscle in my body that doesn't clench when I set eyes upon him. Where I appear to have spent a month in an asylum after our night, he's looks as if he'd just stepped out of a Ralph Lauren spread with a stop by a L'Oreal ad. Blonde hair moussed and golden in the sun, perfectly pressed khakis and white button down with the sleeves rolled up, and designer Aviator sunglasses. The only evidence of last night's events is the deep bruise over his jugular vein not quite hidden by his popped collar. I don't even remember biting him.

"And he shall appear," Bram quips. "Hello, Father. Jane."

"Fancy meeting you here, son," D.J. says as he descends the church steps. I remain at the top. This is more than close enough. "Never seen you up before noon on a Sunday since you were a boy. Come to pray for your mother?"

"She's beyond our prayers now, don't you think? No, I had a late night," he says removing his sunglasses and glancing my way. "Had a shower then got a triple espresso down the street. Just about to head back to my friend's house when I saw y'all out here. Good service?"

"Dull as hell," D.J. says.

Bram's gaze lifts up toward me. "What about you, Jane. Did you enjoy yourself? Wash away all your sins and guilt?"

That glimmer of a smile on his face turns mine cherry red. "Yes, thank you. And I'm sorry for your loss."

"Yes, you do remember you've lost your mama, right?" D.J. asks as if butter wouldn't melt in his mouth. "Because we haven't seen or heard from you since we got word."

"And 'we' is…" Bram counters matching his father's tone. "Have you already moved one of your bimbos into my mother's bed? Fast work, even for you."

That butter melts all over D.J.'s face then sizzles with a glower for his only child. "I don't appreciate what you're insinuating, *son*."

"I don't appreciate you giving me the ammunition to insinuate anything, *Father*."

I want no part of this disgusting display. I start down the remaining steps. "If you gentlemen will excuse me. I have a lot to do today. Nice seeing you both again."

I don't make it but a step past him when Bram clasps my arm to halt my retreat. I draw a quick breath not only from the surprise but because he presses on the bruises he left there last night. "Let me walk you to your car."

"Oh, that's—"

He squeezes tighter. "I insist." Bram's gaze returns to his father. "E-mail me the funeral info. I'm sure you and Betsy have it covered. Jane?"

He gently tugs on my arm to get us moving. As always when I seem to be near him, I don't put up much of a fight. One touch and I lose half my brain cells and all my free will.

When we're out of earshot, Bram says, "Thank you. I was about five seconds from breaking his nose. He is such an asshole. Always has been. He only kept Daphne around because she had so much dirt on him it'd take a bulldozer to push it all. If they ever loved each other, and that is a damn big if, they sure as hell stopped decades ago. Probably before I was born. I can't recall a single memory of them happy together."

"I'm sorry."

"She knew what he was before she married him, just like she knew her role and how to play it to perfection. That woman knew what she wanted and was intelligent enough not only to get it but find a way to keep it against all odds. I have a lot of respect for her for that."

"It sounds so sad to me. A loveless marriage."

"You'd be the expert," Bram counters.

I glance at my escort to gage if he's serious. He stares straight ahead. "My marriage is far from loveless. Us loving one another was never a question."

"Seemed like one last night."

That's it. I attempt to yank my arm from his grasp but he clenches tighter. "Let me go."

"Not until we talk."

I cease moving, the closest thing to a defense I'm capable of. Bram gets the point at last. He takes one step, and when I don't budge, spins around. His mouth opens a smidge in surprise at my sudden defiance, which morphs into confusion as if he cannot fathom why I don't wish to be alone with him. The confusion curdling into pain, soul-crushing pain. It doesn't show on his face, but I sense it as sure as if it were blossoming inside me as well. I've never met anyone with such a never-ending well of sadness inside them as deep and dark as a black hole. And I keep drawing gallons from it with a single gesture.

"I'm sorry," Bram says, claws finally retracting. "I shouldn't have presumed…"

I can't be sure but I believe he literally bites his tongue judging from the wince where there should be words. The last thing on this earth I want is to cause anyone pain, let alone the man I lo—took into my bed.

"It's fine," I say. "And I suppose we should talk."

The grin my words brings to his face could light up all of Bourbon Street. "Yes. Good. Um…how about my office? No one's there."

Which means we'd be alone. Again. The only other option is a public place where people can overhear. Damned if I do, damned if I don't. I'm not drunk now. I can control myself.

"Okay."

Bram doesn't attempt to touch me this time, for which I'm grateful. I follow him a step behind to his office. At least my car's nearby in case I need a quick getaway. The office is as quiet as a tomb when we enter. We ruin the tranquility with our footsteps on the hardwood floor. I used to love silence. Not anymore. Now it's so heavy with dreaded anticipation I'm surprised we're able to pass through it without a sword.

Bram leads me upstairs to his office which is a copy of his father's with antique high-backed chairs the same cherry wood as the desk. The only difference is the artwork on the walls. Where D.J. enjoys maps and sailboats, his son prefers hand drawn sketches of beautiful women, some naked. I want to ask if he's the artist, as they're all obviously done by the same person, but the sight of a brunette reclining on a fainting couch with one breast exposed makes me not want to hear the answer.

"They are mine," Bram says, as if reading my mind. He moves beside me, once again so close I can smell him. Expensive cologne. It's not as intoxicating without the whisky. "When I was fifteen, I got it into my head to move to New York or Paris, train at the Sorbonne and take the art world by storm. D.J. set me straight in the end. He was right to, of course. I just would have slept with every French girl in my orbit and come home with nothing to show for my time but a few sketches and V.D. Instead I became a lawyer who occasionally sketches and sleeps with only half the women in my orbit. Managed to avoid the V.D. part through. I'm usually far more careful than I was last night. Far more tender as well. I was practically bowlegged until the pills kicked in. If I'm this sore, what damage must I have inflicted upon you. I just…"

Though I keep my eyes straight, I can sense his hand reaching to touch me, then thinking better of it. "I have no excuse," he continues. "I'd blame the alcohol, I'd blame my grief and guilt, but I promised never to lie to you. The truth is from the moment I saw you, hell before that, I've wanted you to the point where all logic, all reason, any and all civilized conditioning gets overridden by raw *need*. When you finally allowed me inside, completely inside you in every way possible, self-control proved impossible. A dark part of me even wished to punish you for making me wait so long. I take responsibility for *my* actions last night." He pauses. "But *you* called me. *You* opened that window. *You* kissed me back, ripped off my clothes, opened your legs to me, and matched me thrust for thrust. *You* wanted *me* as much as I wanted you. And Jane, there is nothing wrong with that want. That *need*. Only fools feel guilty about pleasure."

"No, only fools *don't* feel guilty when they hurt other people," I say quietly.

"Your husband? The man who lied to you? Betrayed you? Took steps to deny you what you desire most in the world? You owe him nothing. And if you return to him that is precisely what he will give you, and you him. *Nothing*. Nothing but ever growing resentment."

"No."

"You think you can just return as if the past never happened? As if *we* never happened? Blank slates do not exist. No matter how hard you scrub, a trace always remains. You can return to him, things may even be pleasant for a time, but he will never forget your lies and coldness. And you will never forget either."

"What?"

Bram moves in front of me so close we may as well be pressed to one another already. My skin, my lips, even the tips of every follicle of hair on my body alights with electricity and fire. He stares down at me, that angelic face an unreadable mask. The throbbing between my legs that began the moment we entered this room doubles, stronger than even the pounding of my heart. How does he do this to me?

"*Me*. You will never be able to forget *me*. Every time he touches you, it will be my hands you wish were teasing and caressing your naked body. Every time he kisses you, it will be me you wished you were tasting. When he enters you," Bram whispers, voice tingling every one of my nerve endings, "it will be my cock you're truly craving. As you crave it now. I'm in you, Jane." He leans into my ear, hot, intoxicating breath tickling my already sensitive skin. "Filling your mind, bursting in every one of your atoms, consuming your soul. Just as you're consuming mine. We are two halves of the same whole, beloved. We were created to be with one another. You are mine, and I am yours until eternity ends."

I'm so overwhelmed by his words, his heat like sitting beside a crackling fire on a chilly night, the rightness of everything about him, I barely notice his fingers lightly brushing up the inside of my thigh as my skirt rises. "I love you. No one will ever love you as I do. No man has ever loved a woman as much as I love you. And I never lie, Jane."

Those expert fingers brush aside my panties. He barely brushes my engorged, wet opening and I almost collapse in ecstasy. "You cannot leave me, Jane. Not now. Never. You know I'm right." He traces those petals again, and I shudder. "Even your body knows I'm right. *We* are right." A finger traces my clitoris, saturating it with my own juices. "I swear to you Jane, there is nothing I will not do to bring you happiness. Pure, true joy. I am your slave. Let me pamper you." He caresses me again, soft as silk. My knees almost buckle in ecstasy. "Let me take care of you." Again. A feather light trace. I shudder with pleasure. "Just…let me worship you," he whispers as his finger softly, slowly moves inside me. I open like a blooming flower. "Anything else and you'll be consigning us to your hell, beloved. Save us." His lips caress my cheek. "Save *me*."

All is lost when his lips touch mine. Nothing else matters but satiating the hunger he inspires inside me. His tongue, those infernal digits pressed inside me just make me more famished. It's overwhelming—the *need*—I put up no resistance as he lifts me onto his desk and rips off my panties. I cry out not in pain, not because of his invasion on my already aching center, but because those fingers abandon my body. Not having him inside me is far more unnatural and agonizing. He doesn't have to move between my legs, the moment that cotton barrier is removed I wrap my legs around his waist and pull him where he belongs. When his bulge collides with my still tender womanhood, I whimper in misery. No matter how much I may want him, after last night I don't think I can enjoy it as much as I desire to.

We're so in sync he senses this. After a few seconds of kisses, his lips finally break our seal. He presses me down across his desk before he buries his head between my legs. The kisses and nibbles he bestows on my opening are as expert as his real kisses, and I convulse in pure bliss, my chin tilting toward the heavens with the rest of me. Where last night he was brutal and selfish, now he's gentle to the point of madness with petal kisses on my pulsating labia before his soft tongue breaches the entrance a millimeter a second as his thumb massages my clitoris with a delicate touch. Barely there like a phantom's whisper.

Divine torture.

I clutch onto his hair, urging him in deeper, but he resists, the kisses and licks beginning anew. Sweet torment builds, and builds, and ten seconds later the orgasm rockets through me as I buckle like a cat in heat. Still he continues toying with me, loving me, healing me, burying me in a million glorious sensations until I burst into stardust again. Still…he wants me locked in this pleasure, where he possesses me body and soul. And he does. I am his and he is mine. I was mad to ever fight it. You can't fight fate.

And as he finally, gently sheaths himself in me, whispering, "I love you," and I come for the third time, I finally surrender to it.

"I love you too."

CHAPTER THIRTEEN

The sun kisses my exposed shoulders like a lover would as a gentle breeze caresses my hair, tiny tendrils tickling where God's kisses land. It's so peaceful I could fall asleep in this very chair. Heaven.

"I'm doing your eyes. Keep them open."

I pry my eyelids open and smile at my dashing brother. He truly is the most handsome creature in three counties, especially when the sun dapples his untamed, golden curls. Even his skin glows with vitality. We are truly creatures of the light, he and I. It powers us almost as much as we power one another.

"How much longer?" I ask, the South dripping from my voice like sweet honey.

"An eternity," Romy responds with a grin to rival the sun. "Just keep your eyes open."

I force them far out of their sockets in protest before wiggling in my wooden chair. Shorts and a halter top were a bad idea. The rough wood scratches my skin. I throw one leg over the splintering arm rest and sigh. Romy's impervious to my not-so-subtle complaints. His hands scribble on his pad. He—

Movement on the porch behind Romy snaps my attention that way. Whatever tranquility Mother Nature provided that *thing* snatches away just by being. It. *Him*. The darkness. Always watching. Always waiting. Though it's fifty feet away I can still sense its longing, its melancholia, it's unnaturalness from here. "It's here," I whisper.

Romy glances back then returns his unimpressed gaze to me. "Oh."

"He was standing by my bed this morning, watching me sleep again." I say.

"Well, he wants you, beloved," Romy says, still sketching.

"What?"

"He wants you. He wants to feel your lips on his." He keeps sketching. "He wants to feel the weight of your soft breasts in his hands. The taste of your skin on his tongue. The sensation of your rosebud nipples between his teeth. And your expression of sheer agony as he breaks your maidenhood and the blood seeps out."

"Romy…"

"It's inevitable, beloved. You can't fight fate, can you…?" My brother's eyes finally move up, but they're as black as obsidian. "Jane?"

My own eyes fly open as my gasp startles me awake. What…?

Bram sits in the cream armchair a few feet away, pad and pencil in hand just like… "What are you doing?" I ask still trying to get my bearings.

"You looked so beautiful. I had to sketch you."

I lie on my stomach completely naked save for the white sheet covering my right buttock. I'm more clothed than I've been in four days. "You're not going to hang me on your wall with your other conquests, are you?"

"You're exquisite enough to hang in the Louvre, beloved," he says with a contented smile. "But I'm afraid I'd rip out the eyes of any man who would gaze upon you like this."

"Can't have that. I'd waste away while you were in prison. Can I move?"

"Yes. I'm almost done."

I flip on my side to face him, resting my head on my fist. I don't even bother to pull up the sheet to hide my bare breasts. Bram convinced me that first day the best way to trample my "idiotic Catholic modesty and shame" was to remain as God intended. That and in one of our more desperate couplings my undergarments and clothes didn't survive intact. There hasn't been much call for clothes anyway. We haven't left his house since Sunday. From his office we each drove straight here and since then it's been non-stop lovemaking, eating, drinking, and more lovemaking while eating and drinking. I've crammed in a lifetime of excess into half a week.

And I've never been more content in my life.

Or more exhausted. I don't think Bram sleeps more than an hour or two a night, and even as I slumbered, he gave me no quarter. More than once I've woken with him inside me, bringing me pleasure half asleep himself. There isn't a room, a surface, a position we haven't made love on or in. A look, even something as simple as a sharp intake of breath, and we'd find ourselves giving way to carnality. The man's insatiable in every conceivable way.

"What time is it?" I ask.

"Almost nine."

"Crud. Your mother's funeral starts at ten. I have to get up," I say as I perform the task.

Bram lowers the pad. "No, you don't. There's plenty of time."

"No, I have to go home," I say, rising. Not an easy feat as I'm sore inside and out. "I don't have clothes or make-up here, remember? I can't show up naked."

"If it were up to me you'd do everything naked," my lover purrs, pulling me onto his lap, his erection poking through the slit in his pajama pants.

"If it were up to you, I'd never leave the bed." Or the shower, or couch, kitchen counter, the floor, bent over the banister, against the wall, just to name a few. "Still. It's your mother's funeral. Certain events you just can't miss. Do you still want me to go?"

"*I* don't want to go, beloved."

"Well we're going and that's final," I chuckle. I slide off his lap and even manage a whole step before I'm in his clutches again. He grabs my wrist, rises, then lowers us both onto the bed with him on top. "What are you doing?" I giggle.

"Giving you incentive to stay," he replies as he pulls down his pants.

Before I can utter another word of protest, he glides inside me. At least he's gentle this time. I had to start taking his Vicodin two days ago I hurt so bad. Worked like a dream, but last night's pill must have worn off. Instead of the usual ecstasy I've experienced with one stroke of his tongue, one stroke of his manhood, now it's like he's battering against one deep bruise down there. After the fourth strike at least my body finally responds with lubrication. Still. Even without the pain I need to get home, and I know for a fact he won't stop until I'm satisfied. I dig my fingers into his back, which is a mess of pinpoint scabs—I'm not the only one of us on a Vicodin regimen—and I fake groans and moans before letting out one final wail. Three seconds later that familiar sticky warmth fills me as he comes. Thank God. He pulls out and flops on his back beside me with a sigh. I think he enjoyed that about as much as I did.

"What's the matter?" I ask, caressing his tense cheek. "Is it the funeral?"

"No." My lover takes my hand and presses it to his heart. "It's just…I don't want this to end."

"What?"

"This. Us."

"Bram I'm going ten miles away, not to Venus. You'll see me in less than an hour."

"I know but…in here, you belong only to me. There are no distractions. No one and nothing but us. Once you step out of this house, a million things can snatch you from me again."

"I won't let them. I'm not going anywhere. 'Where you die I will die and there will I be buried. May the Lord deal with me, be it ever so severely, if anything but death separates you and me.'"

"Ruth, Chapter 1: 16-17."

"Ruth kept her promise to Naomi, and I will keep mine to you." I kiss him to seal the pact. "But we have to honor the woman who gave me you. So we'll both shower, change, and meet at the church to do just that."

I give him one final peck before standing, collecting what's left of my clothes from the carpet, and rushing into the bathroom before he finds another way to stop me. My sweater remains intact but the skirt was ripped in half when Bram couldn't get the zipper down fast enough. I'll have to borrow…dear God.

I gasp. Darn mirrors. I look as if I've been in a car crash after being mauled by a bear. Countless black bruises tinged with red welts from his teeth, carpet burns, scabby scratches down my back, my arms, my thighs to rival the damage I inflicted upon him, even the skin he neglected with his bites and battering is pale and waxy. My lips are double their normal size from the swelling and the dark circles under my eyes are as black as the bruises on my inner thighs. I had no idea.

Bram's vanished when I walk out. Jesus, Mary, and Joseph how did I not notice the streaks of blood and crusty stains on the bed before? My ravaged body feels like a petri dish. We have been showering but the actual cleaning part was often neglected. The urge to flee this unclean space knocks me into motion. I slip on a pair of his sweatpants and hurry through the hallway to the stairs. When I had time to notice I realized his house is rather impersonal, like someone just copied a spread in the Pottery Barn catalogue. Beige and brown with furniture I'd swear had never been sat in. Now they need to be deep cleaned. The bed should be burned. My purse and keys are on the floor by the front door.

"See you in half an hour! Love you!" I call as I run outside.

Oh, heck. The sun stings my eyes, but I continue to my car. I half expect Bram to follow me out, even racing after the car like a dog. I do love him, but it feels splendid to finally have some time alone. I couldn't shower, heck I could barely use the toilet, without him around. A sigh escapes me, I think from relief. I can definitely use time to myself. Heck, maybe the night. The thought of sleeping in my own bed, actually sleeping through the night, sounds like bliss. Bram's favorite way to wake me was with kisses down below. One of the best ways to get roused, without question, but I think I've reached the point where eight hours of unmolested slumber is more pleasurable than even cunnalingus. I'll go to the funeral and wake, then slip away and phone him when I'm on my way home. It's mercenary abandoning him after his mother's funeral, but I need this.

Halfway home, I realize I haven't checked my voicemail in days. In our Garden of Eden the thought never crossed my mind. After the first time his own phone rang, Bram took it off the hook. The only outsiders permitted to the house were the food delivery men and I never spoke to them. I still don't want to speak to anyone. I have life altering news to import, news I can barely admit to myself.

Bram was right. I left the house and the magic instantly faded. The million things he worried about—my body, my mind, Owen, reality—are slowly washing me away from him. Because this is ridiculous. I cannot be in love with a man I barely know. I could not have just spent the past four days fornicating, worse *submitting* to a man past the point my body could take. It's...insanity. I literally do not recognize myself. Yes, a night apart is definitely called for.

No ghosts greet me as I return home and hurry upstairs to the shower. Dear Lord I'm still sticky from this morning and last night. I should take twelve showers but one will have to suffice. I'll soak for hours in the tub after the funeral. As the water cleanses me, my cuts sting as if shards of glass plunge into them. In the heat of the moment I barely noticed when he inflicted them on me. More often than not I actually reveled in the pain. It heightened my connection to my own body and flesh. Another bit of magic left behind in our Eden. I should have taken a Vicodin before I left. I perform a gentle yet quick scrub before stepping out. Since I didn't foresee attending a funeral while here, I don't have a black dress. I settle on a black knee-length skirt, dark purple blouse, one of

Felicia's black suit jackets, knee-high black boots, and a white silk scarf to cover as much skin as possible. I have more hickeys than pristine flesh. Slathering on two coats of makeup helps enough I don't resemble a car accident survivor. I still look like I've aged a decade in a week.

Coffee. Coffee will help. After downing three Alleve, I hurry downstairs and into the kitchen, greeted immediately with the sight of an empty wine bottle on the island. That night seems like a lifetime ago. I toss it in the trash before retrieving the instant coffee in the cabinet. Better than noth—

An odd scent, I think hyacinth and sugar, wafts from behind me at the same time the prickling on my neck begins. I twirl around, and it's a good thing the container I hold is plastic because what I see makes me lose motor function. The container drops to the floor, its dull thud overshadowed by my gasp. I should be used to uninvited visitors popping in, but I'm not. Especially when I know she's dead. "Hallie?"

Though I've only seen her in drawings, this has to be her. Afro, mostly gray with streaks of black, pointed chin, full lips pursed in disapproval and black eyes narrowed at me. Even without seeing her face I could sense her displeasure just as strongly as I can smell her. And she's so solid, just like a real person. We stare at one another for a few seconds. I don't know what to do. What to say. The book I skimmed claimed one reason ghosts don't cross over is they have unfinished business. Worth a shot. "Do-do you want help?" Her expression doesn't change. "I-I…don't know what you want."

Slowly, her gaze turns to my right. The moment mine reaches her destination, there's a beep as the answering machine switches on all by itself. "Hello, Mrs. Harrow. This is Bathsheba at London Appraisers. I'm returning your call regarding the property at 187 Fontaine Lane. Please call me back so we can schedule your appointment. Thank you."

Beep.

"Janie, it's Owen." His low baritone is like a punch in the stomach. "I just…wanted to say I enjoyed our talk the other day. And I'm here if you need me. Okay. Bye."

I glance at the specter. Her expression hasn't changed.

Beep. "Janie, it's Owen. Again. Your cell's turned off. I've, uh, been trying you for two days. I'm getting worried here. Melissa said she can't reach you either. Just call be back, okay? Bye."

Beep. "Jane, it's Mel," she says. "I love you to death, but I am getting mighty sick of taking emergency calls from your husband. You had better call me or him ASAP or you'll find the National Guard on your doorstep." A pause. "Whatever's happening, just call me, okay? I'm on your side. Bye."

Beep. "Jane, I don't know what's happened since we last spoke, but I am getting very, *very* worried. Even if you're angry, even if you've changed your mind about leaving, I don't care. Just call me and let me know you're alright. Just let me hear your voice, even if it's to tell me to go to hell. Just call me. I love you."

Beep. End of messages.

Go home…

"This is my home."

Go home before this house becomes your tomb. Burn this place down and never look back.

In a literal blink, she's gone. Or is not visible anymore. I can still smell her, still sense those worried eyes upon me. Par for the course in this house. Okay, forget the coffee, I'll buy some on the way. I almost forget my purse I'm in such a hurry to flee. I need to get the priest here ASAP. I don't want family members, dead or alive, just popping in to judge and lecture me. They're growing stronger too. What she did with the answering machine…

I manage to get into my car and down the driveway before my stomach knots itself with guilt, exactly what my spectral visitors' intention was. The thought that the people I love might be worried about me never crossed my mind these past few days. *They* barely crossed my mind. The few times I allowed myself to conjure up Owen's face or begin to consider what I was going to tell him, Bram seemed to read my thoughts and found a way to distract me. I wish he were here to kiss and caress the guilt back in its pen.

I should call them. It's the right thing to do. But I can't. Because I know what they'll say. That I've finally lost my mind. That I've known Bram two weeks. That I couldn't tell them his middle name. How long his longest relationship lasted. If he wants children. That I've been consumed with lust, not love. And I don't know if I have the correct words to describe the light, the pure bliss, the *rightness* he unleashes inside me just being nearby. God put me on this path. The house, my grandmother's death, the visions, it was all set in motion so I would meet my soul mate. So we would be together. I know it as sure as I know anything. I trust it.

But they won't trust me.

If I phone them now, if we get into a fight, I'll be a wreck, and I can't be a wreck. Bram needs me. We're burying his mother. So I take the coward's way out. At a red light, I text Melissa and Owen, "*Srry. Im fine. Swear.*" Then turn off the phone.

When I reach the center of town, there's no parking again, so I park on a residential street have to walk a quarter mile to the church. I'm not alone making the trek. In fact I think the entire town has come out to pay their respects. There's an actual line down to the street outside on people waiting to give their condolences to D.J. I don't see Bram. He must be inside. I should still give my condolences to his father.

I'm halfway up the church steps when D.J. spots me. After he whispers something to Betsy, she scurries down to me. "Have you seen Bram?" she whispers even before she stops moving.

"He's not here yet?"

"No, and we've been calling and calling. His phone's off and he isn't answering the house or office phones."

"I, uh, just left him not an hour ago. I'm sure he's just running late. He'll be here."

"I certainly hope so," she whispers through gritted teeth before hurrying back to her boss.

Okay, this is odd. Maybe he's inside and just wanted to avoid his father. I leave the line and hurry inside to test my hypothesis. But I don't see him as I circle the church. There is quite the cross-section of society filling the pews. To the left a sea of Chanel, tight faces, and men barking into their phones. To the right, dark roots and platinum hair, polyester, and the scent of Skol wafting up the aisle. The haves shoot a few sneers at the have nots as if the fact they're breathing the same air is an affront. I'm not quite sure which side to sit on. Bram's still nowhere to be found. I position myself by the door to catch him. I even work up the nerve to turn back on my phone and text him. "*Im at church. Wre R U? Call me.*" and slip the phone into my pocket. Oh, he better be here. He has to be. It's his mother's funeral. I—

The phone chirps but my heart leaps into my throat when I read the display. Owen. Crud. I'd turn it off but Bram might—

"You're Felicia's granddaughter, ain't ya?" I spin around to find a man in his eighties with a handlebar mustache dressed in a fraying black coat probably as old as he is. "Heard you was in town. I'm your kin. Your grandpa Dan was my first cousin. Not sure what that makes us, but blood is blood. I'm Merle."

"Jane. Nice to meet you."

He examines me up and down. "Not much Cowan in you, is there? Fontaine's take everything in the end, I guess."

"I wouldn't know. I only ever met two."

"Then count yourself damn lucky, girl. The worst damn mistake Danny made was marrying Felicia. No offence."

"None taken. I heard the story."

"That Cotton shot his ass dead? Yep. Saw that coming a mile away. Told Danny too. Love makes us all mo-rons, huh? He was a sweet guy though. Hope you did get that."

"Me too." I clear my throat. "So, how did you know Daphne?"

"Well, I got the invite cause I'm married to her cousin Starlee, but I've known Daphne since her hell raising days. She spent more time in Vera's than I did."

"Vera's?"

"My bar. It's off Route 78. Hell, it's where Daphne met D.J. Your mama and uncle came in sometimes too. Those two were joined at the damn hip. Only came in without the other once."

My curiosity perks up. "Really? Did my mother ever meet a boy there that you can remember?"

"Juliette? Hell no. Them brave enough to incur Cotton's wrath still had to get past Romy and your mama's shyness. Sorry. If you're fishing for daddies, I ain't got the bait for you, doll. Your mama was as pure as the driven snow as far as I know, and I hear everything. Now your uncle…there was a dark horse. Didn't know he had it in him," he chuckles. "In fact he…well, this ain't the time nor the place. Don't wanna speak ill of the dead at her own damn funeral. No, you come down to Vera's, I'm there most nights. Even give you the family discount. Bram knows where it is."

"Bram…"

"Like I said, I hear everything. Word is you and he are together now. You can bring him too is all."

"How'd you…does everyone know?" I whisper that last part.

"It's been making the rounds. Small town and all. Just know your name ain't the first or even the twentieth to be linked to that boy. Longest I think was CeCe Gardner. They was together about six months. She's over yonder."

He points to the perfectly coiffed, petite redhead in her late twenties. I suddenly feel like an old hag. The peanut gallery shares my sentiment as I spy a few younger women glaring with disgust before whispering to their equally beautiful friends. Nervously, I smooth my hair. I more or less expected to be on display but not with treated with such ire.

"Think you're the star of the funeral, little miss," Merle says. "Poor Daffy. Can't even get top billing at her own damn funeral. Hell, her own son can't even be bothered to show up. Not that I'm all together surprised. No real love lost between those two. Heard they got into a fight the night she died. That true?"

There is no way I'm feeding the gossip mill any more than I have already. "I don't know. Will you please excuse me? I need to use the restroom."

With a gracious grin, I slink off. The bathroom line is as long as the condolence one outside. Once again I'm greeted by sneers and whispers. Excellent thing I don't really have to go. Instead I find a quiet corner to watch people filter in. About a minute later my phone buzzes again. A text. Owen. "*Please talk 2 me.*" I ignore it. I will talk to him, I will, just not today. Maybe another text would do. "*In luv w/someone else. TTYL.*" A Dear John text. There is a special place in hell for those who do such a thing.

I stand in my corner watching the town go by. Most seem more excited than sad. I wonder if a single person here has shed a tear for Daphne. I wouldn't bet on it. They all simply want to be part of the biggest gathering in town. All but her own son.

After meandering in, D.J. breaks away from Father King to rush over to me when he spots me. "Anything yet?" he asks me.

"No. I've texted and called but nothing."

"Typical. Selfish bastard," he mutters.

"No, something must be wrong," I counter.

"Yeah, I raised a selfish brat. This is just like him. Little shithead. Well, we can't wait any longer. Prick," he spews before stalking off.

Now I'm truly worried. What if he got in a car accident too? Or slipped in the shower? I try the house, then his cell, but they just go to voice mail. I text, "*Rlly worried. Plz call me right away.*" Should I stay or go find him? No question. Let the town believe I'm anti-social. I did barely know the woman.

As everyone takes their seats in the pews, I slip out the front and down the church steps at a quick clip. There has to be a good reason he's late. I'll go to his house. I'll trace the route to the church he'd take in case he's unconscious inside his car in a ditch or something. I'm halfway back to my own car when the phone rings. I breathe a literal sigh of relief when I read the display. "Where are you?" I ask, more concerned than angry.

"I'm just, uh, down the street off Packard. I, uh, parked but...I can't seem to get out of the car."

"Are you hurt?"

"No, I just...can't get out."

I stop walking and softly sigh again. "Okay. I'm on my way." I hang up and continue walking. I spot his SUV a block away from my own car. When I see him through the windshield I muster a sympathetic smile, but his lips barely move back. He doesn't even raise his head that rests against his side window as if it's too heavy to lift. I climb into the car and he still doesn't move, just follows me with his eyes. "Hi."

"Hi," I reply, shutting the car door.

"I'm sorry I scared you."

"It's okay. What's going on?"

"I just...I had every intention of going. I really did. I got ready, drove here, but when it came time to open the fucking car door...I just couldn't."

"Why not?"

"Because everyone knows we had an argument. That I'm responsible for her death. Because it'd be fake."

"What would?"

"All the wonderful sentiments about her. Me having to sit there, pretending to agree with them. Us all pretending to mourn. Because I don't mourn her. She was one of the most selfish human beings I have ever met. I was nothing more than an accessory she paraded around when it suited her. She got what she wanted from me the moment I was born and had no real use for me after that. I never liked her. Never. Probably because she didn't like me. I'm sorry she had to die, and she was very beautiful on the outside at least, but if I'm honest…I didn't love her. Not for a second of this life. The woman who gave me life. And I may be many things, but a liar and hypocrite are not among them. Not anymore. She brought me into this world, and a perhaps a miniscule part of me does love her for that, but it's not enough to betray myself. So I've just been sitting here with my disappointment. My self-loathing." He finally lifts his head. "You don't think any less of me, do you?"

I slip my hand into his. "Of course not. You're not a hypocrite. I admire it actually."

"I love you. So much. *So* much. I love you and…" He cups my face in those tender hands, and breathlessly says, "You are my miracle, Jane. When I look at you, when I just think about you, everything feels right, and beautiful, and peaceful. Everything was dark, and you let in the light. Don't ever leave me." He leans across and kisses me. "I could face anything, survive anything but that."

I kiss him, bringing forth the depths of my soul to quell all his torment. "I'm not going anywhere."

Actions and words achieve the desired result. The man I love smiles, truly smiles, before reaching for me once more. We have kissed a hundred, a thousand times in the past days but as always when our lips touch, it's like the first time. We taste one another as if dining on a fine meal, savoring the consumption. It's only been an hour but I was starving for him. An hour. I'm awash is ecstasy, high on just the *being* of this man, until his hand roves up my thigh and under my underwear. A rocket of pain zooms through my womb and up my spine. I shove his hand away while breaking the kiss to wince.

"What?" Bram asks.

"Can you just not…I hurt. A lot. I'm sorry."

"No, I'm sorry," he says, caressing my cheek. "I should have realized. I'm sore too. We do bring out the beast in each other, beloved." He kisses me again. "I just…can't be alone right now. I just want to hold you, okay? We can even go to your house and sleep."

Where we can be accosted by judgmental spirits. "No. That's not a good idea," I say gravely.

"Why? Did something happen?"

"Just the usual."

He pauses before saying, "Then we're definitely going there."

"I don't think that's a good idea."

"Jane, it's *your* house. Someday it will be *our* house. I don't let the living push me around, forget the dead. And neither should you. You're a beast, remember? Let them hear you roar, beloved. Right?"

"Right."

He kisses me again. "Then let's go *home*."

Sitting here gazing at the man I love, the blood of my blood and flesh of my flesh, I'm already there.

CHAPTER FOURTEEN

No one, living or dead, accosts us as we enter the house or as I change into my pajamas and we fall asleep wrapped in each other's arms. Not only does Bram keep the ghosts away but also the bad dreams. I awake clearheaded alone seven hours later. Despite the rest, my body protests with tiny waves of aches from toes to head as I toss off the covers. Luckily Bram left me water and Vicodin on the nightstand. He is so thoughtful. I take the medicine and after stretching, the worst of the pain wanes. I've always recovered from the few illnesses I've gotten and muscle strains quickly, even as I grew older. Hopefully by tomorrow I'll be fighting fit.

I'm on the toilet when I hear something heavy thud downstairs. Then again. "Bram?" I call after flushing. No answer. Maybe he went out. I step into the hallway, calling again. "Bram?"

"Jane?" he shouts from downstairs. "I'm in the servant's rooms."

Oh, thank God. I couldn't handle another spectral visit today.

I think he means those two tiny cells off the kitchen. Each is barely bigger than a closet. I venture downstairs and discover my lover in the first room which has grown both bigger and smaller all at once. Bram walks out of an open panel in the wall carrying another decaying box to add to the three already on the floor. "What the heck is going on?"

"I remembered Felicia mentioning this place. This is Hallie's old bedroom. I found the secret door. Come. Look."

Bram ushers me through the panel door into what must have been a pantry in another incarnation. Now…I have no idea what this is. Cobwebs and centimeters thick dust coat the shelves and floor, making it almost impossible to tell what's in the rows of

178 | C R I M S O N   V A L E

jars. Herbs and roots in most, but some…snakeskin. Dried lizards. Bones. Nails. Yellow powder reeking of sulfur. In the center of the room sits a table with knives, candles, chalk, and two skulls on either side of an iron pot like someone a witch uses. On the walls are strange symbols with hearts, snakes, circles, curls, sometimes all the drawings together and connected.

"What the heck is all this?"

"Hallie's workshop. Where she cast her spells and made her charm bags."

"And these symbols? Are they Satanic?"

"I recognize some. Before you arrived I had the house cleaned and painted, mostly because these symbols were scribbled all over the walls, especially in Jerome's room. Hell, there was even one tattooed on your uncle. When I asked Felicia about them, she said Hallie put them up decades before. I looked them up once, they were a mix of voodoo, Pagan, Wiccan, Nordic, even Christian icons. Think she was hedging her bets. But they were for different purposes too. Keeping evil out, keeping evil in, cleansing, protection, you name it. I think when I removed them, the magic ended."

"So?"

"Well, maybe that's why the ghosts are so strong now. The symbols kept them in line. And if we put them back up, it'll render them powerless again. Maybe we'll even find one to banish the bastards for good. There has to be something in one of these boxes. In one of her books."

"I-I don't know if I'm comfortable with that."

"There's nothing evil about any of this unless that's your intention from the start. The rituals are mostly about nature and energy. It's more like focusing physics. We won't sacrifice any goats or virgins, I promise." He kisses me. "Trust me. Please?"

"I trust you," I say meekly before sighing. "Every time I find out something new about this house it just makes me want to sell it more and more."

"Don't you dare even say that, Jane. This, all of this," he says, gesturing around, "every room, every painting, every piece of wood is your family's history. The culmination of their lives, proof of their existence, just as you are. This is your birthright, and our son's when he's born. Besides, this is where we met. Where we fell in love." I stare at Bram, the sides of my mouth twitching from holding in my words. His eyes narrow as he takes my hand. "Beloved," he says, pulling me against his body, "what is it?"

I was hoping we could avoid this conversation a little longer. I didn't realize how much I dreaded it until now. "I-I need to tell you something."

"What?" he asks, holding onto me even tighter. "That you think you cannot give me children?" I pull away in surprise, but Bram simply smiles down at me. "Doctors are wrong all the time. You were born to be a mother, Jane. You were born to be the mother of *my* children. Just because your body rejected your husband's seed doesn't mean that will happen with us. It *won't* happen with us. I know it." He leans down to kiss me before his grin grows. "And think of all the fun we're going to have trying." He pecks my lips again before releasing me. "Tomorrow. And you had best get away from me because right now it's proving quite difficult to keep my promise from earlier. Why don't you make us dinner while I continue my excavation?"

"Okay."

"Love you," he calls as I walk away.

"Love you too."

I drop the fake smile when I pass through the doorframe. He wants children. Of course he wants children. Despite his confidence the odds are not in our favor. All I can do is pray he won't hate me as the years pass and the nursery gathers dust. I don't think I can go through the years of sighs, of weary eyes, of false starts and dashed hopes poisoning us both. Uh, I don't want to think about any of this now. Not yet. We've only just begun.

Simple hamburgers and salad for dinner I think. No ghosts bother me as I chop and fry dinner. This is nice, almost like normal life. I'm making dinner, the man I love is in the other room working on a project, tonight we'll crawl into bed and watch television before falling asleep wrapped up together. I've missed the simple domesticity of married life. Sure we're not married, and he's looking for way to obliterate ghosts but still. I'm amazed how easy, how right this all seems. With Owen it took a year before I felt really, truly comfortable around him. As I chop the lettuce, humming along to Taylor Swift on the radio, it's as if I'm light as air. Like I want to dance around the house, spinning and twirling like a ballerina. I'd forgotten how wonderful happiness is. I've missed it. I never want to lose it again.

"Smells delicious," the harbinger of my bliss says as he enters the kitchen.

"It's just hamburgers."

He moves in behind me, sliding his hands under my shirt to my chest and stomach as I squish the fat from the patty. "Maybe I'm not talking about the food." He bites my earlobe and kneads my erect, still tender breast. "I really love you, you know." He kisses my neck. "And I'm sorry if I upset you with the baby talk."

"You didn't," I lie.

"I did. It was insensitive of me to talk so blithely about something so sensitive. But I know, I just *know* it won't be the same for us."

"You *can't* know that."

"But I do. The same way I knew you were made for me the moment I laid eyes on you, that's the way I know we will give each other the children we've craved all our lives. It's fate, Jane. *Fate.*"

"But what if you're wrong this time? What if I can't…I lost Owen, I don't want to lose you too because of my toxic womb."

"You will never, *ever* lose me, Jane. I finally found you, I finally have you in my arms, and *nothing* will ever make me give you up now. You're mine, toxic womb and all." He rubs my flat stomach. "Just have faith. Have faith in me. Have faith in us, and I promise on every power this universe holds, I will give you everything your heart and soul desires." With tender care rolls my nipple between his fingers. "Eternal love. Eternal devotion." As he continues to toy with one hand, the other slips down from my stomach into my pants and gently massages that sweet spot in tandem with the rolls. My hips move against his fingers.

"I am your willing slave, Jane," he whispers, breath as hot as the skillet. As hot as he makes me feel from the inside out. Dear God one little touch from his man, and I'm close to orgasm. Not good enough. Nowhere near. I drop the spatula to press my hand to his, adding to the growing pressure, urging his fingers to move harder. Deeper. Faster on my sex as my hips rotate against his now pert erection. He groans, guttural like a wolf on the hunt. I shut my eyes to savor the wonder already rippling through me. "Jesus God, woman, absolve me," Bram growls, fiery breath against my neck. "Absolve me of my promise now or I'll lose my fucking mind."

"Yes! Yes," I cry out through my gritted teeth. I can endure any pain but not the current agony of not having him fill me.

His hands continue their dance as I pull down my sweatpants, leaving me naked from the waist down. Down. Still behind me, Bram lowers me on my knees onto the hardwood floor. His hand leaves my breast only to help me remove my shirt before pinching the bruised nub so tight I groan as his other instrument of torture does the same to my clitoris. A flash of pain rockets down my spine. I revel in it. To love the rose you must take the thorns.

"I'm going to fuck you, Jane," Bram whispers as he clamps down again. "I am going to fuck you like the bitch in heat you are acting like. Like you are." He pinches again, this time thrusting his still clothed bulge against my bare bottom to drive home the point. The words, the acts all just inflame my desire so much I may orgasm before he's even inside me. "Get down on your hands and knees."

I obey without question. When we first tried this position I was mortified what with my breasts hanging down, bare bottom up in the air, and shameful orifices visible if one dared to gaze upon them. The shame's there, on the cusp of consciousness, but is overshadowed by the anticipation, perhaps even intensifying it. I hear him unzip his pants and even that sound heightens the maelstrom inside me, especially the one inside my already engorged, quivering sex. He can't wait any longer than I. As his hands grab my hips, I feel the wet tip of him rake over my anus and perineum. Those same hands yank me backwards onto his rock hard manhood, reaching my very end. The act is so rough, and I'm still so raw, the pain almost blinds me. Or the pleasure. They're one and the same now.

He pulls completely out, leaving nothing but emptiness in his wake. Give me agony, not this. Not this incompleteness. This void after rapture. But even that has its purpose. Without it I wouldn't know what a wonder it is when, as fiercely as the first thrust was, his manhood parts me again. And again. Hard. Ferocious. Crude. Primordial. His end assaults my cervix with the force of a meteor plummeting to earth. His fingernails dig into my hips. His own hip bones batter against my bare bottom. Harder. It hurts. Harder. It all hurts. God, it hurts so good.

Heaven.

He crashes into me again, again, the pressure, the intensity, the frenzy within my body almost reaching its apex. Then again as he picks up a faster rhythm. Brutal. Bestial. Crazed. Raged. I'm sobbing but can't be heard over his grunts, over our bodies colliding. It hurts. God, it hurts. It's too much. It's all too much. Too much pain. Too much ecstasy. No mere human can be the conduit of such divinity.

"I can't hold on much longer," he pants as the frenzied onslaught intensifies. "Come with me, Jane. Come with me, come with me, beloved. My Jane…My Jane…" Bram pleads, moving one hand to my stomach. "*Come*!"

With one final thrust, we each explode into a million tiny pieces as my sex expands and contracts around him, almost suckling his seed into my ravaged womb, healing it. Healing *me*.

When we return from that divine space, we're reassembled. But not as two. As I touch that divine, I know it. I know *him*. The boy in the dream. My son. *Our* son. He's real. Finally. Thank you, God. Thank you.

No longer able to support myself, my body collapses to the ground. Bram lands on top of my back, still inside me but as limp as the rest of him. We both lie on the floor panting, unable to form words, unable to move for several seconds after we re-enter our bodies. Perhaps even afraid to break the spell we just wove. His hand remains on my stomach, and I realize so is mine. "I love you," he whispers. Our fingers entwine over that now sacred spot, and I know he felt it too. Several seconds pass before his body becomes wracked with tiny convulsions. Laughter begins. Pure, triumphant laughter that wanes several seconds later but not the convulsions. I realize he's weeping. "Thank you. Thank you."

"Bram…?"

"For ages. For all my pitiable existence, I dreamed of this. I dreamed of you. It is all that sustained me. The *thought* of you loving me. And no matter what happens, no matter what you find out about me or think of me, know this: I love you. In this moment, no creature has ever or will ever love another as deeply, as purely, as I do you, beloved. You are the blood of my blood. Flesh of my flesh. Soul of my soul. My Alpha and my Omega. My heaven and my hell. You are…*my Jane*." He holds me against him tighter, as if he wants our flesh to merge into one. To trap me under his skin for all eternity. "Never leave me. Promise me, beloved. Never leave. I am nothing without my Jane. Promise. *Promise*."

Before I can promise, the screeching of the smoke alarm begins above our heads. I glance up finally notice the kitchen has filled with white haze. Oh crud, the hamburgers. Even now Bram doesn't release me. "Bram…" I say, removing my hand from his. His grip loosens, and I quickly extract myself to rise. I don't even bother to put on clothes. The hamburgers are charred black along with the rest of the skillet. I grab the handle and toss it into the sink. Jesus wept, we could have burned to death. Bram begins fanning the alarm with a towel as I quickly dress. I need another shower now. I've caked in sweat and—

A second after the alarm stops, I hear the doorbell.

Bram and I exchange a glance. "Are you expecting someone?" I ask.

His face visibly tenses as if he's frightened. "No. Don't answer it. They'll go away—"

It rings again, with a knock following this time. "It could be a delivery. Or your father."

"It's not," he says, not hiding his fear this time. He strides toward me. "Don't answer it."

"Bram, you're being ridiculous."

He grabs my hands, holding on hard enough tendons crack. "*Please.*"

"Bram…" I say, extracting myself from his grip. "They know we're here. I'll be right back. I promise." Shaking my head, I walk out of the sweltering kitchen. The ache inside me begins after the first step like sandpaper grating over glass. Lord, we couldn't even wait twenty-four hours. What happens after we're separated for days? He won't leave anything left of me. Or simply won't let me leave. The doorbell rings again. "Coming!"

Please don't be a nosy neighbor or ghost. Regardless, I cannot greet the person like this. I smooth my hair, rearrange the waistband of my sweats, and open the door. My fake smile twists into a look of shock in time to the rock in my stomach expanding to the size of Pluto. I actually gasp. He's as horrified by the sight of me as I am him, though for entirely different reasons. A lady never wants to open the door to her husband with the semen of her lover still dripping down her leg. "Jesus Christ, Janie, what the hell happened to you?" my husband asks breathlessly.

"Jane, my love, who is it?" Bram calls.

And now the rock is the size of Jupiter.

Owen's thin lip twitches, the only outward sign of the fury that must be churning inside. I cow my head, unable to look at him a second further. This is not happening. I am not ready for this. I haven't worked out what to say or do. I haven't…anything. And when Bram steps beside me, the two opposing gravitational forces of the men I love all but crushing me. It's difficult to breathe let alone speak.

"Um, hello," Bram says, sliding his arm around my waist. I attempt to step away but his grip tightens. "May we help you?"

Owen doesn't utter a word, but I somehow find the courage to glance up. Big mistake. My husband gives my lover the full force of his infamous glower, the same one that has brought drug kingpins to tears. I can only bear it a moment. I look away from Owen. "I'm here to see my wife."

"Then this is awkward," Bram concedes though his smile doesn't waver. "We had no idea you were coming."

"Obviously," Owen grumbles, followed by uncomfortable silence. "And you are?"

"Bram Davenport. Jane's—"

"Lawyer," I cut in before he can utter the other L word. "Well, sort-sort of. What-what are you doing here?"

I sense those sharp brown eyes on me now. Walking across broken glass would prove less painful. "What the hell do you think? Melissa and I were terrified something had happened to you."

I extract myself from Bram's grip to step forward. "Owen, you-you should have called."

"I have been calling. For days," he counters. "Melissa too."

"I did text you."

"Not the same, and you know it."

"Still," Bram says.

Owen glares at my lover again. "I'm sorry, but this doesn't concern you. This is a conversation between *me* and *my* wife. And I am doing my ample best not to give into my first instinct and break your fucking nose, but you are testing my restraint, *sir*."

"I'm sorry, did you just threaten me?" Bram asks, taking a step forward.

I grab his arm to stop a second step as Owen's hands ball into fists, ready to carry out his threat. "Bram…" My lover momentarily forgets my husband and looks at me. "I think Owen and I need to talk. Alone. I'm sorry."

"If you think I am leaving you alone with—"

"You heard the lady," Owen cuts in. "Time to go, asshole."

Bram gazes at me for confirmation. "It's fine. I'll call you later. I promise."

His lip curls up, filling his face with anger and distaste, but quells it a moment later. "As you wish, beloved. I understand." Bram grabs me by the waist again, this time pulling me against him before lowering his lips to mine. There's no love, no tenderness in this kiss, only rage and possession. Hard lips, hard teeth on my already tender flesh. I try not to kiss him back, but as always my body responds against my will. I lean into his contours and match his passion strike for strike. Bite for bite. At least he withdraws quickly. The show only lasts a second or two. The moment he breaks away I glance at Owen, who somehow maintains his poker face, at least on the surface. I can all but feel his fury prickling me like daggers. After that I deserve every torture my husband can inflict. "As you wish."

Point made, Bram retreats into the house. I keep my eyes down to the painted porch like a scolded child until several long, grueling seconds later Bram returns with car keys in hand. "Call me later, beloved," Bram says before smiling at Owen. "Wish I could say it was nice to meet you." I watch as Bram strolls to his car but suddenly spins back around. "Oh, and uh, beloved? Don't forget to clean up the stains we just made on the kitchen floor. Cum bleaches wood." His smile grows. "Love you."

And now I want to die.

I keep my eyes shut, terrified to open them and see my husband's face, until I hear Bram's car drive away. "He was…we didn't—"

"May I come in now?" Owen asks in a tone I never thought him capable of. Snotty.

"Yes," I whisper.

As he passes, I keep my head cowed. I'm petrified to look at him, *really* look at him, in case I burst into tears. This is killing him, it has to be killing him because it's darn sure gutting me, and I'm not even the injured party. I've been on the other end of this situation, and I wouldn't wish it on the devil himself.

"Nice place," Owen deadpans, "if you're a member of the Addams Family."

"It's, um, better in the day," I say, shutting the door. "The light really helps brighten it up." I back against the door. "Did you, uh, come straight from the airport? Would you like something to drink? To eat? I just started making dinner when you…knocked."

"Is that why there's so much smoke? Guess your cooking hasn't improved, huh?"

"Th-the salad should still be good. And I can make other things. There's hamburger meat left over. You like meatloaf. I can—"

"I don't want any goddamn food, Janie," Owen snaps. "I didn't fly two thousand miles for your goddamn meatloaf. Are we not going to talk about what just happened?"

"I-I don't know what to say except…I'm sorry. I'm *so* sorry you had to find out like this," I say, barely a whisper. "I never wanted to hurt you."

"And I didn't want to find out my wife thinks she's seeing ghosts from her best friend."

That rat fink. "Why would she—"

"No, the question is why *you* wouldn't," he snaps. He shakes his head, and for a moment the mask slips. For a moment he cannot hide his fear, his disgust, his pity. And hurt. So much pain for us both. "I saw it in LA. I saw what was happening to you, how lost you'd become, and I should have done more. Stayed. Fought harder."

"There was nothing you could have done," I proclaim.

"The hell there wasn't. I could have not cheated on you. I could have not lied about the vasectomy."

"Hey, I lied to you first about being on the pill, remember? *I* lied when I promised you children. *I* pushed *you* away. *I*…fell in love with someone else and was too afraid to tell you. This was me. This was all me, and the only thing I can do is beg your forgiveness and free you from my dysfunction. You deserve better, so much better than me, Owen."

"Is this why you're doing this to yourself? Driving yourself literally crazy to punish yourself? For the millionth time, I can live without having a child. I have never resented you or blamed you, not for a minute, for the miscarriages. I would be happy if it was you and me on the damn moon without another human being ever to contact us again. I am the one who wanted to look into adoption. You—"

"I know. *I know*. Aren't you hearing me? I take full responsibility, okay? *I* messed up, not you. And I'm sorry. I am so sorry for all the pain I've caused you through the years. I'd give up anything to take it all back, I would. But I can't. Not even God has that power. All I can do now is…let you go. *Really* let you go and support you in finding the woman you are truly meant to be with."

"Jesus Christ, Jane, don't you get it by now? Since the damn night we met there has not been a moment where I have not loved you. Where there has not been a doubt in my mind I will love you until the day I die. All I want, all I have ever wanted, was to spend my life with you. That will *never* change. I am *meant* to be with you."

"But you're not," I say bridging the gap between us. "There's been too much damage, Owen. We're nothing but scar tissue now. I love you, I do and always will, but I cannot do this with you anymore. You think I'm insane? Well, the definition of insanity is doing the same thing over and over again and expecting a different result. I almost lost my mind, Owen, literally because I wouldn't accept that fact. It took coming here, it took Bram for me to realize that and break the cycle. And I know it hurts now, but in a year, two years when *she* comes into your life, when she's walking down the aisle toward you, you'll know I was right. That *this* was right."

"Janie, it sure as hell doesn't look right from where I'm standing. Sweetheart, have you seen yourself? Your skin's gray. You look like you haven't slept in a month. You're bruised, you've lost so much weight since I last saw you, and you think you're seeing ghosts…"

"I don't think, Owen, I know. I know because I'm not the only one who has."

"You mean your boyfriend? He says he saw them too? Anyone else?" he asks with a hard edge.

"I know what you're insinuating. He wouldn't do that."

"Jane, you've only known the guy a few weeks. I looked up his record. The man has three DUIs, has been to rehab twice for cocaine and Oxy addiction, and he was almost disbarred for taking bribes. This is not a good man."

"He had trouble in his past, I am aware of that. He admitted everything, every demon without me even asking. I didn't plan this, I didn't want it, but…I love him. I-I can't explain it, Owen. I just, I *know* as of God himself spoke to me that I'm meant to be with him. And he's not placating me, he's not using me, and he's not lying to me. I trust him. But even if he is lying, that's my burden, not yours." I pause to find the strength to say what I should have years ago. "I love you, I will always love you, and you were a good, *good* husband to me. Better than I deserved. But we're toxic to each other, or I just turned you toxic, I don't know. All I do know is we can't continue like we have. It's killing us, it's poisoning all we meant to one another, and what we can mean to each other in the future. I don't want to lose you, not completely, and I think that's what will happen if we stay married.

"So it's over. We gave it our all, we can't say we didn't, but it just…wasn't meant to be." I reach for his large hand, squeezing it hard. I'm surprised he lets me. "*This* is how it's meant to be. I'm tired of hurting, Owen, and I'm tired of hurting you." I lean in and kiss his cheek. "I'm good. I'm great, I swear I am. And in time you will be too. Just not with me. I'm sorry. *I'm sorry.*"

After one more squeeze, one more touch, I walk past him. I walk past Hallie, the ghost with sadness in her brown eyes, who shakes her head at my folly. I cow my head and continue up the stairs, somehow making it to my bedroom and shutting the door before finally bursting into tears. No matter what anyone says, it had to be done. I know it did. But that doesn't mean it hurts any less.

CHAPTER FIFTEEN

Be it the tension or my long nap, I toss and turn for almost two hours before giving up on sleep. Television only holds my interest for a few minutes. Letting him spend the night here was a mistake, I just didn't have the resolve to break his heart *and* banish him from the house all in the same night. And it is only tonight, I made that quite clear. Bram wasn't too pleased with the news when I phoned him earlier. I'm shocked he actually listened to me and didn't come back "just in case." In case of what, I didn't ask. Owen attacking me or us falling into bed I guess. Regardless I'm glad for his absence. I needed to cry without an audience. God, not even the Mississippi River could hold all the tears I've shed for my marriage. Please God let these be the last.

My stomach grumbles as Nigella whips up fudge on the television. That apple for dinner isn't cutting it. I shut off the TV and listen at the door. Quiet as a crypt. Owen's probably asleep or at least in his room. Good. As quietly as possible, I tip-toe from my room down the stairs to the kitchen. A peanut butter and jelly sandwich and chamomile tea, a perfect not quite midnight snack. I—

Just as I turn on the burner over the tea kettle, I sense her again. The prickling on the back of my neck causes shivers. Sure enough when I spin around Hallie stands in the doorframe of her old bedroom staring at me. I should be used to these spectral visitors by now, but seeing her again, my heart seizes all the same. But only for a moment. I am getting more than a little fed up with all these unwelcome guests, especially the ones silently judging me. I know Bram told me to ignore them that my energy feeds them, but that doesn't seem to be working. Time for a new tactic.

"I know who you are. Hallie," I say to the dead. "You took care of my mother. She named me after you." The ghost actually smiles, the sides of her brown eyes crinkling. We have the same smile. "I wish I could have known you. I've heard only great things." Her smile grows. This seems to be working. "You're not here to hurt me, are you?" She nods no. "Then…what do you want?"

The ghost moves toward me. Instinctively, I back against the counter to escape, but to no avail. She glides toward me faster than I can see her, faster than I can scream. I can't even fight as she enters me. A tumult of sensations overwhelm me. Every of my senses provides contradictory data. It's light, it's dark. It's cold, it's hot. There's no sound but crickets chirp. Then I'm weightless. Insubstantial. Nothing but atoms and stardust as my soul is forced from my body.

One millisecond I'm in my kitchen, and in less than a blink I'm on the porch amid a symphony of crickets. And I'm not alone. Beside me my silent assailant stares out at the bayou into the darkness of the night. Hallie only draws my attention for a second. Haloed in the light from inside the house, *my* house, a man in a seersucker suit puffs a cigar in my rocking chair. This *is* my house. Same railing, same windows, but who is…the familiar man reviews a ledger, I stare, trying to place him. Late twenties, early thirties, with wavy blonde hair, wide blue eyes, with the Fontaine's pointed chin. It couldn't be…he's so young. But it has to be him. It *is* him. Cotton Fontaine, my great-grandfather and family monster. He is handsome, striking even, almost as if charisma oozes from his pores, snaring your attention to him and nothing else. If he knows we're here, he doesn't let on. Nor does the African-American woman in a white gauzy dress and matching turban walking up the porch steps toward him. She's easily eighty, face more wrinkles than skin, but moves like a much younger woman. Like a panther approaching prey. "Everything is in place," she informs the monster.

"The girl?" Cotton asks in the deepest baritone I've ever heard.

"She's aware of what's expected and is prepared."

"Then if there are no troubles, your granddaughter will immediately begin her new post in this household tomorrow morning. You do drive a hard bargain, Camille."

"Yes boy, I am sure it will be such a hardship having a nubile fifteen-year-old you've coveted for a year living under your roof, Cotton Fontaine," the woman spits out. "Your wife must be so pleased."

Cotton rises from the chair, puffing out his broad chest like cock of the walk. "My wife would be less pleased to lose this house and join the bread lines like the rest of the country. Besides, my wife has no right to an opinion in this matter." He reaches into his coat and removes an envelope, handing it to Camille. "Nor do you, Priestess." The woman looks inside then begins counting the bills. "It's all there. That's all the money I have left in this world. Do not come looking for more."

"How the mighty have fallen," Camille says with a smirk.

With one quick movement, Cotton grabs Camille's jaw and yanks her against him, looming over the shocked woman. "Shut your mouth, whore," he snarls. "I still have the whip my grandpappy used to beat your slave ass with, and—"

"*Etrangler*," Camille whispers.

The moment the strange word escapes her lips, the large man doubles over, reduced to a hacking mess. Tears stream from his eyes as he turns purple, as sweat coats his face. He stares at the woman, no doubt wishing looks could kill. Camille merely smiles. "Remember who came to whom for help, Cotton Fontaine, and why. *I* hold the power tonight. Now if you're ready, let's get this over with. I'd rather not spend a moment with you longer than I have to."

Having won the battle, Camille holds her head high as she spins around and steps off the porch. Though vibrating with rage, the monster follows her into the night with Hallie trailing him. I bring up the rear all through the fifty yards of clearing to the dock with a rowboat awaiting us. The boat doesn't tilt as Hallie and I step inside behind the others.

Cotton takes the oars with Camille in the front holding the flickering lantern from the dock to guide us through the inky black swamp. Glowing red eyes poke out of the still water ahead of us. Alligators assessing the trespassers. I wonder if they can sense me. I glance at Hallie, who stares at Cotton with the same expression he had for Camille. Pure, unadulterated hatred. He stares right through her. If I had substance I'd take her hand to comfort her.

At least the ride's short. We row perhaps a hundred yards, mooring the boat on the sandy shore of an island beside three other boats. We're not alone. Even from the shore, through the wispy brush of long grass and tall, dense trees, I can make out the glow of fire that we use as a beacon up the dirt path. Cotton slaps a mosquito on his neck. Then another. "Damn things. Why can't we do this inside the house?" he asks.

"I told you, boy. The magic's strongest here. Three currents intersect this island."

"I don't feel anything."

"I do."

As do I. It ripples through me like an electrical current, the sensation growing stronger as we continue our march inland toward the lights. It's almost unbearable when we reach our destination. Dear God, what is this?

Two women and three African-American men, all dressed in white with the same symbols from Hallie's hidden room painted in glistening blood on their foreheads and bare chests, greet us in the small clearing. Actual torches in a perfect circle flicker against the wind. Inside that circle is another made of salt with more symbols painted around the perimeter in salt and blood.

"Everyone take your places," Camille orders.

Cotton begins removing his clothes as all but one of the others picks up drums and leather pouches. Camille whispers to the youngest of the entourage, a trembling teenager clutching a blanket around her tiny body. She is beautiful with light brown skin the same color as Hallie's. Same everything as Hallie, save for lacking the pointed chin, the teen could be my great-aunt's younger doppelganger. I glance at my companion, who keeps her eyes to the ground.

Whatever Camille says to the girl, the teen nods in agreement and wipes away her tears. God, I can sense her terror from here like mosquitos swarming me, but the girl steps toward the salt circle regardless, dropping the blanket at the perimeter revealing her naked body. Cotton stops unbuttoning his trousers to leer at the girl, all but licking his chops as he drinks in her exposed, trembling flesh. The girl attempts to cover her breasts and privates against the scrutiny. Her eyes never leave the ground and Cotton's never leave her, not even as he yanks down his pants, revealing his thick manhood already at full salute.

"Step into the circle, Fontaine," Camille orders, "and we'll begin."

Cotton obeys, joining the girl inside the salt. That poor girl downright quakes like a palsy patient the moment he's by her side. Petrified. Horrified. The girl's eyes remain down, even as Camille removes a chicken from a crate and the other men begin banging on the drums, the pulse echoing through the night like its heartbeat. Camille moves into the circle with the wailing chicken flapping in an attempt to escape. "Death."

The woman slits the bird's throat, blood instantly flowing down her arm onto the already grotesque ground. She drops the carcass and steps toward the nude duo. As she paints a heart-like symbol with snaking lines around it on the girl's chest from neck to pubis, the girl's tears, coming out in sobs now. Camille ignores her pain, finishing the macabre sigil before moving to Cotton to paint the same drawing on his broad chest as the drumbeat increases in tempo. The women join in the grotesque symphony, chanting in a foreign language, possibly French, in time to that overwhelming beat. Symbols complete, Camille moves beside the chicken and joins in on the chant, nodding at Cotton. The moment she does, my great-grandfather grabs the girl's wrist and lowers the sobbing child to the blood soaked ground. There's no kindness, no preamble. When her back touches dirt, he impales her with his manhood so hard she screams in agony as he literally tears her apart. Thank God I don't have a stomach right now or I'd throw up.

I want to look away. I even force myself to stare up at the stars, away from this horror show, but my resolve only lasts a few seconds. I've become a ghoul. A ghoul who watches as my great-grandfather bucks himself over and over again inside this innocent in time to the beat of the drums. The girl simply lies there, staring at nothing. Or perhaps not. When Hallie bends down to her level, I'd swear the girl's eyes move to the specter's, a peace washing over both their faces, and when Cotton finally cries out as he spills himself inside her, they both smile.

"Life."

Dear God.

Still panting, Cotton rolls off the girl onto his back as Camille steps toward the girl. Smiling sympathetically at her granddaughter, Camille lowers herself beside the girl and caresses her tear stained cheek. She nods reverently at the girl before helping her stand. Camille kisses her granddaughter's forehead and nods again. The girl nods back and lowers her hand between her own legs, fingers returning with blood and semen. What…? Oh. I grimace as the girl paints a symbol that resembles a cross with snakes, on her own grandmother's forehead and steps out of the circle. Her job's complete.

"Rise Cotton DeLaurie Fontaine," Camille commands.

Not even bothering to dress, penis still covered in gore, my great-grandfather obeys, stepping to the rim of the salt circle as Camille takes her place on the opposing side. She removes one of the daggers from her white sash, throwing it to his feet. As he picks it up, she removes the second one. Camille nods, and they slash their palms in perfect unison, the chanting and drums increasing in tempo. Camille begins chanting as well, screeching to the heavens, perhaps to hell, as Cotton says, "I call on you, oh ancient ones of the other realm! I call on you now! I offer you blood! Innocence! Death! Life! Fidelity! Oh, hear my pleas oh powerful, ancient ones, and manifest before us if you deem us worthy! Take my offerings and manifest!" They slice again. "Manifest! I implore you! I am your servant!" Another cut. "I am your slave!" Another. "Manifest!" Both slash their other palm. "Hear my plea! Accept my offerings! I am worthy! Manifest!" They slash their arms. "Manifest!" Slash. "Manif—"

Jesus.

Camille lets out a bloodcurdling scream as her head whips back with enough force to cause damage, her neck elongated to almost a hundred eighty degree angle. All grow quiet, from the people to the animals, as her scream echoes all the way to the bowels of hell. After maybe three seconds of agony, the priestess collapses to the ground like a rag doll. No one moves, I don't think they blink as they stare at the seemingly dead woman with the only noise emanating from Cotton's deep, panting breaths. Even the crickets don't dare made a sound. What—

"I sense your fear, Cotton Fontaine," Camille croaks, voice now several octaves deeper. The old woman slowly gazes up at him, blood dripping from her eyes, ears, and nose. Jesus God.

Cotton cringes. "Camille?"

"She's still in here," the demon says, rising. "She is strong, this one. Unlike you. Fear and weakness reek from your every pore, Cotton Fontaine. They have since your birth, and they will until the grave and beyond."

"How dare you—"

"Is that anyway to speak to your guest, Cotton Fontaine? I thought you offered to be my slave."

"So…you're…" Cotton chokes out.

"I go by many names, Cotton Fontaine, and I shall go by even more as your eons pass." Camille suddenly twitches. Then again as if she has Tourette's. "This one's struggling. We haven't much time. Why have you summoned me?"

"I wish to strike a covenant with you. My business, the business my family built over centuries… it's failing."

"And you wish for me to aid you in restoring it to its former glory."

"Yes. Is that within your power?"

The demon grins from cheek to bloody cheek. "Oh yes, Cotton Fontaine. There is precious little *not* within my power. But there is a price."

"I know. My soul."

The demon bursts into cruel laughter. Cotton cringes. "Oh Cotton Fontaine, what makes you believe you even have one? And if you do, I fear it is even more corrupted than mine."

"Then what *do* you want?" Cotton snaps.

The demon's grin grows. "A new beginning. Substance. *Life*."

For once, my great-grandfather visibly tenses. "Mine?" he asks, voice brittle.

"No. The first born male of your bloodline the day he reaches manhood."

"Done," Cotton says without hesitation. "But until that day, you are bound to me. You do my bidding. I ask, you obey. You are *my* slave."

The demon considers the proposition, but only for a moment. "Then we have our covenant, Cotton Fontaine." He holds out Camille's bleeding hand. "Seal it."

Cotton stares at that hand. The weight, what it means, makes it difficult to raise his own, but after several seconds he shakes it. The moment their blood mingles both jolt. In that same moment something blacker than even the night evaporates out of Camille like smoke to Cotton's side, matching his outline limb for limb. Both people collapse to the dirt but the darkness between them remains upright, staring straight at me just as it had at my home in LA.

Him.

"*Jane*," he whispers mournfully, reaching out for me through time and space. "*My Jane.*"

"JANE!"

The sting of a slap brings me back from wherever I was into my own body. A body that cannot sustain itself. The moment I return my legs give out, and I collapse against something warm, something that wraps its arms around me, anchoring me to this and only this world. What the…?

"It's okay, sweetheart," the man whispers.

Who…Owen. My husband. My brain reboots with this piece of data. I'm in my kitchen. That squealing is the teakettle. I'm home. I'm safe. It's over. They're gone. I'm safe.

I think.

*

"Well, your CAT scan came back clean, Mrs. Harrow," my new tormenter Dr. Fayette says, holding up the black and white negative of my brain. "No signs of stroke, and no indication of a hemorrhage or potential aneurysm. I also reviewed your blood work, and besides your estrogen and progesterone levels being slightly elevated, everything else appears within normal ranges."

"Then what could have caused the episode?" Owen asks.

My poor Owen. He always ends up rushing me to the hospital in the middle of the night then demanding answers that never come. I couldn't talk him out of this trip, and now I've wasted eight more hours of his life. He truly is better off without me.

"I've written down the name and number of an excellent psychiatrist in town," the doctor says. "I am by no means an expert, but it sounds as if your wife may have had a dissociative episode last night."

"Are the hallucinations related?" Owen asks.

"I'm not hallucinating," I insist.

"More than likely yes," the doctor answers, ignoring me. The *men* are talking. Silly me for speaking up. "But the psychiatrist would know more. He will more than likely prescribe antipsychotics, and—"

"I don't need antipsychotics," I say, leaping off the gurney I've been forced to rest on all night. "What I need is to go home."

"Mrs. Harrow, what you've been experiencing is not something to take lightly. It could indicate late onset schizophrenia, which can be managed with medication. Extreme depression can also cause—"

"I am not schizophrenic, and I am not experiencing psychotic depression. What I am experiencing is exhaustion. I have let you poke and prod me and answered each and every one of your embarrassing questions all night long. I'm done. If there is nothing physically wrong with me then you cannot help me, and I am leaving. I demand to be discharged. *Now.*"

Dr. Fayette glances at Owen but still says, "Okay. The nurse will be by with your discharge papers."

"Thank you," I say.

The doctor steps out, closing the curtain behind himself. The moment he does Owen says, "Jane—"

"I need to get dressed," I cut in before the admonishments begin. "I'll be ready in a minute."

Owen stares at me for a few seconds as I retrieve my clothes, but finally takes the hint and leaves me in peace. Thank God. I fall back on the bed, taking a deep breath then slowly releasing it. Alone at last. He's only left my side once when I had the CAT scan, and the doctor practically had to use a crowbar then. I appreciate the concern, I truly do, but I could sense his worry, his anger at his own helplessness. It just brings up bad memories. We've been here far too many times before. And I knew the whole venture would prove fruitless. What happened had nothing to do with my body, it's my spirit that suffered the assault.

All night, when I wasn't being treated like a lab rat, I tried to wrack my mind for a reason Hallie showed me what she did. It must have taken tremendous energy to rip my soul from my body and transport me back in time. To what end? To prove my great-grandfather was a monster? I already knew that. To show me the demon? Without a doubt it was the same entity I saw on my stairs in LA almost a month ago, but I haven't seen or felt it since I came to Crimson. Where is it? Just biding its time? Could it be here now and I just don't sense it because it doesn't want me to? I need to do more research. Get the priest to bless the house. Perhaps perform an exorcism. I'll even call that energist Bram told me about. All I do know is I can't do anything trapped in the hospital.

Owen's waiting not a foot away when I open the curtain. He smartly keeps his mouth shut as I sign the papers and rush out of the medical center to my Kia. He was just biding his time though. The moment we pull out of the parking lot, he says, "Jane—"

"I am not crazy, Owen. I'm *not*. And I am aware that is what crazy people say, I do, but I swear to God in my case it is true."

My husband grips the wheel so tightly it groans. "Why…" He shakes his head. "Why didn't you tell me this was happening to you? Why did you keep this from me? For months? I-I could have helped you. I could have—"

"Had me committed? Drugged until I didn't know who I was? Because in the end it wouldn't have done any good. I don't need a doctor, I don't need a psychologist, what I need is a demonologist or exorcist."

"To help you with the ghosts. And demons," he says harshly.

"Look, I know you don't believe me. *I* wouldn't believe me either, but…what if I can prove it?"

"How?"

I hadn't gotten that far. "I-I don't know exactly, but I think I know the best place to start. We just need a boat."

"A boat?"

"I wanted to buy one anyway. I even know where to get one. Make the next left."

"I don't think—"

"Owen, I'm doing this with or without you," I snap. "I meant what I said last night. Nothing's changed. I'm not your responsibility anymore. This isn't your problem to fix. I don't know, maybe it would be best if you just drop me at home and fly back today. You've done *more* than enough for me."

My husband glances at me, mouth set straight as a vice as if I'd literally thrown acid in his face by this suggestion. Without a word, he makes the left turn. "I stood right in front of you, not a foot away, shouting at the top of my lungs for thirty seconds. You were barely breathing, you weren't blinking, you were just...gone. There is something wrong with you, Jane. You say you want to be friends? Fine. Then as your friend it's my right to say I think you've had some sort of psychotic break. I will say I think your new boyfriend is humoring you with this ghost crap so he can get into your pants. Call it years of experience or just intuition, but there is nothing about that man I trust, not just because he's sleeping with my wife. And you *are* still my wife, at least legally, and I am shit scared for your welfare right now, both mentally and physically. You look like someone is literally draining the life out of you. You're...going against all your morals and beliefs. There is *something wrong*. But the last thing on earth I want to do is commit you, so we'll compromise for now.

"We'll get your damn boat. We'll go wherever you say, but when we find nothing there, I will sit by your side as you call that psychiatrist, make an appointment, and do *everything* he demands. Everything. Do we have a deal?"

That's fair. "And if we do find something?"

"Then...we got bigger problems in this world than I ever thought possible."

CHAPTER SIXTEEN

A third of Jerome's paintings. How did I not notice it before? The dark figure stands on the porch. Behind Hallie on another. Off on the shore watching while my mother lounges in a boat. Did she see it too? Sense it? Has it been stalking my family since the 1930s? Jesus, has it been watching me all my life? I have a million unanswered questions, one more frightening than the last, racing through my mind. Worse, I fear the answers will be equally horrifying, but they need to be uncovered because then I'll know the way to banish this abomination back to hell. That's what Hallie wants. That's why she brought me into that nightmarescape. God give me strength.

The telephone rings in the kitchen, drawing me from my art appreciation. Probably Bram again. When we got home from the hospital there were three messages on the machine and five on my cell. He came by late last night after being woken by the overwhelming fear some evil befell me. By then I was at the hospital, and I forgot my cell. I texted that I was fine and not to come here just yet, but he's probably on his way right now. The men in my life never seem to listen to me. The only thing my husband and lover have in common is their pigheadedness. I always wondered if I had a type.

"I got the motor attached," says Owen, stepping in from the kitchen.

"Come look at this," I order. Owen complies with a sigh. I hold up the painting of my mother. "My uncle painted this over forty years ago. I never met the man. But look." I point to the black figure on the porch. "This is him. That's the demon. Owen, I saw this figure in our home a month ago, *before* I ever saw this painting. And he's in so many of them. That can't be a coincidence."

"It's a black smudge, Janie."

"I thought you were going to keep an open mind," I snap.

"We got the boat, didn't we? You ready?"

"As I'll ever be." I begin walking toward the front door with Owen a pace behind. Just as I'm about to step outside onto the porch, I turn around and say, "An open mind, remember?"

"I promise," my husband solemnly vows.

The rusted johnboat rests on the sandy shore of the calm, black swamp. It was a good deal, five hundred for the boat and motor. Both are ancient but will serve their purpose at least once. I climb in before Owen pushes us off into the murky water. We drift a little before he starts the motor. I'm on navigation duty.

With only last night's vison to guide us, I concentrate on any landmarks but nothing is familiar. Tall, looming hollow cypress trees are almost one on top of another with their weeping branches hanging inches from our heads. An entire ecosystem can change in decades especially when there's no one to tend to it. That doesn't explain why it's so quiet though. Not a bird, not a cricket, just the hum of the motor. In the weeks I've been here I can't recall hearing a single bird chirping from this direction. No snakes, no squirrels, no dragonflies or other bugs have ever emerged from the swamp side of the house. How have I not noticed these things before? It's as if my head's been in the clouds. No, not even in the clouds, more like in outer space. I've crashed back to Earth now. I *have* to find this island. Without a doubt Owen will make good on this promise to commit me. Not that Bram would let him. Still, I want to avoid a battle. And yes I do want to prove I'm right because there's a part of me that believes this is all in my head. I'd be crazy not to.

"Have you noticed there are no birds? No animals besides the alligators?" I ask Owen.

"Yeah, I did. And it is damn odd," Owen concedes.

Score one for not being crazy.

We pass a landmass covered with wild grass taller than me, trees taller than dinosaurs, and alligators sunning themselves on the shore. It could be this one but…no. We haven't gone a hundred yards yet. It was definitely farther out. There's another isle, just sand and grass, but it's too small. Lord, I've become Goldilocks just with demons and alligators instead of bears. Too big, too small…just right. As the third isle drifts into view, almost camouflaged by the army of hollow cypress trees, I *sense* that same prickling from last night against my skin. Under it. It's not negative exactly, not fully, but it still sprouts goosebumps on every one of my limbs. Energy in the air. Not as strong as last night, but I do recognize it.

"Next one on the right," I say.

"Are you sure?"

Not really. "Yes."

When we pull up to the shore, I notice the wild grass isn't as tall here. It's at least a foot or two shorter than on the other islands. Before Owen even shuts off the engine, I leap from the boat into the sea of waist high foliage. "Careful. There might be more alligators," Owen calls. But I'm a woman on God's mission and look where He's guided me already. The years have taken most of my evidence but not all. Amid the grass on the sandy shore I find slats of decayed wood from the dock and a smashed glass and iron lantern still attached to the broken post. Owen kneels beside me a few seconds later. "Huh. Guess someone *was* here."

The path has to be around here somewhere. Still crouching, I examine the approximate location of where it began in my vision. There. I spring up. The grass is even shorter here but only by an inch or two. "Come on," I order, taking the lead.

"Jane, wait!"

The prickling grows more intense as if I were surrounded by a cloud of gnats, as I move inland. "Do you feel that?" I ask.

"Feel what?" he pants behind me.

"Never mind. Look."

About twenty paces ahead the grass ends. It simply ends as if we'd reached the edge of a cliff. I sprint toward that precipice, the figurative gnats growing denser against my flesh with each step. But their oppression doesn't stop me. Be it the sweet relief, the overwhelming power of this place, or just my emotional nature, I almost burst into tears when I reach the small void. It's here. I'm *here*. Last night was real. I'm not crazy.

"Holy shit," Owen says.

It's here, it's all here. The torches, now nothing more but rotted wood amid the grass. Stones with the same strange symbols from last night in a perfect circle. Animal bones and goat skulls starched white from their decades in the sun. As I take everything in, Owen kneels to the ground, running his hands over the dirt. "Looks like they salted the ground," Owen says. He puts a bit of dirt in his mouth then spits it out. "Nope. Just dirt. So why won't anything grow?"

"Because this is a bad place," I say. "Nothing can live here now. That's why there aren't bugs or birds. We should be being eaten alive by now. Alligators won't even come near this place."

"There's a perfectly logical—"

"Owen, I've never been here before," I cut in. "I swear to God I haven't. And I led us right to it. How…?"

As I turn to face my husband, something catches my eye, another shockingly white bone right at the perimeter of the grass. I move toward it. Too big for a chicken or goat. It looks like…my shriek echoes over the island when I realize it's a human femur with a human skull nearby.

"What?" Owen asks as he moves beside me. "Shit. Stay-stay there, sweetheart."

Owen creeps into the grass toward the full skeleton. It's almost like one of those in science class, fully intact but with a few scraps of worn blue fabric on the arms and legs. Owen zeroes in on the gold watch around the wrist and brown square beside the hip bone. He straddles the corpse so as not to disturb the scene but retrieves the square.

"What is it?" I ask.

"Wallet. I think." He opens it and pulls out a piece of plastic. "Driver's license. The name Cotton Fontaine mean anything to you?"

Jesus wept. "He-he was my great-grandfather. He beat my uncle into a coma. Went on the run from the police a few months before I was born."

"Well, he didn't get far, did he?"

I sense someone staring at me and look up. About fifty feet away is the man himself as I saw him last night in all his evil glory, standing in the wafting grass with a huge smile on his handsome face. "Thank you," he mouths before disappearing in the blink of an eye. Off to hell, I hope.

One ghost down I guess. I wonder what other bodies are buried in my backyard. I have the horrible feeling this is just the first of many. I just pray mine doesn't get added to the ever growing list of headstones in the family plot.

CHAPTER SEVENTEEN

If I wasn't the talk of the town already I sure will be now. As a person does when they find a dead body, Owen called the Sheriff's Department, who then brought in the state police crime scene investigators and even the county coroner. My backyard resembles a marina with all the boats and vans parked in the clearing. If Cotton's still around he's probably relishing all the attention. I'm not. At Owen's insistence I stay inside the house, out of everyone's way. This is his wheelhouse, I bow to his experience. About an hour after the horde arrived, Sheriff Hogan with his beer belly and shock of gray hair, walks in with Owen trailing behind, both asking for coffee. I pour us each a mug.

"How's it going out there?" I ask as I add the milk.

"They just started, ma'am," says the Sheriff. "We'll probably be working until tonight, if not tomorrow."

"That's fine. If I can help in any way…" I hand him the mug.

"Thank you. And actually, I do have a few questions for you. Just routine."

I glance at Owen as I hand him his cup. He nods in approval. "Of course," I say. "I just don't know what I can tell you that would help."

The Sheriff sits at the table and Owen and I sit across from him. "Well, the big question is, what were you doing out there today?"

Owen and I already synced our story since the truth would make me sound crazy. "A vision presented to me by a ghost" is far less believable than, "It was Owen's idea. I'd been meaning to survey the entire property since I arrived, but I was too afraid to do it alone. When we went out, Owen noticed the remnants of the dock and that the grass was shorter, so we decided to explore.

When we did, we found the path that led us to…that area," I say with distaste. "I saw the body, and we came right back here to call you. Owen did check the body for ID, but beyond that we didn't disturb that much. Is it Cotton? Really?"

"No reason to think otherwise, not yet anyway. Height matches. Watch too. Same brand as mentioned in the case file. I reviewed it before we left the station. We'll know for sure when we compare the dental records."

"Any idea how he died? Or when?" I ask.

"It's early yet, but it looks like his neck was broke with great force. The cervical vertebrae was obviously damaged, but it's still just a best guess. It'll be weeks before we know for sure. If ever. As for when, the driver's license on the body expired in 1979 so before then."

"Could it have been the night he disappeared?" I ask.

"Can't say for sure, but it is possible." He sips his coffee. "I was there that night, you know. Been on the job for all of a month but even to this day, I remember it. Your grandmamma and Miss Hallie, they were busted up something bad, but your uncle…*that* was brutal. And I hope you won't mind me saying, but if that is Cotton Fontaine out in that swamp, and someone did snap his neck, they did this world a damn service. Still won't stop me from doing my utmost to find out what happened to him. And if the killer is still around, I will bring him to justice, ma'am."

"I'm sure you will, Sheriff," I say.

"Sheriff Hogan?" a man calls from the back porch before stepping inside the kitchen. "Channel 3 just arrived. Bet they're all on their way."

"Shit," the Sheriff says before balking. "Sorry, ma'am."

"She's heard worse," Owen assures him.

The Sheriff rises from the table. "If you don't mind we're gonna block off the driveway. Otherwise they'll swarm the place. And you best stay indoors and screen your calls from now on."

"Okay."

"Thank you for the coffee, ma'am," the Sheriff says before hustling out with his deputy in tow.

As if on cue, the telephone begins ringing. "Miss Fontaine, this is Penny Driscoll from Channel 5 news," a peppy voice says over the machine.

I shake my head. "What a nightmare."

Owen touches my hand. "Maybe we should go to a hotel for a day or two," he suggests. "Or take a trip to the coast. Just get away from all this craziness."

"Maybe. I could use a day or two away from ghosts, demons, dead bodies, and this house…" I glance around the kitchen. "I thought coming here would simplify my life. I'd arrive here and gain clarity. Find some peace. Now I have ghosts ripping my soul from my body, a demon prowling around, and a dead body to explain. And every question I answer just leads to a million new questions."

"Then for fuck's sake Jane, let's just *go*. Let's get the hell out of here and never look back. We'll hire a realtor from L.A., sell this mausoleum, and be done with it."

"Owen…" I say sadly, retracting my hand from his.

"I'm not…I'm not suggesting you and I…" He shakes his head. "If we're over, fine. I won't…I'll come to live with it. In time. But right now all I care about is keeping you safe and healthy. This place, this whole situation, it isn't good for you. Hell, it wouldn't be good for anyone. I've been here less than a damn day and *I* feel like I'm losing my mind."

"So you're starting to believe me?"

"I'm starting to believe…some things should be left in the past. That the future is what matters." He stares into my eyes, his own boring into mine like a drill. "And I believe the longer you stay here, the bleaker that future becomes. I *feel* it Jane, like God himself whispered the words to me. I haven't been this sure of anything since I first saw you at that wedding. I just *know*. Please, baby, *please*, we need to *go*. *Now*."

Jesus, I don't think I've ever seen him this frightened, this stalwart in his belief. It sends a chill down my spine. Maybe he's right. Maybe I should get away. Gain some perspective. Maybe—

"Mrs. Harrow?" a man calls from the doorway. Both Owen and I turn his way. "Your lawyer's at the perimeter. Does he have approval to come in?"

Bram. Oh God, I completely forgot to call him back. He must be out of his mind with worry. Lord knows what he's heard. "Um, yes."

"Yeah, let him pass," the deputy says into his radio before returning the way he came.

"Excuse me," I say, rising from the table.

"We're not done here, Jane," Owen calls as I walk away.

I don't turn back. I hear his footsteps following behind me but keep walking all the way outside. Bram's SUV pulls alongside a police cruiser just as I step onto the front porch. It hasn't even been twenty-four hours since I last saw him, but the moment I lay eyes on his gorgeous, concerned face, it suddenly seems like a decade. For him as well. Worry morphs to sweet yet intense relief. He strides like an Olympic runner toward me, past the cruisers and techs as if they weren't even there. I rush off the porch to meet him halfway. When the man I love scoops me into his arms, all the hell from the past day is forgotten. Unimportant. Nothing matters in this world or the next when I'm in his arms.

"Oh beloved, what am I going to do with you?" he whispers against my cheek before putting those lips to better use. As always his kiss takes my breath away. My lover clutches me tighter, fingers digging into my back hard enough to bruise. I'm actually grateful for the pain. It anchors me. It keeps me aware of the many sets of eyes upon us, including my husband's. I pull away first but Bram won't fully release me, just my lips. "Are you okay? I was so worried. You found a dead body? I-I-I-I heard a rumor you were in the hospital?"

"It was nothing. I'm fine."

His arms drop and he even takes a step back to study me, expression a mix of anger and fright. "You mean you *were* in the hospital? Wh…why…" His gaze whips up to Owen, who watches impassively from the porch. "What the hell did you do to her, you bastard?"

"Excuse me?" Owen snaps, folding his arms across his broad chest.

"You heard me, asshole," Bram responds. He takes a step toward Owen.

"Bram," I say, grabbing his arm to stop him from going further.

"What are you implying?" my husband says, stepping off the porch.

"Against my better judgment I leave her alone with you, and she ends up secretly in the fucking hospital too frightened to call me back?"

"Bram it wasn't—"

"You better watch the next words that come out of your mouth, motherfucker," Owen warns through gritted teeth.

Bram moves toward the fuming Owen who echoes the motion. Two bulls about to charge. "I know your type. She told me all about you. The lying. The cheating. The neglect. What, did you just decide to graduate to wife beater too?"

"Bram!" I shout. "Stop th—"

My lover gets right in my husband's face so close they could kiss. "You just can't stand the fact she's out from under the crush of your thumb," Bram continues. "It's killing you, *killing* you that she's finally found someone who can satisfy her like you can't. That makes her wet with just a touch."

"Bram!" I shout again, pulling at his arm.

"Who can give her something more than a belly full of dead babies. You—"

Owen punches the rest of the insult from Bram's mouth. I shriek as he collapses on the driveway. "Bram!" I drop beside him as the two police officers, who felt the violence in the air as well, swarm Owen whose fist is still cocked. Each grab an arm to hold him back, but Owen holds up his hands in surrender. Bram pants beside me, wiping the blood from his split lip. "Are you okay?"

He ignores me, instead focusing on the once again impassive Owen. "I want this man arrested for assault and battery! Right now!"

"No!" I say. "Bram, no." He finally looks at me as I help him to his feet. I glance at the officers, one of whom actually has his handcuffs out. "Just-Just wait a second, okay? Please? That's not necessary."

"The hell it—"

"Please, wait. Please." I drag Bram away as the officer begins reading Owen his rights. "Don't do this. Please. For me. Don't let them arrest him."

"He hit me."

"Not without provocation," I counter. "What you were saying was disgusting and completely unwarranted. I felt like punching you myself."

"He's dangero—"

"He could lose his job. If you do this...I don't think I could ever forgive you. Ever. Please, Bram. *Please*."

He stares into my eyes for a few seconds, his own icy orbs melting a little. Oh, thank God. Bram caresses my cheek. "I just can't seem to say no to you ever, can I?"

I cup his hand with mine before kissing his palm. "Thank you."

"But he has to go. I don't want him around you. Around *us* anymore."

"Fine. *Fine*. Just don't let them arrest him."

He nods and kisses my palm again, giving it a playful nibble before moving toward the squad car they're maneuvering Owen toward. This is a nightmare. As if this day couldn't get any worse. I'm done. *Done*. Once we get this fresh hell sorted, I'm going to bed for at least two days and not leaving for anything.

As Bram talks to the officers, Owen glances from my lover to me, brow furrowed and doing a terrible job of hiding his scorn. I'm not sure which of us he's angrier at, me for causing this or him for falling into Bram's trap. It takes a full minute, but whatever Bram says works. Owen, though snarling a little, begrudgingly nods. I breathe a literal sigh of relief the cuffs come off and Bram pats one of the officer's shoulders with his best smile affixed. Thank God. But the police escort Owen back inside the house as Bram hustles back to me. "What's happening?" I ask.

"He's getting his suitcase, then he's gone. I told him if he sets foot on this property again I'd call the police and press charges. I'm well within my rights."

"I know. Thank you."

"Like I said," he says, taking me into his arms once more, "I just can't say no to you." He pecks the end of my nose. "You look exhausted. Are you okay?"

"I'm fine."

"Then why the hell were you in the hospital? And what the hell were you doing in the swamp looking for dead bodies?" I give him the short version—Hallie, demon, hospital, swamp—and he just shakes his head and sighs the entire time. "I knew I shouldn't have left last night. I—"

The front door slams shut and Owen, still under guard, steps outside with his suitcase in hand. Bram moves beside me, snaking his arm around my waist as Owen approaches. My husband doesn't take his eyes off me, as if Bram wasn't there at all. "I'll be at the Crimson Vale Motel if you need me."

"Just go back to L.A.," Bram begins. "There's—"

"I will be there as long as you need me," Owen says to me. "I meant what I said. I'm not leaving until I know you're okay. Think about what we talked about earlier. *Really* think about it. Deep down you know I'm right." He finally glares at Bram. "And I'm onto you, pretty boy. You don't fool me for a goddamn minute. You hurt one hair on her head, and I'll take yours. That is a promise."

"Come on," one of the officers says to Owen.

With one final snarl at Bram, Owen tromps to his rental car. My stomach actually lurches when his door shuts. Oh, God. This is horrible. He doesn't deserve this. Once again I've hurt him without meaning it. I *am* poison. "Owen, I'm sorry!" I call as he starts the car.

Bram holds onto me as I attempt to take a step after my husband. "Jane, don't. Let him go. Just let him go."

I've tried. I've tried in L.A., twice here, but I just…can't seem to get it right. Or perhaps I don't want to. Because maybe deep down I *do* know he's right. But I also meant what I said last night. And today just proves it. He's a lot better off without me. I hope he just keeps driving all the way to L.A. the same way I walk into my house beside the man I love. Without looking back.

*

Ghosts, dead bodies, now I'm becoming a darn vampire staying up all night and sleeping through the day. Owen must have taken all my energy with him because the moment I shut the front door, it felt as if I were weighed down by a boulder. I barely had the strength to climb the stairs and plop into bed. I didn't push Bram away as he joined me, or as he wrapped his arms around me. I fell asleep a minute later.

He's gone when I wake. And it seems he's taken the sun with him. How long was I out? I check the clock but it's vanished as well. I sit up and stretch before calling, "Bram?" No answer. In fact there's no noise whatsoever. No crickets, no creaking in the house, it's as if I'm in deep space. In a void. I throw off the covers and get out of bed. "Bram?" Where is he? I pad barefoot out of the bedroom into the hall. The void extends here, as if the air, the earth itself is at a standstill, and dark like black ink save for the glow peeking from under the guest bathroom door. "Bram?"

I open the door, but instead of my lover I find three little girls splashing in the bathtub as the teenage girl from the demonic ritual, now dressed in a liveried maid's black and white uniform, sits on the toilet, watching the girls with a smile. The African-

American girl splashes the other two. The eldest can't be more than seven with the others only a few years younger. I'd still know them anywhere.

"Hallie, baby," the maid chides, "don't splash like that." The eldest girl splashes back. "Helen!"

Little Hallie slowly turns my way, her smile dropping when her gaze reaches the door where I stand. "Mama…it's here again," she whispers.

The other three immediately glance my way. Aunt Helen takes Felicia's hand to comfort the now whimpering youngest. The maid rises from her perch, and without an ounce of fear, faces me. "Leave. *Now*," she says, voice as stony as her expression.

As if a gust of wind pelts me, I'm knocked back a few steps as the door slams shut. What the…? I step forward again and throw open the door, but they've vanished. Nothing but darkness.

"Be careful with her!"

I spin toward the stairs, toward the new interlopers. As if a spotlight were following them, a man and woman, each carrying a baby, walk into the hallway. Even if he didn't look exactly as he did when I saw his ghost in the woods and driveway, I would recognize my grandfather anywhere. He even sports those Buddy Holly glasses. The smiley, bubbly blonde a step behind must be Felicia then. She's no more than eighteen now with the bloom of youth and happiness radiating from her every pore.

"I'm being careful, I promise," Daniel says.

They move right past me before disappearing into the first guest room. I follow. Hallie, still a teenager and almost the exact replica of her mother save for the Fontaine chin, bounces up and down with excitement before Felicia hands the baby to her. "Here's your Godson," says Felicia.

"Oh, he's so gorgeous," Hallie coos.

"No, my son is manly and strong," Daniel corrects. "*She's* gorgeous." He presents his bundle of joy to her aunt. "Juliette."

"And Jerome," Felicia adds. "After Danny's grandfather."

"Fine names," Hallie says. She kisses Jerome's forehead then smiles at the proud parents. "Y'all look exhausted. When'd you last sleep and eat?"

"They're how many days old?" Daniel chuckles.

"Well, y'all are home now and Miss Hallie's here." She sets my uncle inside the blue crib. "Come on, let's get y'all something to eat."

"No, I don't wanna—" Felicia whines.

"They'll be fine for a minute or two," Hallie chides.

Daniel puts my mother in her pink crib. "Are you sure?"

"Cotton ain't gonna be home until tonight," Hallie says. "Seriously, come on. You're no good to them at half-mast."

"She's right, sugarplum," Daniel says, taking his wife's hand. "And we both could use a bath too. Come on."

He leads my reluctant grandmother away from her cooing babies with Hallie close behind. I wait a few seconds before emerging from my corner and walking to the cribs. Oh my word, they are so beautiful. Even at two days old they both have a crop of golden, curly hair. My uncle stares up right into my eyes, cooing and reaching up for me. There's such intelligence behind those baby blues. An old soul as Melissa would call it. Oh, I just want to kiss his tiny nose. "Hello," I whisper. He coos again and even smiles. I think he likes me.

My mother isn't as receptive as her twin. Her eyes jut everywhere, resting only a second on me before moving on. Even now she wants nothing to do with me. "Hi, Mama," I whisper. "I don't know if you can see or hear me, but…I'm your daughter. Jane." She scrunches up that tiny face and whimpers. "Oh, don't—" My mother lets out a louder whimper before wailing. Why am I not surprised? "Sorry," I say, backing away. "Sorry, Mama."

I barely make it three steps before Hallie rushes in again. She stops for a moment to stare at me, gasping even, then quickens her pace to the cribs. "Get out of here. You keep away from them."

"I—"

She holds up her hand and shouts, "*Sortez!*"

In a literal blink I'm back in the pitch black hallway. What…? The sound of bare feet hurrying across hardwood floor cuts through the void. By the time I glance in that direction, a door opens and a figure dashes across the hallway. There's a light knock before another door opens. Jerome's door. As the person opens the door, the dim light from inside his room reveals my mother's beautiful face. She can't be more than fourteen but looks just as I remember her. If she is fourteen, in eight years she'll be dead. Right now, seeing this girl so young with bouncing blonde curls and flowery pink nightgown that fact's unfathomable. "Romy?" she whispers before stepping into the room with me behind her. His room is exactly as it is now right down to the blue plaid comforter my uncle lies under. He sets his book on the nightstand as Mama tip-toes across the room.

"What is it? What's the matter?" my uncle whispers.

"I felt it. I think it was watching me again," my mother whispers back. "Romy, it was right by my damn bed."

"Did you banish it like Hallie does?"

"Yeah, and I think it worked but…can I? Please?"

Jerome sighs but throws the covers off enough for my mother to climb into bed, which she does with a huge grin on her face. They bundle up under the sheets before my mother nestles against her brother's side. "Better?" he asks, putting a protective arm around her.

"Yes. Thanks. I just hate that thing. You *know* it's always around, even when we can't see or feel it. It's *there*. I'd bet it's here right now. Watching us."

"I don't know why you can't just ignore it like we all do. You're just feeding it otherwise."

"I know, I know," she says with a pout. "But it was right next to me. As close as I am to you now. Closer. Romy, it was…I think it was in my brain."

"What?"

"I was dreaming I was playing the piano in Carnegie Hall. 'Moonlight Sonata.'"

"My favorite," Romy says.

"The crowd roared as the spotlight fell on me and only me. But *he* was there, black as a thousand midnights, beside me on the bench playing too. He kept up with me the whole time. It was so intense, like we were dancing toward the edge of a fiery volcano and I was so enraptured I didn't care if I fell in. His…excitement, his loneliness, his passion swirled around me. Intoxicating me. I wanted it to. I reveled in it. It was beautiful. Terrifying. It…spurned me to put every inch of my everything into the only release possible at that moment: the music. And when the song ended, when we reached that last, final crescendo, that climax, when that passion had nowhere else to go, I couldn't help myself. When the final note rang out, I kissed him. I grabbed the back of his neck and pulled his lips to mine, forced myself inside his mouth. But he tasted of ash. Fire. Sulphur and…death. But I didn't care. I didn't mind one whit because inside every particle of that creature there was so much *need*. Like if we didn't kiss we'd both die, and only this, only *I* could save him. But kissing wasn't enough. He began to lay me down on the bench. That's when I woke myself up. But he was still there. The need was still there. That's when I came here before he…before I…couldn't."

"Damn. All that happens in my dreams is I forget to take an Algebra test. How come you get the sexy ones?"

"It wasn't sexy," Mama insists. "It was…dirty."

"Tomato, to-mato," Jerome quips.

"No, *I* feel dirty. Like he took advantage of me."

"Kind of sounds like it was the other way around." She pinches his arm. "Hey!"

"This is serious," Mama says. "He's never been in my dreams before. I-I think he's getting stronger. I mean, we keep seeing him more and more. He's even followed us to school. Janet saw him there too. And he's around you a lot more than me."

"And *I'm* not scared," Jerome assures her. He pecks her forehead. "You know I'll never let anything hurt you. Not man, not beast, certainly not a ghost."

She stares up at her brother, large blue eyes radiating such love and respect for this boy, her protector. And he is just a boy, one who believes every word he utters. As does she. My mother leans up and pecks his lips. "I love you."

He hugs her tighter. Almost as tight as she does him. "I love you too, sissy. Now, let's go to sleep. And no more rounding first with the dead." He pauses. "Or the living."

"I'll join the nunnery tomorrow. I promise."

Jerome chuckles. "Good night, Jules."

My mother flicks off the light, plunging us into darkness again. "Good night, love." He begins humming "Somewhere Over the Rainbow." Once again I find myself in the hallway staring at a closed door. I hope they're still in there, happily wrapped in each other's arms, protected against all the ills of the world. Thank God she had him. Thank God he had her. I just wish He'd given them more time. Who knows what our lives would have been like had he been around. I—

A little girl's giggle rings through the void. I spin sideways down the hall toward the master bedroom. Light. Another burst of laughter echoes around me again. Door number four it is. But when I step inside the room there's no child. No laughter. Only a forty-something Felicia sitting by her young comatose son's bedside reading a book as a machine pumps paste down his throat through a tube. A living corpse. It's unthinkable that the boy I just left, so full of love and light, is the zombie I see before me. Waxy, gray skin that hasn't been touched by the sun in years. Greasy hair a dull tangle of curls. Limbs nothing but sticks. The only sign of life is the beep of the heart monitor. Steady as a surgeon's hand. His mother's not in a better state by any means. Felicia stares at her book but doesn't read it. She's oblivious to everything but her own thoughts. She certainly doesn't seem to care about how disturbing the room itself is. Even without my uncle, the strange symbols I now recognize from Hallie's workshop and island to be voodoo icons mixed with crosses, covering almost every inch of the walls and ceiling.

The girl laughs again, louder than before. In the next room. Felicia doesn't look up from her book, not even when my mother walks through the room toward that bathroom. This is the mother I remember. Lank blonde hair, pasty pallor, vacant expression, skeletal frame. I even recall that lavender dress with pink roses as washed out as she is. The living dead girl. And she is but a girl who shuffles through the room, head cowed without taking her eyes off the floor. As she passes, Jerome twitches, the monitor beeping out of sync the entire time she's in the room. Felicia jolts from her stupor, but I don't linger here. I follow my mother into the bathroom.

But it isn't the master bathroom. Jesus. I'd know this room anywhere. The Cherokee rose wallpaper. The blue sink and toilet. I got my first period in this room. I prepared for my senior prom. And I...

Dear God.

As I move further inside, from the bubbles inside the tub pops the source of the giggling. Me. Little four-year-old me with snow white tresses plastered to her cherubic face. *My* cherubic face. My mother sits across from me on the blue toilet and slumps as if the weight of her own body is too great a burden. Her half hooded eyes are trained my way but like Felicia I don't think she notices I'm there. I start arranging the bubbles into a crown on my head and still nothing. "Mama! Mama look! I'm a princess!"

My mother doesn't even blink. I don't seem to mind. Too many bubbles to play with. I continue building my castle for a few seconds and even humming "Somewhere Over the Rainbow" as I begin the turret. Suddenly Mama comes to life, her greasy head rising to the girl's level as her face contorts into something out of a nightmare, equal parts fear, revulsion, and hate. Such powerful hate it prickles my non-existent skin. The four-year-old me just continues in her own happy world, humming then singing that hopeful tune as a foot away our mother begins breathing heavily and trembling. "Shut up," Mama gasps in a whisper. The girl continues her solo.

"Shut up!" my mother shrieks, leaping off the toilet.

"Mama?" the girl asks, finally looking over at the madwoman.

"*Shut up!*"

Like a wild cat pouncing on a mouse, my mother falls upon the child, forcing her under the water by the shoulders. "Shut up! Shut up! Shut up!" she screams as my limbs flail and break the surface in the tub, water and bubbles splashing everywhere. "I hate you! Demon! Devil! Abomination! I hate you, I hate you, I hate you! Die! Just die!"

Those tiny limbs slow their fight.

Oh God. Oh God. Oh God…

I lunge at the madwoman, grabbing her arms. "Stop it! Stop!"

The moment I touch my mother, her manic gaze whips up, square to my eyes. If possible she plummets deeper into madness, eyes and mouth stretching to their limits as she silently screams in fear. Intense, soul ripping terror. "No! No, no, no, no, no…" she gasps before shrieking, "NO!" My mother leaps up, then backs into the sink as far from me as possible before dashing out of the bathroom. What the…?

The four-year-old me's coughs and sobs snap me back to this odd reality. She's, I mean I'm fine. Aunt Helen's on her way to calm me down and try to kiss it all away. I leave the traumatized child and follow my psychotic mother out of the bathroom. But I don't enter my old farmhouse hallway, instead I'm back in the Fontaine master bedroom. Felicia and Hallie struggle to keep Uncle Jerome in his bed as he flails much as I just did in the tub. A fight for life.

"We need to overdose him! Now!" Hallie shouts.

Mama just continues running out the door, crying, "Not again, not again…"

Without hesitation I shadow her out, leaving the others to their own battle. Mama's just through my current bedroom door when I reach the hallway. When I enter the bedroom, we're back in the Missouri house with its brown wallpaper and large windows. Mama's old room. Mama's old room where she stands in the corner holding a mirrored looking glass trembling as if having a seizure. The moment I step into the room she smashes the mirror against the wall, shards cracking all over the hardwood floor.

"No," I say, holding up my hands to show I mean no harm.

"Not again. Never again," she gasps. "*Never*."

And with one graceful movement, she removes the largest shard of the looking glass and draws it across her pale neck from ear to ear, flesh tearing in twain like the raw meat it is. A burst of blood spurts from the wound before she's even done with the mutilation. Blood pours down her neck from that unnatural smile she created all over her dress and the floor.

"Mama!"

She collapses in her own pool of blood before I can reach her, falling to my knees beside her. "Mama? Mama!" As the life literally drains from her body, she stares up at me. I try to press my hands to the wound but it does nothing. *I* can do nothing.

"You…" she says so quietly I may have imagined it.

"Mama, it's okay," I cry.

"You…" She looks right into my eyes. "Need to die. Die, Jane. *Die*." And she does the very thing she just commanded.

"Jane?" a man calls from the ether.

I simply stare at my mother, the pitiful creature who gave me life then tried to take it back. Madness.

"Jane?" the man calls again.

Madness everywhere. My legacy.

"Jane! Wake up! Now!"

I glance back just as Bram touches my shoulder. The moment he makes contact, I open my eyes. My real eyes. I'm back. My bedroom. Bram stands above me shaking my shoulders just as Mama did. I swat his arms away. "Hey, hey," he says now trying to catch my flailing arms. "It's okay. It's okay." He sits on the bed and pulls me against him into a hug. I cling to him as he pets my hair, each stoke calming me until I can almost breathe normally. "It was just a nightmare. I have you now."

"I-I-I was there," I whisper.

"You were where?"

"Here. There. I-I saw them. My grandparents. My uncle. Mama. I was there. With them. I was *there*. She tried to kill me. She…killed herself. She was so scared. I-I just watched and—"

"Hey. Hey," Bram cuts in as he continues his caresses. "It was just a dream, beloved. Just a dream."

"No, it was real, Bram. It was just like last night. Those things happened, and I was really there. Please believe me. You have to believe me."

He hugs me tighter. "I believe you, Jane." He kisses my temple. "I believe you."

I pull away to search his face to see if he's just placating me, but find sincerity and concern in those blue orbs. "Really?"

"After all we've seen? All we've been through? Of course I do."

"Then what's happening to me?"

Bram tenderly wipes my tears with his thumb. "I don't know, beloved."

"It was-It was like my soul was outside my body. Just like last night. I watched as my mother tried to drown me like I remember, but *I* was *there*. *I* stopped her. She, all of them, thought I was the demon. Wh-why—"

"It's okay," he coos as he pecks my sweaty forehead. "It's all over now. You're back here. With me."

"But what if it doesn't stop? What if it happens again?"

He caresses my wet cheek with his thumb and it sends tingles everywhere. "Then I'll always be here to bring you back to me."

I want to fall into him, have him hug and kiss the fear away, but I hesitate. The moment we stepped into the house after Owen left, I swore he'd have to earn that privilege back. I saw a side to him that disgusted me, and I'm not ready to forgive him.

Yet. "What time is it?" I ask as I move away. I can't think when he's touching me.

"Um, a little after six."

"Really? I slept so long. Are the police gone?"

"Almost. They're wrapping up for the night."

"Any news?"

"Nothing concrete. It'll be days before they have official confirmation on ID or cause of death. They haven't found any more bodies save for a ton of animal bones. They're fairly sure people used to perform voodoo or Satanic rituals out there."

"They did. I saw it. Hallie's great-grandmother raised a demon. It's still around somewhere. Probably watching us. Listening right now," I say, glancing around the room. "I need to get Father King here. If he won't come I'll try a Pastor or Reverend. Maybe *I* need an exorcism. I—"

"You don't need an exorcism," Bram insists. "I had some time on my hands after you kicked me out last night. I read up on hauntings. Every site said if you bring in a priest, it just makes the spirts mad and the activity gets worse. The best thing to do is ignore them. Like I told you before, they feed off your energy. Cut off their supply, they fade away. And we're going to start tonight." He takes my hand and squeezes. "No more ghosts or dead bodies or demons or ex-husbands for the rest of the evening." He brings my hand to his lips to kiss it. "We are going to eat, drink, and be merry."

"'For tomorrow we die,'" I finish, pulling my hand away. I throw the covers off the bed and get out on the opposite side from him. "That's how the quote ends. Isaiah 22:13."

"I try not to dwell on the negative," he says with a grin. It slowly drops the longer he stares at my glaring face. "You're mad at me. I knew it. I knew it! I felt it earlier…" He shakes his head. "You know *I'm* the one who should be pissed, Jane. I spent all last night and all of today stewing in the hell *you* consigned me to. You kicked me out. You chose him over me. You were alone with him all night. You didn't answer any of my calls. Then I hear you're in the hospital? That the police are here?"

"I didn't want to worry you. There was nothing you could do," I counter.

"*I* should have been the one by your side, Jane. Holding your hand. Supporting you. Not *him*," he hisses. "Unless you still love him. You still want him."

"I don't," I say, rounding the bed. "Nothing happened. He was just…here."

"But *I* should have been. You are mine, Jane. Mine to take care of. To protect. To love. Not his. And seeing you defend him, protect him…I lost it. I lost my temper and for that I am sorry. I've just, I've waited decades for you, and now I finally have you…I need you. I need you more than you can fathom. I *cannot* lose you."

"You're not going to lose me," I say, taking his hand.

He draws me in against him. "Then prove it."

"How?" I ask, eyebrow raised.

"Well…" He brushes my hair off my face. "You can put on your sexiest dress and let me take you out to eat…" He kisses my neck. "Drink…" He nibbles my earlobe. "And be merry." His mouth finds mine, kissing, nibbling, probing until I'm putty in his arms. God, this man doesn't just turn me on, he turns me inside out. For once he breaks away first, whispering, "Let me take care of you, Jane. All of you. Mind, body, and soul. I take care of what's mine. And you are mine, right?"

"Forever and always."

A gorgeous grin fills his face. "That's my girl." Those lips are put to better use when he presses them against mine again. Lips made for kissing without question. Made only for mine. Arms made for wrapping around me, making me safe. Tongue, his delicious tongue made to massage mine. We don't need to say another word. Ever. We just need to continue like this. There is no past, there is no future, there is only us. All is forgiven.

The doorbell rings downstairs at the same time my stomach growls like a panther. Bram continues his caresses, oblivious to reality, but for me the moment is officially ruined. I try to pull away but he backs me toward the bed. After the second round of rings a man shouts, "Miz Harrow? Davenport?"

Bram groans in frustration. "Goddamn it."

"Hello?" the interloper calls again.

"Just a minute!" I shout back before looking up at my sneering lover. "Why don't you take care of him, and I'll put on my sexiest dress so we can knock eat off our list? I'm starving."

Bram frowns but says, "Fine. Rain check. But I will collect." He playfully smacks my bottom. "With interest."

"You're on."

After another brilliant smile, Bram saunters out of the room. I plop onto the bed with a sigh. Our first fight. At least it's over and done with. Sort of. Okay, nothing was resolved but the air's been cleared. It's good enough for now. Time to eat, drink, and be merry because if these visions have taught me anything, it's that happiness is darn fleeting and tomorrow is not guaranteed.

For tomorrow, we die.

CHAPTER EIGHTEEN

Oh, I'm drunk. I definitely *definitely* took the "drink" part of the night's festivities too far. Those chocolate martinis were just so delicious. It was all delicious. I've never had crawfish etouffee before, but now I don't think I'll ever order anything else. Delicious food, delicious drink, delicious company, I am blessed. Especially with that last one. His kisses make the food and drink taste like ashes in comparison. I can't even wait until we're inside the house for my fix. I push him up against the car, grab him by the back of the head, and pull his lips to mine. Then again when we reach the porch, his back against the wall this time. "Here," I whisper between the kisses. "Have me right here. On the porch. Screw me against this pillar as the alligators watch."

Bram chuckles. "I've created a monster."

I playfully bite his lip. "And I'm going to eat you up."

"Just not out here. There could be reporters and cops skulking around. Our reputations are already in tatters. We shouldn't add fuel to the fire. We do have to live here."

He's right. If how people treated at the restaurant is any indication we're up there with the Borgias in terms of infamy. The other patrons, even the wait staff, wouldn't stop staring. Some even pointed at us as they whispered to their companions. So much for improving the Fontaine name. Adultery, murder, Satanic worship, and I've only been here a few weeks. Hence the alcohol. One martini, they were mere annoyance. Two, they were almost forgotten. Three, I was ready to make out with Bram right on top of our tiramisu. Bram only imbibed two martinis, so he had the wherewithal to laugh at my suggestion that we give them a show. He didn't seem to mind my toes playing with bulge under the table though.

"Then we should never, ever leave this house ever again," I say. "We'll close all the curtains, bar all the doors, rip out the phones, and never see another soul again."

"As you wish, beloved." He wraps his arms around my thighs and lifts me over his shoulder while I giggle. I yelp when he nips my butt with his teeth.

As he unlocks the door, my giggles continue. We move inside, and he hustles to the living room. After turning on a light, he flings me on the couch. The giggles become full laughs. We are going to have *so* much sex tonight. I'm wet already, and we haven't even begun. How does he do that? It's downright mystical.

As I toss my purse onto the floor, he bends down to kiss me, and I wrap my legs around his waist to pull him on top of me. He's as ready for me as I am him. His bulge thrusts against the thin cotton of my panties and even that's enough for me to lose myself. I grind against him, lost in the delicious sensations of pure pleasure. But only for a few seconds. "Wait, wait," Bram whispers as he extracts himself from my grip to stand.

"No," I whimper.

"Not yet. Hold on."

Not even my pout stops him from hustling out of the room. What the heck? Do I smell or something? I sniff myself. No. What—

Music begins playing, something bluesy, on the record player. Oh. I've never really listened to the blues before. It's so mournful. It does nothing to spoil the mood though. Quite the opposite. I settle into the couch as the mournful notes waft through the air. Sex and death, what an odd pairing. Owen and I had amazing sex after Uncle Robbie's funeral. I think we made our first baby that night. He would be ten by now. I wish I'd gotten to meet you, baby. Even though you never really existed, I still love you. All your brothers and sisters too. I love you all.

Bram returns a few seconds later with a baggie and lighter in his hands. "Thought there might be some left."

"What is that?" I ask, sitting up a little.

"Felicia and I partook some evenings."

"Is that… pot?"

"You ever tried it?" Bram asks, sitting beside me on the hardwood floor.

"My husband's a DEA agent," I remind him.

"*Ex*-husband," Bram insists. He opens the baggie with a whole joint inside. "So I'll take that as a no." He lights the cigarettes and inhales. "Oh, that's good." He hands it to me. "Go on. You'll love it."

I just stare at the smoking thing. "It's illegal."

"Some rules are meant to be broken, beloved," he says. "Come on. Can't be an angel all the time."

Okay, I know if I weren't three sheets already I wouldn't dare. Good thing I am. Before I lose my nerve, I take the joint and inhale. Ugh. The burning begins immediately, and a second later I'm hacking my lungs out as Bram chuckles. He takes another toke before shoving it my way again. Despite the pain I take another hit with the same result. Bram chuckles. "Oh, I do so love corrupting you."

With the world a second behind my consciousness, I realize he's hovering above me on the sofa after it happens. He kisses me, deeply, before pulling away again. Why does he—

Bram grips my dress and rips it apart, buttons popping like popcorn all over the floor. This act is so ridiculous I guffaw like a mad woman. Darn it, I loved this dress. He kisses my neck as the laughs continue. Then downwards to my sternum just above the center of my bra. With another show of force, that rips apart as well, freeing the Harrow two from their prison. Bram stares down at my bare breasts, my nipples erect just from his gaze. He runs his fingers over the tender, baby soft flesh of the right one. I almost come from that one fingertip.

"Jesus Christ, you're fucking beautiful," he whispers huskily. As if it were a fragile, rare jewel, his hand weighs my right breast in his palm. "You know that, right? How goddamn beautiful, how miraculous you are to me?" His thumb runs over the sensitive nipple before suckling it with his warm mouth. My eyes roll back from sheer nirvana. Those lips, that flicking tongue, the suction, all of it pushes me closer to the edge. I barely notice as he lifts up my skirt to pull down my panties. The moment that thumb touches my engorged clitoris in time to his greedy suckles, I whimper. When two fingers press inside my hungry center, expertly stroking the other pleasure center, I darn near lose my mind. This man is Stradivarius and my body is his violin. Every strike is as glorious as a symphony.

The suckling stops but not the fingers. "Your breasts should be worshiped for their perfection."

Those words are so ridiculous I can't help but laugh. "You should have seen them ten years ago."

This must've been the wrong thing to say because lust morphs into anger in those blue eyes, moments ago so adoring. "I hate him," Bram says with utter certainty.

"Who?"

"Your husband."

"Why?"

"Because…" Bram kisses my neglected left nipple. "He did this first."

"What?"

He rolls the right bud in his mouth before gently biting it. My body buckles in pleasure. I barely comprehend as he says, "This." That wet tongue trails down my breast to my belly button. "Kissed you." His hands grope my breasts, fingers pinching and caressing my aching nipples. Those jangling nerves moving closer and closer to the precipice of pleasure. "Touched you." He stops doing that very thing only to move my skirt over my hips as the other hand plays with my throbbing clitoris. Flicking it. Rolling it. Sucking it. Pinching it. My body presses harder into those deft fingers in a bid for deliverance. "Parted you. Invaded you when you were mine. Always mine." His mouth finally replaces that finger. His tongue toys with me before his teeth gently squeeze in reverse time to his fingers on my breast. Pain above, pleasure below. Pleasure below, pain above. Dr. Jekyll and Mr. Hyde both torturing me to utter madness. So sweet. Divine. I'm so close now. Every cell is on the edge of glory. My body bucks to match him stroke for stroke. "So much time stolen from me," he whispers against my pulsating clitoris. Even his hot breath elicits primal need. "I hate him. I hate them all for stealing you away from me."

When I thrust my mound against his mouth, he finally ceases this mad talk to suckle me again. His tongue moves clockwise, then counter before once again plunging his free fingers into me, the other hand still pinching and caressing my nipple. My hips thrust and roll to meet those instruments of bliss. Oh, I'm close.

Fingers still continuing their assault above and below, his mouth moves further down, tongue flicking my perineum. That sensation is a shock, though not an unpleasant one. He does it again, garnering the same response, me pressing against his tongue. Like my clitoris before, like my nipples now, his teeth apply pressure. The feeling is so foreign I can't help but cry out and arch my back to draw him in closer. All the encouragement he needs. As I arch, that mouth finds my anus, circling its tender flesh clockwise until I realize what he's doing and where. I drop my bottom to the couch in surprise.

"What…?" I ask.

Bram gazes up from between my legs. "What? *He* never did that before?"

"No!"

His thumb moves back to that taboo flesh, rimming it as his tongue just had, reaping the same jangle of foreignness. "He never…" That same thumb slowly slides an inch into the tight space. It hurts, burns, but only for a moment before my body squeezes the invader between its folds as he toys with my G-spot, only a thin muscle between both points. It hurts but it hurts so good. The thumb retreats first and a second later his mouth returns to my clitoris. Teeth, tongue, tickle inside me. Teeth, tongue, tickle until tears stream from the corners of my eyes. Until all I can do is pant. Teeth, tongue, tickle until there is nothing but him and the agony rimmed rapture. His fingers leave me only to change places with his tongue. As those wet fingers pinch and roll that aching mound, he kisses the folds of my opening. He nips my labia. Kisses the same spot. Nips again before conquering the rest, licking me like a lollipop. I grab the back of his head to bring him in closer. Deeper. Close. I'm so close. It builds, and builds with each of my thrusts, with each of his pinches. I can barely breathe, but I can groan and whimper so loud it overshadows the mournful blues. My fingernails dig into his scalp, possibly drawing blood, but I don't care. Building…building…almost…almost… "Oh, God," I cry out, "Oh G—"

He's gone.

Just as I'm about to climax, everything vanishes. That tongue, those fingers, they all depart, leaving me desolate. In hell. I open my eyes to find his face still between my sweaty legs, a mere inch from my aggrieved sex, but staring up at me with hard, determined eyes. I release his hair. "What? Why'd you stop?" I pant.

"Tonight's not for you, beloved. You have been a selfish, naughty girl, Jane, and it's up to me to punish you. To torture you. I'm going to fuck you into submission until you beg me to do it all over again. All. Night. Long. Because tonight…your body belongs to *me*." He lightly brushes a fingertip across my inner thigh before digging that nail in hard enough to bruise. "And the things I'm gonna do to it."

He's so darn resolute when he says that, I can't help but laugh. He can't be serious. But my laughs slowly abate when he doesn't join in. Any lingering bliss melts away when I catch his menacing eyes. "Bram…"

His tongue flicks over my clitoris again, pleasure momentarily returning, but he only does it once. Torture. And apparently it's just begun. "You are not to move. You are not to cover yourself. You are not to touch yourself to bring your body relief. If you disobey me…" His mouth moves to that same spot but instead of a soft tongue, hard teeth pinch that extremely sensitive spot, definitely more pain than pleasure that time. I flinch. Bram peers across me again. "Will you be my good girl tonight?"

"Yes," I whisper.

With a sly grin, he kisses my inner thigh before pushing himself up to stand over me. "I'll be back."

Without another glance my way, he walks out of the room toward the foyer. Gone. For once I'm glad to see him go. I sigh. Is this role playing? Is he trying to get me into S&M? Tie me up? I think whips are involved in some capacity. And spanking. If childhood was any indication I'm not a fan of that last one. Well, if that's what he wants I need more to drink. Oh, but I'm not allowed to move.

The joint still smokes in the ashtray beside my purse on the floor. In for a penny, in for a pound as Aunt Helen used to say. I reach down and retrieve the cigarette, inhaling several puffs and doing my best not to cough. Don't want Bram to know I've technically moved. Oh, why do people enjoy smoking this? My throat burns, but at least I relax a bit more. A few more tokes and I stop caring my breasts and lower half are on display. Okay, maybe I do understand why people—

As I flick ash into the receptacle, my purse buzzes. I know who it is. The same person as the dozen times before. Oh, Owen. He must be so worried. Just twenty-four hours ago he was rushing me to the hospital. All that's happened since then...I've put the man through the ringer. He deserves a text back at the very least.

I sit up to make sure Bram isn't coming before I snatch up my purse and the phone inside. Yep, Owen. He's sent a text every hour. The last one just reads, "*Please.*"

I respond: "*Fine. Really. Plz stop worrying.*"

With my thinking a second behind reality, I don't realize Bram's returned until I gaze up. Fudge. He's caught me red handed and doesn't hide his displeasure. "I, uh…" Excuse, excuse. "Off. Turning it off. I was doing…that."

"Of course you were," he responds, words tinged with anger.

Crud. Head bowed, I return my phone to my purse. "Sorry."

"And how is your husband?" he asks, tone growing colder. Darker.

I have to fix this. I gaze up at my furious lover, plastering on a ravishing smirk before slowly standing. "Not here," I reply duskily as I caress the slope of my still exposed breast. Slowly and seductively, making sure to sway my hips, I pad toward Bram. His scowl remains even as I reach him in the foyer doorframe. "If I wanted *him*…" I unbutton his pants. I meet Bram's eyes, still far more hard than I'd like. "If I wanted *him*…" I unzip his fly and reach inside his boxers, gripping his manhood. I trace the head with my thumb. It grows in my hand, expanding and pulsing with heat. "*He'd* be here."

Bram's expression still doesn't change not even as I fall to my knees before him, bringing his trousers and boxers down as well. His penis points straight at me, angry and red. My fault too. I lightly run my index finger along the shaft. The skin's so soft, so velvety over that hard interior. It twitches when I reach the tip already wet for me. It twitches again as I trace the same path with my tongue, ending the march by flicking that small salty slit before going in for the kill. I bring the whole of him into my mouth as deep as I can.

His soft moan is music to my ears. I pull back and gaze up at him through my eyelashes. His head whips down to see why I've released him. If possible, his scowl intensifies. If looks could kill, his would. I smirk before enveloping him again, milking him over and over with my mouth, suckling him with the back of my throat. The next thrust I unleash my teeth, gently scraping them over his skin. He cries out. I stop to roll his tip with my tongue before applying pressure around the foreskin with my teeth. His groan encourages me on further. I bring him in deep again before repeating the maneuver.

"Faster," he groans. I don't obey. I keep the same snail pace, moving a centimeter a second, torturing him. It works. He finally takes control, gripping my head to hold me in place. To use me as he pleases. I barely have time to sheathe my teeth before he thrusts into my mouth. Fucking me. Forcing himself as deep as he can, again and again, hips thrusting into my chin, so deep I fear I may gag. When I actually do, instinct takes over, and I try to pull away. He must notice because he releases his grip to allow me some measure of control, though his hands remain on my head to guide the pace as I gage the depth.

"Fuck me. Fuck me with your sweet mouth. Fuck me, Jane. Fuck me," he whispers. The good girl I am, I comply. Sucking, playing, milking him for every ounce of pleasure my mouth can bring. "His cock isn't this big, is it?" His nails dig into my scalp to increase the pace. He's close. "He can't fuck you half as good as I do, can he?" I bob faster, suck harder. "Fuck me, Jane. Fuck me. Mine. You're mine. Fuck me, beloved. Oh fuck. Oh fu—"

Just as he's about to come, I unleash my teeth. It shocks him enough he releases his grip on me as planned. I fall back, removing my mouth from his aching member. Bram's eyes fly open in shock. I just laugh as I leap to my feet. "Now we're even."

"You—"

I take a step back from the furious man. "I'm a naughty girl, remember?" I giggle. "You want to play?" I pull my dress from my shoulders. "You want to punish me?" I let the fabric fall and stand before him stark naked. "You have to find me first. But I get a thirty second head start. From…now!"

I take off past him into the foyer toward the stairs. He doesn't follow. Good boy.

Naked as a jaybird, I hurry to the second level and quickly open every door. Don't want to make this too easy for him. That task done, I tip-toe to my mother's room. The armoire is perfect.

Just as I carefully close its door, I hear the creak of the steps. Guess my time's up.

He's quick. Light suddenly streams through the cracks of the armoire. Either the record player is attached to the same circuit as the light or Bram switches it on himself because music begins playing. ABBA. Not the best mood music, but we'll make do. I've never—

"When I kissed a teacher…" a girl sings along.

I recognize that high, pretty voice. It was shrieking at me earlier tonight, right before a shard of mirror silenced her I thought forever. No. *No.* Oh God, it's happening again. I don't move. I try not to breathe. I'm naked and my mother is out there. Even by recent standards this is terrifying. What do I—

Someone knocks, "Shave and a haircut" on the bedroom door. "Just a sec!" Mama calls. I hear her bare feet pad along the hardwood floor and the door open. "Hey! I was getting worried!" The floor creaks as the other person walks in. She shuts the door. "What happened? Was I right? Was it a car?" No reply. "Are you okay?"

"Dancing Queen" cues up next. She always loathed this song. A few days before she killed herself, we were attending a church picnic, and it came on. She ran up to the Priest and started screaming at him to turn it off. Even after he did she remained hysterical, trembling and gasping for air as everyone watched her go mad. Aunt Helen hugged her until for a full five minutes before she could even breathe normally.

"Wh-what are you doing?" Mama chuckles nervously.

"I can't believe I'm finally touching you," a man whispers.

"Well, stop it," Mama chuckles again. "Seriously, what's the matter with you? Are you high or something? Did he do something to you out there?"

"He freed me, Juliette. I'm finally free," he laughs, sadness and mirth both coloring the words. "I'm finally *here*. With you."

Mama whimpers for a few seconds before she gasps. There's the sound of a hard slap a moment later. "What the hell is the matter with you? What...let me go."

"You are so beautiful, Juliette," the man whispers. "He thought so too. Deep, deep down he wanted you. He'd dream of you as you did him. Sometimes when he touched himself, it'd be your face he saw. It was your hand, this hand playing with him. You tortured him just as you tortured me. As *I* tortured *you*."

"Let me go."

"I watched you those nights, you know. I was right there with you, watching as you brought your body pleasure in that very bed. Writhing and moaning like a cat in heat. But you knew that, didn't you?"

"What...?"

"You wanted me to watch. You wanted me inside you. Caressing you. Licking you. Parting you. Fucking you. The dreams we shared weren't enough. Not for either of us. But I'm here now, beloved. I'm here...for *you*, Juliette."

"Oh God. You-You...where is he? You're not him. Where is he? Oh God. No. *No*," she whimpers in terror. "Let me go. Let me go!"

"So beautiful," he sighs, ignoring her protests.

"I said let me go! You're hurting me!"

"I've waited so long...an eternity..."

"No! No! Let me go! Hel—" Her words become muffled as I think he covers her mouth. Oh God. Oh God.

"It has to be tonight, beloved. I'm sorry. I'm so sorry I have to do this now. Try to enjoy it..."

I can't listen and do nothing. He's hurting her. He's... "Leave her alone!" I shriek as I open the armoire door.

Darkness. Nothing. The moment I step out, they're gone. The music's faded. Empty. Of course they're not here. But it was so real. I could sense her terror, her pain as if she were mere feet from me. Oh God. Mama. I—

Footsteps grow closer in the hallway, and in my agitated, drug addled state I freeze in terror in case the phantom assailant has returned. But it's Bram who steps into the dim moonlight emanating from the open curtains. "Why'd you yell?"

"Oh, God, it was horrible," I whisper as I rush toward him. "It happened again. I heard my mother. Someone was attacking her. I think he was the—"

"Shush," Bram says as he embraces me. "It's okay, Jane."

"I think it was the demon. I think he possessed someone. God, why won't this stop? Why—"

Bram lifts up my chin with his finger, smiling reassuringly before lowering his lips to mine in a sweet kiss that gradually becomes greedier. I allow myself to let him suck the poison out until nothing but the passion remains inside me. His ardor hasn't waned in the last minute one bit. Peeping out from the slit in his boxers, his tip presses into my bare stomach between us. As the kiss grows deeper still, he digs his fingernails into my bottom, squeezing the flesh as if he were trying to rip out chunks. The fog of lust keeps the pain just this side of pleasure. I hold onto him with equal force as his hands, his tongue play. It isn't until I realize he's backing me deeper into the room toward the bed that reality snaps me out of my haze. I break away to whisper, "Not here, okay?" My back collides with the wooden baseboard. "Not—"

One of those hands leave my bottom to grab the back of my head. He yanks my head up so I have no choice but to gaze up at his snarled face. "I told you," he says, voice as hard as the boulder just dropped into my stomach, "your body belongs to me tonight. It's mine. *You're mine.* Say it." His grip tightens. "Say it."

"I'm yours," I say, voice brittle.

The predatory glint in his eyes dissolves away. He releases my hair and slowly caresses my cheek. "That's right," he whispers tenderly. He traces my swollen lips with this thumb as a smile forms on his. "You're my good girl." My lips part as he presses his thumb into my mouth. "You love me, right?" My tongue toys with his thumb in response. Something deep inside cries out this is wrong. Degrading. Disgusting. But nothing matters but quelling that pulse, that swell between my legs. I suckle his thumb in time to that maddening pulse. Bram's grin widens. "Prove it." He takes a step backwards. "Turn around."

My stomach flutters from nerves, from anticipation, from lust, I don't know. I do know I obey.

"Spread your legs." God help me, I do. "Wider." Without hesitation, I move them wider than shoulder length.

"Now bend over the baseboard."

That pulsing, that burning ache needing to be quenched spurns me on. The hard wood presses into my stomach as I submit once more, bracing myself on the mattress with one hand.

I sense him, his heat, as he steps closer. He lifts me up, my cheek now pressed against the mattress, my bare bum stuck in the air as my feet leave the ground. No preamble. No grace. He thrusts inside me, crashing against my cervix with the force of a tidal wave. It hurts. It's glorious. I clench around him as fire expands everywhere he is. As fast as he enters, he retreats, the tip of him momentarily stopping between the folds of my opening. He grips my hips and pulls against them as he pushes, impaling me again, harder this time. Then again. Again. His pelvis collides against my bum with every blow, every one of my spasms. He retreats again, tormenting me. "Say 'Fuck me, Bram,'" he orders as he withdraws.

"Please," I whimper, my damp folds twitching around that torturing tip.

He brushes it around my engorged labia. Hell. This is hell. "I said, say 'Fuck me, Bram." He rims it again and if I weren't already off my feet my legs would give out.

"Fuck me, Bram," I mutter. "Fuck me. *Please*."

Savagely, cruelly, he drives inside me again. Thank God. Thank God. Again. More. Again. I clutch onto the quilt for dear life, my only anchor to the real world amid the sensory overload. He batters me again. Fucks me. He—

Then he stops. He leaves my body. Even his heat vanishes. What—

"I told you," he pants, "tonight's not for you."

But he returns to me. His thumb parts me once more but only for a moment before that same finger trails up past my perineum to the seam of my bum, leaving my own juices in their wake. Like before his thumb rims my anus before gently pressing inside. My whole body tenses at this strange invasion, but his thumb forces the issue, lining me inside with my own wetness. Real, true panic burns away a large majority of the pleasure. He means to…

"Bram, I don't think—"

He pulls his thumb out. "Relax," he orders. I feel his still lubricated tip press against that tight ring. "This…" Slowly, he advances himself inside centimeter by centimeter. It doesn't want to open. *I* don't want it to. The skin and the muscles fighting this violation burn as if they're already there. "…is for me. Not his. Never his. *Mine*."

"It hurts. Please st—"

One brutal thrust and an almost blinding…I don't know what—agony, burning, nirvana—sensation knocks me out of this world. Literally. One moment it's dark with the only sound coming from my whimpers, and the next the lights are on and "Dancing Queen" continues. I can still sense him inside me but *feel* nothing. No pain, no pleasure, at least not physically.

Mentally I've entered the gates of hell.

My mother lies on her back, her head inches from my own. She stares right at me but wouldn't see me even if I were here in the flesh. Her tear rimmed eyes are empty. Hollow. She's gone away, far far away. She wouldn't scream even if the man's hand weren't pressed against her mouth. That same man is the source of the grunts. My mother's shell jolts in time to that sound. Oh, God. Oh, God he's…oh God. I want to shut my eyes but they won't budge. My head won't turn so I can see her assailant. I'm glued in place staring into my mother's eyes as she's violated. His groans of pleasure, her jolts quicken. "Oh Juliette, I love you." The demon. "I love you so much. I love you. I love you. I love—" The bastard cries out as he finally peaks. If Mama notices she doesn't let on. I was right. She doesn't even scream as he removes his hand.

"I'm sorry, beloved," he whispers. That hand caresses her tear-stained cheek. "I'm so sorry. I know you didn't enjoy that." He caresses her cheek again before his arm moves lower, I think to her stomach. "It had to be tonight. And I waited so long, so long for you, I just couldn't control myself. So long. But I'm sorry. I'm so sorry. The first time is always painful for women anyway. It'll be better next time." There's finally some life in those eyes. They twitch in terror, especially as he moves his head to her chest.

Oh, Jesus Christ. No. *No.*

"I'll make sure of it," Jerome says, kissing her abdomen before staring straight into my eyes. His grin stretches across his face. "I love you. Both."

"Oh, fuck Jane! Fuck!"

In the blink of an eye the room turns black and the music vanishes, replaced with pain. Burning, sharp agony radiating through my bowels to my legs, my abdomen, even my neck where Bram holds my head down against the mattress. His body spasms against me, inside that torn place, as he spurts his hot seed inside my rectum. If possible, the stinging increases. Bram pants for a few seconds before finally removing that instrument of torture from my wrecked body. "Oh, Jane, that was amazing. I—"

Without him supporting me, I haven't the strength to stand on my own. My knees buckle and I crumble to the floor. "Jane?" He seeps out of me, sticky against my bum and thighs. I can't move. I can barely breathe. There's nothing but the agony. "Jane?" Bram asks, voice rising an octave. He bends beside me but I don't have the strength or desire to meet his gaze. "Jane!" He grabs my chin and jerks my head his way. His eyes are stretched to the brink from concern. "Are you okay? Say something. Jane!"

I stare into his terrified eyes yet feel nothing but disgust. With him, with myself, with the world and a God that allows things like that to happen. Why he allows innocents to suffer. Who allows monsters entrance into this world. Monsters like him. Like me. Blood will out.

"I know who my father is."

CHAPTER NINETEEN

The bath water's tinged pink from the blood still seeping from my torn body. I drained it once, but I guess there's more damage than I originally thought. In every way possible. The pain in my body is a paper cut compared to how battered my soul feels. The sitz salts and painkiller have quelled some of the physical torture, though I have to lie on my back and can't put pressure on my bum. His seed, my blood, mucous, feces, it all drains out of me into what should be the warm, clean water. I've been in this tub for an hour, the water's lukewarm, and I've scrubbed my skin raw as the rest of me, yet I'm not clean. I'll never be clean. I was corrupted the moment that *thing* forced me into existence.

I'm damned.

It makes sense, it *all* makes sense now. Why she hated me. Why they sent her away. Why she killed herself. Why my grandmother and Hallie kept Jerome's body alive. Why I can see and do the impossible. Why my body killed all my poor, innocent babies. Because I'm unnatural. An abomination like my father before me. Impure in both body and soul. The spawn of incest. Of rape. The spawn of the devil himself.

The first male of the line. That's what Cotton promised the demon. He brought my uncle to that island on his eighteenth birthday, the night he officially became a man, and the demon took its due. I pray Uncle Jerome's soul found its way to heaven, that he wasn't trapped in that body with that thing all this time. I pray God's not *that* cruel. No, there was none of the sweet boy who comforted Mama, who protected his family, left in that monster. My father.

"Jane, please open the door, beloved. I'm getting worried."

Yeah, worried. Like he was so worried before in Mama's bedroom. After my declaration, I refused to say another word. I wouldn't let him touch me. I picked myself up, hobbled into this bathroom as fast as I could with what felt like shards of glass inside my rectum, shut the door, and haven't spoken since. At least he stopped incessantly knocking and whining apologies. I can't even begin to process what he did. A nightmare for another time.

"Jane? Beloved? If you don't let me know you're alive in there, I'll have to break the door down."

An idle threat. It loses its potency after the fifth time with no follow through. I wish he'd go away. I wish I'd never met him. I wish I'd never come here. The more I discover the less I recognize myself. And I loathe the woman I've become. Doing drugs? Sex games? Sodomy? I may be the offspring of a demon, but I've never acted like one before. This is a test. God's testing me, I know it as sure as I know the earth rotates around the sun. Because if demons are real so is Satan. So is God. And I'm failing His test. Maybe because of who my father is I'll never be granted access to His kingdom, I don't know, but I do know I certainly won't be if I continue down the path I have. With him.

I know what I have to do. I'm not even sad.

As clean as I'll ever physically be, it is now time to begin cleansing my soul. I drain the tub and climb out with care. Even this simple task sends ripples of pain through me. I hobble to retrieve my robe from the hook. After securing it, I find my toiletry bag and throw in the basics like my toothbrush, brush, and make-up. Bag in hand, I finally open the door.

Bram stands on the other side like an overeager dog awaiting its master's return. I keep my head and eyes down as I brush past him into my bedroom. "Jane?" he asks. *Don't look at him. Don't engage.* "Jane?" I find my suitcases in the closet and toss them onto the bed. "What the hell are you doing?" I unzip one. "Jane!"

Bram grabs my arms, but I violently yank them from his grasp. "Don't touch me," I hiss.

"Jane, you're scaring the hell out of me. Talk to me."

I move to the dresser for my clothes. "I'm leaving."

"Okay. We'll go to my house if you—"

"No, I'm *leaving*. This house, this state…all of it."

"Meaning me," he finishes for me. I don't say a word back. I just throw more clothes in. "Will you stop that and talk to me?" He steps right in front of me to block my third trip. "I'm sorry, okay? I'm sorry for what happened. I thought you were enjoying it. You didn't say no."

"You didn't give me the chance. And quite frankly, I don't think it would have mattered if I did."

"Of course it would have!"

"Bull. What you did tonight had nothing to do with love or even sex. You did…that to punish me. To spite me and Owen. And if you can do that to me over nothing…" I shake my head. "I don't trust you. This is insane. This whole *whatever* between us, is insanity. We barely know one another. Heck, after all I've experienced, I barely know *me*. All I do know is I can't stay here anymore. It's corrupting me. It's wrong. *We're* wrong."

"You *can* trust me. Jane, I swear, I swear on everything I hold dear, I will never hurt you again. I got caught up in the game I thought we were both playing. Don't throw what we have together, what we can build together, away because of crossed wires."

"It's not just that. It's…this place is poison, and everything that stems from here is tainted. Including me. And if I stay here, it'll just get inside me more and more until there's nothing of *me* left. There's barely a glimmer now. I have to leave."

"No, you're not thinking clearly, beloved. This is the alcohol, the drugs and whatever you think you know about your father is clouding your mind."

"I don't *think* anything. I *saw*. I heard. I smelled. That demon burnt away my uncle's soul. He stole his body and raped my mother with it, and I'm the product of his crime. Of his unholy design. He wanted me. He literally forced my existence into this world. To what end, I don't know. I don't want to. All I do know is the deck's stacked against me, and I don't want to add any more cards to it. If I stay here, if I stay with you, he'll win."

"That's crazy. This is all crazy, Jane."

"Don't you dare call me crazy," I snap back. "Wh-what's crazy is thinking you're in love with a man you don't even know. It's crazy to let him treat you as nothing more than a sex toy. To leave your whole life behind on a whim. Maybe I was crazy, but I've never felt saner than I do right now. I'm leaving, and I'm going to do my damndest to never look back. Now get out of my way." I move left and he mirrors me. I move right, and he blocks me again. "I said—"

He drops to his knees before me, staring up with tears brimming from his miserable blue eyes. "No. *No*. I love you, and you love me. You know you do. You *know*."

"Bram…"

He wraps his arms around my waist and pulls me into him, resting his forehead on my stomach. "I love you. I've waited so long for you, and you for me. Don't throw that away. Don't throw *me* away because you're scared. What happened in the past, it doesn't matter. All that matters is us. Our future. And it will be so beautiful, Jane. I will dedicate my life to making you happy. I swear it. I'll be your slave. I already am." His warm breath against my almost bare flesh, the need in those words, brings tingles and goose bumps. He kisses my body where just a slit of bare flesh is exposed. "So beautiful, Jane. Our future." His kisses move south, his mouth parting my robe so nothing separates us. "Us." Those kisses continue to that wiry patch of hair, to where I begin to part. "Our babies." Be it those words or just instinct, my legs spread to allow his invasion to continue. "Heaven, beloved. I promise."

His hot mouth then his tongue begin toying with me. I throw my head back and grab his soft hair to steady myself. Those masterful lips, that playful tongue know me so well. After a few seconds all is forgotten save for the bliss be bestows upon me. There's no cruelty, no punishment now, only devotion. Only worship of my flesh. He suckles the tenderest part of me as if he were a baby in need of nourishment. That need infects me, spreading its tendrils from that sweet spot into me, up my back, into my brain. Nothing but rapture and gratification as I convulse with tiny shudders already. My depths ripen and clench in anticipation of him. There's no noise but my gentle moans and his suckling. I look down and he up at the same time. But it's not Bram at my feet, it's Jerome, eyes black as coal. I gasp and stumble backwards. When I blink, it's Bram again staring at me with confusion. "What?"

"Just get out," I order, voice trembling along with the rest of me.

"Jane—"

"*Get out!*" I shriek at the top of my lungs.

His electric eyes double in size in response to my fury. He leaps to his feet. "Jane—"

"Get out! Get out!" I continue roaring like a madwoman as I advance toward him. He backs away. "Get out! Get out!"

The moment he's through the bedroom door, I slam it shut and lock it. I have to take a few seconds to catch my breath my heart races so.

"I-I'm going, Jane. I am. Just, please…I love you. More than anything. More than Jesus loves sinners. I do. And no matter how far apart we are, no matter how long you need, that will never, ever change. And I'll be here. Waiting for you with open arms. Because we're meant for one another, Jane. It's why we were put on this earth. And I have absolute faith you'll come to realize that one day. I have faith in you. I have faith in us. I love you, Jane. I worship you. I adore you. You're mine, and I'm yours. I love you, Jane Harrow." He pauses. I bat away my tears and will myself not to open the door. "*I love you.* Good-bye my love. For now. Good-bye."

It's as if the whole house trembles as his footsteps move away. I don't allow myself to truly shatter until I hear the front door slam. I crumble to the floor and sob until I fear my eyes will bleed.

It was the right thing to do. The only thing I could do to save myself. My head knows that. It does. But my heart? My soul? They've been snapped in twain. He takes them with him. Because he's right. They belong to him. They always have and always will. And that's my penance. My sacrifice to God. I pray it's enough. I pray He'll forgive me.

Both of them.

CHAPTER TWENTY

Owen must have been waiting for my knock because I barely touches his hotel room door when it opens. My husband takes one look at me, and with no recrimination, no concern, steps aside to let me in. As I hobble in, his mouth sets straight and the veins in his neck bulge. My rectum still feels like ground glass moves inside even with the pills. Yet he still doesn't utter a word. He just shuts the door and waits by it. God, what he must be thinking. Whatever it is, it's probably accurate. I don't want to look at him. I barely reassembled myself enough to gather my clothes. I was halfway down the driveway when I realized I'd forgotten my purse. I'm sure I forgot all manner of things. I'll just hire someone to pack and send it wherever I end up. I never intend to set foot in that house again. *Never*.

He's waiting for me to speak, but I don't know what to say. I'm not even sure why I came here besides the fact after all we've been through, he has a right to know everything. "Thank you for, uh, seeing me. I hope I didn't wake you or anything."

"I was up," he says still not moving from the door. "It's not even ten."

"It isn't?" God, I thought it was at least three AM. "Still. I, uh, I just wanted to let you know I'm leaving."

"Leaving? Leaving where?"

"Here. This town. This state. I haven't really made up a plan yet, but I just, I can't stay here. You were right. Coming here was a massive mistake."

My husband remains silent, so silent my still tender stomach clenches again. "What did he do to you?" Owen growls.

"Nothing. I—"

"Bullshit," Owen cuts in.

"It's not what you think. He didn't…this-this isn't about him. What I've seen, what I've done, what I've learned…coming here was supposed to make everything better. Make *me* better down to my very soul."

"There is nothing the matter with your soul, Jane."

"To treat you like I did? To push you away when you did nothing, *nothing* wrong? Yeah, there is. And there always will be. This place just feeds the corruption. So I have to get away from here. I just wanted to tell you in person as soon as possible so you could get back to your life too."

"How considerate of you. What do *you* intend to do?"

"I don't know. Maybe stay with Melissa in St. Louis? I haven't really thought it through."

"Or you can come home. With me. Where you belong," he says, annoyed.

"Owen. We…I…Los Angeles is as haunted as here. You still work with the woman you had an affair with. Our marriage all but died there. We can't go back. And what I discovered about myself…" Even now it makes me want to throw up. "I meant every word I said last night. You deserve better than me. *So* much better than me. I condemned you for *my* crimes. I broke your trust first. I practically shoved you into her arms. I was so lost in my pain and failure I forgot you lost our babies too. It shouldn't have been *you* taking care of *me*, we should have taken care of each other. And I never should have shut you out like I did. I was selfish, so selfish, and I am so sorry. And I—"

"Jane," Owen cuts in.

"What?"

"Shut up."

He takes two strides toward me, wraps his arm around my waist, and pulls me against him, lowering his lips to mine. It isn't the universe shattering, all-consuming kiss Bram bestows, but it's sweet. Comforting. Owen. Even after all the pain, all the betrayal, all the suffering we've inflicted on each other, it's all forgotten. Forgiven. Maybe it has been for months. I've missed him, I've

missed *this* more than I ever admitted to myself. I've been so
stupid. So stubborn. I wrap my arms around his large shoulders
and he around my torso to draw me in closer to his body. The body
I've spent almost every night for over a decade loving. Caressing.
Pressed against during the best and worst times of my life. He
backs me toward the bed then gently lowers me onto it. Just not
gently enough. My backside radiates pain to every part of my
body. My wince and quick intake of breath break the spell and the
kiss. Owen pulls away, at least his lips, to stare down at me, eyes
narrowed in concern and confusion.

"I'm okay," I whisper. "Just…we can't…not-not tonight."

"What did he do to you? Did-did he—"

"No," I assure him. I caress the wrinkles under his eyes to
their corners. "No." I kiss him again. "He doesn't matter. He
doesn't. Only *we* do. Can you really forgive me? Truly? Because I
don't think *I* can forgive me. I've made so many mistakes. And
I'm sorry. I am so, so sorry. I mean it when I say you deserve
better than me. You do—"

My husband kisses the words away again before gazing
into my eyes and says, "I love you. I have loved you from the
minute I saw you, and I will love you until the day I die. We got
lost. Both of us. But we're not anymore. You are my wife. You are
my heart. Nothing you've done can ever change that, even if I
wanted it to. And there have been times I've wanted it too. I've
wanted to hate you, Jane. To turn my back on you. I even tried to."
He pauses. "Since you filed for divorce, I slept with another
woman. Besides Violet."

This revelation is like a knife twist to the heart. "Oh."

"It meant nothing. It just made me realize how in love
with you I still was. And I'll never do it again. I will never stray
again. If you promise the same. That means you can never see him
again. I want you back, I do, but all of you because that's what I'm
giving you. The past happened, we can't change that, but we can
agree on the future. No more secrets. No more lies. And I meant
what I said about children. I'm okay with just you and me."

"I just felt like such a failure. That I failed us both."

"You didn't."

"I know that. Now. Now, I know it was a mercy we didn't. It was God's will. And maybe we can adopt down the road."

He gives me a rare smile. "One thing at a time, okay?" He kisses me. Deeply, cupping my head with his large hands while running his fingers through my hair before pulling away once more. "I love you."

"I love you too," I whisper. "I never stopped. Not for a second."

"Then come home." He caresses my cheek. "Come home, sweetheart."

"Okay," I whisper. I cup his hand with mine. "Okay."

My husband has never been much of a smiler but tonight the biggest, brightest, purest grin stretches across his rugged face. I thought I'd never smile again after tonight but mine almost matches his. He kisses me again. And again. And again until tonight, until the past year, is nothing but a memory. A forgotten nightmare. Thank you, God. Thank you for showing me the way. Thank you for this man and his forgiving heart. I will never stray from the path again. I will earn his love and your Grace from this moment forth. Whatever it takes. Whatever obstacle you see fit for me to endure, I will stay true to those two tenants. I will do right by you both. I will honor my vows. No matter the personal cost. I will never let either one of you down again.

Never.

*

I haven't slept in the same bed with my husband for almost a year. Perhaps that's why I haven't had a good night's sleep in all that time. With his large, warm arms enveloping me, with his strong steady heart beating beneath my ear acting as a lullaby, the moment he shuts off the light I relax enough to begin drifting off. Not even reviewing our plans can stop the trip to slumberland. We'll start driving back to California tomorrow and the moment we get home, I'll call my lawyers to stop the divorce and sell the house in Crimson while Owen puts in for a transfer at work. It'll probably take months for it to go through, but we'll go anywhere, which should expedite the process. A whole new beginning. Moving forward without a glance back. Is it any wonder I fall asleep against my husband with a smile on my face?

Wha—

A vice-like grip on my arm startles me out of a shallow, brief sleep. Ow. What...? As I turn my head toward the source of the pain and groaning, my eyes open. It takes a moment for me to assemble the pieces. My husband's agonized groans. His gentle flailing like a fish on dry land. The figure looming above him so black it's like it's swallowing darkness. My blood runs arctic when everything clicks into place. Owen releases my arm to claw at his chest just over his heart where the darkest darkness reaches inside. I know him. I've seen him. And he's killing my husband. The demon's killing my husband. I don't know what to do.

"Get away from him," I shout as I sit up.

Owen howls in pain as the demon just squeezes tighter.

I don't know what to do. God help—

"In the name of and by the power of God and our Lord Jesus Christ, most cunning serpent, unclean spirit, we drive you from us! God the father commands it! God the Son commands it! God, the Holy Ghost, commands it! Be gone!" I lean over my husband, getting as close to the demon as I dare to. "We said BE GONE!"

I touch the abomination and it vanishes.

Thank you, God. Thank you. "Owen?"

He doesn't answer. He just lies there, unmoving beside me. There's no more noise save for my shaking breath. Though my fingers tremble, I somehow manage to switch on the light. Dear God. Drool and tears run down my husband's crimson, still face. He's not breathing. "Oh, God. Oh, God," I whisper. I reach for the phone on the nightstand to dial 911. "C-Crimson Vale Motel. R-room 7. My-My husband! He-he's not breathing! P-please hurry."

I toss the phone down and flip back to Owen. His skin's clammy as I feel for a pulse. None. "Oh God. Oh God. Okay. Okay." CPR. CPR. He needs CPR. Just like I learned the summer I was a lifeguard, I tilt back his head before beginning chest compressions. After thirty, I breathe twice into his mouth. Nothing. A pulse but only for a second. "No. *No.*" Not him. You've taken everything from me already, everyone, please not him too. He doesn't deserve this. He's a good man. You need him on this Earth. *I* need him. Please. Please. *Please.*

Three minutes. It takes the paramedics three minutes to arrive. Five minutes that seem like an eternity. My arms are about to give out, I'm lightheaded from all the breaths, with nothing to show for it. The EMTs have to physically remove me to try to revive him themselves. I have to stand helpless in the corner as they barrage me with questions about drugs and prior medical conditions all the while cutting off my husband's shirt and prepping needles and machines. "Clear!" His body jolts as they try to shock him back to life. Nothing. "Again!"

Oh, please. Oh, please…I'll give anything. *Please.*

"Again. Clear!"

Owen jerks again, but this time there's a steady beeping emanating from the machine.

"We have a faint pulse," the EMT says to her partner.

My legs give out, and I slide down the wall to my knees. "Thank you," I whisper. "Thank you."

He doesn't wake, he doesn't even twitch as they load him onto a stretcher and wheel him out. Somehow I find the strength to rise again and follow them into the ambulance. I take his cold hand and don't release it until the nurse at the medical center, the same one from the night before, drags me away to fill out forms and fight back a nervous breakdown.

He'll be fine. He's strong. His heart is strong. He won't leave me. Not now. I try to complete the forms, but the words make no sense to my frazzled mind. I can't remember his birthday or middle name. I can't remember…

I burst into tears. This is my fault. He's dying, and it's all my fault. Everything is my fault. It was familiar. What happened was so familiar. My dreams when I lost the babies. A phantom reaching inside me and taking them. It was him. It had to be him. That abomination murdered my babies. It came while I slept and all but ripped them from my womb. Why did he do that? Why did he just try to do the same to their father? To drive me insane with guilt? Because it's working. Owen may die and then I'll be alone. Just how he wants me.

The rightness that last thought jolts the panic from my mind. Because that's it. I know it as sure as I know winter will turn to spring, that's his design. He wants me isolated. Frightened. And he wants me *here*. In this town. He all but steered me here with the visions and voices. But why? What's his endgame? But for certain he won't let me leave until it's reached. Which means Owen isn't safe. My husband's a threat. The demon can materialize anywhere and finish the job. If Owen even survives this attack.

The tears begin anew as I fold in on myself. I can't breathe. The terror seizes not only my lungs but my brain as well. I don't know what to do. How do you fight the epitome of evil? Generations of my family have tried and failed. And they were far stronger women than I. Because I'm not strong. I know that. I never have been. Aunt Helen. Uncle Robbie. Owen. *They* have gotten me this far in life. They propped me up and helped me move one foot in front of the other through my mother's suicide, through their cancers, the miscarriages. I would have crawled into a hole and wasted away if it were up to me.

And now it is.

There's no one left but me. And I don't have Helen's strength. Or Hallie's knowledge. Or Felicia's determination. What I do have is no other choice. That monster's taken my mother, my uncle, my grandmother, and my babies. He's not getting my husband too.

"Mrs. Harrow?"

I glance up to find the nurse who admitted me last night smiling down at me, all tea and sympathy. It's so odd I'm more terrified tonight than when I thought there was something wrong with me. "Y-yes?" I ask, wiping the tears away.

"Your husband's still unconscious, but they're about to take him up to Radiology. I thought you might like to see him before they do."

I leap up and don't wait for her to show me the way. The doctor and two nurses circle him, adjusting the tubes and taking notes. My strong husband seems so diminutive lying there. His eyes flutter above the plastic oxygen mask covering his waxy face. But he's alive. For now. "Owen?" I ask as I rush to his side. I take his clammy hand, pressing it to my lips. He still doesn't wake. My giant of a husband reduced to this. My fault. All my fault. "Is he…" I choke out.

"The paramedics managed to re-start his heart and the rhythm is stabilizing," says the doctor, "but we don't know if there is any brain damage due to oxygen loss. We're taking him for more tests. He has been in and out of consciousness, which is a good sign. You told the paramedics there's been no history of heart disease or drug use?"

"No. None. He-he has yearly physicals. He's always been as healthy as an ox. But-But he'll be fine, right? If-if whatever caused this in the first place doesn't happen again?"

"We'll know more after the tests. Nurse?"

The nurses grab the machines he's attached to and the doctor lifts up the gurney's guard rails. I squeeze his hand tighter and kiss his sweaty forehead. "I love you. I always have and I always will. Do you hear me? I love you. I'm going to make this right. I'm going to keep you safe. I promise. I love you."

I feel hands on my shoulders. "Mrs. Harrow?" the nurse says gently pulling me away from him. "Come on, hon. It'll be okay." They wheel my husband away as the nurse rubs my arms. "It'll all be okay. You'll see. He's a fighter. You can tell. And he's got everything to live for. You just need to be strong for him."

And as they turn the corner out of sight, I have the intense feeling that I'll never see him again. No. *No.* That's not going to happen. I won't let it. She's right, I need to be strong. I need to do what three generations of my family have failed to. For him. For all of them.

It's time to beat the devil.

CHAPTER TWENTY-ONE

This house. This beautiful house. It survived the Civil War, countless hurricanes, and eight generations of Fontaines. When I first arrived here I thought it would provide me sanctuary. A place to heal, to begin anew, an oasis in the cruel world from which I would emerge a new woman. That did happen in a way. It's just that new woman is worse than the one she replaced. I'm weaker. Lustful. Disgusting. But this new me was always inside me. Waiting to bloom and grow and have its tangle of branches blot out the light, allowing the rest of my life to wither and die, leaving me with nothing but the abyss. I swore I'd never come back here. That I'd never set foot inside ever again. I managed to keep that promise all of three hours. So much for keeping my word. Another crime he's forced me to commit.

I leave my car into the cold night. Or that could be the adrenaline withdrawal. I can barely put the key in the lock. What am I doing? This is madness. This is playing right into his hands. It went to so much trouble getting me here in the first place, and now I am giving it what it wants all over again. Even the best of plans can prove downright idiotic. But if it keeps the demon away from Owen, there is nothing I won't do. Including this.

I step inside.

No demon greets me in the foyer. There's nothing but the inky void of the night and silence. Stillness. The reek of marijuana remains on the air. My anus clenches at the memory that stench ignites. The pain pills I took hours ago are wearing off now, but I must keep a clear head. It's the only weapon I have. "I'm here!" I shout through the house. "Do you hear me? I'm here! Like you wanted! I'm not going anywhere! I'm all yours! I'm here…for you!"

Nothing. Fine. I move toward the living room, turning on all the lights as I do. My dress, and panties remain on the floor. My stomach and bum clench again. What he did to me… Cruel. How could I have let him? "Show yourself, you bastard! You coward! I'm right he—"

Chanel #5 mixed with hyacinth.

I spin around and gasp. Not who I expected.

Hallie and Felicia stand shoulder to shoulder not three feet away, faces expressionless as they stare at me. Felicia. This is the first time I've really seen her. She's so haggard. Gray hair a rats nest as if she hadn't brushed it in a decade. Her wrinkled skin's as gray as her hair. Frail, so frail and thin it's as if her ripped t-shirt would weigh too much for her. My grandmother. "Hello," I whisper.

She nods.

"I-I'm…I…I wish I'd gotten to know you. I wish I could have helped you. I wish…" I shake my head to clear the oncoming melancholia and tears. Strong. I need to be strong. "Well, I'm here now. I'm here to help you. Help us all. I know everything now. I know…what I have to do. I—"

Hallie shakes her head. *You know nothing…*

Both women hold out their hands. *But you will.*

Oh, God. Not again. No. No, no, no, no, no. I can't bear it. No more.

Owen…

Felicia smiles sympathetically at me. Owen. Right. No matter the cost. No matter what.

Owen.

No hesitation now. I step forward and take their hands.

There's no pain or confusion like the first time. In a blink I'm standing in my living room yet not *my* living room. The sofa, most of the antique furniture is the same, but instead of night it's twilight, and "Ooh Child" by The Five Stairsteps plays on a nearby radio. Before I wrap my head around these changes, my mother, dressed in a Catholic school uniform with her blonde hair in pigtails, strolls in from the dining room with a huge smile on her face all for the boy at her side. "I'll bet it's a car," Mama says.

"It's not a car," Jerome replies. And it is him. An unsure boy with slightly slumped shoulders, unruly curly blonde hair, and rumpled uniform with the sleeves of his white shirt rolled up. My uncle. My father.

"Or a boat," Mama continues.

"He just said it was a surprise."

"Well, if it is a car or a boat you have to let me borrow them. All he gave *me* was another darn doll. I mean, I'm eighteen, not eight. Hopefully, I can sell it like the others."

"Shush," Jerome orders, even glancing to the two open doorways.

"We're up to two grand," Mama whispers. "It's enough for the first, last, and security deposit at least."

"We don't know if we got in yet. And school isn't—"

"There are high schools in New York. We're eighteen now. We don't need anyone's permission to do anything anymore," Mama points out before taking her brother's hands, squeezing tight. "We *can* do this. We can leave. Tonight. No more Grandfather. No more Mama. No more ghosts. Just us and the Big Apple. I mean, we survived this place. New York will be Candyland in comparison."

"I don't—"

"I can't do it without you," she says as serious as the plague. "And we *need* to do this. Now. As soon as possible. We *need* to leave, Romy. I-I *feel* it. I know it."

"Jules…"

"What are you two conspiring about in here?"

That deep baritone startles every soul in the room, mine included. The twins actually jerk apart and refuse to meet their grandfather's gaze as he enters from the foyer. Those intense blue eyes study the silent and obviously guilty teens. "I asked what you two were discussing," he demands.

"Uh, the party, sir. Tonight," Jerome pipes up. "We were hoping some people would be there. A boy and…girl."

"Hope you weren't the one excited about the boy," Cotton spews back. My uncle stares down at the rug, cowed by the put down. "Are you ready? It's time to go."

"Where are y'all going?" Mama asks.

"None of your goddamn business, girl. I wasn't addressing you."

"Sorry Grandfather," Mama mumbles.

The ogre returns his attention the Jerome. "Are you ready?"

"Yes, Grandfather."

Cotton turns his back on the teens. "Then let's get this over with."

Mama squeezes her brother's hand again with a sympathetic smile, which Jerome returns. "We'll talk more later," he whispers. After pecks Mama's lips, with his head hung, he follows his grandfather out of the room.

Blink.

I'm standing on a sandy bank outside overlooking the bayou. The island. I know it not by sight but by the prickling of power against my soul. By sight, it's much different than how I found it yesterday. Right now the dock extends from the shore to the black water, ready to welcome the oncoming johnboat sailing toward it. The setting sun behind them gives Jerome's hair an orange tint as if he were alight with fire. Cotton sits behind the boy at the helm, stern scowl affixed. Charon ushering a lost soul down the river Styx. Jerome points my way. "Up here?" he asks his grandfather, who doesn't respond. Cotton just maneuvers the boat to the dock.

My uncle is first out, smiling even as he surveys the land. "Wow. This place is beautiful. I never knew it existed."

"Few do," Cotton replies as he secures the boat. "They used to perform hoodoo and voodoo rituals out here."

The boy passes me up the shore toward the path. "Who did?"

"Slaves. Hallie's great-grandmamma Camille mostly. Hallie still comes out here sometimes when I need her to."

"I didn't know that," says Jerome.

"There's a hell of a lot you never have and never will know, boy." Cotton strolls up to his grandson at the foot of the path before moving past him. "Come on. It's up here."

"What is?" Jerome calls, treated once more to only silence. After a lifetime of conditioning Jerome trails after his grandfather without another question with me a clip behind. How can he not sense the wrongness of this place? How can he just blindly obey this monster without hesitation? But he does. And there's nothing I can do to stop him.

We reach the dead space which is the same size in my day it is right now, but that's all that remains the same. The animal cages and lantern posts haven't succumbed to the elements and age yet. Even the grass only reaches our ankles. Jerome meanders around the edge of the circle, taking it all in as Cotton watches his grandson, the sides of the older man's mouth twitching each time Jerome smiles. For the first time, possibly in the whole of his life, he appears nervous, even a tiny bit sad. Regret weighs down his eyes and shoulders as he stares at the boy. His own flesh and blood. But the man's humanity only shines through for a second. "You're a man today."

Jerome turns back to his grandfather. "What?"

"You're officially a man."

"O-okay."

"And part of being a man is doing your duty. For your family."

"I know. I will."

"I don't doubt it, son. You're a good boy. A bit of a pansy but even still...I am sorry for this. Truly. I wish there were another way, but it is what it is."

"What is? I-I don't—"

His words cut short when the black figure materializes shoulder-to-shoulder beside Cotton. It's so solid. If someone dared touch it, it would feel as real as the man beside it. Just as when I first saw it in LA on the top of my stairs. Just like tonight with Owen. It's strong. Real. Even Cotton takes a step to escape its proximity. A monster a monster fears.

"What? What…?" Jerome asks, voice trembling as hard as the rest of him.

"It's time to do your duty. I'm sorry, son."

Jerome quickly glances from Cotton to the figure and finally pieces the chilling tableau come together. That he's been lured to a deserted island by two of the evilest creatures ever to inhabit God's green earth. The boy dashes toward me, toward the path, in an attempt to escape his fate. But he can't. He never could. He was doomed the moment of his conception. He doesn't even make it out of the circle. The demon appears right in front of the boy, who barely has enough time to skid to a stop.

They're the same height, the same build, almost like shadows. His dark self-made manifest. Jerome just stares into the void as the void seems to stare back. They're transfixed, each studying their match. Their fate.

A tear, a single tear falls from my uncle's eye as his bottom lip quivers. That boy. That beautiful boy. So scared. Just a boy who loves his family. Who wanted to move to New York and be an artist. Get married. Have children. My uncle. My *father*. Resigned to his fate. Strong until the end.

As gentle as a lover, the demon raises its hand to caress the tear off before leaning in for a kiss. Jerome closes his eyes. But instead of stopping at the lips the black mass fades into the boy's body, invading his every pore like black poison gas. Killing Jerome Cowan just as dead. The moment it vanishes inside him, the husk collapses onto its back. A second passes. Another. Maybe he—

Suddenly Jerome's body arches from the top of his head to his toes, vertebrae crackling like burnt kindling. He flattens only to arch again, this time his eyes roll back into his head so only the bloodshot whites show. He's fighting. Fighting the corruption. Fighting for his very soul. But the boy's no match. After a final convulsion, he falls flat on the dirt.

He doesn't breathe.

He doesn't blink.

He stares up at the orange and gray sky as a red tear falls from the same eye as Jerome's last. Then it blinks. Once. Twice. It draws in a croaking, gasping gulp of air like its lungs are coated with acid. It begins coughing, hacking as it curls into the fetal position for several seconds until it starts rasping again. Cotton backs away from the demon as it wipes the blood from its eyes. The demon stares at its hands and the blood as if it can't work out what they are. What their purpose is. It licks its fingers of the blood but spits out the foul substance. This is all foreign, all new to it. Air, physics, flesh, form. The demon's nothing more than a newborn in the body of a man. It touches its new face, its hair, its clothes. A laugh escapes it, but the act and sound seem to confuse it. It must like the new sensations, all of them, because it laughs again like the mad creature it is for thirty full seconds.

"I-I'm laughing," the demon says. "Th-this is what laughing feels like. It-It's wh-what's the word…? There-there-there's so much going on. My-my mind…memories. Senses. I-I-my bladder is full, wh-which means I have to—"

The demon rises awkwardly, but staggers like a drunk, tripping on its own feet. "Gravity," it chuckles. "How bracing!" It takes a slow step. Then another toward Cotton. The old man shrinks away from the abomination.

"Wh-what happened to my grandson?"

"Now you care!" the demon says. It stops walking and seems shocked, head jolting backwards, before laughing again. "Sarcasm! Huh." The demon continues to a grassy area before unzipping its pants. "Do you truly care?" It takes out its stolen penis, almost weighing the organ in its hand. "Huh. Not bad."

"Of course I ca—"

"Ooh!" The demon groans rapturously as he pees. "*That is divine.*"

"Is-is he dead? Is he…in heaven?"

"Heaven? You still believe in all that claptrap?"

"Of course. I'm talking to a demon."

The demon finishes its task and zips its pants again. "Labels. I did wonder why you humans felt the need to put everything into such tiny boxes. Now I have a mind, I understand. There's so much to see, feel, hear, experience, a person would go mad without them."

"You're not a demon?"

"No!" it replies, almost offended by the word. "I suppose there could be what you consider a heaven and hell, but in my realm, dimension, sphere of reality—whatever label you need to give it—is nothing like your imagined hell. No brimstone, no large creature with hooves. It's a great deal like here only…better. *We're* better. Evolutionary, by comparison, you humans are still Neanderthals. Oh, that's a fun word to say: Ne-an-der-thal." It smiles again. "Huh. I think I will enjoy having a tongue as much as I love having a prick." He grabs his bulge. "Perhaps not *as* much."

"Bu-but if you're better than us, why did you need my grandson? Why'd you come here at all?"

"What do you always tell yourself, Cotton Fontaine? 'Better to reign in hell than serve in heaven?' Of that we are of the same mind. And to possess a body again? Even one as imperfect as these? That is worth a few years of having to put up with you and your demands. And I won't be stuck in this imperfect shell too long. It's already changing. Adapting to my energy. Infusing with my power. Look." The demon steps toward Cotton, prying open its eye. Even from here I can see that all the blood is gone so only the white remains. It's healed. "And each itineration will get better. Stronger. More powerful. All stemming from your polluted, malicious, evil blood, Cotton Fontaine. Because that's what you are. Evil. The negative energy wafts from you like the stench of rotting meat. And you call *me* a demon? You have raped, cheated, stolen, killed, molested, and terrorized all whom you have come in contact with."

"What I did, I did for my family. For our legacy. You of all, whatever the fuck you are, know if you want an omelet, eggs need to get broken. It was all for the greater good."

The demon's grin stretches across Jerome's beautiful face. "As is this."

As fast as quicksilver, the demon grabs Cotton's head and twists it around almost 180 degrees. Bones and tendons snap as the vertebrae in his neck visibly protrude out of the skin like roots in dirt. The impassive murderer removes its hands from the dead man, who slumps to the ground in the spot I'll find him almost forty years from now.

"You see, I am a being of vision as well. But unlike you, I will take no pleasure in my crimes. Save for this one." It spits on Cotton's body. "It's *my* legacy now. And you will be nothing but a footnote, if remembered at all." The demon looks up from its victim toward the path, letting out a contented sigh. King of all it surveys. With that unwavering grin affixed, the demon leaves the other to join its purloined family and life among us mere mortals.

Blink.

The upstairs hallway. ABBA echoes through the air. "Dancing Queen." Oh, God. Not again. I'm not going in that room again. I'm saved that horror at least. Did it come straight from the island to her room? Was it so consumed with longing and love it couldn't wait an hour to rape my mother? To create me? I—

A door shuts behind me, and I spin around. A frail, forty-something Felicia dressed in a floral nightgown with her hair a mess of tangles, steps into the hallway. Her eyes can't focus, and she blinks slowly. "Hallie?" she croaks. There's no response. "Romy?"

There's noise in Mama's room, the shattering of glass, which draws the zombie's attention. "Julie?" As slow as her cadence, she plods toward the bedroom. The music turns up a little, probably to mask Mama's whimpers, and by the time the demon steps out of the room, Felicia passes me. I was wrong. It took time to shower and change into black pants and sweater before assaulting Mama. Somehow it appears more angelic than before the transformation. Its skin almost glows to the color of its golden hair. It could be the afterglow of sex, but I doubt it. Even its smile lights up the dim hallway. "You're up," it says.

"I…I heard…"

"I broke one of Juliette's dolls. Sorry. Let's get you back to bed, huh?" It wraps its arm around Felicia's torso to support her.

"Did-Did I miss cake?" she asks.

"No. And don't you worry, we'll save you a piece if you do." It pecks the top of her graying head. "Don't you worry about anything, Felicia. Not anymore, okay? I'll take care of everything from now on."

"Okay. Thank you," she says dreamily as she rests her head on its shoulder. "My sweet boy."

"Felicia?" Hallie calls from the foyer. The thirty-something woman dressed in orange bellbottoms with matching kerchief around her afro steps into view below.

"I didn't miss cake," Felicia slurs.

The demon smiles down at Hallie, who has started up the staircase. "It's alright, Hallie. I have her."

"When did you get back?" Hallie asks.

"Not long ago. Let me just…" Still smiling, it nods to Felicia's door before moving toward it. All the while Hallie studies it, eyes narrowing.

"Where's your grandfather?" she asks.

"I have no idea," the demon lies.

"He didn't come back with you?" She reaches the landing. "Where did he take you anyway?"

"Just for a boat ride to talk. What's with the third degree?"

She can sense it. As she moves closer, the muscles in her face, in her back tense and mouth stretched taught like an animal confronted with approaching danger. "*Revelabunt*," she whispers.

The moment that strange word escapes her lips. The demon's head snaps sideways as if he were a vampire confronted by daylight to gaze at Hallie over his shoulder. But it's not Jerome's face that snarls at the woman. It's as if its skin is translucent, a shell, revealing the swirling darkness under the surface. "Jesus," Hallie gasps as she steps away from the abomination.

"Damn it," mutters the demon.

"What?" Felicia asks.

"Get away from her," Hallie commands.

"This is not how I wished for you all to find out," it says as he turns to face Felicia.

"What?" Felicia asks again.

"I said get away from her! *Relinquo*!"

"That doesn't work anymore, beloved," the demon chides.

"Hallie, what—"

Hallie strides toward them. "I said let her go!" She grabs for Felicia's hand, pulling her sister from its clutches. The demon doesn't put up a fight. It releases her then holds up its hands in surrender. "Did it hurt you?" Hallie asks.

"Why would he hurt me?"

"I don't wish to harm any of you," the demon assures them.

Hallie backs herself and Felicia toward the steps, away from it. "What have you done to Romy?"

"Hallie, Romy's right there," Felicia says.

"That's not Romy," Hallie says, voice trembling.

"Of course it is!" Felicia says.

"No, it's not." She's shaking now, even her breath. "Get out of him. You get out of him right now!"

"There's no point in that, beloved. He's gone."

"Who's gone?" Felicia asks.

"No, his soul is still—"

"Part of me now. One in the same, never to be split again," instructs the demon.

Hallie lets out a choked gasp as tears fill her eyes. She releases Felicia to clutch her own stomach. There is not greater agony than losing your child, and that woman was both mother and father to that boy. She's the one who helped with homework, took them to school, guided them and comforted them all the days of their lives when their own mother was too lost in her grief and addiction. *That* woman glances from the deteriorating Hallie to the thing wearing her son's face, eyes narrowed in confusion. "I-I-I don't—"

"It killed him," Hallie gasps. "It killed our boy."

"No. No, he's right there, Hallie. He's right...right?" My grandmother stares at the demon. "Romy?"

"I was hoping you would never have cause to discover the truth, Felicia. I wanted to spare you this."

"Spare me...?" She looks into his sympathetic blue eyes and the pieces finally assemble. Her face slowly falls as the horrific picture comes into focus. "You're *it*."

"Please don't be afraid," the demon requests.

"You killed my son," Felicia gasps. "You killed my son!"

She launches herself at it, screeching like the madwoman everyone always thought she was, but she's no match for it. The demon grabs her outstretched wrists, holding tight, but she struggles against his grasp.

"Let her go!" Hallie shrieks.

"Stop this! I don't want to hurt you," it says soothingly.

"You killed my baby!"

"I said let her go!"

Hallie charges toward the struggling duo. It must deem Hallie the bigger threat because it tosses Felicia against the wall, her nose hitting first and hard enough to leave a streak of blood on the wall, before releasing my grandmother's wrists. The moment Hallie reaches the demon, it grips her by the throat as Felicia slumps to the floor, nose still gushing blood. Before Felicia finishes her fall, the demon picks Hallie up underneath her jaw and lifts her off her feet. It holds her body against the wall, squeezing the life from her lungs.

"I don't want to hurt you!" the demon roars. "I don't want to hurt any of you! You are my family! I love you! All! I don't want to hurt you," it insists, drawing out every word. Yet it squeezes her throat tighter. "But I will. If you try to stop me. If you get in my way, I will. Without hesitation." It releases Hallie, who crumples to the floor beside her half-sister. "But it won't come to that, will it? Because you're both smart women. You both know who I am. What I am capable of, even before I had physical form. You both will be able to recognize that you cannot win. You cannot undo what has already been done. Romy is gone, and I shall mourn him as deeply as you. I loved him too. I was there when he was born. I watched him take his first steps, say his first word. I was there when he went to his first day of school and came home crying. *I loved him.* But what happened was always to be. From the moment he was conceived, that was his fate. Your father made sure of it. The past is gone. All we can do is make the best of things here and now. I will do my utmost if you both agree to as well. I mean, you cannot kill me. This body may die, but as long as there is a drop of Fontaine blood in this world, I remain. You know that. So, truly, what other option do you have but to acquiesce?"

The women stare up at the impassive interloper, both shaking in terror. "Wh-what do you want?" Hallie gasps.

"Right now I want you to tend to Felicia. I fear I accidently broke her nose. We'll go from there. Get up." The demon takes a step back to give the women room to move. Hallie hikes Felicia up and holds onto her for dear life. The demon watches as they disappear into Felicia's bedroom, letting out a sigh when the door closes.

Blink.

My bathroom. Felicia's bathroom. The woman herself violently trembles on the toilet with Hallie kneeling before her, wiping the blood from her sister's face with a washcloth. "What are we going to do?" Felicia pants. "What are we going to do? What are we going to do?"

"I don't know."

"What are we goi—"

"I don't know!" Hallie roars. Felicia jerks back in fright. "I'm sorry. I'm sorry," Hallie cries. She pulls Felicia's head toward hers so their foreheads touch. "I'll think of something. I'll—Juliette." The women break apart.

"He-he came out of her room," Felicia says.

Both women shoot up to their feet and hustle out of the bathroom with me a foot or two behind them. The demon is nowhere to be seen as we rush down the hallway to her room. When they set eyes on my mother I haven't a doubt they wish the demon had just slain them so they didn't have to face this unspeakable horror. I would. Mama lies curled in the fetal position at the edge of the bed staring at nothing. Not blinking, barely breathing, just clutching onto herself, arms folded as if she were already in her coffin. Even without her torn blouse, panties on the floor, and streaks of blood on the sheets, anyone could glean what this girl recently endured.

"Oh Jesus," Hallie gasps.

"No. No, no, no, no, no..." Felicia says, vigorously shaking her head as she backs against the shut door.

Hallie dashes to my mother. "Jules..." She sits on the edge of the bed and touches Mama's shoulder. The girl jerks as if hit with a branding iron. Hallie gasps again and brings her hand to her mouth to muffle her cries.

"I want him *dead*. I want him *dead*," Felicia gasps through gritted teeth. "Dead. *Dead*. Tonight. Now."

"No. No, that's not the way. He might be able to jump bodies. I don't know enough about this. *Him*."

"Then we run."

"He'll find us. He always has before," Hallie says.

"Then what? We do what he wants? Let him be free to do God knows—" Hallie suddenly looks up at Felicia, her mouth in an O. "What? *What*?"

"I-I need to get my books."

"Why?"

"Because…there are worse fates than death. And I'm going to make sure that murderous bastard learns that."

Blink.

A bar. I blink, and I'm in a bar. A dive bar with peanut shells on the worn hardwood floor that matches the counter. The haze of smoke envelops the whole space, especially the pool table area where three bikers in leather chug beer and guffaw over the sound of clacking balls and The Allman Bros Band playing on the jukebox. Them I don't recognize, but the man with the handlebar moustache, who pours Bourbon for the blonde in the cashmere white sweater with her back to me, is familiar.

"Keep 'em coming, Merle," says the blonde. Like the man I cannot place, her voice is familiar.

"That bad, huh?" Merle asks.

Merle. The funeral. Daphne's funeral. My cousin with the honkey-tonk. He's decades younger, a hard forty, but it's him.

The woman downs her booze in one gulp. "Worse." I know that voice. She taps her glass and Merle pours again as I move toward her. When her head whips toward the entrance, and I can see her gorgeous face, if I had a mouth it would drop. Daphne. In her fifties she was pretty but in her early twenties she's a knockout. Especially as a cat that ate the canary grin stretches across her face. "But it just got a little better, cuz."

My gaze follows hers straight to the end of the bar where the shell of Romy Cowan takes a stool. Merle moves down to the demon. "Evening. ID?" Smirking, it removes its wallet and holds up the license. Merle barely glances at it. "Thank you, Mr. Cooper."

"You are welcome my kind sir. May I have your finest, oldest, most expensive glass of whiskey please? I'd be much obliged."

"And put it on my tab, Merle," Daphne says seductively as she slinks toward her quarry.

The demon's stolen smirk grows to match hers. "Why, thank you, ma'am."

"Don't thank me." She lowers herself onto the stool beside him. "Thank my husband."

"Your husband, huh?" the demon asks, eyebrow raised.

"Oh Romy, are you going to break a poor gal's heart by acting like you don't remember me?"

Those blue eyes study her for a few seconds as it accesses its stolen memories. "Daphne Revell. My favorite baby-sitter. It's been awhile."

"So long it's actually Daphne Davenport. At least for now."

"For now? Trouble in paradise?"

She shrugs. "If you count my husband of two years fucking my seventeen-year-old cousin trouble, then yes."

Merle brings him the whisky. "That qualifies," says the demon.

"The bitch actually came over to the house to gloat. It's been going on for months."

"I'm sorry."

"It's not so much the fucking around. I mean, I knew who I was marrying after all. It's the fact he made her the exact same promises he made me. The *exact* ones. I can read the writing on the wall. I promised him a son. I haven't delivered. Case closed. My time's almost up, just like Virginia's was three years ago."

"You're a clever woman. I'm sure you'll come up with something." It raises its eyebrow and leans in, eyes meeting hers again. "If you haven't already."

"Been working on it," she says knowingly.

The demon draws in a deep breath, then slowly releases it in time to its growing grin, lust oozing from its every pore. "Sometimes it just comes down to timing, Mrs. Davenport."

Not taking her eyes from his, she holds up her glass for a toast. "To timing."

They clink glasses. "To fate." The demon takes a slow sip of his whiskey, closing its eyes to savor the taste. "Oh, it is good to be alive." It licks its lips.

"You are nothing like I remember," Daphne says with approval.

"Well, you knew the boy, Mrs. Davenport. Tonight is my first night as a man, at least officially."

"Happy birthday then." They both sip their respective poisons. "So how long do we have before the princess joins us to celebrate?"

"I'm sorry?"

"Juliette, your highness. Siamese twins don't spend as much time together as y'all do."

"Just me tonight. She's a bit under the weather."

"And you left her sickbed to cruise a bar? You *have* changed."

"I just had to get out of that house. I had to think. I couldn't do that around them."

"Care to share?" Daphne asks.

"Just that I think I have to leave town. Pack up Juliette and disappear. At least for a while. The situation at home has become untenable."

"I'm sorry."

"It was inevitable," it sighs. "We'll be back though. This is our home. There should always be a Fontaine in Crimson Vale."

She slides her hand onto its thigh. "Then how about a little going away/birthday present, Mr. Cowan?"

It chugs its whiskey with a shiver then grins. "You read my mind, Mrs. Davenport."

Oh, God.

Please don't. Please—

Daphne tosses a hundred on the bar before both rise from their stools.

Don't leave. Not together. Not tonight. Don't…

Daphne takes the demon's hand and leads the smiling abomination out of the bar.

No. No, no, no, no, no…

It can't be. No. He's not…they won't…he can't be…even though I don't have a stomach I double over and hug it. No. *No.* He's not. He's *not.* But that's why she so desperately wanted me gone. Because she knew we were related. Maybe she even suspected how closely.

Bram's my…no. He's not. It's not…we…I…please no. *Please.*

Blink.

I look up, and I'm back at the house in the foyer. Oh, God. No more. *No more.* No more, no more, no more. Enough. I can't. I—

The front door closes behind me, and the chipper demon strolls in humming, "Somewhere Over the Rainbow," its hair now a wild mess of curls. Dear God. I see it now. The resemblance. Same eyes. Same chin. Same height and build. Even the smile. Exactly like Bram's. Exactly like *mine.*

The demon's song cuts short. I trace his gaze to the living room doorway where Hallie, her head held high and shoulders back, stands tall. The demon's smile grows. "You didn't have to wait up for me, Hallie."

"We should talk," Hallie replies.

"Not now. I didn't anticipate how quickly the energy in the human body depletes. I'm exhausted. Tomorrow." It starts toward the stairs, passing me.

"Juliette's gone," Hallie declares.

The demon stops dead in its tracks and pivots around. "Excuse me?"

"The minute you left we packed her a suitcase and drove her to the bus station. You will never see or touch her again, you son of a bitch."

Those blue eyes stare at her as if it's willing her to drop dead where she stands. "Where did you send her?" it asks, voice as hard as its glare.

"I will never tell you. *Never*."

Its lip twitches, but it says, "You don't need to. As always, you underestimate me."

"No, I didn't. I am aware of your little tricks. Which is why I've warded her." She holds up her palm. There's a familiar symbol, a heart with a triangle and "S" shaped lines around it, recently carved in the flesh, still seeping blood. Mama had a similar scar on her shoulder. "As long as my blood flows, her spirit, her soul will be cut off from you. She's gone. You will never find her. *Never*. Now who underestimated who?"

The demon stares at Hallie, who stares right back. Even with its head cocked slightly to the side, a cruel grin forms on its face. The face of pure evil. The moment its lips stop moving, it lunges at Hallie like a lion after a gazelle. But she's ready for it. Before it can even move a step, she spins around to dash back into the living room. She's halfway to the couch when it crosses the threshold.

The demon makes it one step inside.

"AAAH!"

Thwack!

It happens so fast, it takes both me and the demon a second to work out what occurred. The demon stumbles backwards into the foyer then stops to stare down at the floor and raise its hand to its forehead. The gash begins raining blood from the wound in his temple. What…? From around the corner, Felicia, still holding the fireplace poker, steps into the doorway. Even without the two black eyes and swollen nose I'd barely know this was the simpering woman from before. She stares at the demon with sharp focus, mouth set straight with as much determination as inside her cold eyes. The demon's still touching the blood when Felicia charges toward the monster, raising the poker as she does. *Whack*! The hard metal connects with the side of its head as the demon grunts in pain. With the third hit, the demon collapses to the ground on its side. Felicia brings the poker down on its bloody head again. And again. And again, blonde hair now crimson and uneven as she caves in its skull. Again. Again. Blood rains down from the poker onto its wielder, but she doesn't notice.

"Felicia!" Hallie calls. My grandmother finally stops her onslaught, turning toward her approaching sister. "We need it alive, remember?" Hallie kneels beside the demon and checks its pulse. "Thank Christ. Now go get the book, hammer, and knitting needle. Fast."

Felicia drops the poker and hustles back into the living room. Hallie retrieves the poker and uses her shirt to wipe off Felicia's fingerprints.

"Are-are you sure this is going to work?" Felicia asks, returning with a huge old book, silver needle, and hammer. She kneels and sets the tools beside Hallie.

Hallie opens the book, *Grey's Anatomy,* to a picture of the human brain. "It should. In theory."

"And-and you know how?"

"I read about it in *Time* magazine," Hallie says. She picks up the needle and hammer with her trembling hands. "Okay. Okay," she gasps to herself. "*Just do it*."

Though the demon's face and head are covered with blood and bits of torn scalp and hair, nothing compares to the horror of Hallie shoving that knitting needle through the bottom of its eye. Both Felicia and I look away. My grandmother actually throws up when the hammer clacks against the makeshift lobotomy needle.

"God forgive us," Felicia mutters, wiping her mouth. "Please forgive us."

Several seconds later, the sound of Hallie gagging herself and the hammer clattering draw our gazes back their way. Hallie pants as if she's run a marathon as she shakes and shakes. "Fuck. Fuck," she pants before taking deep breaths to calm herself. "S-still have the knife?" Hallie gasps.

Felicia's head bobs up and down as she once again approaches the gruesome duo. My grandmother reaches behind and removes a knife hidden in the waist of her pants, giving it to Hallie. "W-what if this doesn't work? Wh-what if we can't get Dr. Tanner on board and he tells the police?"

"We pay him enough that man would sell his own child." Hallie uses the knife to re-open the symbol on her hand, wincing the whole time, then lifts up the demon's bloodstained shirt. Felicia turns away again as Hallie carves a similar symbol on the demon's bony hip.

"Are-are you sure *that* will work?" Felicia asks. "It-it'll keep him in that body?"

"Grandmere seemed to think so. At least that's what she wrote in her notes," she replies, finishing the carving. "We'll put up other wards before we bring him back home." Hallie closes her eyes and places her bleeding hand on his carving. I sense a change in the air, a prickling like on the island, as Hallie begins whispering in French. After ten seconds, the body twitches. Then again. Hallie opens her eyes as the air returns to normal. Trapped now. Just not forever.

Hallie leans into the demon's ear. "You wanted this body? You got it, asshole. A crumbling prison you have no control of. I hope you enjoyed your few hours of freedom because from here on out, your existence consists of the same pain, misery, and horror you've inflicted upon us." She spits on him before collecting the book and rising. "Welcome to hell."

"Sh-should we phone the police and doctor now?"

"You pushed Cotton's car into the swamp?" Hallie asks. Felicia nods. "Then one last step. Brace yourself."

"Do we have to?"

"If we want to sell this to the sheriff, yes. Ready?"

"I—"

Before Felicia can finish, Hallie swings the huge hardcover right at Felicia's face. Her nose twists as blood spurts from it again. Before Felicia can even process this pain, Hallie whacks her in the ribs. They crack as well. Felicia collapses to the ground only to have Hallie bring the book down on her arm. Felicia shrieks in agony, that wail almost overshadowing the crack of bone. Breathing heavily, Hallie stares down at the sobbing Felicia. "Sorry. Sorry."

As Felicia continues sobbing, Hallie collects the hammer, pulpy knitting needle, and book before slowly trotting past the broken mother and son in the living room. Calm as can be, she puts the evidence in a plastic bag. Bag still in hand she walks to the doorframe, takes several deep breaths, then tosses her head back before smacking it on the frame. Hard. Before she loses her nerve, she does it again. Moaning she touches her forehead, her eye, and split lip. "*Now* we call the police. But the lawyer first."

On the night of his eighteenth birthday, Jerome Cowan came home and found his mother and housekeeper being attacked by his grandfather, Cotton Fontaine. When the boy came to the women's defense, Cotton beat his grandson into an irreversible coma and fled into the night, never to be seen again. The granddaughter who slept through the whole ordeal was soon shipped off to her aunt's farm only to take her life five years later, leaving behind the daughter she never wanted. The daughter who had no idea her grandmother and aunt had locked themselves in a decaying old plantation house to care for their beloved Jerome until the end of all their days. And that should have been the end of it. All the sacrifice, all the planning to keep him caged from the world was all for nothing. He got out.

He found me.

Blink.

No more. Just no more.

I'm sitting in the passenger seat of a car staring up the driveway at an unfamiliar three-story white Georgian revival house with pristine rosebushes, hedges, and tall wrought iron fence surrounding the beautiful, expensive property. The buzzing to my left draws my attention. I'm not alone. Bram sits beside me, pushing the button on the gate's call box. Jesus, he looks terrible. Wan, waxy pallor, slightly bloodshot eyes, and jittery everything. He can't stop twitching or sniffling. I can't look at him. All I see is Jerome. God, even their hands are the same. Long and elegant. An artist's hands. *My* hands.

"Yes?" a woman asks through the box.

"It's Bram. I'm here to see Mother."

"Is she expecting you?"

"Jesus fucking Christ, Dorothea, just open the goddamn gate already."

There's silence for a few seconds before, "One moment please."

"Fucking bitch," Bram mutters.

Shaking his head, he waits for several more seconds, those graceful hands slightly trembling. At about second five he reaches into his pants pocket and removes a tiny packet of white powder, shaking out some onto his hand. The gate finally buzzes and begins to open as he snorts the cocaine up his nose. He puts the baggie back in his pocket before driving up to the house. Daphne, now very much the woman I met, stands in the doorway with her arms folded across her cashmere covered chest as Bram climbs out of his car.

"You need money," Daphne states as plain fact before he even shuts the door.

"What? I…" He scoffs. "Nice to see you too, Mother."

"We're not giving you another penny."

"Look, can we talk in private, please? I have something you might like to hear."

"I very much doubt that."

"Fontaine house," he says with a grin.

The magic words. Her scowl and tense shoulders both slack a little as she appraises him. "Fine. Five minutes."

His grin growing more mischievous, Bram hurries into the house with me behind. He must have gotten his home décor tips from his mother because this place is exactly like his, classy yet bland. The Davenports were probably keeping Pottery Barn's bottom line very tidy. A woman dressed in an apron stands at the end of the hall glaring at Bram.

"Dorothea, forget waxing the floors for right now. Could you please run to the store? You may have to go to several to find all the pheasants for tonight," Daphne instructs.

"Are you sure, Mrs. Davenport?" the maid asks never removing her eyes from Bram.

"Yes. Thank you. We'll be fine."

"Yes, ma'am."

Daphne nods at the woman before continuing through the beige and white living room to an office. "Dad's not home, is he?" Bram asks.

"No. He told me he went golfing." Daphne shuts the office door. "Of course the only balls he's hitting are his against Betsy. Though better her than me." She sits behind the large desk and Bram across from her, if possible even jittier than before. His knee won't stop bobbing up and down. "So. Fontaine house. I understand you've been there a few times recently."

"Yeah. Dad gave me the case a month ago. Mrs. Cowan's selling the warehouse on Bleeker."

"And how is Boo Radley these days?"

Bram shakes his head. "The woman never shuts up. Besides the priest I don't think she's spoken to another person in months. It's fucking pathetic. And that guy…" Bram shudders.

"You saw Romy?" Daphne asks.

"Yeah. It was fucking disgusting. He's white as paper and skinny as hell. It was sad. Seriously fucking sad."

"Someone should have put him out of his misery at the very start," Daphne says with a twinge of anger.

"Exactly what I've been thinking," Bram says, raising an eyebrow.

"I'm sorry?"

Bram holds up his finger to his lips to signal her to be quiet before he walks to the closed door, opening it to check for eavesdroppers. Finding none, he closes the door again and turns to his mother, all smiles. "It came to me in a dream about a month ago," he says eagerly.

"Oh, Jesus," Daphne mutters. "You and your damn dreams. Did the blonde woman, baby, or alligator give you this idea?"

"No. Listen," he says, sitting again. "It's been consuming me, Mother. Ever since I walked into that house. This is *all* I've been thinking about for a while now, and I've got it all worked out."

"What?"

"I read Felicia's will. As it stands now, when she dies, the house goes to the vegetable with Dad acting as his executor with strict orders that a full medical staff be moved into the house, specifically the nurse Lula and that quack Dr. Linton, until Romy dies. When he does, the Historical Society takes possession of the house."

"And this has what to do with me?"

"What if I can make sure *you* get the house? I know you want it. You're always on Dad to make Felicia an offer. Hell, you used to drive me out there just to look at it."

"That was many years ago. It's falling apart now. And all those weird drawings and crucifixes…"

"Some paint, a few builders in, it'll be good as new. Felicia seemed amenable to the idea. She's a lonely old woman. A little sweet talk and gentle prodding, I'm positive I can get her to agree. Then you get the house *and* don't have to pay for the renovation."

"And dear son do you believe you can also use your golden tongue to convince her to change her will to leave the house to me, a veritable stranger as well?"

"You're on the board of the Historical Society, and Dad's the executor. I'm sure you can work something out."

"One problem, dear. The current inhabitants."

"Well…" He sits back in the chair. "We're talking about an old woman and a severely disabled man who both have one foot in the grave already."

Daphne scowls. "You're not suggesting—" She shuts her collagen filled lips. "No. The less I know the better."

"Agreed."

"So, what's in this little scheme for you, *son*?"

"Fifty grand."

Daphne scoffs. "Excuse me?"

"Half up front, half when you get the deed. But I need the twenty-five now. Within the week or they'll begin foreclosure proceedings on my house."

"Jesus, Bram," Daphne scoffs. "Is it drugs again?"

"What? No," he lies, "I haven't touched that shit since rehab. No, I just made some bad investments."

"Is that supposed to help my nerves? I may not be a lawyer, but I'm fairly sure what you're suggesting is fraud, conspiracy, and possibly…" She just nods.

"If anything goes sideways you can just tell them the twenty-five was you saving my ass again. Not that I would ever sell you down the river, Mother. And besides, *nothing* will go wrong. I've already worked out the best way to do it. No one will question what happens because no one *cares*."

"And you could do…that?"

"You haven't seen what I have, Mother. They shoot horses, don't they?"

Daphne just stares at her son for several more seconds, mulling it all over. This is a joke. They can't really be this evil. This cold blooded. "*If* I agree to this, you'll only get the first half when there's proof that the renovations have begun. Because if you don't deliver on that promise…"

With a huge grin, Bram rises from his chair. "Fair enough. But be ready to transfer the funds by the end of the week. I'm heading over right now to spend the day with that beautiful, dear old lady."

"And this conversation never happened, and you can't prove it ever did," Daphne states. "You ever bring it up, darling son, I will play dumb. If this all blows up in your face, you are on your own."

"Wouldn't expect anything less from you, Mother. Just have my money ready for the *foreclosure*."

Daphne nods. "Give Felicia my warm regards."

Still sporting that cocky grin I once adored, Bram struts out of the study with his head held higher than he deserves. He didn't. He couldn't. He—

Blink.

Beeping. Crosses. Voodoo symbols covering the yellowing walls, even painted on the ceiling and doors. The bed, a hospital bed with half a dozen machines around it, sits directly underneath the same symbol Hallie carved on the demon. The monster itself lies there. Bram was right, it is little more than a corpse now, though it's in far better shape than the concentration camp survivor I'd envisioned. Its skin is albino white, its greasy rat's nest of hair reaches its shoulders, and it's a tad on the skinny side, but is in remarkable shape for a human in a decades long coma. A few wrinkles, some muscle definition, same graceful hands. Felicia's good care or supernatural shenanigans, I don't know. Both perhaps. I do rarely get ill and minor cuts heal within a day or two. I guess I am my father's daughter. And here it is. Here it's been since before I drew my first breath. Defecating and urinating into bags. Being fed by a tube poking out of its throat. Not that it doesn't deserve this.

I'd always wanted a father. Uncle Robbie was beyond fantastic. All that a girl could want. He escorted me to all the Daddy/Daughter dances at church. He worked hard from sunup to sundown literally toiling in fields to keep me in art supplies and books. I even had my own horse. But you still wonder. Kids still make fun of you. You still worry what genetic horrors you'll pass onto your babies. Bram and I inherited his artistic nature. His beautiful smile. At least I avoided the homicidal tendencies, unlike my half-brother.

"I'll get it, Felicia," my lover calls from the hallway.

A second later, Bram slowly creeps into the bedroom, slipping on latex gloves as he does. Without even glancing at Romy, he quietly rushes to the dresser by the window to remove a snub-nose .38, which he shoves into the waist of his black slacks before covering it with his black button down shirt. Task complete, he moves toward the cabinet beside the bed. A man with a plan. Inside is a veritable pharmacy: syringes, vials, pills, and stacks of IVs. All you need to keep a demon locked in its meat prison.

Bram removes a thick syringe and vial of I don't know what. He fills that syringe, using up most of the clear liquid, his hands trembling the entire time. "Okay, okay," he pants as he replaces the vial in the cabinet. For the first time he looks at the comatose man, his pants growing heavier. "I can do this. I *can* do this."

After a second to gain his courage, Bram takes the one step toward the bed. His hands still shaking, he inserts the syringe inside the plastic port in Romy's left arm. He glances at the man, his own father, breath louder than even the steady beeping of the heart monitor. "Fuck. Fuck," Bram mutters. "Just do it, asshole. Don't be a pussy. Just fucking do it!"

Bram closes his eyes and pushes in the plunger before he loses the nerve. Horrific task complete, Bram stumbles backwards, away from his victim.

Nothing happens. The beeping remains steady as a metronome. Bram grows even more anxious, rocking back and forth on his heels. "Come on asshole."

"Bram, dear," Felicia calls, the sound of her voice jolting Bram almost out of his shoes. "Did you find it?"

"Come on," Bram whispers, "come fucking on alr—"

The demon's body jerks upwards, arching its back into almost a U as the beeping instantly becomes erratic. Bram leaps away, then grimaces as the demon falls onto its back only to seize again. And again. The constant beeping almost overshadows the running footfalls coming our way. "Bram?" Felicia shouts.

Her voice knocks my brother out of his stupor. The easy part's over. *She* can fight back. He takes several steps backwards as Felicia hurries into the room. The demon convulses again. His heart rate's two hundred and climbing. Another convulsion. Felicia doesn't give Bram a glance. She races toward the demon. "What happened?" Bram doesn't answer. "Oh God. Oh God." She stands still for a second, unsure what to do. "I…I…" She rounds the bed to the cabinet. "Ca-call an ambulance." Bram doesn't move. He's even stopped shaking. His jaw remains as clenched as his fists. Felicia fails to notice. She's too concerned with rifling through the vials. The demon's heart rate is now 230 and the convulsions haven't stopped. "Bram, call an ambulance!" She fills a new syringe with a drug.

"I'm sorry," Bram says to himself.

"Just call 911."

"God, forgive me."

As Felicia rises, Bram strides toward her. Removing the gun.

Felicia turns her back on him to administer the shot, and that's when the coward strikes. He can't look at her face as he steps behind her, raising the gun to the side of her head. She doesn't have time to even react or glance back. The moment the barrel touches her right temple, he squeezes the trigger, skull and brain and blood spewing out the other side of her gray head. Her body slumps to the ground. Dead. She didn't see it coming. Thank God for small mercies.

Bram watches all this with his mouth gaping open and huffing as if he can't catch his breath. When the body lands, he leaps backwards again and doubles over, kneeling and hugging his legs, whispering "Fuck, fuck," into them.

He only looks up when the beeping finally ceases into a steady whine. Flatline. The body's dead. It's free. At exactly 8:32PM. I saw the black figure at the top of my stairs right after 6:30 Pacific time. Was I his first stop?

I sense him the second before he even arrives.

I wish it were a shock, but when the darkness appears in front of my half-brother, I feel nothing. Not surprise, not horror, not pity. I'm positive the demon had a hand in this whole event. The same way it manipulated me through the years with the dreams, the visits, it must have done the same to Bram. To maneuver him to this very moment. But you can't foster something to grow if it hasn't already been planted. My brother had a darkness inside him, and our father simply guided it to a target. And before him now is his payment in kind. I'm glad I never met the bastard.

Bram gasps at the sight of the demon and quickly gets to his feet. "Wha—"

Whatever he sees in that abyss cuts short his words. Like Romy before, Bram stands transfixed, not breathing, not blinking as he stares into that darkness. At death itself. The figure leans in and the moment their lips meet, the demon fades inside that beautiful body I've kissed every inch of. That has been inside me. That I worshiped to the point of idolatry. The demon infects it. Corrupts it. Transforms it.

My brother doesn't put up as much of a fight as my uncle did. He drops to the floor, but after only one convulsion, the body's still. The demon blinks its new eyes, takes a deep breath with its new lungs, and smiles with its new lips before letting out a laugh that chills me even in this form. The laugh of the victorious. The laugh of a creature who has thwarted all its enemies and has every confidence it will continue to in the future. The same laugh he had after we made love in the kitchen, and like then the laughs quickly give way to tears of pure happiness. My hand touches my stomach, and I feel it. A pinpoint of otherness inside me. Growing. His ultimate triumph.

Oh, God. No more. No more.

"No more!" I shriek to the heavens.

I'm still shrieking when I'm forced back into my body. I fall on all fours and vomit onto the rug, twice, before curling into the fetal position on the floor. "No more," I whisper, my throat raw. "No more. No more." I start pounding on my stomach. "Oh, God. Oh, God."

Chanel.

Through my tears, I gaze at my grandmother kneeling beside me, gently stroking my hair though I can't feel her hand. I can sense her sympathy, her heartbreak for me with each stroke. I want to die. I want to scrub off my skin in every place he ever touched me. I pound my womb as hard as I can. How could I have been so blind? How could I have been so stupid? What am I going to do? What am I going to do?

You know.

I look up and gasp.

Hallie. Daniel. Great-Grandma Cecile. Ada. Aunt Helen. Uncle Robbie. Daphne.

Mama.

They surround me, staring with their melancholy, sympathetic eyes boring into me. His victims. My family. Those stolen from me and I them. Who sacrificed their sanity, their very lives to stop this very moment from occurring. All begging. All pleading. Because I do know what I have to do. For them. For me. For Owen. For all that was stolen from us all. For all the lives that will continue to be corrupted. I know what I have to do because it is the *only* thing to do. "Okay." I meet my mama's eyes and for the first time ever I find love in them, especially when she kneels in front of me and smiles. Truly smiles like I never thought her capable of. "Okay."

My girl. My beautiful, brave girl. Thank you. She bends beside her own mother and kisses me on the forehead. I feel it. I feel her lips. I feel her love. My mother loves me.

Thank you.

CHAPTER TWENTY-TWO

Dawn.

I sit in a rocking chair on my back porch wrapped in one of my grandmother's quilts enjoying a perfect cup of coffee as the sun slowly climbs over the still, black water of my bayou amid the hollow cypress trees with their weeping leaves. The sky transforming from black to a warm orange finally fading into pink mixed with blue. A new day. So full of promise. Of hope. No matter how wretched yesterday was, as long as the sun rises, there's always a chance the next day will be better. God giving you an opportunity to begin anew. Not to make the same mistakes. It could be the day you finally get the promotion you've been striving for. The day you meet the man of your dreams. The day you win the lotto. All possible.

What we never think is perhaps this is the day your house burns down. The day you're given a terminal cancer diagnosis. The day your spouse leaves you. We don't like to dwell on that fact, nor should we. It's what keeps us going. A little self-delusion is healthy. But what happens when it's all been stripped away? When the sun rises only to reveal all the dark crevices of the world? When the cruelty, the unfairness, the horror is all laid bare for you to see? To understand. What do you do when that understanding burns your soul to ashes? I know the answer now. Perhaps I always did. The knowledge flows in the Fontaine blood.

And blood will out.

The sound of tire on gravel cuts through the tranquility. It's here. No matter the time, no matter the distance, no matter the request, I call and it comes running. I could ask it to rob a bank, murder someone, and I don't doubt he'd be by my side in less than a heartbeat. It's already proven that. There is *nothing* it wouldn't do for me. For love. Or its twisted view of it.

Even after all I've seen and experienced, I don't doubt it believes it loves me. Just as I don't doubt it believed it loved Hallie. Felicia. Romy. Mama. But love is unselfish. It's putting those you care about before yourself. As the Bible reads, "*Love is patient, love is kind. It does not envy, it does not boast, it is not proud, it is not self-seeking. It always protects, always trusts, always hopes, always perseveres*." -Corinthians. I read that quote to Owen as part of my wedding vows. Time to finally prove I meant them. He has time and again, even when he shouldn't have. And last night he almost died because of me. The doctor said he's resting comfortably. Out of danger.

Not just yet.

I rise from my chair and return inside to the kitchen. The doorbell rings as I rinse out the coffee mug. For whom the bell tolls. I'm surprised it didn't just walk in. I'm sure it considers this more its house than mine. I wouldn't disagree. The bell chimes again as I retrieve his surprise and my cell phone from the kitchen table. I straighten my long pink sweater and smooth my hair.

It's time.

I'm halfway to the door when it chimes again, this time followed by an impatient knock. I should be nervous. I should be falling apart. If this were a week ago, heck two days ago, I would be. But that's what clarity does to a person. Knowing your purpose in life. Being shown the right, dare I say it, righteous path makes it easier to continue down it. Especially when given so much love and support along the way. I cannot see them but I know they're here. I will not stumble. I will not fall. *I will not let them down.*

Without hesitation, I open the front door. Nothing. I feel nothing when I set eyes on him. *It.* Not hate, not love, only the ever present lust. Is it magic? Did it bespell me? Make it seem as if becoming its lover was of my own free will? Rape me without force? Gazing at this blonde Adonis with electric blue eyes brought out by its matching blue sweater, not a single soul would believe him capable of any atrocity. Of course Lucifer was an angel before his fall. The Morningstar. Speak of the Devil and he shall appear.

"Hello," I say.

"Hi," the demon replies with a million watt smile. It hasn't even been twelve hours and as always it gazes at me as if it hasn't seen me in a millennia. As if I possessed all the answers to the universe that it'd been searching for since the dawn of time. Every woman, every man should be looked at like this at least once in their lifetime. It used to move me, down to my very soul. God help me, even now a part of me revels in it.

"Were you surprised to hear from me?" I ask.

"Not even a little," it says, that grin growing. "You can't stay away from me anymore than I can you, beloved." Its smile slowly drops when I don't return it. "Last night…everything you accused me of was correct. I allowed ridiculous, unwarranted jealousy warp my mind. I was selfish. Cruel to the one person in this and any universe I would rather die than harm. All I can do is apologize until the end of my days and do all in my power to make up for it." The demon takes a step toward me. I force myself not to move away. "And it will never, *ever* happen again."

"I know it won't."

There goes that smile again. So much like Uncle Jerome's. And mine. Blind. I was so blind. Or worse I just didn't wish to see. A large part of me still aches for that darkness still. To leap into its arms, shower it with kisses, and make love until the end of eternity. But I will be strong. I *must* be strong. "Would you like to come in?"

"Only if you want me to," it replies.

"*Want* doesn't factor into it. *Need* is more accurate when it comes to us, no?" I step aside. "Come in."

The demon brushes past me and as usual, that slight touch sends my body alight as if its kissing me everywhere at once. I hold my breath, I don't even blink until the sensation passes. "It didn't work, you know," I say as I shut the door.

"I'm sorry?" it asks.

I spin around, placing my back to the wall. "Owen's alive."

The demon's a good actor. Or Bram was and the abomination simply absorbed that trait. Its eyes narrow as its mouth opens in confusion. "What are you talking about?"

"The paramedics were able to restart his heart. He's fine. Up. Talking. *Alive*. Despite your best efforts."

Its stolen face falls further. "What…something happened? I don't—"

"*Revelabunt.*"

The demon hisses and looks away, but I see it. The abyss underneath. My creator. My nightmare. "Hello, father."

"Jane—"

"Did you truly believe it was all for the greater good? That's what you told Cotton before you snapped his neck. That it was all for the greater good. Is that how you justify all your crimes? Like raping my mother? Obliterating my uncle from existence? Manipulating my half-brother into murdering our grandmother? Ripping…my children from my womb? What good has it served? Because I need to understand. I need to know. Tell me." It doesn't utter a word. "*Tell me!*" I roar.

The beautiful abomination finally looks at me again, staring with its mouth agape, for once at a loss for words. I've tongue tied the devil itself. That devil meets my eyes for the answer, finding only scorn. Hatred. The fact I finally see it in all its vile glory. The demon's shoulders slump and false puzzlement vanishes, replaced with a sad smile. "Oh, beloved. How can you ask me that when you yourself are the answer?"

"What?"

"You…are my greatest good. You are my masterpiece, Jane. You are better than I ever hoped, ever dreamed you would be. You're beautiful. Intelligent. Talented. Funny. Kind. Thoughtful. Everything a human should be. But without all that came before, there would be no *you*. And how poor the world would be then."

"You're insane."

"No, beloved, I'm a being of vision. Of hope. I was summoned here, I was given the chance at life anew, for a purpose."

"Yeah, to make sure Cotton Fontaine didn't go bankrupt."

"You're thinking micro, Jane. I'm talking macro. I was *meant* to come here. To put all of this into motion. Here. On earth."

"You want to take over the world?"

"I want to *improve* this world," it corrects desperately. "Improve human bodies, human minds. In my realm, we live longer. Our minds are capable of processes humans cannot even begin to fathom. Most only use ten percent of their brains. In just one generation, I have increased that by one percent. The shared dreams, our psychic link, your ability to see the dead and have your consciousness traverse through time and space, all of that is possible because we're of the same blood. The same energy. That's why our bodies, our souls are so drawn to one another. Even if I were still in that rotting carcass of a prison upstairs, and you passed this body on the street, you would have the same reaction. You and this body were *made* for one another. Though you should be thankful it was me and not him you encountered first. Bram Davenport didn't have a loyal bone in this body. Selfish, cruel, closed minded, self-destructive. He never would have appreciated you. Never could have loved you. He didn't know how to love. My poor boy." The demon shakes its head. "Daphne was never meant to be a mother, not like you were. She was beautiful, determined, willing, but little else. The only time she truly showed motherly interest was in her attempt to keep us apart. She suspected you were Romy's child as well and wanted to avert disaster, as she called it. And she was mad about the will. I didn't keep Bram's promise. I forged a new will and cut her out. Her revenge was to try to take you away from me."

"So you killed her," I say without a shadow of a doubt.

"I reached into her chest while she was driving here to tell you the truth. She lost control of the car and went straight into a

bayou. Drowned. She should consider herself fortunate, though.
My incarceration allowed her decades of life I might not otherwise
would have seen fit to grant her. I wouldn't have allowed that
sociopath to raise my son. That bitch almost ruined him. Our
beautiful boy was a means to an end for her, nothing more, and he
knew that. His so-called parents didn't even pretend to love him.
Even with that extra evolutionary push my genes gifted him he
barely survived the two overdoses. And no cheap trick like I used
to save you in that bathtub would have worked on him. It took so
much effort and energy to break out when Juliette tried to drown
you. Then that bitch Hallie entombed me one more. I couldn't even
sense you again until she died. She taught Felicia the spells and
sigils, but thankfully your grandmother had none of her half-
sister's inherent power."

"Felicia was a big enough threat you manipulated Bram
into killing her," I point out.

"Do you have any notion, even an inkling, what it is like
to be imprisoned within your own body? Knowing all that's
occurring around you, but not being able to do a damn thing about
it? Literally not being able to lift a finger? Being at the mercy of
others while your body decays. Being physically and emotionally
tortured for decades? I felt *everything*. Every procedure. Every
lobotomy, tracheotomy, colon resection. And you think *me* a
monster?"

"You didn't leave them much choice, did you? You killed
my great-grandfather. My uncle. You *raped* my mother."

"I never meant to do that. Truly," it says regretfully. "I
loved your mother…almost as much as I love you. I watched her
come into this world. I watched her grow into a spectacular,
sensual young woman. I intended to woo her as she deserved. I
did. But instinct told me it had to be that night. *Then*. And I was
right. Without that horrendous act I regret even now, there would
be no you, Jane. And I would have spent the remainder of my days
making up for my crime. I would have given my Juliette
everything, done anything, denied her nothing. In time, she would

have forgiven me. Because she loved me. And she did love me, Jane. Whenever I visited her in her dreams, she told me so. She showed me so. We had already consummated that love many times before I was made flesh. We would have had a wonderful life together. You would have had siblings to play with. Parents who adored you. Freedom from ridiculous shame and guilt those religious zealots brainwashed within you. There wouldn't have been a moment when you felt unloved. Lost. Because I know you have. All your life, everything just seemed...wrong. Like you didn't belong. Even with Owen. *He* felt wrong. Because he was. You weren't living the life you were meant to be. So don't you dare feel sad for Hallie and Felicia. They stole as much from you as they did me."

"So that's why you tried to kill Owen? Why you...killed my babies? Because they were wrong for me?"

"I didn't cause your miscarriages, Jane," it says offensively.

"Liar," I hiss.

"I didn't," it proclaims with utter conviction.

"I saw you. I saw you loom over our bed. I saw you squeeze Owen's heart just like you did to me."

"I admit to last night. I do. I knew you'd go back to him. I knew I'd gone too far and you were leaving me. I couldn't bear for that to happen. I panicked." It takes a step toward me, and I tense. "But *I* would never hurt *you* like that. I would never deny you motherhood. It was why you were put on this earth, Jane. My blood, our blood should spread far and wide. That's why I came to this realm. To make it better. And *she* knew that. *She* has been snuffing out every drop of my blood to spite me, even in death. She would have murdered Bram and you before you were born if it were within her power then. Because as long as there is a drop of my blood in this universe, I remain. I have a home. Isn't that right," its head jerks to the left, "Hallie?"

I follow its gaze to the living room where the ghost stands, mouth set straight in defiance. "So she stored up all her energy, all her power, and reached inside your body to destroy those fragile blessings. Just to hurt *me*. She doesn't give a damn about you, Jane. None of them truly love you.

"No," I say. "*No*. You did it so I'd come here. To you. So I wouldn't be tied to Owen. And she wouldn't do that to me..." But when I meet her cold eyes, see that tight jaw and head held high with pride, my words stops. No. No, no, no, no. no...

"You were always going to come home, Jane. Husband or no. You were always going to be drawn to Bram. To me. And if I were stuck in that prison this generation, between my son and daughter, there would always be a next. Not as strong or powerful with diluted blood, but it would still be within my power to change that fact. She knew that. So she went out of her way to make sure there wouldn't be a next. She doesn't love you, Jane. None of them love you. They all wish you dead. Some even attempted to make it so. So why would you waste a moment of your time or energy on them? Why would you chose them over me? When we're together, just us two, aren't we happy? Haven't these been the happiest days of your life? And it's only the beginning. Just imagine what it will be like when you hold our son. Our beautiful boy growing inside you now." The demon takes another step but glares at Hallie. "You won't get this one. I've found a way to banish you. To vaporize you all into oblivion." It turns back to me, eyes as hard and determined as Hallie's. "Nothing and no one will ever harm you again. *Ever*.

"Look at me, Jane. Look at me!" He takes the final step, leaving no room between us. Even now my body reacts, arching toward him. I force my eyes to meet his. "I promised I would never lie to you, and I have kept that promise. I keep my promises, Jane. And I promise, I *promise* I don't want to hurt you. I don't want to hurt anyone, least of all you. I love you. I love you with all my heart and all my soul. Do you believe me?" My eyes lower but he grabs my jaw, forcing me to look up. "*Do you believe me*?"

I gaze into his eyes. "I believe you love me as best as you can. Yes."

"And do you believe we were meant to be together? To love one another?"

"Yes," I say with utter certainty.

"And that is all I want, Jane. You and me…" He touches my stomach. "And our *children*. That is all I want. That is all I have ever wanted and will ever want. Just like you. And we can have that, Jane. No matter how strange, how sordid the beginning may have been, we have each other now. The journey is complete. We've only one minor inconvenience to cast out…and we're done. We can have our paradise on this earth. You…me…and *he* are just the beginning. The first of many blessings to both us and the world."

"But it's wrong. They'll be monsters."

"Are you a monster? Are you not perfect in every way? Forget convention. Forget what other people might say or believe. We know the truth. Those rules don't apply to us. Because…" his hand caresses my cheek, "we're better than them. We're *more*. And the best of us will grow stronger through the generations. That is what our children and our children's children will inherit. They'll be world leaders. Influential artists and musicians. Brilliant doctors who will save millions of lives. And, beloved, it all begins here. With us." He presses his hand harder against my belly. "With *him*."

"The Anti-Christ."

The demon rolls his eyes. "Oh, Jane. There is no devil. There are no demons. There is no *God*. There is no man on a cloud watching over everything and everyone. It's a fable created by man to keep others in line. When you die your energy, your life force simply rejoins the current that binds this universe together. Good and evil don't factor into it. Positive and negative, yes, but within all humans which side the energy gravitates toward is always in flux. But no one is watching. No one is judging. No one *cares*. A great father figure isn't waiting to pass or fail you, Jane. We are only accountable for what we choose to be accountable for. Who and what we choose is worthy of our energy. There is only this. There is only *us*. And our beautiful future."

He leans in, pressing his lips to mine. A wave of divine images and emotions flow through me. Bram and I lying in bed as he sings to my huge belly while I laugh and stroke his soft hair. Standing on the porch holding my cherubic, blonde, blue-eyed boy I've dreamed of all my life as Bram walks up from behind, enveloping us both in his strong arms. Bram helping our now toddler son hang an ornament on the Christmas tree as I sit watching with our newborn daughter swaddled in my arms. Me fixing breakfast while Bram and our now four children make funny faces at one another. Our first born, the spitting image of his grandfather at that age, receiving his high school diploma. Bram walking our youngest daughter down the porch steps toward the rose covered arch where her future husband waits with tears in his eyes. Bram and I, ancient now, sitting in the rocking chairs on that same porch, holding hands while our children and their children run around in the backyard. Talking. Laughing. Playing tag. All beautiful. All healthy. All *good*.

Heaven on earth.

My beloved's lips leave mine and the images, the majesty vanishes. All but the love. Because despite it all, all the pain and harm he's inflicted, I do love him. He has my heart, my body, even my soul. This being that tore a hole in two universes. Who brought wealth and glory to my family. Who did all in his considerable power just to bring me into his life. My missing piece. My soul mate.

I caress his cheek with my left hand and rest my forehead against his. "I love you," I whisper. "It was always you. Always going to be you, be *this*. *This* is our fate. We were always…damned."

The demon I love stares up at me, eyes narrowed in confusion. "You're right," I continue. "It doesn't matter if there is a God or not. Some things do transcend good and evil. Right and wrong. But not this. *This* is right." He gasps when I put the barrel of the gun to his chest. "*We* are wrong."

BANG!

His body jerks as the bullet penetrates his cold, corrupted heart. He doesn't move again, he doesn't blink. He just stares into my tear filled eyes, betrayal and shock brimming from his. "I'm sorry."

The demon collapses to the floor, blood spewing from his mouth as he lands. Every breath brings up more and more. I haven't much time. I remove my cell phone from my pocket and punch in 911. "Hello, this is Jane Harrow. I need the police at 187 Fontaine Lane. I've just shot Bram Davenport IV. He admitted…to murdering my uncle, my grandmother, his own mother, and attempting to kill my husband. I did…the only thing I could do. To end this nightmare. To bring them peace.

His breathing is slowing now. His accusing eyes are slowly losing their battle to remain open. Not yet. *Not yet.*

"Please…Owen…please play this message for him. For my husband. Please know…I love you. Know you are the best thing that ever happened to me. The best man, the best husband, the best friend I ever could have hoped for. You were my gift from God."

The demon's eyes close.

"And know…none of this is your fault. Know there is nothing you could have done to change it." I bite my lip to stop the oncoming tears. I am strong. I will be strong. "Thank you for showing me love. For being…the best human being I ever knew. I never deserved you, Owen Harrow. *Never.*"

I sense the moment he dies. It's the same moment the darkness lifts out of him to stand before me.

"Please find someone who does. Good-bye, my love."

I put the gun to my temple. For him. For them all. I stare into the abyss. "Good-bye."

I squeeze the trigger.

And the abyss swallows me whole.

ACKNOWLEDGEMENTS

As always, thanks to my Beta Bunch: Susan Dowis, Jill Kardell, and Ginny Dowis. This one was really out of their taste wheelhouse but they managed to get through it and make it better.

Thanks to the Prince William, Fairfax, and Fayette County Public Library systems for giving me a place to work.

Thanks to everyone who has bought a book, checked one out from the library, recommended one to a friend, and especially those who write me to let me know how much you enjoy my books.

To all my fellow FREAKS out there…you are relevant. There is nothing wrong with you. Don't let the bastards get you down.

ABOUT THE AUTHOR

Jennifer Harlow spent her restless childhood fighting with her three brothers and scaring the heck out of herself with horror movies and books. She grew up to earn a degree at the University of Virginia which she put to use as a radio DJ, crisis hotline volunteer, bookseller, lab assistant, wedding coordinator, and government investigator. Currently she calls Atlanta home but that restless itch is ever present. In her free time, she continues to scare the beejepers out of herself watching scary movies and opening her credit card bills. She is the author of the Amazon best-selling F.R.E.A.K.S. Squad, Midnight Magic Mystery series and The Galilee Falls Trilogy. For the soundtrack to her books and other goodies, visit her at www.jenniferharlowbooks.com

www.ingramcontent.com/pod-product-compliance
Lightning Source LLC
Chambersburg PA
CBHW070304260626
47160CB00003B/715